26/10/17

45

D0716888

NDERSON

First Published in Great Britain 2017
By Mills & Boon, an imprint of HarperCollins*Publishers*
1 London Bridge Street, London, SE1 9GF

THE BEAUMONT BROTHERS © 2017 Harlequin Books S. A.

Not The Boss's Baby, *Tempted By A Cowboy* and *A Beaumont Christmas Wedding* were first published in Great Britain by Harlequin (UK) Limited.

Not The Boss's Baby © 2014 Sarah M. Anderson
Tempted By A Cowboy © 2014 Sarah M. Anderson
A Beaumont Christmas Wedding © 2014 Sarah M. Anderson

ISBN: 978-0-263-92951-5

05-0217

Award-winning author **Sarah M. Anderson** may live east of the Mississippi River, but her heart lies out west on the Great Plains. With a lifelong love of horses and two history teachers for parents, she had plenty of encouragement to learn everything she could about the tribes of the Great Plains.

When she started writing, it wasn't long before her characters found themselves out in South Dakota among the Lakota Sioux. She loves to put people from two different worlds into new situations and to see how their backgrounds and cultures take them someplace they never thought they'd go.

Sarah's book *A Man of Privilege* won the 2012 RT Reviewers' Choice Award for Best Mills & Boon Desire.

When not helping out at her son's school or walking her rescue dogs, Sarah spends her days having conversations with imaginary cowboys and American Indians, all of which is surprisingly well-tolerated by her wonderful husband. Readers can find out more about Sarah's love of cowboys and Indians at www.sarahmanderson.com.

NOT THE BOSS'S BABY

BY
SARAH M. ANDERSON

To Leah Hanlin. We've been friends for over twenty years now, and I'm so glad I've been able to share this journey—and my covers!—with you.
Let's celebrate by getting more sleep!

One

"Ms. Chase, if you could join me in my office."

Serena startled at the sound of Mr. Beaumont's voice coming from the old-fashioned intercom on her desk. Blinking, she became aware of her surroundings.

How on earth had she gotten to work? She looked down—she was wearing a suit, though she had no memory of getting dressed. She touched her hair. All appeared to be normal. Everything was fine.

Except she was pregnant. Nothing fine or normal about *that*.

She was relatively sure it was Monday. She looked at the clock on her computer. Yes, nine in the morning— the normal time for her morning meeting with Chadwick Beaumont, President and CEO of the Beaumont Brewery. She'd been Mr. Beaumont's executive assistant for seven years now, after a yearlong internship and a year working in Human Resources. She could count the number of times they'd missed their 9:00 a.m. Monday meeting on two hands.

No need to let something like a little accidental pregnancy interrupt that.

Okay, so everything had turned upside down this past weekend. She wasn't just a little tired or a tad stressed out. She wasn't fighting off a bug, even. She was, in all likelihood, two months and two or three weeks pregnant. She knew that with certainty because those were the last times she'd slept with Neil.

Neil. She had to tell him she was expecting. He had a right to know. God, she didn't want to see him again—to be rejected again. But this went way beyond what she wanted. What a huge mess.

"Ms. Chase? Is there a problem?" Mr. Beaumont's voice was strict but not harsh.

She clicked the intercom on. "No, Mr. Beaumont. Just a slight delay. I'll be right in."

She was at work. She had a job to do—a job she needed now more than ever.

Serena sent a short note to Neil informing him that she needed to talk to him, and then she gathered up her tablet and opened the door to Chadwick Beaumont's office. Chadwick was the fourth Beaumont to run the brewery, and it showed in his office. The room looked much as it might have back in the early 1940s, soon after Prohibition had ended, when Chadwick's grandfather John had built it. The walls were mahogany panels that had been oiled until they gleamed. A built-in bar with a huge mirror took up the whole interior wall. The exterior wall was lined with windows hung with heavy gray velvet drapes and crowned with elaborately hand-carved woodwork that told the story of the Beaumont Brewery.

The conference table had been custom-made to fit the

room—Serena had read that it was so large and so heavy that John Beaumont had to have the whole thing built in the office because there was no getting it through a doorway. Tucked in the far corner by a large coffee table was a grouping of two leather club chairs and a matching leather loveseat set. The coffee table was supposedly made of one of the original wagon wheels that Phillipe Beaumont had used when he'd crossed the Great Plains with a team of Percheron draft horses back in the 1880s on his way to settle in Denver and make beer.

Serena loved this room—the opulence, the history. Things she didn't have in her own life. The only changes that reflected the twenty-first century were a large flat-screen television that hung over the sitting area and the electronics on the desk, which had been made to match the conference table. A door on the other side of the desk, nearly hidden between the bar and a bookcase, led to a private bathroom. Serena knew that Chadwick had added a treadmill and a few other exercise machines, as well as a shower, to the bathroom, but only because she'd processed the orders. She'd never gone into Chadwick's personal space. Not once in seven years.

This room had always been a source of comfort to her—a counterpoint to the stark poverty that had marked her childhood. It represented everything she wanted—security, stability, *safety*. A goal to strive for. Through hard work, dedication and loyalty, she could have nice things, too. Maybe not this nice, but better than the shelters and rusted-out trailers in which she'd grown up.

Chadwick was sitting behind his desk, his eyes focused on his computer. Serena knew she shouldn't think of him as Chadwick—it was far too familiar. Too personal. Mr. Beaumont was her boss. He'd never made a move on her, never suggested that she "stay late" to work on a project that didn't exist—never booked them on a weekend conference that didn't exist. She worked hard for him, pulling long hours whenever necessary. She did good work for him and he rewarded her. For a girl who'd lived on free school lunches, getting a ten-thousand-dollar bonus *and* an eight-percent-a-year raise, like she had at her last performance review, was a gift from heaven.

It wasn't a secret that Serena would go to the ends of the earth for this man. It *was* a secret that she'd always done just a little more than admire his commitment to the company. Chadwick Beaumont was an incredibly handsome man—a solid six-two, with sandy blond hair that was neatly trimmed at all times. He was probably going gray, but it didn't show with his coloring. He would be one of those men who aged like a fine wine, only getting better with each passing year. Some days, Serena would catch herself staring at him as if she were trying to savor him.

But that secret admiration was buried deep. She had an excellent job with benefits and she would never risk it by doing something as unprofessional as falling in love with her boss. She'd been with Neil for almost ten years. Chadwick had been married as well. They worked together. Their relationship was nothing but business-professional.

She had no idea how being pregnant was going to change things. If she'd needed this job—and health benefits—before, she needed them so much more now.

Serena took her normal seat in one of the two chairs set before Chadwick's desk and powered up her tablet. "Good morning, Mr. Beaumont." Oh, heavens—she'd forgotten to see if she'd put on make-up this morning in her panic-induced haze. At this point, she could only pray she didn't have raccoon eyes.

"Ms. Chase," Chadwick said by way of greeting, his

gaze flicking over her face. He looked back at his monitor, then paused. Serena barely had time to hold her breath before she had Chadwick Beaumont's undivided attention. "Are you okay?"

No. She'd never been less okay in her adult life. The only thing that was keeping her together was the realization that she'd been less okay as a kid and survived. She'd survive this.

She hoped.

So she squared her shoulders and tried to pull off her most pleasant smile. "I'm fine. Monday mornings, you know."

Chadwick's brow creased as he weighed this statement. "Are you sure?"

She didn't like to lie to him. She didn't like to lie to anyone. She had recently had her fill of lying, thanks to Neil. "It'll be fine."

She had to believe that. She'd pulled herself out of sheer poverty by dint of hard work. A bump in the road—a baby bump—wouldn't ruin everything. She hoped.

His hazel eyes refused to let her go for a long moment. But then he silently agreed to let it pass. "Very well, then. What's on tap this week, beyond the regular meetings?"

As always, she smiled at his joke. What was on tap was beer—literally and figuratively. As far as she knew, it was the only joke he ever told.

Chadwick had set appointments with his vice presidents, usually lunch meetings and the like. He was deeply involved in his company—a truly hands-on boss. Serena's job was making sure his irregular appointments didn't mess up his standing ones. "You have an appointment at ten with your lawyers on Tuesday to try and reach a settlement. I've moved your meeting with Matthew to later in the afternoon."

She carefully left out the facts that the lawyers were divorce attorneys and that the settlement was with his soon-to-be-ex-wife, Helen. The divorce had been dragging on for months now—over thirteen, by her count. She did not know the details. Who was to say what went on behind closed doors in any family? All she knew was that the whole process was wearing Chadwick down like waves eroding a beach—slowly but surely.

Chadwick's shoulders slumped a little and he exhaled with more force. "As if this meeting will go any differently than the last five did." But then he added, "What else?" in a forcefully bright tone.

Serena cleared her throat. That was, in a nutshell, the extent of the personal information they shared. "Wednesday at one is the meeting with the Board of Directors at the Hotel Monaco downtown." She cleared her throat. "To discuss the offer from AllBev. Your afternoon meeting with the production managers was cancelled. They're all going to send status reports instead."

Then she realized—she wasn't so much terrified about having a baby. It was the fact that because she was suddenly going to have a baby, there was a very good chance she could lose her job.

AllBev was an international conglomerate that specialized in beer manufacturers. They'd bought companies in England, South Africa and Australia, and now they had their sights set on Beaumont. They were well-known for dismantling the leadership, installing their own skeleton crew of managers, and wringing every last cent of profit out of the remaining workers.

Chadwick groaned and slumped back in his chair. "That's this week?"

"Yes, sir." He shot her a wounded look at the *sir*, so she corrected herself. "Yes, Mr. Beaumont. It got moved up to accommodate Mr. Harper's schedule." In addition to owning one of the largest banks in Colorado, Leon Harper was also one of the board members pushing to accept AllBev's offer.

What if Chadwick agreed or the board overrode his wishes? What if Beaumont Brewery was sold? She'd be out of a job. There was no way AllBev's management would want to keep the former CEO's personal assistant. She'd be shown the door with nothing more than a salvaged copier-paper box of her belongings to symbolize her nine years there.

Maybe that wouldn't be the end of the world—she'd lived as frugally as she could, tucking almost half of each paycheck away in ultra-safe savings accounts and CDs. She couldn't go back on welfare. She *wouldn't*.

If she weren't pregnant, getting another job would be relatively easy. Chadwick would write her a glowing letter of recommendation. She was highly skilled. Even a temp job would be a job until she found another place like Beaumont Brewery.

Except...except for the benefits. She was pregnant. She *needed* affordable health insurance, and the brewery had some of the most generous health insurance around. She hadn't paid more than ten dollars to see a doctor in eight years.

But it was more than just keeping her costs low. She couldn't go back to the way things had been before she'd started working at the Beaumont Brewery. Feeling like her life was out of control again? Having people treat her like she was a lazy, ignorant leech on society again?

Raising a child the way she'd been raised, living on food pantry handouts and whatever Mom could scavenge from her shift at the diner? Of having social workers threaten to take her away from her parents unless they could do better—*be* better? Of knowing she was always somehow less than the other kids at school but not knowing why—until the day when Missy Gurgin walked up to her in fourth grade and announced to the whole class that Serena was wearing the exact shirt, complete with stain, she'd thrown away because it was ruined?

Serena's lungs tried to clamp shut. *No,* she thought, forcing herself to breathe. It wasn't going to happen like that. She had enough to live on for a couple of years—longer if she moved into a smaller apartment and traded down to a cheaper car. Chadwick wouldn't allow the family business to be sold. He would protect the company. He would protect her.

"Harper. That old goat," Chadwick muttered, snapping Serena back to the present. "He's still grinding that ax about my father. The man never heard of letting bygones be bygones, I swear."

This was the first that Serena had heard about this. "Mr. Harper's out to get you?"

Chadwick waved his hand, dismissing the thought. "He's still trying to get even with Hardwick for sleeping with his wife, as the story goes, two days after Harper and his bride got back from their honeymoon." He looked at her again. "Are you sure you're all right? You look pale."

Pale was probably the best she could hope for today. "I...." She grasped at straws and came up with one. "I hadn't heard that story."

"Hardwick Beaumont was a cheating, lying, philandering, sexist bigot on his best day." Chadwick repeated all of this by rote, as if he'd had it beaten into his skull with a dull spoon. "I have no doubt that he did exactly that—or something very close to it. But it was forty years ago. Hardwick's been dead for almost ten years.

Harper…." He sighed, looking out the windows. In the distance, the Rocky Mountains gleamed in the spring sunlight. Snow capped off the mountains, but it hadn't made it down as far as Denver. "I just wish Harper would realize that I'm not Hardwick."

"I know you're not like that."

His eyes met hers. There was something different in them, something she didn't recognize. "Do you? Do you, really?"

This…this felt like dangerous territory.

She didn't know, actually. She had no idea if he was getting a divorce because he'd slept around on his wife. All she knew was that he'd never hit on her, not once. He treated her as an equal. He respected her.

"Yes," she replied, feeling certain. "I do."

The barest hint of a smile curved up one side of his lips. "Ah, that's what I've always admired about you, Serena. You see the very best in people. You make everyone around you better, just by being yourself."

Oh. *Oh.* Her cheeks warmed, although she wasn't sure if it was from the compliment or the way he said her name. He usually stuck to Ms. Chase.

Dangerous territory, indeed.

She needed to change the subject. *Now.* "Saturday night at nine you have the charity ball at the Denver Art Museum."

That didn't erase the half-cocked smile from his face, but it did earn her a raised eyebrow. Suddenly, Chadwick Beaumont looked anything but tired or worn-down. Suddenly, he looked hot. Well, he was always hot—but right now? It wasn't buried beneath layers of responsibility or worry.

Heat flushed Serena's face, but she wasn't entirely sure why one sincere compliment would have been enough to set her all aflutter. Oh, that's right—she was pregnant. Maybe she was just having a hormonal moment.

"What's that for, again? A food bank?"

"Yes, the Rocky Mountain Food Bank. They were this year's chosen charity."

Every year, the Beaumont Brewery made a big splash by investing heavily in a local charity. One of Serena's job responsibilities was personally handling the small mountain of applications that came in every year. A Beaumont Brewery sponsorship was worth about $35 million in related funds and donations—that's why they chose a new charity every year. Most of the non-profits could operate for five to ten years with that kind of money.

Serena went on. "Your brother Matthew planned this event. It's the centerpiece of our fundraising efforts for the food bank. Your attendance will be greatly appreciated." She usually phrased it as a request, but Chadwick had never missed a gala. He understood that this was as much about promoting the Beaumont Brewery name as it was about promoting a charity.

Chadwick still had her in his sights. "You chose this one, didn't you?"

She swallowed. It was almost as if he had realized that the food bank had been an important part of her family's survival—that they would have starved if they hadn't gotten groceries and hot meals on a weekly basis. "Technically, I choose all the charities. It's my job."

"You do it well." But before the second compliment could register, he continued, "Will Neil be accompanying you?"

"Um…." She usually attended these events with Neil. He mostly went to hobnob with movers and shakers, but Serena loved getting all dressed up and drinking champagne. Things she'd never thought possible back when she was a girl.

Things were different now. So, *so* different. Suddenly, Serena's throat closed up on her. God, what a mess.

"No. He…" *Try not to cry, try not to cry.* "We mutually decided to end our relationship several months ago."

Chadwick's eyebrows jumped up so high they almost cleared his forehead. "Several *months* ago? Why didn't you tell me?"

Breathe in, breathe out. Don't forget to repeat.

"Mr. Beaumont, we usually do not discuss our personal lives at the office." It came out pretty well—fairly strong, her voice only cracking slightly over the word *personal*. "I didn't want you to think I couldn't handle myself."

She was his competent, reliable, loyal employee. If she'd told him that Neil had walked out after she'd confronted him about the text messages on his phone and demanded that he recommit to the relationship—by having a baby and finally getting married—well, she'd have been anything but competent. She might be able to manage Chadwick's office, but not her love life.

Chadwick gave her a look that she'd seen before—the one he broke out when he was rejecting a supplier's offer. A look that blended disbelief and disdain into a potent mix. It was a powerful look, one that usually made people throw out another offer—one with better terms for the Brewery.

He'd never looked at her like that before. It bordered on terrifying. He wouldn't fire her for keeping her private life private, would he? But then everything about him softened as he leaned forward in his chair, his elbows on the table. "If this happened several months ago, what happened this weekend?"

"I'm sorry?"

"This weekend. You're obviously upset. I can tell, although you're doing a good job of hiding it. Did he…" Chadwick cleared his throat, his eyes growing hard. "Did he do something to you this weekend?"

"No, not that." Neil might have been a jerk—okay, he *was* a cheating, commitment-phobic jerk—but she couldn't have Chadwick thinking Neil had beaten her. Still, she was afraid to elaborate. Swallowing was suddenly difficult and she was blinking at an unusually fast rate. If she sat there much longer, she was either going to burst into tears or black out. Why couldn't she get her lungs to work?

So she did the only thing she could. She stood and, as calmly and professionally as possible, walked out of the office. Or tried to, anyway. Her hand was on the doorknob when Chadwick said, "Serena, stop."

She couldn't bring herself to turn around and face him—to risk that disdainful look again, or something worse. So she closed her eyes. Which meant that she didn't see him get up or come around his desk, didn't see him walk up behind her. But she heard it—the creaking of his chair as he stood, the footsteps muffled by the thick Oriental rug. The warmth of his body as he stood close to her—much closer than he normally stood.

He placed his hand on her shoulder and turned her. She had no choice but to pivot, but he didn't let go of her. Not entirely. Oh, he released her shoulder, but when she didn't look up at him, he slid a single finger under her chin and raised her face. "Serena, look at me."

She didn't want to. Her face flushed hot from his touch—because that's what he was doing. *Touching* her. His finger slid up and down her chin—if she didn't know better, she'd say he was caressing her. It was the most intimate touch she'd felt in months. Maybe longer.

She opened her eyes. His face was still a respectable foot away from hers—but this was the closest they'd ever been. He could kiss her if he wanted and she wouldn't be able to stop him. She *wouldn't* stop him.

He didn't. This close up, his eyes were such a fine blend of green and brown and flecks of gold. She felt some of her panic fade as she gazed up into his eyes. She was not in love with her boss. Nope. Never had been. Wasn't about to start falling for him now, no matter how he complimented her or touched her. It wasn't going to happen.

He licked his lips as he stared at her. Maybe he was as nervous as she was. This was several steps over a line neither of them had ever crossed.

But maybe…maybe he was hungry. Hungry for her.

"Serena," he said in a low voice that she wasn't sure she'd ever heard him use before. It sent a tingle down her back that turned into a shudder—a shudder he felt. The corner of his mouth curved again. "Whatever the problem is, you can come to me. If he's bothering you, I'll have it taken care of. If you need help or…" She saw his Adam's apple bob as he swallowed. His finger stroked the same square inch of her skin again and she did a whole lot more than shudder. "Whatever you need, it's yours."

She needed to say something here, something professional and competent. But all she could do was look at his lips. What would they taste like? Would he hesitate, waiting for her to take the lead, or would he kiss her as if he'd been dying to do for seven years?

"What do you mean?" She didn't know what she wanted him to say. It *should* sound like an employer expressing concern for the well-being of a trusted employee—but it didn't. Was he hitting on her after all this time? Just because Neil was a jerk? Because she was obviously having a vulnerable moment? Or was there something else going on there?

The air seemed to thin between them, as if he'd leaned forward without realizing it. Or perhaps she'd done the leaning. *He's going to kiss me,* she realized. *He's going to kiss me and I want him to. I've always wanted him to.*

He didn't. He just ran his finger over her chin again, as if he were memorizing her every feature. She wanted to reach up and thread her fingers through his sandy hair, pull his mouth down to hers. Taste those lips. Feel more than just his finger.

"Serena, you're my most trusted employee. You always have been. I want you to know that, whatever happens at the board meeting, I will take care of you. I won't let them walk you out of this building without anything. Your loyalty *will* be rewarded. I won't fail you."

All the oxygen she'd been holding in rushed out of her with a soft "*oh.*"

It was what she needed to hear. God, how she needed to hear it. She might not have Neil, but all of her hard work was worth something. She wouldn't have to think about going back on welfare or declaring bankruptcy or standing in line at the food pantry.

Then some of her good sense came back to her. This would be the time to have a business-professional response. "Thank you, Mr. Beaumont."

Something in his grin changed, making him look almost wicked—the very best kind of wicked. "Better than *sir,* but still. Call me Chadwick. Mr. Beaumont sounds too much like my father." When he said this, a hint of his former weariness crept into his eyes. Suddenly, he dropped his finger away from her chin and took a step back. "So, lawyers on Tuesday, Board of Directors on Wednesday, charity ball on Saturday?"

Somehow, Serena managed to nod. They were back on familiar footing now. "Yes." She took another deep breath, feeling calmer.

"I'll pick you up."

So much for that feeling of calm. "Excuse me?"

A little of the wickedness crept back into his smile. "I'm going to the charity gala. You're going to the charity gala. It makes sense that we would go to the charity gala together. I'll pick you up at seven."

"But…the gala starts at nine."

"Obviously we'll go to dinner." She must have looked worried because he took another step back. "Call it…an early celebration for the success of your charity selection this year."

In other words, don't call it a date. Even if that's what it sounded like. "Yes, Mr. Beau—" He shot her a hot look that had her snapping her mouth shut. "Yes, Chadwick."

He grinned an honest-to-God grin that took fifteen years off his face. "There. That wasn't so hard, was it?" Then he turned away from her and headed back to his desk. Whatever moment they'd just had, it was over. "Bob Larsen should be in at ten. Let me know when he gets here."

"Of course." She couldn't bring herself to say his name again. Her head was too busy swimming with everything that had just happened.

She was halfway through the door, already pulling it shut behind her, when he called out, "And Serena? Whatever you need. I mean it."

"Yes, Chadwick."

Then she closed his door.

Two

This was the point in his morning where Chadwick normally reviewed the marketing numbers. Bob Larsen was his handpicked Vice President of Marketing. He'd helped move the company's brand recognition way, way up. Although Bob was closing in on fifty, he had an intrinsic understanding of the internet and social media, and had used it to drag the brewery into the twenty-first century. He'd put Beaumont Brewery on Facebook, then Twitter—never chasing the trend, but leading it. Chadwick wasn't sure exactly what SnappShot did, beyond make pictures look scratched and grainy, but Bob was convinced that it was the platform through which to launch their new line of Percheron Seasonal Ales. "Targeting all those foodies who snap shots of their dinners!" he'd said the week before, in the excited voice of a kid getting a new bike for Christmas.

Yes, that's what Chadwick *should* have been thinking

about. He took his meetings with his department heads seriously. He took the whole company seriously. He rewarded hard work and loyalty and never, ever allowed distractions. He ran a damn tight ship.

So why was he sitting there, thinking about his assistant?

Because he was. Man, was he.

Several months.

Her words kept rattling around in his brain, along with the way she'd looked that morning—drawn, tired. Like a woman who'd cried her eyes out most of the weekend. She hadn't answered his question. If that prick had walked out several months before—and no matter what she said about what 'we decided,' Chadwick had heard the 'he' first—what had happened that weekend?

The thought of Neil Moore—mediocre golf pro always trying to suck up to the next big thing every time Chadwick had met him—doing anything to hurt Serena made him furious. He'd never liked Neil. Too much of a leech, not good enough for the likes of Serena Chase. Chadwick had always been of the opinion that she deserved someone better, someone who wouldn't abandon her at a party to schmooze a local TV personality like he'd witnessed Neil do on at least three separate occasions.

Serena deserved so much better than that ass. Of course, Chadwick had known that for years. Why was it bothering him so much this morning?

She'd looked so...different. Upset, yes, but there was something else going on. Serena had always been unflappable, totally focused on the job. Of course Chadwick had never done anything inappropriate involving her, but he'd caught a few other men assuming she was up for grabs just because she was a woman in Hardwick Beaumont's old office. Chadwick had never done business with those men again—which, a few times, meant going with the higher-priced vendor. It went against the principles his father, Hardwick, had raised him by—the bottom line was the most important thing.

Hardwick might have been a lying, cheating bastard, but that wasn't Chadwick. And Serena knew it. She'd said so herself.

That had to be why Chadwick had lost his mind and done something he'd managed not to do for eight years—touch Serena. Oh, he'd touched her before. She had a hell of a handshake, one that betrayed no weakness or fear, something that occasionally undermined other women in a position of power. But putting his hand on her shoulder? Running a finger along the sensitive skin under her chin? Hell.

For a moment, he'd done something he'd wanted to do for years—engage Serena Chase on a level that went far beyond his scheduling conflicts. And for that moment, it'd felt wonderful to see her dark brown eyes look up at him, her pupils dilating with need—reflecting his desire back at him. To feel her body respond to his touch.

Some days, it felt like he never got to do what he wanted. Chadwick was the responsible one. The one who ran the family company and cleaned up the family messes and paid the family bills while everyone else in the family ran amuck, having affairs and one-night stands and spending money like it was going out of style.

Just that weekend his brother Phillip had bought some horse for a million dollars. And what did his little brother do to pay for it? He went to company-sponsored parties and drank Beaumont Beer. That was the extent of Phillip's involvement in the company. Phillip always did exactly what he wanted without a single thought for how it might affect other people—for how it might affect the brewery.

Not Chadwick. He'd been born to run this company. It wasn't a joke—Hardwick Beaumont had called a press conference in the hospital and held the newborn Chadwick up, red-faced and screaming, to proclaim him the future of Beaumont Brewery. Chadwick had the newspaper articles to prove it.

He'd done a good job—so good, in fact, that the Brewery had become the target for takeovers and mergers by conglomerates who didn't give a damn for beer or for the Beaumont name. They just wanted to boost their companies' bottom lines with Beaumont's profits.

Just once, he'd done something he wanted. Not what his father expected or the investors demanded or Wall Street projected—what *he* wanted. Serena had been upset. He'd wanted to comfort her. At heart, it wasn't a bad thing.

But then he'd remembered his father. And that Chadwick seducing his assistant was no better than Hardwick Beaumont seducing his secretary. So he'd stopped. Chadwick Beaumont was responsible, focused, driven, and in no way controlled by his baser animal instincts. He was better than that. He was better than his father.

Chadwick had been faithful while married. Serena had been with—well, he'd never been sure if Neil was her husband, live-in lover, boyfriend, significant other, life partner—whatever people called it these days. Plus, she'd worked for Chadwick. That had always held him back because he was not the apple that had fallen from Hardwick's tree, by God.

All of these correct thoughts did not explain why Chadwick's finger was hovering over the intercom button, ready to call Serena back into the office and ask her again what had happened this weekend. Selfishly, he almost wanted her to break down and cry on his shoulder, just so he could hold her.

Chadwick forced himself to turn back to his monitor and call up the latest figures. Bob had emailed him the analytics Sunday night. Chadwick hated wasting time having something he could easily read explained to him. He was no idiot. Just because he didn't understand *why* anyone would take pictures of their dinner and post them online didn't mean he couldn't see the user habits shifting, just as Bob said they would.

This was better, he thought, as he looked over the numbers. Work. Work was good. It kept him focused. Like telling Serena he was taking her to the gala—a work function. They'd been at galas and banquets like that before. What difference did it make if they arrived in the same car or not? It didn't. It was business related. Nothing personal.

Except it was personal and he knew it. Picking her up in his car, taking her out to dinner? Not business. Even if they discussed business things, it still wouldn't be the same as dinner with, say, Bob Larsen. Serena usually wore a black silk gown with a bit of a fishtail hem and a sweetheart neckline to these things. Chadwick didn't care that it was always the same gown. She looked fabulous in it, a pashmina shawl draped over her otherwise bare shoulders, a small string of pearls resting against her collarbone, her thick brown hair swept up into an artful twist.

No, dinner would not be business-related. Not even close.

He wouldn't push her, he decided. It was the only compromise he could make with himself. He wasn't like his father, who'd had no qualms about making his secretaries' jobs contingent upon sex. He wasn't about to trap Serena into doing anything either of them would regret. He would take her to dinner and then the gala, and would do nothing more than enjoy her company. That was that. He could restrain himself just fine. He'd had years of practice, after all.

Thankfully, the intercom buzzed and Serena's normal, level voice announced that Bob was there. "Send him in," Chadwick replied, thankful to have a distraction from his own thoughts.

He had to fight to keep his company. He had no illusions that the board meeting on Wednesday would go well. He was in danger of becoming the Beaumont who lost the brewery—of failing at the one thing he'd been raised to do.

He did not have time to be distracted by Serena Chase. And that was final.

The rest of Monday passed without a reply from Neil. Serena was positive about this because she refreshed her email approximately every other minute. Tuesday started much the same. She had her morning meeting with Chadwick where, apart from when he asked her if everything was all right, nothing out of the ordinary happened. No lingering glances, no hot touches and absolutely no near-miss kisses. Chadwick was his regular self, so Serena made sure to be as normal as she could be.

Not to say it wasn't a challenge. Maybe she'd imagined the whole thing. She could blame a lot on hormones now, right? So Chadwick had stepped out of his prescribed role for a moment. She was the one who'd been upset. She must have misunderstood his intent, that's all.

Which left her more depressed than she expected. It's not like she *wanted* Chadwick to make a pass at her. An

intra-office relationship was against company policy—
she knew because she'd helped Chadwick rewrite the
policy when he first hired her. Flings between bosses and
employees set the company up for sexual harassment lawsuits when everything went south—which it usually did.

But that didn't explain why, as she watched him walk
out of the office on his way to meet with the divorce lawyers with his ready-for-battle look firmly in place, she
wished his divorce would be final. Just because the process was draining him, that's all.

Sigh. She didn't believe herself. How could she convince anyone else?

She turned her attention to the last-minute plans for
the gala. After Chadwick returned to the office, he'd
meet with his brother Matthew, who was technically in
charge of planning the event. But a gala for five hundred
of the richest people in Denver? It was all hands on deck.

The checklist was huge, and it required her full attention. She called suppliers, tracked shipments and checked
the guest list.

She ate lunch at her desk as she followed up on her
contacts in the local media. The press was a huge part of
why charities competed for the Beaumont sponsorship.
Few of these organizations had an advertising budget.
Beaumont Brewery put their name front and center for
a year, getting television coverage, interviews and even
fashion bloggers.

She had finished her yogurt and wiped down her desk
by the time Chadwick came back. He looked *terrible*—
head down, hands jammed into his pockets, shoulders
slumped. Oh, no. She didn't even have to ask to know
that the meeting had not gone according to plan.

He paused in front of her desk. The effort to raise his
head and meet her eyes seemed to take a lot out of him.

Serena gasped in surprise at how *lost* he looked. His eyes were rimmed in red, like he hadn't slept in days.

She wanted to go to him—put her arms around him and tell him it'd all work out. That's what her mom had always done when things didn't pan out, when Dad lost his job or they had to move again because they couldn't make the rent.

The only problem was, she'd never believed it when she was a kid. And now, as an adult with a failed long-term relationship under her belt and a baby on the way?

No, she wouldn't believe it either.

God, the raw pain in his eyes was like a slap in the face. She didn't know what to do, what to say. Maybe she should just do nothing. To try and comfort him might be to cross the line they'd crossed on Monday.

Chadwick gave a little nod with his head, as if he were agreeing they shouldn't cross that line again. Then he dropped his head, muttered, "Hold my calls," and trudged into his office.

Defeated. That's what he was. *Beaten.* Seeing him like that was unnerving—and that was being generous. Chadwick Beaumont did not lose in the business world. He didn't always get every single thing he wanted, but he never walked away from a negotiation, a press conference—anything—looking like he'd lost the battle *and* the war.

She sat at her desk for a moment, too stunned to do much of anything. What had happened? What on earth would leave him that crushed?

Maybe it was the hormones. Maybe it was employee loyalty. Maybe it was something else. Whatever it was, she found herself on her feet and walking into his office without even knocking.

Chadwick was sitting at his desk. He had his head

in his hands as if they were the only things supporting his entire weight. He'd shed his suit coat, and he looked smaller for having done it.

When she shut the door behind her, he started talking but he didn't lift his head. "She won't sign off on it. She wants more money. Everything is finalized except how much alimony she gets."

"How much does she want?" Serena had no business asking, but she did anyway.

"Two hundred and fifty." The way he said it was like Serena was pulling an arrow out of his back.

She blinked at him. "Two hundred and fifty dollars?" She knew that wasn't the right answer. Chadwick could afford that. But the only other option was…

"Thousand. Two hundred and fifty thousand dollars."

"A year?"

"A month. She wants three million a year. For the rest of her life. Or she won't sign."

"But that's—that's insane! No one needs that much to live!" The words burst out of her a bit louder than she meant them to, but seriously? Three million dollars a year forever? Serena wouldn't earn that much in her entire lifetime!

Chadwick looked up, a mean smile on his face. "It's not about the money. She just wants to ruin me. If I could pay that much until the end of time, she'd double her request. Triple it, if she thought it would hurt me."

"But why?"

"I don't know. I never cheated on her, never did anything to hurt her. I tried…" His words trailed off as he buried his face in his hands.

"Can't you just buy her out? Make her an up-front offer she can't refuse?" Serena had seen him do that before, with a micro-brew whose beers were undercutting

Beaumont's Percheron Drafts line of beers. Chadwick had let negotiations drag on for almost a week, wearing down the competitors. Then he walked in with a lump sum that no sane person would walk away from, no matter how much they cared about the "integrity" of their beer. Everyone had a price, after all.

"I don't have a hundred million lying around. It's tied up in investments, property...the horses." He said this last bit with an edge, as if the company mascots, the Percherons, were just a thorn in his side.

"But—you have a pre-nup, right?"

"Of *course* I have a pre-nup," he snapped. She flinched, but he immediately sagged in defeat again. "I watched my father get married and divorced four times before he died. There's no way I wouldn't have a pre-nup."

"Then how can she do that?"

"Because." He grabbed at his short hair and pulled. "Because I was stupid and thought I was in love. I thought I had to prove to her that I trusted her. That I wasn't my father. She gets half of what I earned during our marriage. That's about twenty-eight million. She can't touch the family fortune or any of the property—none of that. But..."

Serena felt the blood drain from her face. "Twenty-eight *million*?" That was the kind of money people in her world only got when they won the lottery. "But?"

"My lawyers had put in a clause limiting how much alimony would be paid, for how long. The length of the marriage, fifty thousand a month. And I told them to take it out. Because I wouldn't need it. Like an idiot." That last bit came out so harshly—he really did believe that this was his fault.

She did some quick math. Chadwick had gotten married near the end of her first year at Beaumont Brewery—her internship year. The wedding had been a big thing, obviously, and the brewery had even come out with a limited-edition beer to mark the occasion.

That was slightly more than eight years ago. Fifty thousand—still an absolutely insane number—times twelve months times eight years was...*only* $4.8 million. And somehow, that and another $28 million wasn't enough. "Isn't there...anything you can do?"

"I offered her one fifty a month for twenty years. She laughed. *Laughed.*" Serena knew the raw desperation in his voice.

Oh, sure, she'd never been in the position of losing a fortune, but there'd been plenty of desperate times back when she was growing up.

Back then, she'd just wanted to know it was going to be okay. They'd have a safe place to sleep and a big meal to eat. To know she'd have both of those things the next day, too.

She never got those assurances. Her mother would hum "One Day At a Time" over and over when they had to stuff their meager things into grocery bags and move again. Then they finally got the little trailer and didn't have to move any more—but didn't have enough to pay for both electricity and water.

One day at a time was a damn fine sentiment, but it didn't put food on the table and clothes on her back.

There had to be a way to appease Chadwick's ex, but Serena had no idea what it was. Such battles were beyond her. She might have worked for Chadwick Beaumont for over seven years, might have spent her days in this office, might have attended balls and galas, but this was not her world. She didn't know what to say about someone who wasn't happy with *just* $32.8 million.

But she could sympathize with staring at a bill that could never be paid—a bill that, no matter how hard your mom worked as a waitress at the diner or how many overtime shifts as a janitor your dad pulled, would never, ever end. Not even when her parents had filed for bankruptcy had it truly ended, because whatever little credit they'd been able to use as a cushion disappeared. She loved her parents—and they loved each other—but the sinking hopelessness that went with never having enough…

That's not how she was going to live. She didn't wish it on anyone, but especially not on Chadwick.

She moved before she was aware of it, her steps muffled by the carpeting. She knew it would be a lie, but all she had to offer were platitudes that tomorrow was a new day.

She didn't hesitate when she got to the desk. In all of the time she'd spent in this office, she'd never once crossed the plane of the desk. She'd sat in front of the massive piece of furniture, but she'd never gone around it.

Today she did. Maybe it was the hormones again, maybe it was the way Chadwick had spoken to her yesterday in that low voice—promising to take care of her.

She saw the tension ripple through his back as she stepped closer. The day before, she'd been upset and he'd touched her. Today, the roles were reversed.

She put her hand on his shoulder. Through the shirt, she felt the warmth of his body. That's all. She didn't even try to turn him as he'd turned her. She just let him know she was there.

He shifted and, pulling his opposite hand away from his face, reached back to grab hers. Yesterday, he'd had all the control. But today? Today she felt they were on equal footing.

She laced their fingers together, but that was as far as

it went. She couldn't make the same kinds of promises he had—she couldn't take care of him when she wasn't even sure how she was going to take care of her baby. But she could let him know she was there, if he needed her.

She chose not to think about exactly what *that* might mean.

"Serena," Chadwick said, his voice raw as his fingers tightened around hers.

She swallowed. But before she could come up with a response, there was a knock on the door and in walked Matthew Beaumont, Vice President of Public Relations for the Beaumont Brewery. He looked a little like Chadwick—commanding build, the Beaumont nose— but where Chadwick and Phillip were lighter, sandier blondes, Matthew had more auburn coloring.

Serena tried to pull her hand free, but Chadwick wouldn't let her go. It was almost as if he wanted Matthew to see them touching. Holding hands.

It was one thing to stick a toe over the business-professional line when it was just her and Chadwick in the office—no witnesses meant it hadn't really happened, right? But Matthew was no idiot.

"Am I interrupting?" Matthew asked, his eyes darting between Serena's face, Chadwick's face, and their interlaced hands.

Of course, Serena would rather take her chances with Matthew than with Phillip Beaumont. Phillip was a professional playboy who flaunted his wealth and went to a lot of parties. As far as Serena could tell, Phillip might be the kind of guy who wouldn't have stopped at a simple touch the day before. Of course, with his gorgeous looks, he probably had plenty of invitations to keep going.

Matthew was radically different from either of his brothers. Serena guessed that was because his mother was Hardwick's second wife, but Matthew was always working hard, as if he were trying to prove he belonged at the brewery. But he did so without the intimidation that Chadwick could wear like a second skin.

With a quick squeeze, Chadwick released her hand and she took a small step back. "No," Chadwick said. "We're done here."

For some inexplicable reason, the words hurt. She didn't know why. She had no good reason for him to defend their touch to his half brother. She had absolutely no reason why she would want Chadwick to defend their relationship—because they didn't have one outside of boss and trusted employee.

She gave a small nod of her head that she wasn't sure either of them saw, and walked out of his office.

Minutes passed. Chadwick knew that Matthew was sitting on the other side of the desk, no doubt waiting for something, but he wasn't up for that just yet.

Helen was out to ruin him. If he knew why, he'd try to make it up to her. But hadn't that pretty much described their marriage? She got her nose bent out of shape, Chadwick had no idea why, but he did his damnedest to make it up to her? He bought her diamonds. She liked diamonds. Then he added rubies to the mix. He'd thought it made things better.

It hadn't. And he was more the fool for thinking it had.

He replayed the conversation with Serena. He hadn't talked much about his divorce to anyone, beyond informing his brothers that it was a problem that would be taking up some measure of his time. He didn't know why he'd told Serena it was his fault that negotiations had gotten to this point.

All he knew was that he'd had to tell someone. The

burden of knowing that this whole thing was a problem he'd created all by himself was more than he could bear.

And she'd touched him. Not like he'd touched her, no, but not like she'd ever touched him before. More than a handshake, that was for damn sure.

When was the last time a woman had touched him aside from the business handshakes that went with the job? Helen had moved out of the master bedroom almost two years before. Not since before then, if he was being honest with himself.

Matthew cleared his throat, which made Chadwick look up. "Yes?"

"If I thought you were anything like our father," Matthew began, his voice walking the fine line between sympathetic and snarky, "I'd assume you were working on wife number two."

Chadwick glared at the man. Matthew was only six months younger than Chadwick's younger brother, Phillip. It had taken several more years before Hardwick's and Eliza's marriage had crumbled, and Hardwick had married Matthew's mother, Jeannie, but once Chadwick's mother knew about Jeannie, the end was just a matter of time.

Matthew was living proof that Hardwick Beaumont had been working on wife number two long before he'd left wife number one.

"I haven't gotten rid of wife number one yet." Even as he said it, though, Chadwick flinched. That was something his father would have said. He detested sounding like his father. He detested *being* like his father.

"Which only goes to illustrate how you are *not* like our father," Matthew replied with an easy-going grin, the same grin that all the Beaumont men had. A lingering gift from their father. "Hardwick wouldn't have cared. Marriage vows meant nothing to him."

Chadwick nodded. Matthew spoke the truth and Chadwick should have taken comfort in that. Funny how he didn't.

"I take it Helen is not going quietly into the night?"

Chadwick hated his half brother right then. True, Phillip—Chadwick's full brother, the only person who knew what it was like to have both Hardwick and Eliza Beaumont as parents—wouldn't have understood either. But Chadwick hated sitting across from the living symbol of his father's betrayal of both his wife and his family.

It was a damn shame that Matthew had such a good head for public relations. Any other half relative would have found himself on the street long ago, and then Chadwick wouldn't have had to face his father's failings as a man and a husband on a daily basis.

He wouldn't have had to face his own failings on a daily basis.

"Buy her out," Matthew said simply.

"She doesn't want money. She wants to hurt me." There had to be something wrong with him, he decided. Since when did he air his dirty laundry to anyone—including his executive assistant, including his half brother?

He didn't. His personal affairs were just that, personal.

Matthew's face darkened. "Everyone has a price, Chadwick." Then, in an even quieter voice, he added, "Even you."

He knew what that was about. The whole company was on pins and needles about AllBev's buyout offer. "I'm *not* going to sell our company tomorrow."

Matthew met his stare head-on. Matthew didn't flinch. Didn't even blink. "You're not the only one with a price, you know. Everyone on that board has a price, too—and probably a far sight less than yours." Matthew paused, looking down at his tablet. "Anyone else would have already made the deal. Why you've stuck by the family name for this long has always escaped me."

"Because, unlike *some* people, it's the only name I've ever had."

Everything about Matthew's face shut down, which made Chadwick feel like an even bigger ass. He remembered his parents' divorce, remembered Hardwick marrying Jeannie Billings—remembered the day Matthew, practically the same age as Phillip, had come to live with them. He'd been Matthew Billings until he was five. Then, suddenly, he was Matthew Beaumont.

Chadwick had tortured him mercilessly. It was Matthew's fault that Eliza and Hardwick had fallen apart. It was Matthew's fault that Chadwick's mom had left. Matthew's fault that Hardwick had kept custody of both Chadwick and Phillip. And it was most certainly Matthew's fault that Hardwick suddenly hadn't had any time for Chadwick—except to yell at him for not getting things right.

But that was a child's cop-out and he knew it. Matthew had been just a kid. As had Phillip. As had Chadwick. Hardwick—it had been all *his* fault that Eliza had hated him, had grown to hate her children.

"I'm…that was uncalled for." Nearly a lifetime of blaming Matthew had made it damn hard to apologize to the man. So he changed the subject. "Everything ready for the gala?"

Matthew gave him a look Chadwick couldn't quite make out. It was almost as if Matthew was going to challenge him to an old-fashioned duel over honor, right here in the office.

But the moment passed. "We're ready. As usual, Ms.

Chase has proven to be worth far more than her weight in gold."

As Matthew talked, that phrase echoed in Chadwick's head.

Everyone did have a price, he realized.

Even Helen Beaumont. Even Serena Chase.

He just didn't know what that price was.

Three

"The Beaumont Brewery has been run by a Beaumont for one hundred and thirty-three years," Chadwick thundered, smacking the tabletop with his hand to emphasize his point.

Serena jumped at the sudden noise. Chadwick didn't normally get this worked up at board meetings. Then again, he'd been more agitated—more abnormal—this entire week. Her hormones might be off, but he wasn't behaving in a typical fashion, either.

"The Beaumont name is worth more than $52 dollars a share," Chadwick went on. "It's worth more than $62 a share. We've got one of the last family-owned, family-operated breweries left in America. We have the pleasure of working for a piece of American history. The Percherons? The beer? That's the result of hard American work."

There was an unsettled pause as Serena took notes. Of

course there was a secretary at the meeting, but Chadwick liked to have a separate version against which he could cross-check the minutes.

She glanced up from her seat off to the side of the hotel ballroom. The Beaumont family owned fifty-one percent of the Beaumont Brewery. They'd kept a firm hand on the business for, well, forever—easily fending off hostile takeovers and not-so-hostile mergers. Chadwick was in charge, though. The rest of the Beaumonts just collected checks like any other stockholders.

She could see that some people were really listening to Chadwick—nodding in agreement, whispering to their neighbors. This meeting wasn't a full shareholders' meeting, so only about twenty people were in the room. Some of them were holdovers from Hardwick's era—handpicked back in the day. They didn't have much power beyond their vote, but they were fiercely loyal to the company.

Those were the people nodding now—the ones who had a personal stake in the company's version of American history.

There were some members—younger, more corporate types that had been brought in to provide balance against the old-boys board of Hardwick's era. Chadwick had selected a few of them, but they weren't the loyal employees that worked with him on a day-to-day basis.

Then there were the others—members brought in by other members. Those, like Harper and his two protégées, had absolutely no interest in Beaumont beer, and they did nothing to hide it.

It was Harper who broke the tense silence. "Odd, Mr. Beaumont. In my version of the American dream, hard work is rewarded with money. The buyout will make you a billionaire. Isn't that the American dream?"

Other heads—the younger ones—nodded in agreement.

Serena could see Chadwick struggling to control his emotions. It hurt to watch. He was normally above this, normally so much more intimidating. But after the week he'd had, she couldn't blame him for looking like he wanted to personally wring Harper's neck. Harper owned almost ten percent of this company, though. Strangling him would be frowned upon.

"The Beaumont Brewery has already provided for my needs," he said, his voice tight. "It's my duty to my company, my *employees*...." At this, he glanced up. His gaze met Serena's, sending a heated charge between them.

Her. He was talking about her.

Chadwick went on, "It's my duty to make sure that the people who *choose* to work for Beaumont Brewery also get to realize the American dream. Some in management will get to cash out their stock options. They'll get a couple of thousand, maybe. Not enough to retire on. But the rest? The men and women who actually make this company work? They won't. AllBev will walk in, fire them all, and reduce our proud history to nothing more than a brand name. No matter how you look at it, Mr. Harper, that's not the American dream. I take care of those who work for me. I reward loyalty. I do not dump it by the side of the road the moment it becomes slightly inconvenient. I cannot be bought off at the expense of those who willingly give me their time and energy. I expect nothing less from this board."

Then, abruptly, he sat. Head up, shoulders back, he didn't look like a man who had just lost. If anything, he looked like a man ready to take all comers. Chadwick had never struck her as a physical force to be reckoned with—but right now? Yeah, he looked like he could fight for his company. To the death.

The room broke out into a cacophony of arguments—the old guard arguing with the new guard, both arguing with Harper's faction. After about fifteen minutes, Harper demanded they call a vote.

For a moment, Serena thought Chadwick had won. Only four people voted to accept AllBev's offer of $52 a share. A clear defeat. Serena breathed a sigh of relief. At least something this week was going right. Her job was safe—which meant her future was safe. She could keep working for Chadwick. Things could continue just as they were. There was comfort in the familiar, and she clung to it.

But then Harper called a second vote. "What should our counteroffer be? I believe Mr. Beaumont said $62 a share wasn't enough. Shall we put $65 to a vote?"

Chadwick jolted in his seat, looking far more than murderous. They voted.

Thirteen people voted for the counteroffer of $65 a share. Chadwick looked as if someone had stabbed him in the gut. It hurt to see him look so hollow—to know this was another fight he was losing, on top of the fight with Helen.

She felt nauseous, and she was pretty sure it had nothing to do with morning sickness. Surely AllBev wouldn't want to spend that much on the brewery, Serena hoped as she wrote everything down. Maybe they'd look for a cheaper, easier target.

Everything Chadwick had spoken of—taking care of his workers, helping them all, not just the privileged few, reach for the American dream—that was why she worked for him. He had given her a chance to earn her way out of abject poverty. Because of him, she had a chance to raise her baby in better circumstances than those in which she'd been raised.

All of that could be taken away from her because Mr. Harper was grinding a forty-year-old ax.

It wasn't fair. She didn't know when she'd started to think that life was fair—it certainly hadn't been during her childhood. But the rules of Beaumont Brewery had been more than fair. Work hard, get promoted, get benefits. Work harder, get a raise, get out of a cube and into an office. Work even harder, get a big bonus. Get to go to galas. Get to dream about retirement plans.

Get to feel secure.

All of that was for sale at $65 a share.

The meeting broke up, everyone going off with their respective cliques. A few of the old-timers came up to Chadwick and appeared to offer their support. Or their condolences. She couldn't tell from her unobtrusive spot off to the side.

Chadwick stood stiffly and, eyes facing forward, stalked out of the room. Serena quickly gathered her things and went after him. He seemed to be in such a fog that she didn't want him to accidentally leave her behind.

She didn't need to worry. Chadwick was standing just outside the ballroom doors, still staring straight ahead.

She needed to get him out of there. If he was going to have another moment like he'd had yesterday—a moment when his self-control slipped, a moment where he would allow himself to be lost—by no means should he have that moment in a hotel lobby.

She touched his arm. "I'll call for the car."

"Yes," he said, in a weirdly blank voice. "Please do." Then his head swung down and his eyes focused on her. Sadness washed over his expression so strongly that it brought tears to her eyes. "I tried, Serena. For you."

What? She'd thought he was trying to save his company—the family business. The family name. What did he mean, he'd tried for *her*?

"I know," she said, afraid to say anything else. "I'll go get the car. Stay here." The driver stayed with the car. The valet just had to go find him.

It took several minutes. During that time, board members trickled out of the ballroom. Some were heading to dinner at the restaurant up the street, no doubt to celebrate their brilliant move to make themselves richer. A few shook Chadwick's hand. No one else seemed to realize what a state of shock he was in. No one but her.

Finally, after what felt like a small eternity, the company car pulled up. It wasn't really a car in the true sense of the word. Oh, it was a Cadillac, but it was the limo version. It was impressive without being ostentatious. Much like Chadwick.

The doorman opened the door for them. Absent-mindedly, Chadwick fished a bill out of his wallet and shoved it at the man. Then they climbed into the car.

When the door shut behind them, a cold silence seemed to grip the car. It wasn't just her security on the line.

How did one comfort a multi-millionaire on the verge of becoming an unwilling billionaire? Once again, she was out of her league. She kept her mouth shut and her eyes focused on the passing Denver cityscape. The journey to the brewery on the south side of the city would take thirty minutes if traffic was smooth.

When she got back to the office, she'd have to open up her resume—that was all. If Chadwick lost the company, she didn't think she could wait around until she got personally fired by the new management. She *needed* uninterrupted health benefits—prenatal care trumped any thought of retirement. Chadwick would understand that, wouldn't he?

When Chadwick spoke, it made her jump. "What do you want?"

"Beg pardon?"

"Out of life." He was staring out his own window. "Is this what you thought you'd be doing with your life? Is this what you wanted?"

"Yes." Mostly. She'd thought that she and Neil would be married by now, maybe with a few cute kids. Being single and pregnant wasn't exactly how she'd dreamed she'd start a family.

But the job? That was exactly what she'd wanted.

So she wasn't breaking through the glass ceiling. She didn't care. She was able to provide for herself. Or had been, anyway. That was the most important thing.

"Really?"

"Working for you has been very…stable. That's not something I had growing up."

"Parents got divorced too, huh?"

She swallowed. "No, actually. Still wildly in love. But love doesn't pay the rent or put food on the table. Love doesn't pay the doctor's bills."

His head snapped away from the window so fast she thought she'd heard his neck pop. "I…I had no idea."

"I don't talk about it." Neil knew, of course. He'd met her when she was still living on ramen noodles and working two part-time jobs to pay for college. Moving in with him had been a blessing—he'd covered the rent for the first year while she'd interned at Beaumont. But once she'd been able to contribute, she had. She'd put all her emphasis on making ends meet, then making a nest egg.

Perhaps too much emphasis. Maybe she'd been so focused on making sure that she was an equal contributor to the relationship—that money would never drive them apart—that she'd forgotten a relationship was more than a bank account. After all, her parents had nothing *but* each other. They were horrid with money, but they loved each other fiercely.

Once, she'd loved Neil like that—passionately. But somewhere along the way that had mellowed into a balanced checkbook. As if love could be measured in dollars and cents.

Chadwick was staring at her as if he'd never seen her before. She didn't like it—even though he no longer seemed focused on the sale of the company, she didn't want to see pity creep into his eyes. She hated pity.

So she redirected. "What about you?"

"Me?" He seemed confused by the question.

"Did you always want to run the brewery?"

Her question worked; it distracted Chadwick from her dirt-poor life. But it failed in that it created another weary wave that washed over his expression. "I was never given a choice."

The way he said it sounded so…cold. Detached, even. "Never?"

"No." He cut the word off, turning his attention back to the window. Ah. Her childhood wasn't the only thing they didn't talk about.

"So, what *would* you want—if you had the choice?" Which he very well might have after the next round of negotiations.

He looked at her then, his eyes blazing with a new, almost feverish, kind of light. She'd only seen him look like that once before—on Monday, when he'd put his finger under her chin. But even then, he hadn't looked quite this…heated. The back of her neck began to sweat under his gaze.

Would he lean forward and put his hand on her again? Would he keep leaning until he was close enough to kiss? Would he do more than just that?

Would she let him?

"I want…" He let the word trail off, the raw need in his voice scratching against her ears like his five-o'clock shadow would scratch against her cheek. "I want to do something for me. Not for the family, not for the company—just for me."

Serena swallowed. The way he said that made it pretty clear what that 'something' might be.

He was her boss, she was his secretary, and he was still married. But none of that seemed to be an issue right now. They were alone in the back of a secure vehicle. The driver couldn't see through the divider. No one would barge in on them. No one would stop them.

I'm pregnant. The words popped onto her tongue and tried frantically to break out of her mouth. That would nip this little infatuation they both seemed to be indulging right in the bud. She was pregnant with another man's baby. She was hormonal and putting on weight in odd locations and wasn't anyone's idea of desirable right now.

But she didn't. He was already feeling the burden of taking care of his employees. How would he react to her pregnancy? Would all those promises to reward her loyalty and take care of her be just another weight he would struggle to carry?

No. She had worked hard to take care of herself. So she was unexpectedly expecting. So her job was possibly standing on its last legs. She would not throw herself at her boss with the hopes that he'd somehow "fix" her life. She knew first-hand that waiting for someone else to fix your problems meant you just had to keep on waiting.

She'd gotten herself into her current situation. She could handle it herself.

That included handling herself around Chadwick.

So she cleared her throat and forced her voice to sound light and non-committal. "Maybe you can find something that doesn't involve beer."

He blinked once, then gave a little nod. He wasn't going to press the issue. He accepted her dodge. It was the right thing to do, after all.

Damn it.

"I like beer," he replied, returning his gaze to the window. "When I was nineteen, I worked alongside the brew masters. They taught me how to *make* beer, not just think of it in terms of units sold. It was fun. Like a chemistry experiment—change one thing, change the whole nature of the brew. To those guys, beer was a living thing—the yeast, the sugars. It was an art *and* a science." His voice drifted a bit, a relaxed smile taking hold of his mouth. "That was a good year. I was sorry to leave those guys behind."

"What do you mean?"

"My father made me spend a year interning in each department, from the age of sixteen on. Outside of my studies, I had to clock in at least twenty hours every week at the brewery."

"That's a lot of work for a teenager." True, she'd had a job when she was sixteen, too, bagging groceries at the local supermarket, but that was a matter of survival. Her family needed her paycheck, plus she got first crack at the merchandise that had been damaged during shipping. She kept the roof over their heads and occasionally put food on the table. The satisfaction she'd gotten from accomplishing those things still lingered.

His smile got less relaxed, more cynical. "I learned

how to run the company. That's what he wanted." She must have given him a look because he added, "Like I said—I wasn't given any choice in the matter."

What his father had wanted—but not what Chadwick had wanted.

The car slowed down and turned. She glanced out the window. They were near the office. She felt like she was running out of time. "If you had a choice, what would you want to do?"

It felt bold and forward to ask him again—to demand he answer her. She didn't make such demands of him. That's not how their business relationship worked.

But something had changed. Their relationship was no longer strictly business. It hadn't crossed a line into pleasure, but the way he'd touched her on Monday? The way she'd touched him yesterday?

Something had changed, all right. Maybe everything.

His gaze bore into her—not the weary look he wore when discussing his schedule, not even the shell-shocked look he'd had yesterday. This was much, much closer to the look he'd had on Monday—the one he'd had on his face when he'd leaned toward her, made the air thin between them. Made her want to feel his lips pressing against hers. Made her want things she had no business wanting.

A corner of his mouth curved up. "What are you wearing on Saturday?"

"What?"

"To the gala. What are you wearing? The black dress?"

Serena blinked at him. Did he seriously *want* to discuss the shortcomings of her wardrobe? "Um, no, actually…." It didn't fit anymore. She'd tried it on on Monday night, more to distract herself from constantly refreshing her email to see if Neil would reply than anything else.

The dress had not zipped. Her body was already changing. How could she not have realized that before she peed on all those sticks? "I'll find something appropriate to wear by Saturday."

They pulled up in front of the office building. The campus of Beaumont Brewery was spread out over fifteen acres, with most of the buildings going back to before the Great Depression.

That sense of permanence had always attracted Serena. Her parents moved so frequently, trying to stay one step ahead of the creditors. The one time Serena had set them up in a nice place with a reasonable rent—and covered the down payment and security deposit, with promises to help every month—her folks had fallen behind. Again. But instead of telling her and giving her a chance to make up the shortfall, they'd done what they always did—picked up in the middle of the night and skipped out. They didn't know how to live any other way.

The Beaumonts had been here for over a century. What would it be like to walk down halls your grandfather had built? To work in buildings your great-grandfather had made? To know that your family not only took care of themselves, but of their children and their children's children?

The driver opened up their door. Serena started to move, but Chadwick motioned for her to sit. "Take the afternoon off. Go to Neiman Marcus. I have a personal shopper there. He'll make sure you're appropriately dressed."

The way he said it bordered on condescending. "I'm sorry—was my black dress inappropriate somehow?"

It had been an amazing find at a consignment shop. Paying seventy dollars for a dress and then another twenty to get it altered had felt like a lot of money, but she'd worn it more than enough to justify the cost, and it had always made her feel glamorous. Plus, a dress like that had probably cost at least five hundred dollars originally. Ninety bucks was a steal. Too bad she wouldn't be able to wear it again for a long time. Maybe if she lost the baby weight, she'd be able to get back into it.

"On the contrary, it would be difficult to find another dress that looks as appropriate on you. That's why you should use Mario. If anyone could find a better dress, it would be him." Chadwick's voice carried through the space between them, almost as if the driver wasn't standing three feet away, just on the other side of the open car door.

Serena swallowed. He didn't have her backed against a door and he certainly wasn't touching her, but otherwise? She felt exactly as she had Monday morning. Except then, she'd been on the verge of sobbing in his office. This? This was different. She wouldn't let her emotions get the better of her today, hormones be damned.

So she smiled her most disarming smile. "I'm afraid that won't be possible. Despite the generous salary you pay me, Neiman's is a bit out of my price range." Which was not a lie. She shopped clearance racks and consignment stores. When she needed some retail therapy, she hit thrift stores. Not an expensive department store. Never Neiman's.

Chadwick leaned forward, thinning the air between them until she didn't care about the driver. "We are attending a work function. Dressing you appropriately is a work-related expense. You will put the dress on my account." She opened her mouth to protest—that was not going to happen—when he cut her off with a wave of his hand. "Not negotiable."

Then, moving with coiled grace, he exited the vehicle. And made the driver shut the door before Serena could follow him out. "Take her to Neiman's," she heard Chadwick say.

No. No, no, no, *no*. This wasn't right. This was wrong on several levels. Chadwick gave her stock options because she did a good job on a project—he did not buy her something as personal, as *intimate*, as a dress. She bought her own clothing with her own money. She didn't rely on any man to take care of her.

She shoved the door open, catching the driver on the hip, and hopped out. Chadwick was already four steps away. "*Sir,*" she said, putting as much weight on the word as she could. He froze, one foot on a step. Well, she had his attention now. "I must respectfully decline your offer. I'll get my own dress, thank you."

Coiled grace? Had she thought that about him just moments ago? Because, as Chadwick turned to face her and began to walk back down toward where she was standing, he didn't look quite as graceful. Oh, he moved smoothly, but it was less like an athlete and more like a big cat stalking his prey. *Her*.

And he didn't stop once he was on level ground. He walked right up to her—close enough that he could put his finger under her chin again, close enough to kiss her in broad daylight, in front of the driver.

"You asked, Ms. Chase." His voice came out much closer to a growl than his normal efficient business voice. "Did you not?"

"I didn't ask for a dress."

His smile was a wicked thing she'd never seen on his face before. "You asked me what I wanted. Well, this is what I want. I want to take you out to dinner. I want you to accompany me to this event. And I want you to feel as beautiful as possible when I do it."

She sucked in a breath that felt far warmer than the ambient air temperature outside.

His gaze darted down to her lips, then back up to her eyes. "Because that black dress—you feel beautiful in it, don't you?"

"Yes." She didn't understand what was going on. If he was going to buy her a dress, why was he talking about how she felt? If he was going to buy her a dress and look at her with this kind of raw hunger in his eyes—talk to her in this voice—shouldn't he be talking about how beautiful he *thought* she was? If he was going to seduce her—because that's what this was, a kind of seduction—wasn't he going to tell her she was pretty? That he'd always thought she was pretty?

"It is a work-related event. This is a work-related expense. End of discussion."

"But I couldn't possibly impose—"

Something in him seemed to snap. He did touch her then—not in the cautious way he'd touched her on Monday, and not in the shattered way he'd laced his fingers with hers just yesterday.

He took her by the upper arm, his fingers gripping her tightly. He moved her away from the car door, opened it himself, and put her inside.

Before Serena could even grasp what was happening, Chadwick had climbed in next to her. "Take us to Neiman's," he ordered the driver.

Then he shut the door.

Four

What was wrong with this woman?

That was the question Chadwick asked himself over and over as they rode toward the Cherry Creek Shopping Center, where the Neiman Marcus was located. He'd called ahead and made sure Mario would be there.

Women in his world loved presents. It didn't matter what you bought them, as long as it was expensive. He'd bought Helen clothing and jewelry all the time. She'd always loved it, showing off her newest necklace or dress to her friends with obvious pride.

Of course, that was in the past. In the present, she was suing him for everything he had, so maybe there were limits to the power of gifts.

Still, what woman didn't like a gift? Would flatly refuse to even entertain the notion of a present?

Serena Chase, that's who. Further proving that he didn't know another woman like her.

"This is ridiculous," she muttered.

They were sitting side by side in the backseat of the limo, instead of across from each other as they normally did. True, Serena had scooted over to the other side of the vehicle, but he could still reach over and touch her if he wanted to.

Did he want to?

What a stupid question. Yes, he wanted to. Wasn't that why they were here—he was doing something he wanted, consequences be damned?

"What's ridiculous?" he asked, knowing full well she might haul off and smack him at any moment. After all, he'd forced her into this car with him. He could say this was a work-related expense until he was blue in the face, but that didn't make it actually true.

"This. *You.* It's the middle of the afternoon. On a Wednesday, for God's sake. We have *things* to do. I should know—I keep your schedule."

"I hardly think..." He checked his watch. "I hardly think 4:15 on a Wednesday counts as the middle of the afternoon."

She turned the meanest look onto him that he'd ever seen contort her pretty face. "*You* have a meeting with Sue Colman this afternoon—your weekly HR meeting. *I* have to help Matthew with the gala."

Chadwick got his phone and tapped the screen. "Hello, Sue? Chadwick. We're going to have to reschedule our meeting this afternoon."

Serena gave him a look that was probably supposed to strike fear in his heart, but which only made him want to laugh. Canceling standing meetings on a whim—just because he felt like it?

If he didn't know better, he'd think he was having fun.

"Did the board meeting run long?" Sue asked.

"Yes, exactly." A perfect excuse. Except for the fact that someone might have seen them return to the brewery—and then leave immediately.

"It can wait. I'll see you next week."

"Thanks." He ended the call and tapped on the screen a few more times. "Matthew?"

"Everything okay?"

"Yes, but Serena and I got hung up at the board meeting. Can you do without her for the afternoon?"

There was silence on the other end—a silence that made him shift uncomfortably.

"I suppose I could make do without *Ms. Chase*," Matthew replied, his tone heavy with sarcasm. "Can you?"

If I thought you were anything like our father, Matthew had said the day before, *I'd assume you were working on wife number two.*

Well, he wasn't, okay? Chadwick was not Hardwick. If he were, he'd have Serena flat on her back, her prim suit gone as he feasted on her luscious body in the backseat of this car.

Was he doing that? No. Had he ever done that? *No*. He was a complete gentleman at all times. Hardwick would have made a new dress the reward for a quick screw. Not Chadwick. Just seeing her look glamorous was its own reward.

Or so he kept telling himself.

"I'll talk to you tomorrow." He hung up before Matthew could get in another barb. "There," he said, shoving his phone back into his pocket. "Schedule's clear. We have the rest of the afternoon, all forty-five minutes of it."

She glared at him, but didn't say anything.

It only took another fifteen minutes to make it to the shopping center. Mario was waiting by the curb for them. The car had barely come to a complete stop when he had the back door open. "Mr. Beaumont! What a joy to see you again. I was just telling your brother Phillip that it's been too long since I've had the pleasure of your company."

"Mario," Chadwick said, trying not to roll his eyes at the slight man. Mario had what some might call a *flamboyant* way about him, what with his cutting-edge suit, faux-hawk hair and—yes—eyeliner. But he also had an eagle eye for fashion—something Chadwick didn't have the time or inclination for. Much easier to let Mario put together outfits for him.

And now, for Serena. He turned and held a hand out to her. When she hesitated, he couldn't help himself. He notched an eyebrow in challenge.

That did it. She offered her hand, but she did not wrap her fingers around his.

Fine. Be like that, he thought. "Mario, may I introduce Ms. Serena Chase?"

"Such a delight!" Mario swept into a dramatic bow—but then, he didn't do anything that wasn't dramatic. "An honor to make your acquaintance, Ms. Chase. Please, come inside."

Mario held the doors for them. It was only when they'd passed the threshold that Serena's hand tightened around Chadwick's. He looked at her and was surprised to see something close to horror on her face. "Are you all right?"

"Fine," she answered, too quickly.

"But?"

"I've just…never been in this particular store before. It's…" She stared at the store. "It's different than where I normally shop."

"Ah," he said, mostly because he didn't know what else to say. What if she hadn't been refusing his offer due to stubborn pride? What if there was another reason?

Mario swept around them and clapped his hands in what could only be described as glee. "Please, tell me how I can assist you today." His gaze darted to where Chadwick still had a hold of Serena's hands, but he didn't say anything else. He was far too polite to be snide.

Chadwick turned to Serena. "We have an event on Saturday and Ms. Chase needs a gown."

Mario nodded. "The charity gala at the Art Museum, of course. A statement piece or one of refined elegance? She could easily pull off either with her shape."

Serena's fingers clamped down on Chadwick's, and then she pulled her hand away entirely. Perhaps Mario's extensive knowledge of the social circuit was a surprise to her. Or perhaps it was being referred to in the third person by two men standing right in front of her. Surely it wasn't the compliment.

"Elegant," she said.

"Fitting," Mario agreed. "This way, please."

He led them up the escalator, making small talk about the newest lines and how he had a spotted a suit that would be perfect for Chadwick just the other day. "Not today," Chadwick said. "We just need a gown."

"And accessories, of course," Mario said.

"Of course." When Chadwick agreed, Serena shot him a stunned look. He could almost hear her thinking that he'd said nothing about accessories. He hadn't, but that was part of the deal.

"This way, please." Mario guided them back to a private fitting area, with a dressing room off to the side, a seating area, and a dais surrounded by mirrors. "Champagne?" he offered.

"Yes."

"No." Serena's command was sudden and forceful. At first Chadwick thought she was being obstinate again, but then he saw the high blush that raced across her cheeks. She dropped her gaze and a hand fluttered over her stomach, as if she were nervous.

"Ah." Mario stepped back and cast his critical eye over her again. "My apologies, Ms. Chase. I did not realize you were expecting. I shall bring you a fruit spritzer—non-alcoholic, of course." He turned to Chadwick. "Congratulations, Mr. Beaumont."

Wait—what? *What*?

Chadwick opened his mouth to say something, but nothing came out.

Had Mario just said…*expecting*?

Chadwick looked at Serena, who suddenly seemed to waver, as if she were on the verge of passing out. She did not tell Mario that his critical eye was wrong, that she was absolutely *not* expecting. She mumbled out a pained "Thank you," and then sat heavily on the loveseat.

"My assistant will bring you drinks while I collect a few things for Ms. Chase to model," Mario said. If he caught the sudden change in the atmosphere of the room, he gave no indication of it. Instead, with a bow, he closed the door behind him.

Leaving Chadwick and Serena alone in the silence.

"Did he just say…."

"Yes." Her voice cracked, and then she dragged in a ragged breath.

"And you're…"

"Yes." She bent forward at the waist, as if she could make herself smaller. As if she wanted to disappear from the room.

Or maybe she was on the verge of vomiting and was merely putting her head between her knees.

"And you—you found out this weekend. That's why you were upset on Monday."

"Yes." That seemed to be the only word she was capable of squeezing out.

"And you didn't tell me?" The words burst out of him. She flinched, but he couldn't stop. "Why didn't you *tell* me?"

"Mr. Beaumont, we usually do not discuss our personal lives at the office." At least that was more than a syllable, but the rote way she said it did nothing to calm him down.

"Oh? Were we going to *not* discuss it when you started showing? Were we going to not discuss it when you needed to take maternity leave?" She didn't reply, which only made him madder. Why was he so mad? "Does Neil know?" He was terrified of what she might say. That Neil might not be the father. That she'd taken up with someone else.

He had no idea why that bothered him. Just that it did.

"I…" She took a breath, but it sounded painful. "I sent Neil an email. He hasn't responded yet. But I don't need him. I can provide for my child by myself. I won't be a burden to you or the company. I don't need help."

"Don't lie to me, Serena. Do you have any idea what's going to happen if I lose the brewery?"

Even though she was looking at her black pumps and not at him, he saw her squeeze her eyes shut tight. Of course she knew. He was being an idiot to assume that someone as smart and capable as Serena wouldn't already have a worst-case plan in place. "I'll be out of a job. But I can get another one. Assuming you'll give me a letter of reference."

"Of course I would. You're missing the point. Do you know how hard it'll be for a woman who's eight months pregnant to get a job—even if I sing your praises from the top of the Rocky Mountains?"

She turned an odd color. Had she been breathing, beyond those few breaths she'd taken a moment before?

Jesus, what an ass he was being. *She* was pregnant—so *he* was yelling at her.

Something his father would have done. Dammit.

"Breathe," he said, forcing himself to speak in a quiet tone. He wasn't sure he was nailing "sympathetic," but at least he wasn't yelling. "Breathe, Serena."

She gave her head a tiny shake, as if she'd forgotten how.

Oh, hell. The absolute last thing any of them needed was for his pregnant assistant to black out in the middle of the workweek in an upscale department store. Mario would call an ambulance, the press would get wind of it, and Helen—the woman he was still technically married to—would make him pay.

He crouched down next to Serena and started rubbing her back. "Breathe, Serena. Please. I'm sorry. I'm not mad at you."

She leaned into him then. Not much, but enough to rest her head against his shoulder. Hadn't he wanted this just a few days before? Something that resembled his holding her?

But not like this. Not because he'd lost his temper. Not because she was...

Pregnant.

Chadwick didn't have the first clue how to be a good father. He had a great idea of how to be a really crappy father, but not a good one. Helen had said she didn't want kids, so they didn't have kids. It had been easier that way.

But Serena? She was soft and gentle where Helen, just like his own mother, had been tough and brittle. Serena worked hard and wasn't afraid to learn new things—wasn't afraid to get her hands dirty down in the trenches.

Serena would be a good mother. A *great* mother.

The thought made him smile. Or it would have, if he hadn't been watching her asphyxiate before his very eyes.

"Breathe," he ordered her. Finally, she gasped and exhaled. "Good. Do it again."

They sat like that for several minutes, her breathing and him reminding her to do it again. The assistant knocked on the door and delivered their beverages, but Serena didn't pull away from him and he didn't pull away from her. He sat on his heels and rubbed her back while she breathed and leaned on him.

When they were alone again, he said, "I meant what I said on Monday, Serena. This doesn't change that."

"It changes *everything*." He'd never heard her sound sadder. "I'm sorry. I didn't want anything to change. But it did. *I* did."

They'd lived their lives in a state of stasis for so long—he'd been not-quite-happily married to Helen, and Serena had been living with Neil, not quite happily, either, it turned out. They could have continued on like that forever, maybe.

But everything had changed.

"I won't fail you," he reminded her. Failure had not been an option when he was growing up. Hardwick Beaumont had demanded perfection from an early age. And it was never smart to disappoint Hardwick. Even as a child, Chadwick had known that.

No, he wouldn't fail Serena.

She leaned back—not away from him, not enough to break their contact, but far enough that she could look at him. The color was slowly coming back into her face, which was good. Her hair was mussed up from where her head had been on his shoulder and her eyes were wide. She looked as if she'd just woken up from a long nightmare, like she wanted him to kiss her and make it all better.

His hand moved. It brushed a few strands of hair from her cheek. Then his fingers curved under her cheek, almost as if he couldn't pull away from her skin.

"I won't fail you," he repeated.

"I know you won't," she whispered, her voice shaking.

She reached up—she was going to touch him. Like he was touching her. She was going to put her fingers on his face and then pull him down and he would kiss her. God, how he would kiss her.

"Knock, knock!" Mario called out from the other side of the door. "Is everybody decent in there?"

"Damn."

But Serena smiled—a small, tense smile, but a smile all the same. In that moment, he knew he hadn't let her down yet.

Now he just had to keep it that way.

Five

"Breathe in," Mario instructed as he held up the first gown.

Serena did as she was told. Breathing was the only thing she was capable of doing right now, and even that was iffy.

She'd almost kissed Chadwick. She'd almost let herself lean forward in a moment of weakness and *kiss him*. It was bad enough that she'd been completely unprofessional and had a panic attack, worse that she'd let him comfort her. But to almost kiss him?

She didn't understand why that felt worse than letting him kiss her. But it did. Worse and better all at the same time.

"And breathe *all* the way out. All the way, Ms. Chase. There!" The zipper slid up the rest of the way and she felt him hook the latch. "Marvelous!"

Serena looked down at the black velvet that clung to

every single size-ten curve she had and a few new ones. "How did you know what size I'd need?"

"Darling," Mario replied as he made a slow circle around her, smoothing here and tugging up there, "it's Mario's job to know such things."

"Oh." She remembered to breathe again. "I've never done this before. But I guess you figured that out." He'd guessed everything else. Her dress size, her shoe size—even her bra size. The strapless bra fit a lot better than the one she owned.

"Which part—trying on gowns or being whisked out of the office in the middle of the day?"

Yeah, she wasn't fooling anyone. "Both." Mario set a pair of black heels before her and balanced her as she stepped into them. "I feel like an imposter."

"But that's the beauty of fashion," Mario said, stepping back to look her over yet again. "Every morning you can wake up and decide to be someone new!" Then his face changed. "Even Mario." His voice changed, too—it got deeper, with a thicker Hispanic accent. "I'm really Mario from the barrio, you know? But no one else does. That's the beauty of fashion. It doesn't matter what we were. The only thing that matters is who we are today. And today," he went on, his voice rising up again, "you shall be a queen amongst women!"

She looked at him, more than a little surprised at what he'd said. Was it possible that he really was Mario from the barrio—that he might understand how out of place she felt surrounded by this level of wealth? She decided it didn't matter. All that mattered was that he'd made her feel like she could do this. She felt herself breathe again—and this time it wasn't a strain. "You really are fabulous, you know."

"Oh," he said, batting her comment away with a

pleased grin, "I tell my husband that all the time. One of these days, he's going to believe me!" Then he clapped his hands and turned to the cart that had God only knew how many diamonds and gems on it. "Mr. Beaumont is quite the lucky man!"

But he wasn't. He wasn't the father of her baby and he wasn't even her boyfriend. He was her boss. The walls started to close in on her again.

She needed to distract herself and fast. "Does this happen a lot? Mr. Beaumont showing up with a fashion-challenged woman?" The moment she asked the question, she wished she could take it back. She didn't want to know that she was the latest in a string of afternoon makeovers.

"Heavens, no!" Mario managed to look truly shocked at the suggestion as he turned with a stunning diamond solitaire necklace the size of a pea. "His brother, Mr. Phillip Beaumont? Yes. But not Mr. Chadwick Beaumont. I don't believe he ever even joined his wife on such an afternoon. Certainly not here. I would recall *that*."

Serena breathed again. There wasn't a particularly good reason for that to make her so happy. She had no claim on Chadwick, none at all. And just because he hadn't brought a girl shopping didn't mean he hadn't been seeing anyone else.

But she didn't think he had. He worked too much. She knew. She managed his schedule.

"Now," Mario went on, draping the necklace around her neck and fastening it, "you may have woken up this morning a frugal..." He tilted his head to the side and looked at her suit, now neatly hanging by the door. "Account executive?"

"Close," she said. "Executive assistant."

He snapped his fingers in disappointment, but it didn't

last. "By the time Mario gets done with you, you will *be* royalty."

He held his arm out to her, for which she was grateful—those heels were at least two inches higher than her dress shoes. Then he opened the door and they walked out into the sitting room.

Chadwick was reclined in the loveseat, a glass of champagne in one hand. He'd loosened his tie, a small thing that made him look ten times more relaxed than normal.

Then he saw her. His eyes went wide as he sat up straight, nearly spilling his drink. "Serena...wow."

"And this is just the beginning!" Mario crowed as he led her not to Chadwick but over to the small dais in front of all the mirrors. He helped her up and then guided her in a small turn.

She saw herself in the mirrors. Mario had smoothed her hair out after he'd gotten her suit off her. Her face still looked a little ashen, but otherwise, she couldn't quite believe that was her.

Royalty, indeed. Chadwick had been right. This dress, just like her black dress at home, made her feel beautiful. And after the day she'd had, that was a gift in itself.

She got turned back around and saw the look Chadwick was giving her. His mouth had fallen open and he was now standing, like he wanted to walk right up to her and sweep her into his arms.

"Now," Mario said, although it didn't feel like he was talking to either Serena or Chadwick. "This dress would be perfect for Saturday, but half the crowd will be wearing black and we don't want Ms. Chase to blend, do we?"

"No," Chadwick agreed, looking at her like she hadn't announced half an hour ago that she was pregnant. If anything, he was looking at her like he'd never really seen her before. And he wanted to see a lot more. "No, we don't want that."

"Plus, this dress is not terribly forgiving. I think we want to try on something that has more flow, more grace. More..."

"Elegant," Chadwick said. He seemed to shake back to himself. He backed up to the loveseat and sat again, one leg crossed, appraising her figure again. "Show me what else you've got, Mario."

"With pleasure!"

The next dress was a pale peachy pink number with a huge ball gown skirt and a bow on the back that felt like it was swallowing Serena whole. "A classic style," Mario announced.

"Too much," Chadwick replied, with a shake of his hand. She might have been hurt by this casual dismissal, but then he caught her gaze and gave her a smile. "But still beautiful."

Then came a cornflower blue dress with an Empire waist, tiny pleats that flowed down the length of the gown, and one shoulder strap that was encrusted with jewels. "No necklace," Mario informed her as he handed her dangling earrings that looked like they were encrusted with real sapphires. "You don't want to compete with the dress."

When she came out this time, Chadwick sat up again. "You are...*stunning*." There was that look again—like he was hungry. Hungry for her.

She blushed. She wasn't used to being stunning. She was used to being professional. Her black dress at home was as stunning as she'd ever gotten. She wasn't sure how she was going to pull off stunning while pregnant. But it didn't seem to be bothering Chadwick.

"This one has a much more forgiving waistline. She'll

be able to wear it for several more months and it'll be easier to get back into it." Mario was talking to Chadwick, but Serena got the feeling that he was really addressing her—greater wearability meant better value.

Although she still wasn't looking at the price tags.

"I don't know where else I'd wear it," she said.

Chadwick didn't say anything, but he gave her a look that made her shiver in the best way possible.

They went through several dresses that no one particularly loved—Mario kept putting her in black and then announcing that black was too boring for her. She tried on a sunflower yellow that did horrible things to her skin tone. It was so bad, Mario wouldn't even let her go out to show Chadwick.

She liked the next, a satin dress that was so richly colored it was hard to tell if it was blue or purple. It had an intricate pattern in lace over the bodice that hid everything she didn't like about her body. That was followed by a dark pink strapless number that reminded her of a bridesmaid gown. Then a blue-and-white off-the-shoulder dress where the colors bled into each other in a way that she thought would be tacky but was actually quite pretty.

"Blue is your color," Mario told her. She could see he was right.

She didn't think it was possible, but she was having fun. Playing dress-up, such as it was. High-end dress-up, but still—this was something she'd had precious little of during her childhood. Chadwick was right—she *did* feel beautiful. She twirled on the dais for him, enjoying the compliments he heaped upon her.

It was almost like...a fairy tale, a rags-to-riches dream come true. How many times had she read some year-old fashion magazine that she'd scavenged from a recycling bin and dreamed about dressing up in the pretty things?

She'd thought she'd gotten that herself with her consign-ment store dress, but that was nothing compared to being styled by the fabulous Mario.

Time passed in a whirl of chiffons and satins. Soon, it was past seven. They'd spent almost four hours in that dressing room. Chadwick had drunk most of a bottle of champagne. At some point, a fruit-and-cheese tray had been brought in. Mario wouldn't let Serena touch a bite while she was wearing anything, so she wound up standing in the dressing room in her underthings, eat-ing apple slices.

She was tired and hungry. Chadwick's eyes had begun to glaze over, and even Mario's boundless energy was seeming to flag.

"Can we be done?" Serena asked, drooping like a wilted flower in a pale green dress.

"Yes," Chadwick said. "We'll take the blue, the pur-ple, the blue-and-white and…was there another one that you liked, Serena?"

She goggled at him. Had he just listed *three* dresses? "How many times do you expect me to change at this thing?"

"I want you to have all options available."

"One is plenty. The blue one with the single strap."

Mario looked at Chadwick, who repeated, "All three, please. With all necessary accessories. Have them sent to Serena's house."

"Of course, Mr. Beaumont." He gathered up the gowns in question and hurried from the room.

Still wearing the droopy green dress, Serena kicked out of her towering shoes and stalked over to Chadwick. She put her hands on her hips and gave him her very best glare. "*One*. One I shouldn't let you buy me in the first place. I do *not* need three."

He had the nerve to look down at her and smile his ruthless smile, the one that let everyone in the room know that negotiations were finished. Suddenly, she was aware that they were alone and she wasn't wearing her normal suit. "Most women would jump at the chance to have someone buy them nice things, Serena."

"Well," she snapped, unable to resist stamping her foot in protest, "I'm not most women."

"I know." Then—almost as if he were moving in slow motion, he stood and began taking long strides toward her, his gaze fastened on her lips.

She should do…something. Step back. Cross her arms and look away. Flee to the dressing room and lock the door until Mario came back.

Yes, those were all truly things she *should* do.

But she *wanted* him to kiss her.

He slipped one arm around her waist, and his free hand caught her under the chin again. "You're not like any woman I've ever known, Serena. I could tell the very first time I saw you."

"You don't actually remember that, do you?" Her voice had dropped down to a sultry whisper.

His grin deepened. "You were working for Sue Colman in HR. She sent you up to my office with a comparison of new health-care plans." As he spoke, he pulled her in tighter, until she could feel the hard planes of his chest through the thin fabric of the gown. "I asked you what you thought. You told me that Sue recommended the cheaper plan, but the other one was better. It would make the employees happier—would make them want to stay with the brewery. I made you nervous—you blushed—but—"

"You picked the plan I wanted." The plan she'd needed. She'd just been hired full-time. She'd never had health benefits before and she wanted the one with a lower copay and better prescription coverage. She couldn't believe he remembered—but he did.

Her arms went around his chest, her hands flat on his back. She wasn't pushing him away. She couldn't. She wanted this. She had since that day. When she'd knocked on the door, he'd looked up at her with those hazel eyes. Instead of making her feel like she was an interruption, he'd focused on her and asked for her opinion—something he did *not* have to do. She was the lowest woman on the totem pole, barely ranking above unpaid intern—but the future CEO had made her feel like the most important worker in the whole company.

He had looked at her then the same way he was looking at her right now...like she was far more than the most important worker in the company. More like she was the most important woman in the world. "You were honest with me. And what's more than that, you were *right*. It's hard to expect loyalty if you don't give people something to be loyal to."

She'd been devoted to him from that moment on. When he'd been named the new CEO a year later, she'd applied to be his assistant the same day. She hadn't been the most qualified person to apply, but he'd taken a chance on her.

She'd been so thankful then. The job had been a gift that allowed her to take care of herself—to not rely on Neil to pay the rent or buy the groceries. Because of Chadwick, she'd been able to do exactly what she'd set out to do—be financially independent.

She was still thankful now.

Still in slo-mo, he leaned down. His lips brushed against hers—not a fierce kiss of possession, but something that was closer to a request for permission.

Serena took a deep breath in satisfaction. Chadwick's scent surrounded her with the warmth of sandalwood on top of his own clean notes. She couldn't help it—she clutched him more tightly, tracing his lips with her tongue.

Chadwick let out a low growl that seemed to rumble right out of his chest. Then the kiss deepened. She opened her mouth for him and his tongue swept in.

Serena's knees gave in to the heat that suddenly flooded her system, but she didn't go anywhere—Chadwick held her up. Her head began to swim again but instead of the stark panic that had paralyzed her earlier, she felt nothing but sheer desire. She'd wanted that kiss since the very first time she'd seen Chadwick Beaumont. Why on God's green earth had she waited almost eight years to invite it?

Something hard and warm pressed against the front of her gown. A similar weight hung heavy between her legs, driving her body into his. This was what she'd been missing for months. Years. This raw passion hadn't just been gone since Neil had left—it'd been gone for much longer.

Chadwick wanted her. And oh, how she *wanted him*. Wanted to forget about bosses and employees and companies and boards of directors and pregnancies and everything that had gone wrong in her world. This—being in Chadwick's arms, his lips crushed against hers—this was right. So very *right*. Nothing else mattered except for this moment of heat in his arms. It burned everything else away.

She wanted to touch him, find out if the rest of him was as strong as his arms were—but before she could do anything of the sort, he broke the kiss and pulled her into an even tighter hug.

His lips moved against her neck, as if he were smiling

against her. She liked how it felt. "You've always been special, Serena," he whispered against her skin. "So let me show you how special you are. I *want* to buy you all three dresses. That way you can surprise me on Saturday. Are you going to refuse me that chance?"

The heat ebbed between them. She'd forgotten about the dresses—and how much they probably cost. For an insane moment, she'd forgotten everything—who she was. Who he was.

She *absolutely* should refuse the dress, the dinner, the way he had looked at her all afternoon like he couldn't wait to strip each and every dress right off her, and the way he was holding her to his broad chest right now. She had no business being here, doing this—no business letting her attraction to Chadwick Beaumont cloud her thinking. She was pregnant and her job was on the line, and at no point in the past, present or future did she require three gowns that probably cost more than her annual salary.

But then that man leaned backward and cupped her cheek in his palm and said, "I haven't had this much fun in...well, I can't remember when. It was good to get out of the office." His smile took a decade of worry off his face.

She was about to tell him that the champagne had gone to his head—although she was painfully aware that she had no such excuse as to why she'd kissed him back—when he added, "I'm glad I got to spend it with you. Thank you, Serena."

And she had nothing. No refusal, no telling him off, no power to insist that Mario only wrap up one dress and none of the jewelry, no defense that she did not need him to buy her anything because she was perfectly able to buy her own dresses.

He'd had fun. With her.

"The dresses are lovely, Chadwick. Thank you."

He leaned down, his five-o'clock shadow and his lips lightly brushing her cheek. "You're welcome." He pulled back and stuck out his arm just like Mario had done to escort her to the dais. "Let me take you to dinner."

"I…" She looked down at the droopy green dress, which was now creased in a few key areas. "I have to get back to work. I have to go back to being an executive assistant now." Funny how that sounded off all of a sudden. She'd been nothing but an executive assistant for over seven years. Why shouldn't putting the outfit back on feel more…natural?

A day of playing dress-up had gone right to her head. She must have forgotten who she was. She was really Serena Chase, frugal employee. She wasn't the kind of woman who had rich men lavish her with exorbitant gifts. She *wasn't* Chadwick's lover.

Oh God, she'd let him kiss her. She'd kissed him back. What had she *done*?

Chadwick's face grew more distant. He, too, seemed to be realizing that they'd crossed a line they couldn't uncross. It made her feel even more miserable. "Ah, yes. I probably have work to do as well."

"Probably." They might have been playing hooky for a few hours that afternoon, but the world had kept on turning. The fallout from the board meeting no doubt had investors, analysts and journalists burning up the bandwidth, all clamoring for a statement from Chadwick Beaumont.

But more than that, she needed to be away from him. This proximity wasn't helping her cause. She needed to clear her head and stop having fantasies about her boss. Fantasies that now had a very real feel to them—the feeling of his lips against hers, his body pressed to hers.

Fantasies that would probably play out in her dreams that night.

She couldn't accept dinner on top of the dresses. She had to draw the line somewhere.

But she'd already crossed that line.

How much farther would she go?

Six

Chadwick did not sleep well.

He told himself that it had everything to do with the disastrous board meeting and nothing to do with Serena Chase, but what the hell was the point in lying? It had *everything* to do with Serena.

He shouldn't have kissed her. Rationally, he knew that. He'd fired other executives for crossing that very same line—one strike and they were out. For way too long, Beaumont Brewery had been a business where men took all kinds of advantage of the women who worked for them. That was one of the first things he'd changed after his father died. He'd had Serena write a strict sexual harassment policy to prevent exactly this situation.

He'd always taken the higher road. Fairness, loyalty, equality.

He was not Hardwick Beaumont. He would not seduce his secretary. Or his executive assistant, for that matter.

Except that he'd already started. He'd told her he was taking her to the gala. He'd taken her shopping and bought tens of thousands of dollars worth of gowns, jewels and handbags for her.

He'd kissed her. He'd wanted to do so much more than just kiss her, too. He'd wanted to leave that gown in a puddle on the floor and sit back on the loveseat, Serena's body riding his. He wanted to feel the full weight of her breasts in his hands, her body taking his in.

He'd wanted to do something as base and crass as take her in a dressing room, for God's sake. And that was exactly what Hardwick would have done.

So he'd stopped. Thankfully, she'd stopped, too.

She hadn't wanted the dresses. She'd fought him tooth and nail about that.

But the kiss?

She'd kissed him back. Tracing his mouth with her tongue, pressing those amazing breasts against him—holding him just as tightly as he had been holding her.

He found himself in his office by five-thirty the next morning, running a seven-minute mile on his treadmill. He had the international market report up on the screen in front of him, but he wasn't paying a damn bit of attention to it.

Instead, he was wondering what the hell he was going to do about Serena.

She was pregnant. And when she'd come out in those gowns, she'd *glowed*. She'd always been beautiful—a bright, positive smile for any occasion with nary a manipulating demand in sight—but yesterday she'd taken his breath away over and over again.

He was totally, completely, one hundred percent confounded by Serena Chase. The women in Chadwick's world did not refuse expensive clothing and jewelry. They spent their days planning how to get more clothes, better jewels and a skinnier body. They whimpered and pleaded and seduced until they got what they wanted.

That's what his mother had always done. Chadwick doubted whether Eliza and Hardwick had ever really loved each other. She'd wanted his money, and he'd wanted her family prestige. Whenever Eliza had caught Hardwick *in flagrante delicto*—which was often—she'd threaten and cry until Hardwick plunked down a chunk of change on a new diamond. Then, when one diamond wasn't enough, he started buying them in bulk.

Helen had been like that, too. Oh, she didn't threaten, but she did pout until she got what she wanted—cars, clothes, plastic surgery. It had been so much easier to just give in to her demands than deal with the manipulation. In the last year before she filed for divorce, she'd only slept with him when he'd bought her something. Not that he'd enjoyed it much, even then.

Somehow, he'd convinced himself he was fine with that. He didn't need to feel passion because passion left a man wide open for the pain of betrayal. Because there was always another betrayal around the next corner.

But Serena? She didn't cry, didn't whine and didn't pout. She never treated him like he was a pawn to be moved until she got what she wanted, never treated him like he was an obstacle she had to negotiate around.

She didn't even want to let him buy her a dress that made her feel beautiful.

He punched the treadmill up another mile per hour, running until his lungs burned.

He could not be lusting after his assistant and that was final.

This was just the result of Helen moving out of their bedroom over twenty-two months before, that was all.

And they hadn't had sex for a couple of months before that. Yes, that was it. Two years without a woman in his arms—without a woman looking at him with a smile, without a woman who was glad to see him.

Two years was a hell of a long time.

That's all this was. Sexual frustration manifesting itself in the direction of his assistant. He hadn't wanted to break his marriage vows to Helen, even in the middle of their never-ending divorce. Part of that was a wise business decision—if Helen found out that he'd had an affair, even after their separation, she wouldn't sign off on the divorce until he had nothing left but his name.

But part of that was refusing to be like his father.

Except his father totally would have lavished gifts on his secretary and then kissed her.

Hell.

Finally his legs gave out, but instead of the normal clarity a hard run brought him, he just felt more muddled than ever. Despite the punishing exercise, he was no closer to knowing what he was supposed to do when Serena came in for their morning meeting.

Oh, he knew what he wanted to do. He wanted to lay her out on his desk and lavish her curves with all the attention he had. He wanted her to straddle him. He wanted to bring her to a shuddering, screaming climax, and he wanted to hold her afterwards and fall asleep in her arms.

He didn't just want to have sex.

He wanted to have Serena.

Double damn.

He threw himself into his shower without bothering to touch the hot water knob. The cold did little to shock him back to his senses, but at least it knocked his erection down to a somewhat manageable level.

This was beyond lust. He had a need to take care of

her—to *not* fail her. That was why he'd bought her nice things, right? Sure. He was just rewarding her loyalty.

She'd said that her ex hadn't responded to her email. There—that was something he could do. He could get that jerk to step up to the plate and at least acknowledge that he'd left Serena in a difficult situation. Yeah, he liked that idea—making Neil Moore toe the line was a perfectly acceptable way of looking out for his best employee, and it didn't involve kissing her. He doubted that Serena would hold Neil responsible for his legal obligations—but Chadwick had no problem putting that man's feet to the fire.

He shut the water off and grabbed his towel. He was pretty sure he had Neil's information in his phone. But where had he left it?

He rummaged in his pants pocket for a few minutes before he remembered he'd set it down on his desk when he came in.

He opened the door and walked into his office—and found himself face-to-face with Serena.

"Chadwick!" she gasped. "What are you—"

"Serena!" It was then that he remembered the only thing he had on was a towel. He hadn't even managed to dry off.

Her mouth was frozen in a totally kissable "oh," her eyes wide as her gaze traveled down his wet chest.

Desire pumped through him, hard. All he'd have to do would be to drop the towel and show her exactly what she did to him. Hell, at the rate he was going, he wouldn't even have to drop the towel. She wasn't blind and his body wasn't being subtle right now.

"I'm...I'm sorry," she sputtered. "I didn't realize...."

"Just checking my phone." *Just thinking about you.*

He glanced at his clock. She was at least an hour ahead of schedule. "You're early."

"I wanted…I mean, about last night…" She seemed to be trying to get herself back under control, but her gaze kept drifting down. "About the kiss…" A furious blush made her look innocent and naughty at the same time.

He took a step forward, all of his best intentions blown to hell by the look on her face. The same look she'd had the night before when he'd kissed her. She wanted him.

God, that made him feel good.

"What about the kiss?"

Finally, she dropped her gaze from his body to the floor. "It shouldn't have happened. I shouldn't have kissed you. That was unprofessional and I apologize." She rushed through the words in one breath, sounding like she'd spent at least half the night rehearsing that little speech. "It won't happen again."

Wait—what? Was she taking all the blame for that? No. It's not like she'd shoved him against the wall and groped him. He was the one who'd pulled her into his arms. He was the one who'd lifted her chin. "Correct me if I'm wrong, but I thought I was the one who kissed *you*."

"Yes, well, it was still unprofessional, and it shouldn't have happened while I was on the job."

For a second, Chadwick knew he'd screwed up. She was serious. He'd be lucky if she didn't file suit against him.

But then she lifted her head, her bottom lip tucked under her teeth as she peeked at his bare torso. There was no uncertainty in her eyes—just the same desire that was pumping through his veins.

Then he realized what she'd said—while she was on the job.

Would she be "on the job" on Saturday night? Or off the clock?

"Of course," he agreed. Because, even though she was looking at him like that and he was wearing nothing more than a towel, he was not his father. He could be a reasonable, rational man. Not one solely driven by his baser needs. He could rein in his desires.

Sort of.

"What time shall I pick you up for dinner on Saturday?"

Her lower lip still held captive by her teeth—God, what would it feel like if she bit his lip like that?—he thought he saw her smile. Just a little bit. "The gala starts at nine. We should arrive by nine-twenty. We don't want to be unfashionably late."

He'd take her to the Palace Arms. It would be the perfect accompaniment to the gala—a setting befitting Serena in a gown. "Ms. Chase," he said, trying to use his normal business voice. It was harder to do in a towel than he would have expected. "Please make dinner reservations for two at the Palace Arms for seven. I'll pick you up at six-thirty."

Her eyes went wide again—like they had the day before when he'd informed her he was sending her to Neiman's to get a dress. Like they had when he'd impulsively ordered all three dresses. Why was she so afraid of him spending his money as he saw fit? "But that's..."

"That's what I want," he replied.

And then, because he couldn't help himself, he let the towel slip. Just a little—not enough to flash her—but more than enough to make her notice.

And respond. No, she didn't like it when he flashed his wealth around—but his body? His body appeared to be a different matter entirely. Her mouth dropped open into that "oh" again and then—God help him—her tongue flicked out and traced over her lips. He had to bite down to keep the groan from escaping.

"I'll…I'll go make those reservations, Mr. Beaumont," she said breathlessly.

He couldn't have kept the grin off his face if he tried. "Please do."

Oh, yeah, he was going to take her out to dinner and she was going to wear one of those gowns and he would…

He would enjoy her company, he reminded himself. He did not expect anything other than that. This was not a quid pro quo situation where he bought her things and expected her to fall into bed out of obligation. Sex was not the same as a thank-you note.

Then she held up a small envelope. "A thank-you note. For the dresses."

He almost burst out laughing, but he didn't. He was too busy watching Serena. She took two steps toward the desk and laid the envelope on the top. She was close enough that, if he reached out, he could pull her back into his arms again, right where she'd been the night before.

Except he'd have to let go of the towel.

When had restraint gotten this hard? When had he suddenly had trouble controlling his urges? Hell, when was the last time he'd had an urge he had to control?

Years, really. Long, dry years in a loveless marriage while he ran a company. But Serena woke up something inside of him—and now that it was awake, Chadwick felt it making him wild and impulsive.

The tension in the room was so thick it was practically visible.

"Thank you, Ms. Chase." He was trying to hide behind last names, like he'd done for years, but it wasn't working. All his mouth could taste was her kiss.

"You have Larry coming in for his morning meeting." She didn't step back, but he saw the side-eye she was giving him. "Shall I reschedule him or do you think you can be dressed by then?"

This time, he didn't bother to hold back his chuckle. "I suppose I can be dressed by then. Send him in when he gets here."

She gave a curt nod with her head and, with one more glance at his bare chest, turned to leave.

He couldn't help himself. "Serena?"

She paused at the door, but she didn't look back. "Yes?"

"I..." He snapped off the part about how he wanted her. Even if it was the truth. "I'm looking forward to Saturday."

She glanced back over her shoulder and gave him the same kind of smile she'd had when she'd been twirling in the gowns for him—warm, nervous and excited all at once. "Me, too."

Then she left him alone in his office. Which was absolutely the correct thing to have done.

Saturday sure seemed like a hell of a long time off.

He hoped he could make it.

Serena made sure to knock for the rest of the week.

Not that she didn't want to see Chadwick's bare chest, the light hairs that covered his body glistening with water, his hair damp and tousled....

And certainly not because she'd been fantasizing about Chadwick walking in on her in the shower, leaning her back against the tiled wall, kissing her like he'd kissed her in the store, those kisses going lower and lower until she was blind with pleasure, then her returning the favor....

Right. She knocked extra hard on his door because it was the polite thing to do.

Thursday was busy. The fallout from the board meeting had to be dealt with, and the last-minute plans for the gala could not be ignored. Once Chadwick got his clothes on, she hardly had more than two minutes alone with him before the next meeting, the next phone call.

Friday was the same. They were in the office until almost seven, soothing the jittery nerves of employees worried about their jobs and investors worried about not getting a big enough payout.

She still hadn't heard from Neil. She did manage to get a doctor's appointment scheduled, but it wasn't for another two weeks. If she hadn't heard anything after that, she'd have to call him. That was all.

But she didn't want to think about that. Instead, she thought about Saturday night.

She was not going to fall into bed with Chadwick. Above and beyond the fact that he was still her boss for the foreseeable future, there were too many problems. She *was* pregnant, for starters. She was still getting over the end of a nine-year relationship with Neil—and Chadwick wasn't divorced quite yet. She didn't want whatever was going on with her and Chadwick to smack of a rebound for either of them.

That settled it. If, perhaps in the near future—a future in which Serena was not pregnant, Chadwick was successfully divorced and Serena no longer worked for him because the company had been sold—*then* she could be brazen and call him up to invite him over. *Then* she could seduce him. Maybe in the shower. Definitely near a bed.

But not until then. Really.

So this was just a business-related event. Sure, an extra fancy one, but nothing else had changed.

Except for that kiss. That towel.
Those fantasies.
She was in *so* much trouble.

Seven

Her hair fixed into a sleek twist, Serena stood in her bedroom in her bathrobe and stared at the gowns like they were menacing her. All three were hung on her closet door.

With the price tags still on them.

Somehow, she'd managed to avoid looking at the tags in the store. The fabulous Mario had probably been working overtime to keep them hidden from her.

She had tens of thousands of dollars worth of gowns. Hanging in her house. Not counting the "necessary accessories."

The one she wanted to wear—the one-shoulder, cornflower blue dress that paired well with the long, dangly earrings? That one, on sale, cost as much as a used car. *On sale*! And the earrings? Sapphires. Of course.

I can't do this, she decided. This was not her world and she did *not* belong. Why Chadwick insisted on dressing her up and parading her around was beyond her.

She'd return the dresses and go back to being frugal Serena Chase, loyal assistant. That was the only rational thing to do.

Then her phone buzzed. For a horrifying second, she was afraid it was Neil, afraid that he'd come to his senses and wanted to talk. Wanted to see her again. Wanted frugal, loyal Serena back.

Just because she was trying not to fall head over heels for Chadwick didn't mean she wanted Neil.

She picked up her phone—it was a text from Chadwick.

On my way. Can't wait to see you.

Her heart began to race. Would he wear a suit like he usually did? Would he look stiff and formal or...would he be relaxed? Would he look at her with that gleam in his eye—the one that made her think of things like towels and showers and hot, forbidden kisses?

She should return these things. *All* of them.

She slipped the blue dress off the hanger, letting the fabric slide between her fingers. On the other hand... what would one night hurt? Hadn't she always dreamed about living it up? Wasn't that why she'd always gone to the galas before? It was a glimpse into a world that she longed to be a part of—a world where no one went hungry or wore cast-off clothing or moved in the middle of the night because they couldn't make rent?

Wasn't Chadwick giving her exactly what she wanted? Why shouldn't she enjoy it? Just for the night?

Fine, she decided, slipping into the dress. One night. One single night where she wasn't Serena Chase, hardworking employee always running away from poverty. For one glorious evening, she would be Serena Chase, queen amongst women. She would be escorted by a man who wouldn't be able to take his eyes off her—a man who made her feel beautiful.

If she ever saw the fabulous Mario again, she was going to hug that man.

She dressed carefully. She felt like she was going too slowly, but she wasn't about to rush and accidentally pop a seam on such an expensive dress. She decided to go with a bolder eye, so she spent more time putting on eyeliner and mascara than she had in the last month.

She'd barely gotten her understated lipstick into the tiny purse that Mario had put with this dress—even though it was a golden yellow—when she heard the knock on the door. "One moment!" she yelled, as she grabbed the yellow heels that had arrived with everything else.

Then she took a moment to breathe. She looked good. She felt good. She was going to enjoy tonight or else. Tomorrow she could go back to being pregnant and frugal and all those other things.

Not tonight. Tonight was hers. Hers and Chadwick's.

She opened the door and felt her jaw drop.

He'd chosen a tux. And a dozen red roses.

"Oh," she managed to get out. The tux was exquisitely cut—probably custom-made.

He looked over the top of the roses. "I was hoping you'd pick that one. I brought these for you." He held the flowers out to her and she saw he had a matching rose boutonnière in his lapel.

She took the roses as he leaned forward. "You look amazing," he whispered in her ear.

Then he kissed her cheek. One hand slid behind her back, gripping her just above her hip. "Simply amazing," he repeated, and she felt the heat from his body warm hers from the inside out.

They didn't have to go anywhere. She could pull him

inside and they could spend the night wrapped around each other. It would be perfectly fine because they weren't at work. As long as they weren't in the office, they could do whatever they wanted.

And he was what she wanted to do.

No. No! She could not let him seduce her. She could not let herself *be* seduced. At least, not that easily. This was a business-related event. They were still on the clock.

Then he kissed her again, just below the dangly earring, and she knew she was in trouble. She had to do something. Anything.

"I'm pregnant," she blurted out. Immediately her face flushed hot. And not the good kind of hot, either. But that was exactly what she'd needed to do to slam on the brakes. Pregnant women were simply not amazing. Her body was crazy and her hormones were crazier and that had to be the *only* reason she was lusting after her boss this much.

Thank heavens, Chadwick pulled back. But he didn't pull away, damn him. He leaned his forehead against hers and said, "In all these years, Serena, I've never seen you more radiant. You've always been so pretty, but now… pregnant or not, you are the most beautiful woman in the world."

She wanted to tell him he was full of it—not only was she not the most beautiful woman in the world, but she didn't crack the top one hundred in Denver. She was plain and curvy and wore suits. Nothing beautiful about that.

But he slipped his hand over her hip and down her belly, his hand rubbing small circles just above the top of her panties. "This," he said, his voice low and serious and intent as his fingers spread out to cover her stomach, "just makes you better. I can't control myself around you anymore and I don't think I want to." As he said it, his hand circled lower. The tips of his fingers crossed over the demarcated line of her panties and dipped down.

The warmth from his touch focused heat in her belly—and lower. A weight—heavy and demanding and pulsing—pounded between her thighs. She didn't want him to stop. She wanted him to keep going until he was pressing against the part of her that was heaviest. To feel his touch explore her body. To make her *his*.

If she didn't know him, she'd say he was feeding her a line of bull a mile long. But Chadwick didn't BS people. He didn't tell them what they wanted to hear. He told them the truth.

He told *her* the truth.

Which only left one question.

Now that she knew the truth, what would she do with it?

The absolute last place Chadwick wanted to be was at this restaurant. The only possible exception to that statement was the gala later. He didn't want to be at either one. He wanted to go back to Serena's place—hell, this restaurant was in a hotel, he could have a room in less than twenty minutes—and get her out of that dress. He wanted to lay her down and show her *exactly* how little he could control himself around her.

Instead, he was sitting across from Serena in one of the best restaurants in all of Denver. Since they'd left her apartment, Serena had been...quiet. He'd expected her to push back against dinner like she'd pushed back against the gown that looked so good on her, but she hadn't. Which was not a bad thing—she'd been gracious and perfectly well-mannered, as he knew she would be—but he didn't know what to talk about. Discussing work was both boring and stressful. Even though this was supposed to be a business dinner, he didn't want to talk about losing the company.

Given how she'd reacted to him touching her stomach—soft and gently rounded beneath the flowing dress—he didn't think making small talk about her pregnancy was exactly the way to go, either. That wasn't making her feel beautiful. At least, he didn't think so. He was pretty sure if they talked about her pregnancy, they'd wind up talking about Neil, and he didn't want to think about that jerk. Not tonight.

Chadwick's divorce was out, too. Chadwick knew talking about exes and soon-to-be-exes at dinner simply wasn't done.

And there was the part where he'd basically professed how he felt about her. Kind of hard to do the chitchat thing after that. Because doing the chitchat thing seemed like it would minimize what he'd said.

He didn't want to do that.

But he didn't know what else to talk about. For one of the few times in his life, he wished his brother Phillip was there. Well, he *didn't*—Phillip would hit on Serena mercilessly, not because he had feelings for her but because she was female. He didn't want Phillip anywhere near Serena.

Still, Phillip was good at filling the silence. He had an endless supply of interesting stories about interesting celebrities he'd met at parties and clubs. If anyone could find *something* to talk about, it'd be his brother.

But that wasn't Chadwick's life. He didn't jet around making headlines. He worked. He went to the office, ran, showered, worked, worked some more and then went home. Even on the weekends, he usually logged in. Running a corporation took most of his time—he probably worked a hundred hours a week.

But that's what it took to run a major corporation. For so long, he'd done what was expected of him—what his father had expected of him. The only thing that mattered was the company.

Chadwick looked at Serena. She was sitting across from him, her hands in her lap, her eyes wide as she looked around the room. This level of luxury was normal for him—but it was fun seeing things through her eyes.

It was fun *being* with her. She made him want to think about something other than work—and given the situation, he was grateful for that alone. But what he felt went way beyond simple gratitude.

For the first time in his adult life—maybe longer—he was looking at someone who meant more to him than the brewery did.

That realization scared the hell out of him. Because, really—who *was* he if he wasn't Chadwick Beaumont, the fourth-generation Beaumont to run the brewery? That was who he'd been raised to be. Just like his father had wanted, Chadwick had always put the brewery first.

But now…things were changing. He didn't know how much longer he'd have the brewery. Even if they fended off this takeover, there might be another. The company's position had been weakened.

Funny, though—he felt stronger after this week with Serena.

Still, he had to say *something*. He hadn't asked her to dinner just to stare at her. "Are you doing all right?"

"Fine," she answered, breathlessly. She did look fine. Her eyes were bright and she had a small, slightly stunned smile on her face. "This place is just so…fancy! I'm afraid I'm going to use the wrong fork."

He felt himself relax a bit. Even though she looked like a million dollars, she was still the same Serena.

His.

No. He pushed that thought away as soon as it cropped up. She was not his—she was only his assistant. That was the extent of his claim to her. "Your parents never dressed you up and took you out to eat at a place like this just for fun?"

"Ah, no." A furious blush raced up her cheeks.

"Really? Not even for a special event?"

That happened a lot. He'd be eating some place nice— some place like this—and a family with kids who had no business being in a five-star restaurant would come in, the boys yanking on the necks of their ties and tipping over the drinks, the girls being extra fussy over the food. He'd sort of assumed that all middle-class people did something like that once or twice.

She looked up at him, defiance flashing in her eyes. The same defiance that had her refusing dresses. He liked it on her—liked that she didn't always bow and scrape to him just because he was Chadwick Beaumont.

"Did your parents ever put you in rags and take you to a food pantry just for fun?"

"What?"

"Because that's where we went 'out to eat.' The food pantry." As quickly as it had come, the defiance faded, leaving her looking embarrassed. She studied her silverware setting. "Sorry. I don't usually tell people that. Forget I said anything."

He stared at her, his mouth open. Had she really just said…*the food pantry?* She'd mentioned that her family had gone through a few financial troubles but—

"You picked the food bank for this year's charity."

"Yes." She continued to inspect the flatware, everything about her closed off.

This wasn't the smooth, flowing conversation he'd wanted. But this felt more important. "Tell me about it."

"Not much to tell." Her chin got even lower. "Poverty is not a bowl full of cherries."

"What happened to your parents?" Not that his parents had particularly loved him—or even liked him—but he'd never wanted for anything. He couldn't imagine how parents could let that happen to their child.

"Nothing. It's just that…Joe and Shelia Chase did everything to a fault. They still do. They're loyal to a fault, forgiving to a fault—generous to a fault. If you need twenty bucks, they'll give you the last twenty they have in the bank and then not have enough to buy dinner or get the bus home. My dad's a janitor."

At this, a flush of embarrassment crept over her. But it didn't stop her. "He'll give you the shirt off his back—not that you'd want it, but he would. He's the guy who always stops when he sees someone on the side of the road with a flat tire, and helps the person change it. But he gets taken by every stupid swindle, every scam. Mom's not much better. She's been a waitress for decades. Never tried to get a better job because she was so loyal to the diner owners. They hired her when she was fifteen. Whenever Dad got fired, we lived on her tips. Which turns out to not be enough for a family of three."

There was so much hurt in her voice that suddenly he was furious with her parents, no matter how kind or loyal they were. "They had jobs—but you still had to go to the food pantry?"

"Don't get me wrong. They love me. They love each other…but they acted as if money were this unknown force that they had no power over, like the rain. Sometimes, it would rain. And sometimes—most of the time—it wouldn't. Money flows into and out of our lives independent of anything we do. That's what they thought. Still think."

He'd never questioned having money, just because there had always been so much of it. Who had to worry about their next meal? Not the Beaumonts, that was for damn sure. But he still worked hard for his fortune.

Serena went on, "They had love, Mom always said. So who needed cars that ran or health insurance or a place to live not crawling with bugs? Not them." Then she looked up at him, her dark brown eyes blazing. "But I do. I want more than that."

He sat there, fully aware his mouth had dropped open in shock, but completely unable to get it shut. Finally, he got out, "I had no idea."

She held his gaze. He could see her wavering. "No one does. I don't talk about it. I wanted you to look at me for what I am, not what I was. I don't want *anyone* to look at me and see a welfare case."

He couldn't blame her for that. If she'd walked into the job interview acting as if he owed her the position because she'd been on food stamps, he wouldn't have hired her. But she hadn't. She'd never played the sympathy card, not once.

"Did Neil know?" Not that he wanted to bring Neil into this.

"Yes. I moved in with him partly because he offered to cover the rent until I could pay my share. I don't think... I don't think he ever really forgot what I'd been. But he was stable. So I stayed." Suddenly, she seemed tired. "I appreciate the dresses and the dinner, Chadwick—I really do. But there were years where my folks didn't clear half of what you paid. To just *buy* dresses for that much..."

Like a bolt out of the blue, he understood Serena in a way he wasn't sure he'd ever understood another person. She was kind and she was loyal—not to a fault, not at the sacrifice of her own well-being—but those were traits that he'd always admired in her. "Why did you pick the brewery?"

She didn't look away from him this time. Instead, she leaned forward, a new zeal in her eyes. "I had internship offers at a couple of other places, but I looked at the employee turnover, the benefits—how happy the workers were. I couldn't bear the thought of changing jobs every other year. What if I never got another one? What if I couldn't take care of myself? The brewery had all these workers that had been there for thirty, forty years—entire careers. It's been in your family for so long…it just seemed like a stable place. That's all I wanted."

And now that was in danger. He wasn't happy about possibly failing to keep the company in family hands, but he had a personal fortune to fall back on. He'd been worried about the workers, of course—but Serena brought it home for him in a new way.

Then she looked up at him through her dark lashes. "At least, that's all I *thought* I wanted."

Desire hit him low and hard, a precision sledgehammer that drove a spike of need up into his gut. Because, unlike Helen and unlike his mother, he knew that Serena wasn't talking about the gowns or the jewels or the fancy dinner.

She was talking about *him*.

He couldn't picture the glamorous, refined woman sitting across from him wearing rags and standing in line at a food pantry. And he didn't have to. That was one of the great things about being wealthy. "I promised you I wouldn't fail you, Serena. I keep my promises." Even if he lost the company—if he failed his father—

he wouldn't leave Serena in a position in which welfare was her only choice.

She leaned back, dropping her gaze again. Like she'd just realized she'd gone too far and was trying to backtrack. "I know. But I'm not your responsibility. I'm just an employee."

"The hell you are." The words were out a little faster than he wanted them to be, but what was the point of pretending anymore? He hadn't lied earlier. Something about her had moved him beyond his normal restraint. She was so much *more* than an employee.

Her cheeks took on that pale pink blush that only made her more beautiful. Her mouth opened and she looked like she was about to argue with him when the waiter came up. When the man left with their orders—filet mignon for him, lobster for her—Chadwick looked at her. "Tell me about you."

She eyed him with open suspicion.

He held up his hands in surrender. "I swear it won't have any bearing on how I treat you. I'll still want to buy you pretty things and take you to dinner and have you on my arm at a gala." *Because that's where you belong,* his mind finished for him.

On his arm, in his bed—in his life.

She didn't answer at first, so he leaned forward and dropped his voice. "Do you trust me when I say I'll never use it against you?"

She tucked her lower lip up under her teeth. It shouldn't look so sexy, but on her it did. Everything did.

"Prove it."

Oh, yeah, she was challenging him. But it didn't feel like a battle of wills.

He didn't hesitate. "My dad beat me. Once, with a belt." He kept his voice low, so no one could hear, but it didn't matter. The words ripped themselves out of a place deep inside of his chest.

Her eyes went wide with shock and she covered her open mouth with her hand. It hurt to look at her, so he closed his eyes.

But that was a mistake. He could see his father standing over him, that nice Italian leather belt in his hand, buckle out—screaming about how Chadwick had gotten a C on a math test. He heard the belt whistle through the air, felt the buckle cut into his back. Felt the blood start to run down his side as the belt swung again—all because Chadwick had messed up how to subtract fractions. Future CEOs knew how to do math, Hardwick had reminded him again and again.

That's all Chadwick had ever been—future CEO of Beaumont Brewery. He'd been eleven. It was the only time Hardwick Beaumont had ever left a mark on him, but it was a hell of a mark. He still had the scar.

It was all such a long time ago. Like it had been part of a different life. He thought he'd buried that memory with his father, but it was still there, and it still had the capacity to cause him pain. He'd spent his entire life trying to do what his father wanted, trying to avoid another beating, but what had that gotten him? A failed marriage and a company that was about to be sold out from under him.

Hardwick couldn't hurt him now.

He opened his eyes and looked at Serena. Her face was pale and there was a certain measure of horror in her eyes, but she wasn't looking at him like he feared she would—like she'd forgotten about the man he was now and only saw a bleeding little boy.

Just like he saw a woman he trusted completely, and not a little girl who ate at food pantries.

He kept going. "When I didn't measure up to expectations. As far as I know, he never hit any of his other kids. Just me. He broke my toys, sent my friends away and locked me in my room, all because I had to be the perfect Beaumont to run his company."

"How…how could he do that?"

"I was never his son. Just his employee." The words tasted bitter, but they were the unvarnished truth. "And, like you said, I don't tell people about it. Not even Helen. Because I don't want people to look at me with pity."

But he'd told her. Because he knew she wouldn't hold it against him. Helen would have. Every time they fought, she would have thrown that back in his face because she thought she could use his past to control him.

Serena wouldn't manipulate him like that. And he wouldn't do that to her.

"So," he said, leaning back in his chair, "tell me about it."

She nodded. Her face was still pale, but she understood what he was saying. She understood him. "Which part?"

"All of it."

So she did.

Eight

Serena clung to Chadwick's arm as they swept up the red-carpeted stairs, past the paparazzi and into the Denver Art Museum. Part of her clinginess was because of the heels. Chadwick took huge, masterful strides that she was struggling to keep up with.

But another part of it was how unsettled she was feeling. She'd told him about her childhood. About the one time she and her mom had lived in a women-only shelter for three days because her dad didn't want them to have to sleep on the streets in the winter—but her mom had missed him so much that she'd bundled Serena up and they'd gone looking for him. She'd told him about Missy Gurgin in fourth grade making fun of Serena for wearing her old clothes, about the midnight moves to stay ahead of the due rent, about eating dinner that her mom had scavenged from leftovers at the diner.

Things she'd never told anyone. Not even Neil knew about all of that.

In turn, he'd told her about the way his father had controlled his entire life, about punishments that went way
beyond cruel. He'd talked in a dispassionate tone, like
they were discussing the weather and not the abuse of
a child too young to defend himself, but she could hear
the pain beneath the surface. He could act like it was
all water under the bridge, but she knew better. All the
money in the world hadn't protected Chadwick.

She put her hand over her stomach. No one would ever
treat her child like that. And she would do everything
in her power to keep her baby from ever being cold and
hungry—or wondering where her next meal was coming from.

They walked into the Art Museum. Serena tried to
find the calm in her mind. God knew she needed it. She
pushed aside the horror of what Chadwick had told her,
the embarrassment of sharing her story with him.

This was more familiar territory. She'd come to the
Art Museum for this gala for the previous seven years.
She knew where the galleries were, where the food was.
She'd helped arrange that. She knew how to hold her
champagne glass—oh, wait. No champagne for her to-
night.

Okay, no need to panic. She was still perfectly at ease.
She was only wearing a wildly expensive dress, four-inch
heels and a fortune in jewels. Not to mention she was
pregnant, on a date with her boss and....

Yeah, champagne would be *great* right about now.

Chadwick leaned over and whispered, "Are you
breathing?" in her ear.

She did as instructed, the grin on her face making it
easier. "Yes."

He squeezed her hand against his arm, which she
found exceptionally reassuring. "Good. Keep it that way."

It was almost ten o'clock. Once they'd started sharing stories at dinner, it had been hard to stop. Serena was both mortified that she'd told any of that to Chadwick and, somehow, relieved. She'd buried those secrets deep, but they hadn't been dead. They'd lived on, terrorizing her like a monster under the bed.

At some point during dinner, she'd relaxed. The meal had been fabulous—the food was a little out there, but good. She'd been able to just enjoy being with Chadwick.

Now they were arriving at the gala slightly later than was fashionable. People were noticing as Chadwick swept her into the main hall. She could see heads tilting as people craned their necks for a better view, could hear the whispers starting.

Oh, this was not a good idea.

She'd loved her black dress because it looked good—but it had also blended, something Mario had forbidden. Now that she was here and standing out in the crowd in a bold blue, she wished she'd gone with basic black. People were *staring*.

A woman wearing a fire engine red gown that matched her fire engine red hair separated from the crowd just as Serena and Chadwick hit the middle of the room. She fought the urge to excuse herself and bolt for the ladies room. Queens amongst women did not hide in the bathroom, and that was *that*.

"There you are," the woman said, leaning to kiss Chadwick on the cheek. "I thought maybe you weren't coming, and Matthew and I would have to deal with Phillip all by ourselves."

Serena exhaled in relief. She should have recognized Frances Beaumont, Chadwick's half sister. She was well liked at the Beaumont Brewery, a fact that had a great deal to do with Donut Friday. Once a month, she personally delivered a donut to every single employee. Apparently, she'd been doing it since she was a little girl. As a result, Serena had heard more than a few of the workers refer to her as "our Frannie."

Frances was the kind of woman people described as "droll" without really knowing what that meant. But her razor-sharp wit was balanced with a good nature and an easy laugh.

Unlike everyone else at the brewery, though, Chadwick didn't seem to relax around his half sister. He stood ramrod straight, as if he were hoping to pass inspection. "We were held up. How's Byron?"

Frances waved her hand dismissively as Serena wondered, *Byron?*

"Still licking his wounds in Europe. I believe he's in Spain." Frances sighed, as if this revelation pained her, but she said nothing else.

Chadwick nodded, apparently agreeing to drop the topic of Byron. "Frannie, you remember Serena Chase, my assistant?"

Frances looked her up and down. "Of course I remember Serena, Chadwick." She leaned over and carefully pulled Serena into a light hug. "Fabulous dress. Where did you get it?"

"Neiman's." Breathing in, breathing out.

Frances gave her a warm smile. "Mario, am I right?"

"You have a good eye."

"Of course, darling." She drawled out this last word until it was almost three whole syllables. "It's a job requirement when you're an antiquities dealer."

"Your dress is stunning." Serena couldn't help but wonder how much it cost. Was she looking at several thousand dollars of red velvet and rubies? The one good thing was that, standing next to Frances Beaumont in that dress, no one was noticing Serena Chase.

Chadwick cleared his throat. She glanced up to find him smiling down at her. Well, no one but him would notice her, anyway.

He turned his attention back to his sister. "You said Phillip is already drunk?"

Frances batted away this question with manicured nails that perfectly matched the color of her dress. "Oh, not yet. But I'm sure before the evening is through he'll have charmed the spirits right out of three or four bottles of the good stuff." She leaned forward, dropping her voice to a conspiratorial whisper. "He's just that charming, you know."

Chadwick rolled his eyes. "I know."

Serena giggled, feeling relieved. Frances wasn't treating her like a bastard at a family picnic. Maybe she could do this.

Then Frances got serious, her smile dropping away. "Chadwick, have you thought more about putting up some money for my auction site?"

Chadwick made a huffing noise of disapproval, which caused a shadow to fall over Frances's face. Serena heard herself ask, "What auction site?"

"Oh!" Frances turned the full power of her smile on Serena. "As an antiquities dealer, I work with a lot of people in this room who'd prefer not to pay the full commission to Christie's auction house in New York, but who would never stoop to the level of eBay."

Ouch. Serena had bought more than a few things off the online auction site.

"So," Frances went on, unaware of the impact of her words on Serena, "I'm funding a new venture called Beaumont Antiquities that blends the cachet of a traditional art auction house with the power of social media. I have some partners who are handling the more technical aspects of building our platform, while I'm bringing the family name and my *extensive* connections to the deal." She turned back to Chadwick. "It's going to be a success. This is your chance to get in on the ground floor. And we could use the Chadwick Beaumont Seal of Approval. It'd go a long way to help secure additional funding. Think of it. A Beaumont business that has nothing to do with beer!"

"I like beer," Chadwick said. His tone was probably supposed to be flat, but it actually came out sounding slightly wounded, as if Frances had just told him his life's work was worthless.

"Oh, you know what I mean."

"You always do this, Frannie—investing in the 'next big idea' without doing your homework. An exclusive art auction site? In this market? It's not a good idea. If I were you, I'd get out now before you lose everything. Again."

Frances stiffened. "I haven't lost *everything*, thank you very much."

Chadwick gave her a look that was surprisingly paternal. "And yet, I've had to bail you out how many times?" Frances glared at him. Serena braced for another cutting remark, but then Chadwick said, "I'm sorry. Maybe this one will be a success. I wish you the best of luck."

"Of course you do. You're a good brother." Instantly, her droll humor was back, but Serena could see a shadow of disappointment in her eyes. "We're Beaumonts. You're the only one of us who behaves—well, you and maybe Matthew." She waved her hand in his general direction. "All respectable, while the rest of us are desperately trying to be dissolute wastrels." Her gaze cut between Chadwick and Serena. "Speaking of, there's Phillip now."

Before Serena could turn, she felt a touch slide down her bare arm. Then Phillip Beaumont walked around her, his fingers never leaving her skin. He was quite the golden boy. Only an inch shorter than his brother, he wore a tux without a bow tie. It made him look disheveled and carefree—which, according to all reports, he was. Where Chadwick was more of a sandy blond, Phillip's coloring was brighter, as if he'd been born for people to look at him.

Phillip took her hand in his and bent low over it. "*Mademoiselle*," he said as he held the back of her hand against his lips.

An uncontrollable shiver raced through her body. She did not particularly like Phillip—he caused Chadwick no end of grief—but Frances was one-hundred-percent right. He was exceedingly charming.

He looked up at Serena, his lips curled into the kind of grin that pronounced him fully aware of the effect he was having on her. "*Where* did you come from, enchantress? And, perhaps more importantly, why are you on *his* arm?"

Enchantress? That was a new one. And also a testament to Mario's superpowers. Phillip stopped by the office on a semi-regular basis to have meetings with Chadwick and Matthew about his position as head of special promotions for the brewery. She'd talked to him face-to-face dozens, if not hundreds, of times.

Chadwick made a sound that was somewhere between clearing his throat and growling. "Phillip, you remember Serena Chase, my executive assistant."

If Phillip was embarrassed that he hadn't recognized her, he gave no sign of it. He didn't even break eye contact with her. Instead, he favored her with the kind of smile that probably made the average woman melt into his bed. As it was, she was feeling a little dazzled by his sheer animal magnetism.

"How could I forget Ms. Chase? You are," he went on, leaning into her, "*unforgettable*."

Desperate, she looked at Frances, who gave a small shrug.

"That's *enough*." No mistaking it this time—that was nothing but a growl from Chadwick.

If Chadwick had growled at anyone else like that, he would have sent them diving for cover. But not Phillip. Good heavens, he didn't even look ruffled. He did give her a sly little wink before he touched her hand to his lips again. Chadwick tensed next to her and she wondered if a brawl was about to break out.

But then he released his grip on her hand and turned his full attention to his brother. Serena heaved a sigh of relief. No wonder Phillip had such a reputation as a ladies' man.

"So, news," he said in a tone that was only slightly less sultry than the one he'd been using on her. "I bought a horse!"

"Another one?" Frances and Chadwick said at the same time. Clearly, this was something that happened often.

"You've got to be kidding me." Chadwick looked… murderous. There really was no other way to describe it. He looked like he was going to throttle his brother in the middle of the Art Museum. "I don't suppose this one was only a few thousand?"

"Chad—hear me out." At this use of his shortened name, Chadwick flinched. Serena had never heard anyone call him that but Phillip. "This is an Akhal-Teke horse."

"*Gesundheit*," Frances murmured.

"A *what*?" Chadwick was now clutching her fingers against his arm in an almost desperate way. "How much?"

"This breed is extremely rare," Phillip went on. "Only about five thousand in the world. From Turkmenistan!"

Serena felt like she was at a tennis match, her head was turning back and forth between the two brothers so quickly. "Isn't that in Asia, next to Afghanistan?"

Phillip shot her another white-hot look and matching smile. "Beautiful *and* smart? Chadwick, you lucky dog."

"I swear to God," Chadwick growled.

"People are staring," Frances added in a light, sing-song tone. Then, looking at Serena for assistance, she laughed as if this were a great joke.

Serena laughed as well. She'd heard Chadwick and Phillip argue before, but that was usually behind Chadwick's closed office door. Never in front of her. Or in front of anyone else, for that matter.

For once, Phillip seemed to register the threat. He took an easy step back and held out his hands in surrender. "Like I was saying—this Akhal-Teke. They're most likely the breed that sired the Arabians. Very rare. Only about five hundred in this country, and most of those come from Russian stock. Kandar's Golden Sun isn't a Russian Akhal-Teke."

"*Gesundheit*," Frances murmured again. She looked at Serena with a touch of desperation, so they both laughed again.

"He's from Turkmenistan. An incredible horse. One to truly found a stable on."

Chadwick pinched the bridge of his nose. "How much?"

"Only seven." Phillip stuck out his chest, as if he were proud of this number.

Chadwick cracked open one eye. "Thousand, or hundred thousand?"

Serena tried not to gape. Seven thousand for a horse wasn't too much, she guessed. But seven *hundred* thousand? That was a lot of money.

Phillip didn't say anything. He took a step back, though, and his smile seemed more…forced.

Chadwick took a step forward. "Seven *what*?"

"You know, one Akhal-Teke went for fifty million—and that was in 1986 dollars. The most expensive horse ever. Kandar's Golden Sun—"

That was as far as he got. Chadwick cut him off with a shout. "You spent seven *million* on a horse while I'm working my ass off to keep the company from being sold to the wolves?"

Everything about the party stopped—the music, the conversations, the movement of waiters carrying trays of champagne.

Someone hurried toward them. It was Matthew Beaumont. "Gentlemen," he hissed under his breath. "We are having a *charity* event here."

Serena put her hand on Chadwick's arm and gave it a gentle tug. "A very good joke, Phillip," she said in a slightly too-loud voice.

Frances caught Serena's eye and nodded in approval. "Chadwick, I'd like to introduce you to the director of the food bank, Miriam Young." She didn't know where, exactly, the director of the food bank was. But she was sure Ms. Young wanted to talk with Chadwick. Or, at least, had wanted to talk to him before he'd started yelling menacingly at his relatives.

"Phillip, did I introduce you to my friend Candy?" Frances added, taking her brother by the arm and pulling him in the opposite direction. "She's *dying* to meet you."

The two brothers held their poses for a moment longer, Chadwick glaring at Phillip, the look on Phillip's face almost daring Chadwick to hit him in full view of the assembled upper crust of Denver society.

Then the men parted. Matthew walked on the other side of Chadwick, ostensibly to lead the way to the director. Serena got the feeling it was more to keep Chadwick from spinning and tackling his brother.

"Serena," Matthew said simply. "Nicely done. *Thus far*," he added in a heavy tone, "the evening has been a success. Now if we can just get through it without a brawl breaking out—"

"I'm fine," Chadwick snapped, sounding anything but. "I'm just *fine*."

"Not fine," Matthew muttered, guiding them into a side gallery. "Why don't I get you a drink? Wait here," he said, parking Chadwick in front of a Remington statue. "Do *not* move." He looked at Serena. "Okay?"

She nodded. "I've got him."

She hoped.

Nine

Chadwick had never really believed the old cliché about being so mad one saw red. Turns out, he'd just never been mad enough, because right now, the world was drenched in red-hot anger.

"How could he?" he heard himself mutter. "How could he just buy a horse for that much money without even thinking about the consequences?"

"Because," a soft, feminine voice said next to him, "he's not you."

The voice calmed him down, and some of the color bled back into the world. He realized Serena was standing next to him. They were in a nearly empty side gallery, in front of one of the Remington sculptures that made the backbreaking work of herding cattle look glorious.

She was right. Hardwick had never expected anything from Phillip. Never even noticed him, unless he did something outrageous.

Like buy a horse no one had ever heard of for seven million damn dollars.

"Remind me again why I work myself to death so that he can blow the family fortune on horses and women? So Frances can sink money into another venture that's bound to fail before it gets off the ground? Is that all I'm good for? A never-ending supply of cash?"

Delicate fingers laced through his, holding him tightly. "Maybe," Serena said, her voice gentle, "you don't have to work yourself to death at all."

He turned to her. She was staring at the statue as if it were the most interesting thing in the world.

Phillip had done whatever the hell he wanted since he was a kid. It hadn't mattered what his grades were, who his friends were, how many sports cars he had wrecked. Hardwick just hadn't cared. He'd been too focused on Chadwick.

"I…" He swallowed. "I don't know how else to run this company." The admission was even harder than what he'd shared over dinner. "This is what I was raised to do."

She tilted her head to one side, really studying the bronze. "Your father died while working, didn't he?"

"Yes." Hardwick had keeled over at a board meeting, dead from the heart attack long before the ambulance had gotten there. Which was better, Chadwick had always figured, than him dying in the arms of a mistress.

She tilted her head in the other direction, not looking at him but still holding his hand. "I rather like you alive."

"Do you?"

"Yes," she answered slowly, like she really had to think about it. But then her thumb moved against the palm of his hand. "I do."

Any remaining anger faded out of his vision as the room—the woman in it—came into sharp focus.

"You told me a few days ago," she went on, her voice quiet in the gallery, "that you wanted to do something for yourself. Not for the family, not for the company. Then you spent God only knows how much on everything I'm wearing." He saw the corner of her mouth curve up into a sly smile. "Except for a few zeros, this isn't so different, is it?"

"I don't need to spend money to be happy like he does."

"Then why am I wearing a fortune's worth of finery?"

"Because." He hadn't done it because it made him happy. He'd done it to see her look like this, to see that genuine smile she always wore when she was dressed to the nines. To know he could still *make* a woman smile.

He'd done it to make her happy. *That* was what made him happy.

She shot him a sidelong glance that didn't convey annoyance so much as knowing—like that was exactly what she'd expected him to say. "You are an impossibly stubborn man when you want to be, Chadwick Beaumont."

"It has been noted."

"What do you want?"

Her.

He'd wanted her for years. But because he was not Hardwick Beaumont, he'd never once pursued her.

Except now he was. He was walking a fine line between acceptable actions and immoral, unethical behavior.

What he really wanted, more than anything, was to step over that line entirely.

She looked up at him through her thick lashes, waiting for an answer. When he didn't give her one, she sighed. "The Beaumonts are an intelligent lot, you know. They'll learn how to survive. You don't have to protect them.

Don't work for them. They won't ever appreciate it because they didn't earn it themselves. Work for you." She reached up and touched his cheek. "Do what makes *you* happy. Do what *you* want."

She did realize what she was telling him, didn't she? She had to—her fingers wrapped around his, her palm pressed against his cheek, her dark brown eyes looking into his with a kind of peace that he couldn't remember ever feeling.

What he wanted was to leave this event behind, drive her home, and make love to her all night long. She *had* to know that was all he wanted—however not-divorced he was, pregnant she was, or employed she was by him.

Was she giving him permission? He would not trap his assistant into any sexual relationship. That wasn't him.

God, he wanted her permission. *Needed* it. Always had.

"Serena—"

"Here we are." Matthew strode into the gallery leading Miriam Young, the director of the Rocky Mountain Food Bank, and a waiter with a tray of champagne glasses. He gave Serena a look that was impossible to miss. "How is everything?"

She withdrew her hand from his cheek. "Fine," she said, with one of those beautiful smiles.

Matthew made the introductions and Serena politely declined the champagne. Chadwick only half paid attention. Her words echoed around his head like a loose bowling ball in the trunk of a car.

Don't work for them. Work for you.

Do what makes you happy.

She was right. It was high time he did what he wanted—above and beyond one afternoon.

It was time to seduce his assistant.

* * *

Standing in four-inch heels for two hours turned out to be more difficult than Serena had anticipated. She resorted to shifting from foot to foot as she and Chadwick made small talk with the likes of old-money billionaires, new-money billionaires, governors, senators and foundation heads. Most of the men were in tuxes like Chadwick's, and most of the women were in gowns. So she blended in well enough.

Chadwick had recovered from the incident with Phillip nicely. She'd like to think that had something to do with their conversation in the gallery. With the way she'd told him to do what he wanted and the way he'd looked at her like the only thing he wanted to do was *her*.

She knew there was a list of reasons not to want him back. But she was tired of those reasons, tired of thinking she couldn't, she *shouldn't*.

So she didn't. She focused on how painful those beautiful, beautiful shoes were. It kept her in the here and now.

Shoes aside, the evening had been delightful. Chadwick had introduced her as his assistant, true, but all the while he'd let one of his hands rest lightly on her lower back. She'd gotten a few odd looks, but no one had said anything. That probably had more to do with Chadwick's reputation than anything else, but she wasn't about to question it. Even without champagne, she'd been able to fall into small talk without too much panic.

She'd had a much nicer time than when she used to come with Neil. Then, she'd stood on the edge of the crowd, judiciously sipping her champagne and watching the crowd instead of interacting with it. Neil had always talked to people—always looking for another sponsor for his golf game—but she'd never felt like she was a part of the party.

Chadwick had made her a part of it this time. She wasn't sure she'd ever truly feel like she fit in with the high roller crowd, but she hadn't felt like an interloper. That counted for a great deal.

The evening was winding down. The crowd was trailing out. She hadn't seen Phillip leave, but he was nowhere to be seen. Frances had bailed almost an hour before. Matthew was the only other Beaumont still there, and he was deep in discussion with the caterers.

Chadwick shook hands with the head of the Centura Hospital System and turned to her. "Your feet hurt."

She didn't want to seem ungrateful for the shoes, but she wasn't sure her toes would ever be the same. "Maybe just a little."

He gave her a smile that packed plenty of heat. But it wasn't indiscriminately flirtatious, like his brother's. All night long, that goodness had been directed at only one woman.

Her.

He slid a hand around her waist and began guiding her toward the door. "I'll drive you home."

She grinned at this statement. "Don't worry. I didn't snag a ride with anyone else."

"Good."

The valet brought up Chadwick's Porsche, but he insisted on holding the door for her. Then he was in the car and they were driving at a higher-than-average speed, zipping down the highway like he had someplace to be.

Or like he couldn't wait to get her home.

The ride was quick, but silent. What was going to happen next? More importantly, what did she want to happen next? And—most importantly of all—what would she *let* happen?

Because she wanted this perfect evening to end perfectly. She wanted to have one night with him, to touch the body she'd only gotten a glimpse of, to feel beautiful and desirable in his arms. She didn't want to think about pregnancies or exes or jobs. It was Saturday night and she was dressed to the nines. On Monday, maybe they could go back to normal. She'd put on her suit and follow the rules and try not to think about the way Chadwick's touch made her feel things she'd convinced herself she didn't need.

Soon enough, he'd pulled up outside her apartment. His Porsche stuck out like a sore thumb in the parking lot full of minivans and late-model sedans. She started to open her door, but he put a hand on her arm. "Let me."

Then he hopped out, opened her door and held his hand out for her. She let him help her out of the deep seats of his car.

Then they stood there.

His strong hand held tight to hers as he pulled her against his body. She looked up into his eyes, feeling lightheaded without a drop of champagne. All night long, he'd only had eyes for her—but they'd been surrounded by people.

Now they were alone in the dark.

He reached up and traced the tips of his fingers over her cheek. Serena's eyelids fluttered shut at his touch.

"I'll walk you to your door," he said, his voice thick with strain. He stroked her skin—a small movement, similar to the way he'd touched her on Monday.

But this was different. Everything was different now.

This was the moment. This was her decision. She didn't want sex with Chadwick to be one of those things that "just happened," like her pregnancy. She was in control of her own life. She made the choices.

She could thank him for the lovely evening and tell

him she'd see him bright and early Monday morning. She could even make a little joke about seeing him in a towel again. Then she could walk into her apartment, close the door and...

Maybe never have another moment—another chance—to be with Chadwick.

She made her choice. She would not regret it.

She opened her eyes. Chadwick's face was inches from hers, but he wasn't pressing her to anything. He was waiting for her.

She wouldn't make him wait any longer. "Would you like to come in?"

He tensed against her. "Only if I can stay."

She kissed him then. She leaned up in the painful, beautiful shoes and pressed her lips to his. There was no "kissing him back," no "waiting for him to make the first move."

This was going to happen because she wanted it to. She'd wanted it for years and she was darn tired of waiting. That was reason enough.

"I'd like that."

The next thing she knew, Chadwick had physically swept her off her feet and was carrying her up to her door. When she gave him a quizzical look, he grinned sheepishly and said, "I know your feet hurt."

"They do."

She draped her arms around his neck and held on as he took the stairs, carrying her as if she were one of the skinny women from the party instead of someone whose size-ten body was getting bigger every day. But then, she'd seen all his muscles a few days before. If anyone could carry her, it was him. His chest was warm and hard against her body.

Things began to tighten. Her nipples tensed underneath the gown, and that heavy weight between her legs seemed to be pulling her down into his body. Oh, yes. She wanted him. But the thing that was different from all her time with Neil was how intense it felt to want Chadwick.

Obviously, it'd only been a few months since the last time she'd had sex with Neil. Just about three months. That was how far along she was. But she hadn't felt the physical weight of desire for much, much longer than that. She couldn't remember the last time just thinking about sex with Neil had turned her on this much. Maybe it was her crazy hormones—or maybe Chadwick did this to her. Maybe he'd always done this to her and she'd forced herself to ignore the attraction because falling for her boss just wasn't convenient.

He set her down at the door so she could get her key out of the tiny purse. But he didn't let her go. He put his hands on her hips and pulled her back into his front. They didn't talk, but the huge bulge that pressed against her backside said *lots* of things, loud and clear.

She got the door open and they walked inside. She kicked off the pretty shoes, which made Chadwick loom an extra four inches over her. He hadn't let go of her. His hands were still on her hips. He was *grabbing* her in a way that was quickly going from gentle to possessive. The way he filled his palms with her hips didn't make her feel fat. It made her feel like he couldn't get enough of her—he couldn't help himself.

Yes. That was what she needed—to be wanted so much that he couldn't control himself.

He leaned down, his mouth against her ear. "I've been waiting for you for years." The strain of the wait made his voice shake. He pulled her hips back again, the ridge in his pants unmistakable. "*Years*, Serena."

"Me, too." Her voice came out breathy, barely above a

whisper. She reached behind her back and slid her hand up the bulge. "Is that for me?"

"Yes," he hissed, his breath hot against her skin. One hand released a hip and found her breast instead. Even through the strapless bra, he found her pointed nipple and began to tease it. "You deserve slow and sensual, but I need you too much right now."

As if to prove his point, he set his teeth against her neck and bit her skin. Not too hard, but the feeling of being consumed by desire—by him—crashed through her. Her knees began to shake.

"Slow later," she agreed, wiggling her bottom against him.

With a groan, he stepped away from her. She almost toppled over backward, but then his hands were unzipping her dress. The gown slid off her one shoulder and down to the ground with a soft rustle.

She was extra glad she hadn't gone with the Spanx. Bless Mario's heart for putting her in a dress that didn't require them. Instead, a matching lacy thong had arrived with the bra. Which meant Chadwick currently had one heck of a view. She didn't know if she should strut, or pivot so he couldn't see her bottom.

Once the gown was gone, she stepped free of it. Chadwick moaned. "Serena," he got out as he slid his hands over her bare backside. "You are…amazing." His fingers gripped her skin, and he pressed his mouth to the space between her neck and her shoulder.

Strut, she decided. Nothing ruined good sex like being stupidly self-conscious when he already thought she was amazing. She pulled away from him before he could take away her power to stand.

"This way," she said over her shoulder as she, yes, *strutted* toward the bedroom, her hips swaying.

Chadwick made a noise behind her that she took as a compliment, before following her.

She headed toward the bed, but he caught up with her. He grabbed her hips again. "You are better than I thought," he growled as his hands slipped underneath the lace of the thong. He pulled the panties down, his palms against her legs. "I've dreamed of having you like this."

"Like how?"

He nimbly undid her bra, tossing it aside. She was naked. He was not.

He directed her forward, but not toward the bed. Instead, he pushed her in the direction of her dresser.

The one with the big mirror over it.

Serena gasped at the sight they made. Her, nude. Him, still in his tux, towering over her.

"This. Like this." He bent his head until his lips were on her neck again, just below the dangling earrings. "Is this okay?" he murmured against her skin.

"Yes." She couldn't take her eyes off their reflections, the way her pale skin stood out against his dark tux. The way his arms wrapped around her body, his hands cradled her breasts. The way his mouth looked as he kissed her skin.

The driving weight of desire between her legs pounded with need. "Yes," she said again, reaching one arm over her head and tangling her fingers in his hair. "Just like this."

"Good. So good, Serena." Without the bra, she could feel the pads of his fingertips trace over her sensitive nipple, pulling until it went stiff with pleasure.

She moaned, letting her head fall back against his shoulder. "Just like that," she whispered.

Then his other hand traced lower. This time, he didn't pause to stroke her stomach. His fingers parted her neatly trimmed hair and pressed against her heaviest, hottest place.

"Oh, Chadwick," she gasped as he moved his fingers in small, knowing circles, his other hand stroking her nipple, his mouth finding the sensitive spot under her ear—his bulge rubbing against her.

Her knees gave, but she didn't go far. Her wet center rode heavy on his hand as his other arm caught her under both breasts.

"Put your hands on the dresser," he told her. His voice was shaking as badly as her knees were, which made her smile. He might be pushing her to the brink, but she was pulling him along right behind her. "Don't close your eyes."

"I won't." She leaned forward and braced herself on the dresser. "I want to see what you do to me."

"Yeah," he groaned, a look of pure desire on his face as he met her gaze in the mirror. A finger slipped inside. So much, but not enough. She needed more. "You're so ready for me." Then she felt him lean back and work his own zipper.

"Next time, I get to do that for you."

"Any time you want to strip me down, you just let me know. Hold on, okay?" Then he withdrew his fingers.

She watched as he removed a condom from his jacket pocket. It wasn't like she could get more pregnant than she already was, but she appreciated that he didn't question protecting her.

He rolled the condom on and leaned into her. She quivered as she waited for his touch. He bent forward, placing a kiss between her shoulder blades. Then he was against her. Sliding into her.

Serena sucked in air as he filled her. And filled her. And *filled* her. In the mirror, her eyes locked onto his as he entered her. She almost couldn't take it. "Oh, Chadwick," she panted as her body took him in. "Oh—oh—*oh*!"

The unexpected orgasm shook her so hard that she almost pulled off him—but he held her. "Yeah," he groaned. "You feel so beautiful, Serena. So beautiful."

He gripped her hips as he slid almost all the way out before he thrust in again. "Okay?" he asked.

"Better than okay," she managed to get out, wiggling against him. The boldness of her action shocked her. Was she really having sex with Chadwick Beaumont, standing up—in front of a mirror?

Oh, hell yes, she was. And it was the hottest thing she'd ever done.

"Naughty girl," he said with a grin.

Then he began in earnest. From her angle, she couldn't see where their bodies met. She could only see his hands when he cupped her breasts to tweak a nipple or slid his fingers between her legs to stroke her center. She could only see the need on his face when he leaned forward to nip at her neck and shoulder, the raw desire in his eyes when their gazes met.

She held on to that dresser as if her life depended on it while Chadwick thrust harder and harder. "I need you so much," he called out as he grabbed her by the waist and slammed his hips into hers. "I've always needed you *so* much."

"Yes—like that," she panted, rising up to meet him each time. His words pushed her past the first orgasm. She couldn't remember ever feeling this needed, this sexual. "I'm going to—I'm—" Her next orgasm cut off her words, and all she could do was moan in pleasure.

But she didn't close her eyes. She saw how she looked

when she came—her mouth open, her eyes glazed with desire. So hot, watching the two of them together.

A roar started low in Chadwick's chest as he pumped once, twice more—then froze, his face twisted in pleasure. Then he sort of fell forward onto her, both of them panting.

"My Serena," he said, sounding spent.

"My Chadwick," she replied, knowing it was the truth. She was his now. And he was hers.

But he wasn't. He couldn't be. He was still married. He was still her boss. One explosive sexual encounter didn't change those realities.

For tonight, he was hers.

Tomorrow, however, was going to be a problem.

Ten

Chadwick laid in Serena's bed, his eyes heavy and his body relaxed.

Serena. How long had he fantasized about bending her over the desk and taking her from behind? Years. But the mirror? Watching her watch him?

Amazing.

She came back in and shut the door behind her. Her hair was down now, hanging in long, loose waves around her shoulders. He couldn't remember ever seeing her hair down. She always wore it up. He could see her nude figure silhouetted by the faint light that trickled through her drapes. Her body did things to him—things he didn't realize he could still feel. It'd been so long....

She paused. "You need anything?"

"You." He held out his hand to her. "Come here."

She slipped into bed and curled up against his chest. "That was...wow."

Grinning, he pulled her in for a kiss. A long kiss. A kiss that involved a little more than just kissing. He could *not* get enough of her. The feeling of her filling his hands, pressed against him—she was so much a woman. He'd brought three condoms, just in case. He had the remaining two within easy reach on her bedside table.

So he broke the kiss.

"Mmmm," she hummed. "Chadwick?"

"Yes?"

She paused, tracing a small circle on his chest. "I'm pregnant."

"A fact we've already established."

"But why doesn't that bother you? I mean, everything's changing and I feel so odd and I'm going to blow up like a whale soon. I just don't think...I don't feel beautiful."

He traced a hand down her back and grabbed a handful of her bountiful backside. "You are amazingly beautiful. I guess you being pregnant just reminds me how much of a woman you are."

She was quiet for a moment. "Then why didn't you ever have kids with Helen?"

He sighed. He didn't want Helen in this room. Not now. But Serena had a right to know. Last week, they might not have discussed their personal lives at the office—but this was a different week entirely. "Did you ever meet her? Of course you did."

"At the galas. She never came by the office."

"No, she never did. She didn't like beer, didn't like my job. She only liked the money I made." Part of that was his fault. If he'd put her before the job, well, things might have been different. But they might not have been. Things might have been exactly the same.

"She was very pretty. Very—"

"Very plastic." She'd been pretty once, but with every

new procedure, she'd changed. "She had a lot of work done. Lipo, enlargements, Botox—she didn't want to have a baby because she didn't want to be pregnant. She didn't want me."

That was the hard truth of the matter. He'd convinced himself that she did—convinced himself that he wanted to spend the rest of his life with her, that it would be different from his father's marriages. That's why he'd struck the alimony clause from the pre-nup. But he'd never been able to escape the simple fact that he was Hardwick's son. All he'd ever been able to do was temper that fact by honoring his marriage vows long after there was nothing left to honor.

"She moved out of our bedroom about two years ago. Then filed for divorce almost fourteen months ago."

"That's a *very* long time." The way she said it—air rushing out of her in shock—made him hold her tighter. "Did you want to have a kid? I mean, I get her reasons, but…"

Had he ever wanted kids? It was no stretch to say he didn't know. Not having kids wasn't so much his choice as it had been the path of least resistance. "You haven't met my mother, have you?"

"No."

He chuckled. "You don't want to know her. She's— well, in retrospect, she's a lot like Helen. But that's all I knew. Screaming fights and weeks of silent treatment. And since I was my father's chosen son, she treated me much the same way she treated Hardwick. I ruined her figure, even though she got a tummy tuck. I was a constant reminder that she'd married a man she detested."

"Is that what Helen did? Scream?"

"No, no—but the silent treatment, yes. It got worse over time. I didn't want to bring a child into that. I didn't want a kid to grow up with the life I did. I didn't…I didn't want to be my father."

He couldn't help it. He took her hand and guided it around to his side—to where the skin had never healed quite right.

Serena's fingertips traced the raised scar. It wasn't that bad, he told himself. He'd been telling himself that same thing for years. Just an inch of puckered skin.

Helen had seen it, of course, and asked about it. But he hadn't been able to tell her the truth. He'd come up with some lie about a skiing accident.

"Oh, Chadwick," Serena said, in a voice that sounded like she was choking back tears.

He didn't want pity. As far as the world was concerned, he had no reason to be pitied. He was rich, good-looking and soon to be available again. Only Serena saw something else—something much more real than his public image.

He still didn't want her to feel sorry for him. So he kept talking even as she rubbed his scar. "Do you know how many half siblings I have?"

"Um, Frances and Matthew, right?"

"Frances has a twin brother, Byron. And that's just with Jeannie. My father had a third wife and had two more kids with her, Lucy and David. Johnny, Toni and Mark with his fourth wife. We know of at least two other kids, one with a nanny and one with…" He swallowed, feeling uncertain.

"His secretary?"

He winced. "Yes. There are probably more. That was why I fought against *this*," he said, pressing his lips against her forehead, "for so long. I didn't want to be him. So when Helen said she wanted to wait before we had kids—and wait and wait—I said fine. Because that's different than what Hardwick did."

Serena pulled her hand away from his scar to trace small circles on his chest again. "Those are all really good reasons. Mine were more selfish. I didn't marry Neil because my parents were married and that piece of paper didn't save them or me. I always thought we'd have kids one day, but I wanted to wait until my finances could support us. I put almost every bonus you've ever given me into savings, building up my nest egg. I thought I'd like to take some time off, but the thought of not getting that paycheck every other week scared me so much. So I waited. Until I messed up." She took a ragged breath. "And here I am."

He chewed over what she'd said. "Here with me?"

"Well…yes. Unmarried, pregnant and sleeping with my boss in clear violation of company policy." She sighed. "I've spent my adult life trying to lead a stable life. I stayed with a man I didn't passionately love because it was the safe thing to do. I've stayed in this apartment—the same place I've lived since I moved in with Neil nine years ago—because it's rent-controlled. I drive the same car I bought six years ago because it hasn't broken down. And now? This is not the most secure place in the world. It…it scares me. To be here with you."

Her whole life had been spent running away from a hellish childhood. Was that any different from his? Trying so hard to not let the sins of the father revisit the son.

Yet here he was, sleeping with his secretary. And here she was, putting her entire livelihood at risk to fall into bed with him.

No. This would not be a repeat of the past. He would not let her fall through the cracks just because he wasn't strong enough to resist her. At the very least, he hadn't gotten her pregnant and abandoned her like his father would have—even if someone else had done just that.

"I want to be here with you, even if it complicates matters. You make me feel things I didn't know I was still capable of feeling. The way you look at me...I was never a son, never really a husband. Just an employee. A bank account. When I'm with you, I feel like...like the man I was always supposed to be, but never got the chance to."

She clutched him even tighter. "You never treated me like I was an afterthought, a welfare kid. You always treated me with respect and made me feel like I could be better than my folks were. That I *was* better."

He tilted her face back. "I will *not* fail you, Serena. This complicates things, but I made you a promise. I *will* keep it."

She blinked, her eyes shining. "I know you will, Chadwick. That means everything to me." She kissed him, a tender brush that was sweeter than any other touch he'd ever felt. "I won't fail you, either."

The next kiss wasn't nearly as tender. "Serena," he groaned as she slipped her legs over his thighs, heat from her center setting his blood on fire. "I need you."

"I need you, too," she whispered, rolling onto her back. "I don't want to look at you in a mirror, Chadwick. I want to see you."

He sat back on his knees and grabbed one of the condoms. Quickly, he rolled it on and lowered himself into her waiting arms. His erection found her center and he thrust in.

She moaned as he propped himself up on one arm and filled his other hand with her breast. "Yes, just like that."

He rolled his thumb over her nipple and was rewarded when it went stiff. Her breast was warm and full and *real*.

Everything about her was real—her body, her emotions, her honesty.

Serena ran her nails down his back as she looked him in the eye, spurring him on. Over and over he plunged into her welcoming body. Over and over, waves of emotion flooded his mind.

Now that he was with her, he felt more authentic than he had in years—maybe ever. The closest he'd ever come to feeling real was the year he'd spent making beer. The brewmasters hadn't treated him with distrust, as so many people in the other departments had. They'd treated him like a regular guy.

Serena worked hard for him, but she'd never done so with the simpering air of a sycophant. Had never treated him like he was a stepping stool to bigger and better things.

This was real, too. The way her body took his in, the way he made her moan—the way he wanted to take her in his arms and never let her go....

Without closing her eyes—without breaking the contact between them—she made a high-pitched noise in the back of her throat as she tightened on his body then collapsed back against her pillow.

He drove hard as his climax roared through his ears so loudly that it blotted out everything but Serena. Her eyes, her face, her body. *Her.*

He wanted her. He always had.

This didn't change anything.

"Serena..." He wanted to tell her he loved her, but then what did that mean? Was he actually in love with her? What he felt for her was far stronger than anything he'd ever felt for another woman, but did that mean it was love?

So he bit his tongue and pulled her into his arms, burying his face into her hair.

"Stay with me," she whispered. "Tonight. In my bed."

"Yes." That was all he needed right now. Her, in his arms.

What if this was love? With Serena tucked against his chest, Chadwick started to drift off to sleep on that warm, happy thought. He and Serena. In love.

But then a horrifying idea popped into his mind, jerking him back from peaceful sleep. What if this wasn't love? What if this was mere infatuation, something that would evaporate under the harsh light of reality—reality that they might have ignored tonight but that would be unavoidable come Monday morning?

He'd slept with his assistant. Before the divorce was final.

It was exactly what his father would have done.

Eleven

The smell of crisp bacon woke him.

Chadwick rolled over to find himself alone in an unfamiliar bed. He found a clock on the side table. Half past six. He hadn't slept that late in years.

He sat up. The first thing he saw was the mirror. The one he'd watched as he made love to his assistant.

Serena.

His blood began to roar in his ears as his mind replayed the previous night. Had he really crossed that line—the one he'd sworn he would never cross?

Waking up naked in her bed, his body already aching for her, seemed to say one hell of a *yes*.

He buried his head in his hands. What had he done?

Then he heard it—the soft sound of a woman humming. It was light and, if he didn't know better, filled with joy.

He got out of bed and put his pants on. Breakfast

first. He'd think better once he had a meal in him. As he walked down the short hallway toward the kitchen, he was surprised at how sore his body was. Apparently, not having sex for a few years and then suddenly having it twice had been harder on him than running a few extra miles would have been.

He looked around Serena's place. It was quite small. There was the bedroom he'd come out of. He made another stop at the bathroom, which stood between the bedroom and another small room that was completely empty. Then he was out into the living room, which had a shabby-looking couch against one wall and a space where a flat-screen television must have been on the other. A table stood between the living room space and the kitchen. The legs and the chairs looked a bit beat up, but the table was covered by a clean, bright blue cloth and held a small, chipped vase filled with the roses he'd brought her.

His wine cellar was bigger than this apartment. The place was clearly assembled from odds and ends, but he liked it. It looked almost exactly how he'd imagined a real home would look, one in which babies might color on the walls and spill juice on the rug. One filled with laughter and joy. A place that was a *home*, not just a piece of real estate.

He found Serena standing in front of the stove, a thin blue cotton robe wrapped around her shoulders, her hair hanging in long waves down her back. Something stirred deep in his chest. Did she have anything on under the robe? She was humming as she flipped the bacon. It smelled *wonderful*.

He had a cook, of course. Even though he didn't eat at home very often, George was in charge of feeding the household staff. If Chadwick gave him enough warning, George would have something that rivaled the best restaurants in Denver waiting for him. But if Chadwick didn't, he'd eat the same thing that the maids did. Which was the norm.

He leaned against the doorway, watching Serena cook for him. This felt different than knowing that, somewhere in his huge mansion, George was making him dinner. That was George's job.

Serena frying him bacon and, by the looks of it, eggs?

This must be what people meant by "comfort food." Because there was something deeply comforting about her taking care of him. As far as he could remember, no one but a staff cook had ever made him breakfast.

Was this what normal people did? Woke up on a Sunday morning and had breakfast together?

He came up behind her and slid his arms around her waist, reveling in the way her hair smelled—almost like vanilla, but with a hint of breakfast. He kissed her neck. "Good morning."

She startled but then leaned back, the curve of her backside pressing against him. "Hi." She looked up at him.

He kissed her. "Breakfast?"

"I'm normally up before six, but I made it until a little after," she said, sounding sheepish about it.

"That's pretty early." Those were basically the same hours he kept.

"I have this boss," she went on, her tone teasing as she flipped another strip of bacon, "who keeps insane hours. You know how it is."

He chuckled against her ear. "A real bastard, huh?"

She leaned back, doing her best to look him in the eye. "Nope. I think he's amazing."

He kissed her again. This time he let his hands roam away from her waist to other parts. She pulled away and playfully smacked the hand that had been cupping her breast. "You don't want your breakfast burned, do you? The coffee's ready."

She already had a cup sitting in front of the coffee-maker. Like everything else in her place, the coffeemaker looked like it was either nine years old or something she'd bought secondhand.

She hadn't been kidding. By the looks of her apartment, she really had put every bonus in savings.

It was odd. In his world, people spent money like it was always going out of style. No one had to save because there would always be more. Like Phillip, for example. He saw a horse he wanted, and he bought it. It didn't matter how much it was or how many other horses he had. Helen had been the same, except for her it was clothing and plastic surgery. She had a completely new wardrobe every season from top designers.

Hell, he wasn't all that different. He owned more cars than he drove and a bigger house than he'd ever need, and he had three maids. The only difference was that he'd been so busy working that he hadn't had time to start collecting horses like his brother. Or mistresses, like his father. For them, everything had been disposable. Even the horses. Even the people.

Serena wasn't like that. She didn't need a new coffee-pot just because the old one was *old*. It still worked. That seemed to be good enough for her.

He filled his mug—emblazoned with the logo of a local bank—and sat at the table, watching her. She moved comfortably around her kitchen. He wasn't entirely sure where the kitchen was in his family mansion. "You make breakfast often?"

She put some bread into a late-model toaster. "I've gotten very good at cooking. It's…"

"Stable?"

"*Reassuring,*" she answered with a grin. "I bring home my own bacon *and* fry it up in the pan." She brought plates with bacon and eggs to the table, and then went back for the toast and some strawberry jam. "I clip coupons and shop the sales—that saves a lot of money. Cooking is much cheaper than eating out. I think last night was the first time I'd gone out to dinner in…maybe three months?" Her face darkened. "Yes. Just about three months ago."

He remembered. Three months ago, Neil and she had "mutually" decided to end their relationship.

"Thank you for making me breakfast. I've never had someone cook for me. I mean, not someone who wasn't on staff."

She blushed. "Thank you for dinner. And the dresses. I think it's pretty obvious that I've never had anyone spend that kind of money on me before."

"You handled yourself beautifully. I'm sorry if I made you uncomfortable."

That had been his mistake. It was just that she fit in so well at the office, never once seeming out of place among the high rollers and company heads Chadwick met with. He'd assumed that was part of her world—or at least something close to it.

But it wasn't. Now that he saw her place—small, neatly kept but more "shabby" than "shabby chic"—he realized how off the mark he'd been.

She gave him a smile that was part gentle and part hot. "It was fun. But I think I'll get different shoes for next time."

Next time. The best words he'd heard in a long, long time.

They ate quickly. Mostly because he was hungry and the food was good, but also because Serena shifted in her seat and started rubbing his calf with her toes. "When do you have to leave?"

He wanted to stay at least a little bit longer. But he had things to do, even though it was Sunday—for starters, he had an interview with *Nikkei Business*, a Japanese business magazine, at two. He couldn't imagine talking about the fate of the brewery from the comfort of Serena's cozy place. How could those two worlds ever cross?

The moment the thought crossed his mind, he felt like he'd been punched in the stomach. Really, how *could* their two worlds cross? His company was imploding and his divorce was draining him dry—and that wasn't even counting the fact that Serena was pregnant. And his assistant.

He'd waited so long for Serena. She'd done admirably the night before at dinner and then the gala, but how comfortable would she really be in his world?

They still had this morning. They finished breakfast and then he tried to help her load the dishwasher. Only he kept trying to put the cups on the bottom rack, which made her giggle as she rearranged his poor attempts. "Never loaded a dishwasher before, huh?"

"What gave me away?" He couldn't bring himself to be insulted. She was right.

"Thanks for trying." She closed the dishwasher door and turned to him. "Don't worry. You're better at other things."

She put her arms around his neck and kissed him. Yeah, he didn't have to leave yet.

He stripped the robe from her shoulders, leaving it in a

heap on the floor. No, nothing underneath. Just her wonderful body. With the morning light streaming through
the sheers she had hung over her windows, he could finally, fully see what he'd touched the night before.

Her breasts were large and firm. He bent down and
traced her nipple with his tongue. Serena gasped as the
tip went hard in his mouth, her fingers tangling through
his hair. *Sensitive.* Perfect.

"Bed," she said in a voice that walked the fine line
between fluttery and commanding.

"Yes, ma'am," he replied, standing back to give her a
mock salute before he swept her off her feet.

"Chadwick!" Serena clutched at him, but she giggled
as he carried her back down the short hall.

He laid her down on the bed, pausing only long enough
to get rid of his pants. Then he was filling his hands with
her breasts, her hips—covering her body with his—loving the way she touched him without abandon.

This was what he wanted—not the company, not
Helen, not galas and banquets and brothers and sisters
who took and took and never seemed to give back.

He wanted Serena. He wanted the kind of life where
he helped cook and do the dishes instead of having an
unseen staff invisibly take care of everything. He wanted
the kind of life where he ate breakfast with her and then
went back to bed instead of rushing off for an interview
or a meeting.

He wanted to have a life outside of Beaumont Brewery. He wanted it to be with Serena.

He had no idea how to make that happen.

As he rocked into Serena's body and she clung to him,
all he could think about was the way she made him feel—
how he hadn't felt like this in…well, maybe ever.

This was what he wanted.

There had to be a way.

Finally, after another hour of lying in her arms, he managed to tear himself away from Serena's bed. He put on his tuxedo pants and shirt and headed for the car after a series of long kisses goodbye. How amazing did Serena look, standing in the doorway in her little robe, a coffee cup in her hand as she waved him off? It almost felt like a wife kissing her husband goodbye as he went off to work.

He was over-romanticizing things. For starters, Serena wouldn't be happy as a stay-at-home wife. It would probably leave her feeling too much like she wasn't bringing home that bacon. He knew now how very important that was to her. But they couldn't carry on like this at work. The office gossips would notice something sooner or later—and once she began to show, things would go viral in a heartbeat. He didn't want to subject her to the rumor mill.

There had to be a way. The variables ran through his mind as he drove home. He was about to lose the company. She worked for him. A relationship was against company policy. But if he lost the company...

If he lost the company, he wouldn't be her boss anymore. She might be out of a job, too, but at least they wouldn't be violating any policy.

But then what? What was next? What did he *want* to do? That was what she'd asked him. Told him, in fact. Do what he wanted.

What was that?

Make beer, he realized. That was the best time he'd had at Beaumont Brewery—the year he'd spent making beer with the brewmasters. He *liked* beer. He knew a lot about it and had played a big role in selecting the seasonal drafts for the Percheron Drafts line of craft beers. What if...

What if he sold the brewery, but kept Percheron Drafts for himself, running it as a small private business? Beaumont would be dead, but the family history of brewing would live on in Percheron Drafts. He could be rid of his father's legacy and run this new company the way he wanted to. It wouldn't be Hardwick's. It would be Chadwick's.

He could hire Serena. She knew as much about what he did as anyone. And if they formed a new company, well, they could have a different company policy.

And if they got sixty-five dollars a share for the brewery...maybe he could walk into Helen's lawyer's office and make her that offer she couldn't refuse. Everyone had a price, Matthew had said, and he was right. He quickly did the math.

If he liquidated a few extraneous possessions—cars, the jet, property, *horses*—he could make Helen an offer of $100 million to sign the papers. Even she wouldn't be able to say no to a number like that. And he'd still have enough left over to re-incorporate Percheron Drafts.

As he thought about the horses, he realized this plan would only work if he did it on his own. He would get $50 million because he actually worked for the company. But his siblings would get about $15 to $20 million each. He couldn't keep working for them. Serena had been right about that, too. If he took Percheron Drafts private, he would have to sever all financial ties with his siblings. He couldn't keep footing the bill for extravagant purchases, and what's more, he didn't want to.

The more he thought about it, the more he liked this idea. He'd be done with Beaumont Brewery—free from his father's ideas of how to run a company. Free to do things the way he wanted, to make the beer he wanted. It would be a smaller company, sure—one that wouldn't be able to pay for the big mansion or the staff or the garage full of cars he rarely drove.

He'd have to downsize his life for a while, but would that really be such a horrible thing? Serena had lived small her entire life and she seemed quite happy—except for the pregnancy thing.

He wanted to give her everything he could—but he knew she wouldn't be comfortable with extravagance. If he gave her a job in a new company, paid her a good wage, made sure she had the kind of benefits she needed…

That was almost the same thing as giving her the world. That was giving her stability.

This could work. He'd call his lawyers when he got home and run the idea past them.

This *had* to work. He had to make this happen. Because it was what he wanted.

After Serena watched Chadwick's sports car drive away, she tried not to think about what the neighbors would say about the late arrival and very late departure of such a vehicle.

But that didn't mean she didn't worry. What had she done? Besides have one of the most romantic nights in memory. A fancy dinner, glamorous gala, exquisite sex? It'd been like something out of a fairy tale, the poor little girl transformed into the belle of the ball.

How long had it been since she'd enjoyed sex that much? Things with Neil had been rote for a while. A long while, honestly. Something that they *tried* to do once a week—something that didn't last very long or feel very good.

But sex with Chadwick? Completely different. Completely *satisfying*. Even better than she'd dreamed it would be. Chadwick hadn't just done what he wanted and left it at that. He'd taken his time with her, making sure she came first—and often.

What would it be like to be with a man who always brought that level of excitement to their bed? Someone she couldn't keep her hands off—someone who thought she was sexy even though her body was getting bigger?

It would be *wonderful*.

But how was that fantasy—for that's what it was, a fantasy of epic proportions—going to become a reality? She couldn't imagine fitting into Chadwick's world, with expensive clothes and fancy dinners and galas all the time. And, as adorably hot as he'd looked standing in her kitchen in nothing but his tux trousers, she also couldn't imagine Chadwick being happy in her small apartment, clipping coupons and shopping consignment stores for a bargain.

God, how she wanted him. She'd been waiting for her chance for years, really. But she had no idea how she could bridge the gap between their lives.

In a fit of pique, Serena started cleaning. Which was saying something, as she'd already cleaned in anticipation of Chadwick possibly seeing the inside of her apartment—and her bedroom.

But there was laundry to be done, dishes to be washed, beds to be made—more than enough to keep her busy. But not enough to keep her mind off Chadwick.

She changed into her grubby sweat shorts and a stained T-shirt. What the heck was going to happen on Monday? It was going to be hard to keep her hands off him, especially behind the closed door of his office. But doing anything, even touching him, was a violation of company policy. It went against her morals to violate policies, especially ones she'd helped write.

How was she supposed to be in love with Chadwick while she worked for him?

She couldn't be. Not unless...

Unless she didn't work for him.

No. She couldn't just quit her job. Even if the whole company was about to be sold off, she couldn't walk away from a steady paycheck and benefits. The sale and changeover might take months, after all—months during which she could be covered for prenatal care, could be making plans. Or some miracle could occur and the whole sale could fall through. Then she'd be safe.

So what was she going to do about Chadwick? She didn't want to wait months before she could kiss him again, before she could hold him in her arms. She was tired of pretending she didn't have feelings for him. If things stayed the same...

Well, one thing she knew for certain was that things wouldn't stay the same. She'd slept with him—multiple times—and she was pregnant. Those two things completely changed *everything*.

She was transferring the bedsheets from the washer to the dryer when she heard something at the door. Her first thought was that maybe Chadwick had changed his mind and decided to spend the day with her.

But, as she raced for the door, it swung open. *Chadwick doesn't have a key*, she thought. And she always kept her door locked.

That was as far as she got in her thinking before Neil Moore, semi-pro golf player and ex-everything, walked in.

"Hey, babe."

"Neil?" The sight of him walking in like he'd never

walked out caused such a visceral reaction that she almost threw up. "What are you doing here?"

"Got your email," he said, putting his keys back on his hook beside the door as he closed it. He looked at her in her cleaning clothes. "You look…good. Have you put on weight?"

The boldness of this insult—for that's what it was—shook her back to herself. "For crying out loud, Neil. I sent you an email. Not an invitation to walk in, unannounced."

Another wave of nausea hit her. What if Neil had shown up two hours before—when she was still tangled up with Chadwick? Good lord. She fought the emotion down and tried to sound pissed. Which wasn't that hard, really.

"You don't live here anymore, remember? *You* moved out."

Then he said, "I missed you."

Nothing about his posture or attitude suggested this was the case. He slouched his way over to the couch—*her* couch—and slid down into it, just like he always had. What had she seen in this man, besides the stability he'd offered her?

"Is that so? I've been here for three months, Neil. Three months without a single call or text from you. Doesn't seem like you've missed me very much at all."

"Well, I did," he snapped. "I see that nothing's changed here. Same old couch, same old…" He waved his hand around in a gesture that was probably supposed to encompass the whole apartment but mostly seemed directed at her. "So what did you want to talk to me about?"

She glared at him. Maybe it would have been better if Chadwick *had* still been here. For starters, Neil would have seen that nothing was the same anymore—

she wasn't, anyway. She wasn't the same frugal executive assistant she'd been when he'd left. She was a woman who went shopping in the finest stores and made small talk with the titans of industry and looked damn good doing it. She was a woman who invited her boss into her apartment and then into her bed. She was pregnant and changing and bringing home her own bacon and frying it up in her own pan, thank you very much.

Neil didn't notice her look of death. He was staring at the spot where the TV had been before he'd taken that with him. "You haven't even gotten a new television yet? Geez, Serena. I didn't realize you were going to take me leaving so hard."

"I don't need one. I don't watch TV." A fact she would have thought he'd figured out after nine years of cohabitating—or at least figured out after she told him to take the TV when he moved. "Did you come here just to criticize me? Because I can think of a lot better ways to spend a Sunday morning."

Neil rolled his eyes, but then he sat up straighter. "You know, I've been thinking. We had nine good years together. Why did we let that get away from us?"

She could not believe the words coming out of this man's mouth. "Correct me if I'm wrong, but I believe 'we' let that get away from 'us' when you started sleeping with groupies at the country club."

"That was a mistake." He agreed far more quickly than he had when Serena had found the incriminating text messages. They'd gone out to dinner that night to try and "work things out," but it'd all fallen apart instead. "I've changed, babe. I know what I did was wrong. Let me make it up to you."

This was Neil "making it up to her"—criticizing her appearance and her apartment?

"I'll do better. Be better for you." For a second, he managed to look sincere, but it didn't last. "I heard that the brewery might get sold. You own stock in the company, right? We could get a bigger place—much nicer than this dump—and start over. It could be really good, babe."

Oh, for the love of Pete. That's what this was. He'd gotten wind of the AllBev offer and was looking for a big payout.

"What happened? Your lover go back to her husband?"

The way Neil's face turned a ruddy red answered the question for her, even though he didn't. He just went back to staring at the space where the television used to be.

The more she talked to him, the less she could figure out what she had ever seen in him. The petty little criticisms—it wasn't that those were new, it was just that she'd gotten used to not having her appearance, her housekeeping and her cooking sniped at.

In three months, she'd realized how much she'd settled by staying with Neil. No wonder the passion had long since bled out of their relationship. Hard to be passionate when the man who supposedly loved you was constantly tearing you down.

Chadwick didn't do that to her. Even before this last week had turned everything upside down, he'd always let her know how much he appreciated her hard work. That had just carried over into her bed. Boy, had he appreciated her hard work.

Serena shook her head. This wasn't exactly an either/or situation. Just because she didn't want Neil didn't necessarily mean her only other option was Chadwick. Even if whatever was going on between her and Chadwick was nothing more than a really satisfying rebound—for both of them—well, that didn't mean she wanted to throw herself at Neil. She was no longer a scared college girl existing just above the poverty line. She was a grown woman fully capable of taking care of herself.

It was a damn good thing to realize.

"I'm pregnant. You're the father." There. She'd gotten it out. "That's what I needed to talk to you about. And because *you* were sleeping around, *I* have to get tested."

For a moment, Neil was well and truly shocked. His mouth flopped open and his eyes bugged out of his head. "You're…"

"Pregnant. Have been for three months."

"Are you sure I'm the father?"

Her blood began to boil. "Of course you're the father, you idiot. Just because you were sleeping around doesn't mean I was. I was faithful to you—to *us*—until the very end. But that wasn't enough for you. And now you're not enough for me."

"I…I…" He seemed stuck.

Well, he could just stick. She was the one that was pregnant. She'd spend the rest of her life raising his— *her*—baby. But that didn't mean she had to spend the rest of her life with him. "I thought you should know."

"I didn't want—I can't—" He wasn't making a lot of progress. "Can't you just *end* it?"

"Get out." The words flew from her mouth. "Get out *now*."

"But—"

"This is my child. I don't need anything from you, and what's more is I don't *want* anything from you. I won't sue you for child support. I never want to see you again." She hadn't said that when he'd left the last time. Maybe because she hadn't believed the words. But now she did.

Neil's eyes hadn't made a lot of progress back into

his skull. "You don't want money? Damn—how much is Beaumont paying you now?"

Was that all she was—a back-up source of funding? "If you're still here in one minute, I'm calling the police. Goodbye, Neil."

He got up, looking like she'd smacked him. "Leave your key," she called after him. She didn't want any more surprise visits.

He took the key off his key ring and hung it back on the hook.

Then he closed the door on his way out.

And that was that.

She looked around the apartment as if the blinders had suddenly been lifted from her eyes. This wasn't her place. It had never been hers. This had been *their* place—hers and Neil's. She'd wanted to stay here because it was safe.

But Neil would always feel like he was entitled to be there because it had been his apartment before she'd moved in.

She didn't want to raise her baby in a place that was haunted by unfaithfulness and snide put-downs.

She needed a fresh start.

The thought terrified her.

Twelve

"Ms. Chase, if you could join me in my office."

Serena tried not to grin as she gathered up her tablet. He was paging her a full forty minutes earlier than their normal meeting time. What a difference a week made. Seven days before, she'd been shell-shocked after realizing she was pregnant. This week? She was sort of her boss's secret lover.

No, best not to think of it in those terms. Company policy and all that.

She opened the door to Chadwick's office and shut it behind her. That was what she normally did, but today the action had an air of secrecy about it.

Chadwick was sitting behind his desk, looking as normal as she'd ever seen him. Well, maybe not *that* normal. He glanced up and his face broke into one huge grin. God, he was so handsome. It almost hurt to look at him, to know that he was so happy because of her.

He didn't say anything as she walked toward her regular seat. Instead, he got up and met her halfway with the kind of kiss that melted every single part of her body. He pulled her in tight, and his lips explored hers.

"I missed you," he breathed in her ear as he wrapped his arms around her.

She took in his clean scent, her body responding to his touch. How different was this from Neil telling her he missed her the day before? Chadwick wasn't all talk. He followed up everything he said with actions.

"Me, too." Now that she knew exactly what was underneath that suit jacket, she couldn't stop running her hands over the muscles of his back. "I've never wanted Monday to get here so fast."

"Hmmm" was all he replied as he took another kiss from her. "When can I see you again?"

She gave him a look that was supposed to be stern. It must not have come across the way she intended it to, because he cracked a goofy grin. "This doesn't count?"

"You know what I mean."

She did. When could they spend another night wrapped in each other's arms? She wanted to say tonight. Right now. They could leave work and not come back until much, much later.

That wasn't an option.

"What are we going to do? I hate breaking the rules."

"You wrote the rule."

"That makes it even worse."

Instead of looking disgruntled with her, his grin turned positively wicked. "Look, I know this is a problem. But I'm working on a solution."

"Oh?"

"It's in process." She must have given him a look because he squeezed her a little tighter. "Trust me."

She stared into his eyes, wanting nothing more than to go back to Saturday night. Or even Sunday morning.

But reality was impossible to ignore. "If you need any help solving things, you just let me know."

"Done. When's your doctor's appointment?"

She touched the cleanly shaven line of his chin. "Friday next week."

"You want me to come with you?"

Love. The word floated up to the top of her consciousness, unbidden. That's what this was—love. Even if she hadn't said the exact word, she felt it with all of her heart.

Her throat closed up as tears threatened. Oh, God, she was in love with Chadwick Beaumont. It was both the best thing that had ever happened to her and one hell of a big problem.

He ran his finger under her chin again—much like he had the week before—and smiled down at her. "You all right?"

"I am. You wouldn't mind coming with me?"

"I've recently discovered that it's good to get out of the office every so often. I'd love to accompany you."

She had to swallow past the lump in her throat.

"Are you sure you're all right?"

She leaned her head against his shoulder, loving the solid, strong way he felt against her. "I hope you get that solution figured out soon."

"I won't fail you, Serena." He sounded so serious about it that she had no choice but to believe him. To hope that whatever he was planning would work. "Now, I believe I have time tonight to have a business dinner with my assistant, don't I? We can discuss my schedule in a little more...detail."

How could she say no to that? It was a business-professional activity, after all. "I believe we can make that happen."

"So," Chadwick said, pulling back and leading her toward the couch. "Tell me about your weekend."

"Funny about that." Sitting on the couch, her head against his shoulder, she related what had happened with Neil.

"You want me to take care of it?"

The way he said it—sounding much like he had when he'd nearly started a fight with his brother at the gala—made her smile. It should have been him being something of a Neanderthal male. As it was, it made her feel...secure.

"No, I think he got the message. He's not getting anything out of me or this company."

She then told Chadwick how she was thinking of moving to a new place and making a clean break with the past.

He got an odd look on his face as she talked. She knew that look—he was thinking.

"Got a solution to this problem yet?"

He cupped her face in his hands and kissed her—not the heated kiss from earlier, but something that was softer, gentler. Then he touched his forehead to hers. "You'll be the first to know."

That lump moved up in her throat again. She knew he'd keep his promise.

But what would it cost him?

"Mr. Beaumont." Serena's voice over the intercom sounded...different. Like she was being strangled.

"Yes?" He looked at Bob Larsen sitting across the desk from him, who froze mid-pitch. It wasn't like Serena to interrupt a meeting without a damn good reason.

There was a tortured pause. "Mrs. Beaumont is here to see you."

Stark panic flooded Chadwick's system. There were only a few women who went by that name and all of the options were less than pleasant. Blindly, he chose the least offensive option. "My mother?"

"Mrs. *Helen* Beaumont is here to see you."

Oh, *hell*.

Chadwick locked eyes with Bob. Sure, he and Bob had worked together for a long time, and yes, Chadwick's never-ending divorce was probably watercooler fodder, but Chadwick had worked hard to keep his personal drama and business life separate.

Until now.

"One moment," he managed to get out before he shut the intercom off. "Bob…"

"Yeah, we can pick this up later." Bob was hastily gathering his things and heading for the door. "Um… good luck?"

"Thanks." Chadwick was going to need a lot more than luck.

What was Helen doing there? She'd never come to the office when they were semi happily married. He hadn't talked to her without lawyers present in over a year. He couldn't imagine she wanted to reconcile. But what else would bring her there?

He knew one thing—he had to play this right. He could not give her something to use against him. He took a second to straighten his tie before he opened his door.

Helen Beaumont was not sitting in the waiting chairs across from Serena's desk. Instead, she was standing at one of the side windows, staring out at the brewery campus. Or maybe at nothing at all.

She was so thin he could almost see through her, like

she was a shadow instead of an actual woman. She wore a high-waisted skirt that clung to her frame, and a silk blouse topped with a fur stole. Diamonds—ones he'd paid for—covered her fingers and ears. She wasn't the same woman he'd married eight years before.

He looked at Serena, who was as white as notebook paper. Serena gave him a panicked little shrug. So she didn't have any idea what Helen was doing there, either.

"Helen." In good faith, he couldn't say it was nice to see her. So he didn't. "Shall we talk in my office?"

She pivoted on her five-inch heels and tried to kill him with a glare. "Chadwick." Her eyes cut to Serena. "I don't concern myself with what servants might hear."

Chadwick tried his best not to show a reaction. "Fine. To what do I owe the honor of a visit?"

"Don't be snide, Chadwick. It doesn't suit you." She looked down her nose at him, which was quite a feat given that she was a good eight inches shorter than he was. "My lawyer said you were going to make a new offer—the kind of offer you've refused to make for the last year."

Damn it. His lawyers were going to find themselves short one influential client for jumping the gun. Floating a trial balloon was different than telling Helen he had an offer. He hadn't even had the time to contact AllBev's negotiating team yet, for crying out loud. There was no offer until the company was sold.

He couldn't take control of his life—get the company he wanted, live the *way* he wanted—until Beaumont Brewery and AllBev reached a legally binding agreement. And what's more, none of this was going to happen overnight or even that week. Even if things moved quickly, negotiations would take months.

Plus, he hadn't told Serena about the plan to sell Beaumont but keep Percheron. God, he'd wanted to keep this all quiet until he had everything set—no more ugly surprises like this one.

"There's a difference between 'refused' and 'been unable' to make."

"Is there? Are you trying to get rid of me, Chadwick?" She managed to say it with a pout, as if he were trying to hurt her feelings.

"I've been trying to end our relationship since the month after you filed for divorce. Remember? You refused to go to marriage counseling with me. You made your position clear. You didn't want me anymore. But here we are, closing in on fourteen months later, and you insist on dragging out the proceedings."

She tilted her head to the side as she fluttered her eyelashes. "I'm not dragging anything out. I'm just…trying to get you to notice me."

"*What*? If you want to be noticed, suing a man is a piss-poor way of going about it."

Something about her face changed. For a moment he almost saw the woman who'd stood beside him in a church, making vows about love and honor.

"You *never* noticed me. Our honeymoon was only six days long because you had to get back early for a meeting. I always woke up alone because you left for the office by six every morning and then you wouldn't come back until ten or eleven at night. I guess I could have lived with that if I'd gotten to see you on the weekends, but you worked every Saturday and always had calls and interviews on Sunday. It was like…it was like being married to a ghost."

For the first time in years, Chadwick felt sympathy for Helen. She was right—he'd left her all alone in that big house with nothing to do but spend money. "But you knew this was my job when you married me."

"I—" Her voice cracked.

Was she on the verge of crying? She'd cried some, back when they would actually fight about…well, about how much he worked and how much money she spent. But it'd always been a play on his sympathies then. Was this a real emotion—or an old-fashioned attempt at manipulation?

"I thought I might be able to make you love me more than you loved this company. But I was wrong. You had no intention of ever loving me. And now I can never have those years back. I lost them to this damn brewery." She brightened, anything honest about her suddenly gone. He was looking at the woman who glared at him from across the lawyers' conference room table. "Here we are. I'm just getting what I deserve."

"We were married for less than ten years, Helen. What is it you think you deserve?"

She gave him a simpering smile and he knew the answer. *Everything.* She was going to take the one thing that had always mattered to him—the company—and she wouldn't stop until it was gone.

Until he had nothing left.

The phone rang on Serena's desk, causing him to jump. She answered it in something that sounded like her normal voice. "I'm sorry, but Mr. Beaumont is in a…meeting. Yes, I can access that information. One moment, please."

"My office," he said under his breath. "*Now.* We don't need to continue this conversation in front of Ms. Chase."

Helen's eyes narrowed until she looked like a viper mid-strike. "Oh? Or is it that you don't want to have *Ms. Chase* in front of me?"

Oh, no. He'd finally done something he wanted— taken Serena out, spent a night in her arms—and he was going to pay for it. Damn it all, why hadn't he kept his hands off her?

Because he wanted Serena. Because she wanted him. It'd all seemed so simple two days before. But now?

"I beg your pardon," Serena said in an offended tone as she hung up the phone.

Helen's mouth twisted into a smirk. "You should. Sleeping with other people's husbands is never a good career move for a secretary."

"You can't talk to me like that," Serena said, sounding more shocked than angry.

Helen continued to stare at her, fully aware she held the upper hand in this situation. "How could you, Chadwick? Dressing up this dumpy secretary and parading her about as if she was *worth* something? I heard it was a pitiable sight."

Damn it all. He'd forgotten about Therese Hunt, Helen's best friend. Serena's face went a blotchy shade of purplish red, and she actually seemed to sway in her seat, like she might faint.

If Helen wanted his attention, she had it now. He was possessed with a crazy urge to throw himself between Serena and Helen—to protect Serena from Helen's wrath. He didn't do that, but he did take a step toward Helen, trying to draw her attention back to him.

"You will watch your mouth or I will have security escort you out of this building and, if you ever set foot on brewery property again, I'll file a restraining order so fast your head will spin. And if you think I'm not making a big enough offer now, just wait until the cops get involved. You will get nothing."

"After what you put me through, you owe me," she screeched.

Keeping his cool was turning out to be a lot of work. "I already offered you terms that are in line with what I owe you. You're the one who won't let this end. I'd like to move on with my life, Helen. Usually, when someone files for divorce, they're indicating that they, too, would like to move on with their lives—separately."

"You've been *sleeping* with her, haven't you?" Her voice was too shrill to be shouting, but loud enough to carry down the halls. Office doors opened and heads cautiously peeked out. "For how long?"

This whole situation was spiraling out of control. "Helen—"

"How long? It's been years, right? Were you banging her before we got married? *Were you*?"

Once, Helen had seemed sweet and lovely. But it had all been so long ago. The vengeful harpy before him was not the woman he had married.

It took everything he had to keep his voice calm. "I *was* faithful to you, Helen. Even after you moved out of our bedroom. But you're not my wife anymore. I don't owe you an explanation for what I do or who I love."

"The hell I'm not your wife—I haven't signed off!"

Anger roared through his body. "You are *not* my wife. You can't cling to the refuge of that technicality anymore, Helen. I've moved on with my life. For the love of God, move on with yours. My lawyers will be in contact with yours."

"You lying bastard! You stand here and take it like a man!"

"I'm not doing this, Helen. Ms. Chase, if you could join me in my office."

Serena gathered her tablet and all but sprinted through his open office door.

"You can't ignore me. I'll take everything. *Everything*!"

He positioned himself between her and the doorway to his office. "Helen, I apologize that I wasn't the man you needed me to be. I'm sorry you weren't the woman I thought you were. We both made mistakes. But move on. Take my next offer. Start dating. Find the man who *will* notice you. Because it's not me. Goodbye, Helen."

Then, over the hysterical sound of her calling him every name in the book, he shut the door.

Serena hunched in her normal chair, her head near her knees.

Chadwick picked up his phone and dialed the security office. "Len? I have a situation outside my office—I need you to make sure my ex-wife makes it out of the building as quietly as possible without you laying a hand on her. Whatever you do, *don't* provoke her. Thanks."

Then he turned his attention to Serena. Her color was not improving. "Breathe, honey."

Nothing happened. He crouched down in front of her and raised her face until he could see that her eyes were glazed over.

"Breathe," he ordered her. Then, because he couldn't think of anything else to shock her back into herself, he kissed her. Hard.

When he pulled back, her chest heaved as she sucked in air. He leaned her head against his shoulder and rubbed her back. "Good, hon. Do it again."

Serena gulped down air as he held her. What a mess. This was all his fault.

Well, his and his lawyers'. *Former* lawyers.

Outside the office, the raging stopped. Neither he nor

Serena moved until his phone rang some minutes later. Chadwick answered it. "Yes?"

"She's sitting in her car, crying. What do you want me to do?"

"Keep an eye on her. If she gets back out of the car, call the police. Otherwise, just leave her alone."

"Chadwick," Serena whispered so quietly that he almost didn't hear her.

"Yes?"

"What she said…"

"Don't think about what she said. She's just bitter that I took you to the gala." The blow about Serena being a dumpy secretary had been a low one.

"No." Serena pushed herself off his shoulder and looked him in the eye. Her color was better, but her eyes were watery. "About her being alone all the time. Because you work *all the time*."

"I did."

But that wasn't the truth, and they both knew it. He still worked that much.

She touched her fingertips to his cheek. "You *do*. I know you. I know your schedule. You left my apartment on Sunday exactly for the reason she said—because you had an interview."

All of his plans—plans that had seemed so great twenty-four hours before—felt like whispers drifting into the void.

"Things are going to change," he promised her. She didn't look like she believed him. "I'm working on it. I won't work a hundred hours a week. Because Helen was right about something else, too—I didn't love her more than I loved the company. But that's…" His voice choked up. "But that's different now. I'm different now, because of you."

Her lip trembled as two matching tears raced down either cheek. "Don't you see the impossible situation we're in? I can't be with you while I work for you—but if I don't work for you, will I ever see you?"

"Yes," he said. She flinched. It must have come out more harshly than he'd meant it to, but he was feeling desperate. "You will. I'll make it happen."

Her mouth twisted into the saddest smile he'd ever seen. "I've made your life so much harder."

"Helen did—not you. You are making it better. You always have."

She stroked his face, tears still silently dripping down her cheeks. "Everything's changed. If it were just you and me...but it's not anymore. I'm going to have a baby and I have to put that baby first. I can't live with the fear of Helen or even Neil popping up whenever they want to wreak a little havoc."

The bottom of his stomach dropped out. "I'm going to sell the company, but it'll take months. You'll be able to keep your benefits, probably until the baby's born. It doesn't have to change right now, Serena. You can stay with me."

Tears streaming, she shook her head. "I can't. You understand, don't you? I can't be your dumpy secretary and your weekend lover at the same time. I can't live that way, and I won't raise my child torn between two worlds like that. I don't belong in your world, and you—you can't fit in mine. It just won't work."

"It will," he insisted.

"And this company," she went on. "It's what you were raised to do. I can't ask you to give that up."

"Don't do this," he begged. The taste of fear was so strong in the back of his mouth that it almost choked him. "I'll take care of you, I promise."

Helen had left him, of course. But underneath the drama, he'd been relieved she was gone. It meant no more fights, no more pain. He could get on with the business of running his company without having to gauge everything against what Helen would do.

This? This meant no more seeing Serena first thing every morning and last thing every night. No more Serena encouraging him to get out of the office, reminding him that he didn't have to run the world just so his siblings could spend even more money.

The loss of Helen had barely registered on his radar. But the loss of Serena?

It would be devastating.

"I can't function without you." Even as he said it, he knew it was truer than he'd realized. "Don't leave me."

She leaned forward, pressing her wet lips to his cheek. "You can. You will. I have to take care of myself. It's the only way." She stood, letting her fingers trail off his skin. "I hereby resign my position of executive assistant, effective immediately."

Then, after a final tear-stained look that took his heart and left it lying in the middle of his office, she turned and walked out the door.

He watched her go.

So this was a broken heart.

He didn't like it.

Thirteen

The door to Lou's Diner jangled as Serena pulled it open. Things had been so crazy that she hadn't even had time to tell her mom and dad that she was pregnant. Or that she had quit her great job because she was in love with her great boss.

Mom and Dad had an old landline phone number that didn't have voice mail or even an answering machine, if it worked at all. The likelihood of her getting a "this number is out of service" message when Serena called was about fifty percent. Catching her mom at work was pretty much the only guaranteed way to talk to her parents.

She'd put off going there for a few nights. Seeing her parents always made her feel uncomfortable. She'd tried to help them out through the years—got them into that apartment, helped make the payments on her dad's car—and there'd been the disastrous experiment with prepaid cell phones. It always ended with them not being able to keep up with payments, no matter how much Serena put toward them. She was sure it had something to do with sheer, stubborn pride—they would not rely on their daughter, thank you very much. It drove Serena nuts. Why wouldn't they work a little harder to improve their situation?

Why hadn't they worked harder for her? Sure, if they wanted to be stubborn and barely scrape by, she couldn't stop them. But what about her?

Yes, she loved her parents and yes, they were always glad to see her. But she wanted better than a minimum wage job for the rest of her life, pouring coffee until the day she died because retirement was something for rich people. And what's more, she wanted better for her baby, too.

Still, there was something that felt like a homecoming, walking into Lou's Diner. Shelia Chase had worked here for the better part of thirty years, pulling whatever shift she could get. Lou had died and the diner had changed hands a few times, but her mom had always stuck with it. Serena didn't think she knew how to do anything else.

Either that, or she was afraid to try.

It'd been nine days since Serena had walked out of Chadwick's office. Nine long, anxious days that she'd tried to fill by keeping busy planning her new life.

She'd given her notice to her landlord. In two weeks, she was going to be moving into a new place out in Aurora, a good forty minutes away from the brewery. It wasn't a radically different apartment—two bedrooms, because she was sure she would need the space once the baby started crawling—but it wasn't infused with reminders of Neil. Or of Chadwick, for that matter. The rent was almost double what she was paying now, but if she bought her baby things used and continued to clip coupons, she had enough to live on for a year, maybe more.

She'd applied for ten jobs—office manager at an insurance firm, administrative assistant at a hospital, that sort of thing. She'd even sent her resume to the food bank. She knew the director had been pleased with her work and that the bank was newly flush with Beaumont cash. They could afford to pay her a modest salary—but health insurance…well, she was covered by a federal insurance extension plan. It wasn't cheap, but it would do. She couldn't go without.

She hadn't had any calls for interviews yet, but it was still early. At least, that's what she kept telling herself. Now was not the time to panic.

Except that, as she slid into a booth that was older than she was, the plastic crackling under her growing weight, the old fear of being reduced to grocery shopping in food pantries gripped her.

Breathe, she heard Chadwick say in her head. Even though she knew he wasn't here, it still felt…comforting.

Flo, another old-timer waitress with a smoker's voice, came by. "'Rena, honey, you look good," she said in a voice so gravelly it was practically a baritone. She poured Serena a cup of coffee. "Shelia's waiting on that big table. She'll be over in a bit."

So just the thought of being back in this place that had barely kept her family above water was enough to make breathing hard. There was still something comforting about the familiar—Flo and her scratchy voice, Mom waiting tables. Serena's world might have been turned completely on its ear in the last few weeks, but some things never changed.

She smiled at Flo. "Thanks. How are the grandkids?"

"Oh, just adorable," Flo said, beaming. "My daughter got a good job at Super-Mart stocking shelves, so I watch the kids at night after I get off work. They sleep like angels for me."

As Flo went to make her coffee rounds, Serena pushed back a new wave of panic. A good job stocking shelves? Having her mom watch the kids while she worked the night shift?

Yes, a job was better than no job, but this?

She'd thought that she could never be a part of Chadwick's world and he could never be a part of hers—they were just too different. But now, sitting here and watching her mother carry a huge tray of food over to a party of ten, Serena realized how much her world had really and truly changed. Once upon a time, when she was in college, a night job stocking shelves *would* have been a good job. It would have paid the rent and the grocery bills, and that was all she would have needed.

But now?

She needed more. No, she didn't need the five-thousand-dollar dresses that she hadn't been able to bring herself to pack up and return to the store. But now that she'd had a different kind of life for so long—a life that didn't exist in the spaces between paychecks—she knew she couldn't go back to one of menial labor and night shifts.

A picture of Chadwick floated before her eyes. Not the Chadwick she saw every day sitting behind his desk, his eyes glued to his computer, but the Chadwick who had stood across from her in a deserted gallery. He had been trying just as hard as she was to make things work—even if those "things" were radically different for each of them. He had been a man hanging on to his sanity by the tips of his fingers, terrified of what would happen if he let go.

In that moment, Chadwick hadn't just been a handsome or thoughtful boss. He'd been a man she understood on a fundamental level.

A man who'd understood her.

But then Helen Beaumont had come in and reminded Serena exactly how far apart her world and Chadwick's really were.

Deep down, Serena had known she couldn't carry on with Chadwick while she worked for him. An affair with her boss—no matter how passionate or torrid—wasn't who she was. But hearing how Chadwick had neglected his wife in favor of his company?

It'd been like a knife in the back. Were she and Chadwick only involved because they'd spent more time together in the past seven years than he'd ever spent with his wife—because, as Chadwick's employee, she was the only woman he spent any time with at all?

What if he was only with her because she was available? Hadn't she stayed with Neil for far too long for the exact same reason—because that was the path of least resistance?

No. She would not be the default anymore. Stability wasn't the safest route. That's what had kept her mother chained to this diner for her entire life—it was a guaranteed job. Why risk a bird in the hand when two in the bush was no sure thing?

If whatever was going on between Chadwick and Serena was more than just an affair of convenience, it would withstand her not being his executive assistant. She was sure of it.

Except for one small thing. He hadn't called. Hadn't even texted.

She hadn't really expected him to, but part of her was still disappointed. Okay, *devastated*. He'd said all those lovely things about how he was going to change, how she made him a better person—words that she had longed to hear—but actions spoke so much louder. And he hadn't done anything but watch her go.

She might love Chadwick. The odds were actually really good. But she couldn't know for sure while she worked for him. More than anything else, she didn't want to feel like he held all the cards in their relationship. She didn't want to feel like she owed everything to him—that he controlled her financial well-being.

That was why, as painful as it had been, she'd walked away from his promise to take care of her. Even though she wanted nothing more than to know that the man she loved would be there for her and that she'd never have to worry about sliding back into poverty again, she couldn't bank on that.

She was in control of her life, her fate. She had to secure her future by herself.

Serena Chase depended on no one.

Which was a surprisingly lonely way to look at the rest of her life.

Her head swimming, Serena was blinking back tears when her mother came to her table. "Sweetie, look at you! What's wrong?"

Serena smiled as best she could. Her mother was not many things, but she'd always loved her *sweetie*. Serena couldn't hide her emotional state from her mom.

"Hi, Mom. I hadn't talked to you for a while. Thought I'd drop in."

"I'm kinda busy right now. Can you sit tight until the rush clears out? Oh, I know—I'll have Willy make you some fried chicken, mashed potatoes and a chocolate shake—your favorite!"

Mom didn't cook. But she could order comfort food like a boss. "That'd be great," Serena admitted. She was eating for two now, after all. "Dad coming to get you tonight?"

That was their normal routine. If he still had a car that worked, that was.

Mom patted her on the arm. "Sure is. He got a promotion at work—he's now the head janitor! He'll be by in a few hours if you can wait that long."

"Sure can." Serena settled into the booth, enjoying the rare feeling of her mother spoiling her. She pulled out her phone and checked her email.

There was a message from Miriam Young. "Ms. Chase," it read, "I'm sorry to hear that you're no longer with the Beaumont Brewery. I'd be delighted to set up an interview. The Rocky Mountain Food Bank would be lucky to have someone with your skills on board. Call me at your earliest convenience."

Serena felt her shoulders relax. She would get another job. She'd be able to continue being her own stability.

Mom brought her a plate heaped with potatoes and chicken. "Everything okay, sweetie?"

"I think so, Mom."

Serena ate slowly. There was no rush, after all. Yes, if she could get another job lined up, that would go a long way toward being *okay*.

Yes, she'd be fine. Her and the baby. Just the two of them. Tomorrow, at her first appointment, she might get to hear the heartbeat.

The appointment Chadwick had offered to attend with her.

She knew she'd be fine on her own. She'd hardly missed Neil after a couple of weeks. It'd been a relief not to have to listen to his subtle digs, not to clean up after his messes.

Even though she'd only had Chadwick in her bed for

a night, that night had changed everything. He had been passionate and caring. He'd made her feel things she'd forgotten she needed to feel. In his arms, she felt beautiful and desirable and wanted. Very much wanted. Things she hadn't felt in so long. Things she couldn't live without.

Now that she'd tasted that sort of heat, was she really going to just do without it?

As she ate, she tried to figure out the mess that was her life. If she got a job at the food bank, then she would be able to start a relationship with Chadwick on equal footing. Well, he'd still be one of the richest men in the state and she'd still be middle class. *More* equal footing, then.

Finally, the rush settled down just as Joe Chase came through the door. "Well, look who's here! My baby girl!" he said with obvious pride as he leaned down and kissed her forehead.

Mom got him some coffee and then slid into the booth next to him. "Hey, babe," her dad said, pulling her mom into the kind of kiss that bordered on not-family-friendly.

Serena studied the tabletop. Her parents had never had money, never had true security—but they'd always had each other, for better or worse. In a small way, she was jealous of that. Even more so now that she'd glimpsed it with Chadwick.

"So," Dad said as he cleared his throat. Serena looked back at them. Dad was wearing stained coveralls and Mom looked beat from a day on her feet, but his arm was around her shoulder and she was leaning into him as if everything about the world had finally gone right.

"How's the job?"

Serena swallowed. She'd had the same job, the same apartment, for so long that she didn't know how her parents would deal with this. "Well…"

She told them how she'd decided to change jobs and

apartments. "The company may be sold," she said as both of her parents looked at her with raised eyebrows. "I'm just getting out while I can."

Her mom and dad shared a look. "This doesn't have anything to do with that boss of yours, does it?" Dad asked in a gruff voice as he leaned forward. "He didn't do nothing he shouldn't have, did he?"

"No, Dad, he's fine." She wished she could have sounded a little more convincing when she said it, because her parents shared another look.

"I don't have to work weekends now," her dad said. "I can round up a few buddies and we can get you moved in no time."

"That'd be really great," she admitted. "I'll get some beer and some pizzas—dinner for everyone."

"Nah, I got a couple of bucks in my sock drawer. I'll bring the beer."

"*Dad...*" She knew he meant it. A couple of bucks was probably all he had saved away.

Mom wasn't distracted by this argument. "But sweetie, I don't understand. I thought you liked your job and your apartment. I know it was rough on you when you were young, always moving around. Why the big change now?"

It was hard to look at them and say this out loud, so she didn't. She looked at the table. "I'm three months pregnant."

Her mom gasped loudly while her dad said, "You're *what* now?"

"Who—" was as far as her mom got.

Her dad finished the thought for her. "Your boss? If he did this to you, 'Rena, he should pay. I got half a mind to—"

"No, no. Neil is the father. Chadwick wasn't a part of

this." Or, at least, he hadn't been two weeks ago. "I've already discussed it with Neil. He has no interest in being a father, so I'm going to raise the baby by myself."

They sat there, stunned. "You—you okay doing that?" her dad said.

"We'll help out," her mom added, clearly warming to the idea. "Just think, Joe—a baby. *Flo!*" she hollered across the restaurant. "I'm gonna be a grandma!"

After that, the situation sort of became a big party. Flo came over, followed by Willy the cook and then the busboys. Her dad insisted on buying ice cream for the whole restaurant and toasting Serena.

It almost made Serena feel better. They couldn't give her material things—although her proud dad was hell-bent on trying—but her parents had always given her love in abundance.

It was nine that night before she made it back to her cluttered apartment. Boxes were scattered all over the living room.

Serena stood in the middle of it all, trying not to cry. Yes, the talk with her parents had gone well. Her dad would have all of her stuff moved in an afternoon. Her mom was already talking about layettes. Serena wasn't even sure what a layette was, but by God, Shelia Chase was going to get one. The best Serena had been able to do was to get her mom to promise she wouldn't take out another payday loan to pay for it.

Honestly, she wasn't sure she'd ever seen her parents so excited. The change in jobs and apartment hadn't even fazed them.

But the day had left her drained. Unable to deal with the mess of the living room, she went into her bedroom. That was a mistake.

There, hanging on the closet door, were the dresses. Oh, the dresses. She could hardly bear to look at the traces of finery Chadwick had lavished on her without thinking of how he'd bent her over in front of the dresser, how he'd held her all night long. How he'd promised to go with her to the doctor tomorrow. How he'd promised that he wouldn't fail her.

He was going to break his promise.

It was going to break her heart.

Fourteen

Serena got up and shaved her legs in preparation for her doctor's appointment. It seemed like the thing to do. She twisted up her hair and put on a skirt and a blouse. The formality of the outfit was comforting, somehow. It didn't make sense. But then, nothing made a lot of sense anymore.

For example, she needed to leave for the doctor's office by ten-thirty. She was dressed by eight. Which left her several hours to fret.

She was staring into her coffee cup, trying to figure out the mess in her head, when someone knocked on the door.

Neil? Surely he wouldn't have come back. She'd done a pretty thorough job of kicking him out the last time.

Maybe it was her mom, stopping in early to continue celebrating the good news. But, after another round of knocks, she was pretty sure it wasn't her mom.

Serena hurried to the door and peeked through the peephole. There, on her stoop, stood Chadwick Beaumont.

"Serena? I need to talk to you," he called, staring at the peephole.

Damn. He'd seen her shadow. She couldn't pretend she wasn't home without being totally rude.

She was debating whether or not she wanted to be *totally* rude when he added, "I didn't miss your appointment, did I?"

He hadn't forgotten. Sagging with relief, she opened the door a crack.

Chadwick was wearing a button-up shirt and trousers, with no tie or jacket. The informality looked good on him, but that might have had something to do with the grin on his face. If she didn't know better, she'd say he looked...giddy?

"I didn't think you were going to come."

He stared at her in confusion. "I told you I would." Then he looked at what she was wearing. "You already have an interview?"

"Well, yes. I quit my job. I need another one." She cleared her throat, suddenly nervous about this conversation. "I was counting on a letter of recommendation from you."

The grin on Chadwick's face broadened. It was as if all his worry from the last few years had melted away. "I should have guessed that you wouldn't be able to take time off. But you can cancel your interview. I found a job for you."

"You *what*?"

"Can I come in?"

She studied him. He'd found her a job? He'd come for her appointment? What was going on? Other than him being everything she'd hoped he'd be for the last week and a half. "It's been ten days, you know. Ten days without so much as a text from you. I thought…"

He stepped into the doorway—not pushing her aside, but cupping her face with his hand and stroking her chin with his fingertips. She shuddered into his touch, stunned by how much it affected her. "I was busy."

"Of course. You have a business to run. I know that."

That's why Serena walked out. She needed to see if he would still have feelings for her if she wasn't sitting outside his office door every day.

"Serena," he said, his voice deep with amusement. "Please let me come in. I can explain."

"I understand, Chadwick. I really do." She took a deep breath, willing herself not to cry. "Thank you for remembering the appointment, but maybe it's best if I go by myself."

He notched up an eyebrow as if she'd thrown down the gauntlet. "Ten minutes. That's all I'm asking. If you still think we need some time apart after that, I'll go. But I'm not walking away from you—from what we have."

Then, just because he apparently could, he stroked his fingers against her chin again.

The need to kiss him, to fall back into his arms, was almost overpowering. But that emotion was in a full-out war with her sense of self-preservation.

"What did we have?"

The grin he aimed at her made her knees suddenly shake. He leaned in, his cheek rubbing against hers, and whispered in her ear, *"Everything."*

Then he slipped a hand around her waist and pulled her into his chest. His lips touched the space underneath her ear, sending heat rushing from her neck down her back and farther south.

God, how she wanted this. Why had she thought she could walk away from him? From the way he made her feel? "Ten minutes," she heard herself murmur as she managed to push him far enough back that she could step to the side and let him in.

So she could stop touching him.

Chadwick walked into her apartment and looked around. "You're already moving?"

"Yes. This was where I lived with Neil. I need a fresh start. All the way around," she added, trying to remember why. Oh, yes. Because she couldn't fall for Chadwick while she worked for him. And work was all he did.

She expected him to say something else, but instead he gave her a look she couldn't quite read. Was he... amused? She didn't remember making a joke.

As he stood in the middle of the living room, she saw for the first time that he was holding a tablet. "I had this plan." He began tapping the screen. "But Helen forced my hand. So instead of doing this over a couple of months, I had to work around the clock for the last ten days."

If this was him convincing her that he'd find a way to see her outside of work, he was doing a surprisingly poor job of it. "Is that so?"

He apparently found what he was looking for because he grinned up at her and handed her the tablet. "It won't be final until the board votes to accept it and the lawyers get done with it, but I sold the company."

"You *what*?" She snatched the tablet out of his hands and looked at the document.

Letter of intent, the header announced underneath the insignia of the brewery's law firm. *AllBev hereby agrees to pay $62 a share for The Beaumont Brewery and all related Beaumont Brewery brands, excluding Percheron Drafts. Chadwick Beaumont reserves the right to* *keep the Percheron Drafts brand name and all related recipes....*

The whole thing got bogged down in legalese after that. Serena kept rereading the first few lines. "Wait, what? You're keeping Percheron?"

"I had this crazy idea," he said, taking the tablet back from her and swiping some more. "After someone told me to do what I wanted—for me and no one else—I remembered how much I liked to actually make beer. I thought I might keep Percheron Drafts and go into business for myself, not for the Beaumont name. Here." He handed her back the tablet again.

She looked down at a different lawyer's letter—this one from a divorce attorney. *Pursuant to the case of Beaumont v. Beaumont, Mrs. Helen Beaumont (hereby known as Plaintiff) has agreed to the offer of Mr. Chadwick Beaumont (hereby known as Defendant) for alimony payments in the form of $100 million dollars. Defendant will produce such funds no later than six months after the date of this letter....*

Serena blinked at the tablet. The whole thing was shaking—because she was shaking. "I...I don't understand."

"Well, I sold the brewery and I'm using the money I got for it to make my ex-wife an offer she can't refuse. I'm keeping Percheron Drafts and going into business myself." He took the tablet from her and set it down on a nearby box. "Simple, really."

"*Simple?*"

He had the nerve to nod as if this were all no big deal—just the multi-billion dollar sale of an international company. Just paying his ex-wife $100 million.

"Serena, breathe," he said, stepping up and wrapping his arms around her. "Breathe, babe."

"What did you do?" she asked, unable to stop herself from leaning her head against his warm, broad chest. It was everything she wanted. He was everything she wanted.

"I did something I should have done years ago—I stopped working for Hardwick Beaumont." He leaned her back and pressed his lips against her forehead. She felt herself breathe in response to his tender touch. "I'm free of him, Serena. Well and truly free. I don't have to live my life according to what he wanted, or make choices solely because they're the opposite of what he would have done. I can do whatever I want. And what I want is to make beer during the day and come home to a woman who speaks her mind and pushes me to be a better man and is going to be a great mother. A woman who loves me not because I'm a Beaumont, but in spite of it."

She looked up at him, aware that tears were trickling down her cheeks but completely unable to do anything about it. "This is what you've been doing for the last ten days?"

He grinned and wiped a tear off her face. "If I could have finalized the sale, I would have. It'll still take a few months for all the dust to settle, but Harper should be happy he got his money *and* got even with Hardwick, so I don't think he'll hold up the process much."

"And Helen? The divorce?"

"My lawyers are working to get a court date next week. Week after at the latest." He gave her a look of pure wickedness. "I made it clear that I couldn't wait."

"But...but you said a job? For me?"

His arms tightened around her waist, pulling her into his chest like he wasn't ever going to let her go. "Well, I'm starting this new business, you see. I'm going to need someone working with me who can run the offices, hire the people—a partner, if you will, to keep things going while I make the beer. Someone who understands how I operate. Someone who's not afraid of hard work. Someone who can pick a good health care plan and organize a party and understand spreadsheets." He rubbed her back as he started rocking from side to side. "I happen to know the perfect woman. She comes very highly recommended. Great letter of reference."

"But I can't be with you while I work for you. It's against company policy!"

At that, he laughed. "First off—new company, new policies. Second off, I'm not hiring you to be my underling. I'm asking you to be my partner in the business." He paused then and cleared his throat. "I'm asking you to marry me."

"You *are*?"

"I am." He dropped to his knees so suddenly that she almost toppled forward. "Serena Chase, would you marry me?"

Her hand fluttered over her stomach. "The baby…"

He leaned forward and kissed the spot right over her belly button. "I want to adopt this baby, just as soon as your old boyfriend severs his parental rights."

"What if he won't?" She was aware the odds of that were small—Neil had shown no interest in being a father. But she wasn't going to just throw herself into Chadwick's arms and believe that love would solve all the problems in the world.

Even if it felt like that were true right now.

Chadwick looked up at her, his scary businessman face on. "Don't worry. I can be *very* persuasive. Be my wife, Serena. Be my family."

Could they do that? Could she work with him, not *for* him? Could they be partners *and* a family?

Could she trust that he'd love her more than he loved his company?

He must have sensed her worry. "You told me to do what makes me happy," he told her as he stood again, folding her back into his arms. "*You* make me happy, Serena."

"But…where will we live? I don't want to live in that big mansion." The Beaumont Estate was crawling with too many ghosts—both dead and living.

He smiled down at her. "Anywhere you want."

"I…I already signed a lease for an apartment in Aurora."

He notched an eyebrow at her. "We can live there if you really want. Or you can break the lease. I'll have enough left from my golden parachute that we won't have to worry about money for a long, long time. And I promise not to drop thousands on gowns or jewels for you anymore. Except for this one."

He reached into his pocket and pulled out a small dark blue box. It was just the right size for a ring.

As he opened it, he said, "Would you marry me, Serena? Would you make me a happy man for the rest of my life and give me the chance to do the same for you? I won't fail you, I promise. You are the most important person in my life and you will always come first."

Serena stared at the ring. The solitaire diamond was large without being ostentatious. It was perfect, really.

"Well," she replied, taking the box from him. "Maybe a gown every now and then…."

Chadwick laughed and swept her into his arms. "Is that a yes?"

He was everything she wanted—passion and love and stability. He wouldn't fail her.

"*Yes.*"

He kissed her then—a long, hard kiss that called to mind a certain evening in front of a mirror. "Good," he said.

It was.

* * * * *

TEMPTED BY
A COWBOY

BY
SARAH M. ANDERSON

To Phil Chu, who kept his promise and got me on
television—that's what friends are for, right?
I can't believe we've been friends for twenty years!
Here's your book, Phil!

One

Jo got out of the truck and stretched. Man, it'd been a long drive from Kentucky to Denver.

But she'd made it to Beaumont Farms.

Getting this job was a major accomplishment—a vote of confidence that came with the weight of the Beaumont family name behind it.

This wouldn't be just a huge paycheck—the kind that could cover a down payment on a ranch of her own. This was proof that she was a respected horse trainer and her nontraditional methods worked.

A bowlegged man came out of the barn, slapping a pair of gloves against his leg as he walked. Maybe fifty, he had the lined face of a man who'd spent most of his years outside.

He was *not* Phillip Beaumont, the handsome face of the Beaumont Brewery and the man who owned this farm. Even though she shouldn't be, Jo was disappointed.

It was for the best. A man as sinfully good-looking as

Phillip would be…tempting. And she absolutely could not afford to be tempted. Professional horse trainers did not fawn over the people paying their bills—especially when those people were known for their partying ways. Jo did *not* party, not anymore. She was here to do a job and that was that.

"Mr. Telwep?"

"Sure am," the man said, nodding politely. "You the horse whisperer?"

"Trainer," Jo snapped, unable to help herself. She detested being labeled a "whisperer." Damn that book that had made that a thing. "I don't *whisper*. I *train*."

Richard's bushy eyebrows shot up at her tone. She winced. So much for *that* first impression. But she was so used to having to defend her reputation that the reaction was automatic. She put on a friendly smile and tried again. "I'm Jo Spears."

Thankfully, the older man didn't seem too fazed by her lack of social graces. "Miz Spears, call me Richard," he said, coming over to give her a firm handshake.

"Jo," she replied. She liked men like Richard. They'd spent their lives caring for animals. As long as he and his hired hands treated her like a professional, then this would work. "What do you have for me?"

"It's a—well, better to show you."

"Not a Percheron?" The Beaumont Brewery was world-famous for the teams of Percherons that had pulled their wagons in all their commercials for—well, for forever. A stuffed Beaumont Percheron had held a place of honor in the middle of her bed when she'd been growing up.

"Not this time. Even rarer."

Rarer? Not that Percheron horses were rare, but they weren't terribly common in the United States. The massive draft horses had fallen out of fashion now that people weren't using them to pull plows anymore.

"One moment." She couldn't leave Betty in the truck. Not if she didn't want her front seat destroyed, anyway.

Jo opened the door and unhooked Betty's traveling harness. The donkey's ears quivered in anticipation. "Ready to get out?"

Jo scooped Betty up and set her on the ground. Betty let off a serious round of kicks as Richard said, "I heard you traveled with a—well, what the heck is *that?*" with a note of amusement in his voice.

"That," Jo replied, "is Itty Bitty Betty. She's a mini donkey." This was a conversation she'd had many a time. "She's a companion animal."

By this time, Betty had settled down and had begun investigating the grass around her. Barely three feet tall, she was indeed mini. At her size and weight, she was closer to a medium sized dog than a donkey—and acted like it, too. Jo had trained Betty, of course, but the little donkey had been Jo's companion ever since Granny bought Betty for Jo almost ten years ago. Betty had helped Jo crawl out of the darkness. For that, Jo would be forever grateful.

Richard scratched his head in befuddlement at the sight of the pint-size animal. "Danged if I've ever seen a donkey that small. I don't think you'll be wanting to put her in with Sun just yet." He turned and began walking.

Jo perked up. "Sun?" She fell in step with Richard and whistled over her shoulder. Betty came trotting.

"Danged if I've ever," Richard repeated.

"Sun?" she said.

"Kandar's Golden Sun." Richard blew out hard, the frustration obvious. "You ever heard of an Akhal-Teke?"

The name rang a bell. "Isn't that the breed that sired the Arabian?"

"Yup. From Turkmenistan. Only about five thousand in the world." He led the way around the barn to a paddock off to one side, partially shaded by trees.

In the middle of the paddock was a horse that probably *was* golden, as the name implied. But sweat matted his coat and foam dripped from his mouth and neck, giving him a dull, dirty look. The horse was running and bucking in wild circles and had worked himself up to a lather.

"Yup," Richard said, the disappointment obvious in his voice. "That's Kandar's Golden Sun, all right."

Jo watched the horse run. "Why's he so worked up?"

"We moved him from his stall to the paddock. Three hours ago." Jo looked at the older man, but he shrugged. "Took three men. We try to be gentle, but the damn thing takes one look at us and goes ballistic."

Three hours this horse had been bucking and running? Jesus, it was a miracle he hadn't collapsed in a heap. Jo had dealt with her share of terrified horses but sooner or later, they all wore themselves out.

"What happened?"

"That's the thing. No one knows. Mr. Beaumont flew to Turkmenistan himself to look at Sun. He understands horses," Richard added in explanation.

Heat flooded her cheeks. "I'm aware of his reputation."

How could anyone *not* be aware of Phillip Beaumont's reputation? He'd made the *People Magazine* "Most Beautiful" list more than a few years in a row. He had the sort of blond hair that always looked as if he'd walked off a beach, a strong chin and the kind of jaw that could cut stone. He did the Beaumont Brewery commercials but also made headlines on gossip websites and tabloid magazines for some of the stunts he pulled at clubs in Vegas and L.A. Like the time he'd driven a Ferrari into a pool. At the top of a hotel.

No doubt about it, Phillip was a hard-partying playboy. Except...except when he wasn't. In preparing for this job, she'd found an interview he'd done with *Western Horseman* magazine. In that interview—and the accompanying photos—he hadn't been a jaded playboy but an honest-to-God cowboy. He'd talked about horses and herd management and certainly looked like the real McCoy in his boots, jeans, flannel shirt and cowboy hat. He'd said he was building Beaumont Farms as a preeminent stable in the West. Considering the Beaumont family name and its billions in the bank—it wasn't some lofty goal. It was within his reach.

Which one was he? The playboy too sinfully handsome to resist or the hard-working cowboy who wasn't afraid to get dirt on his boots?

No matter which one he was, she was not interested. She couldn't *afford* to be interested in a playboy, especially one who was going to sign her checks. Yes, she'd been training horses for years now, but most wealthy owners of the valuable horses didn't want to take a chance on her nontraditional methods. She'd taken every odd job in every out-of-the-way ranch and farm in the lower forty-eight states to build her clientele. The call from Beaumont Farms was her first major contract with people who bought horses not for thousands of dollars, but for *millions*. If she could save this horse, her reputation would be set.

Besides, the odds of even meeting Phillip Beaumont were slim. Richard was the man she'd be working with. She pulled her thoughts away from the unattainable and focused on why she was here—the horse.

Richard snorted. "We don't deal too much with the partying out here. We just work horses." He waved a hand at Sun, who obliged by rearing on to his back legs and whinnying in panic. "Best we can figure is that maybe something happened on the plane ride? But there were no marks, no wounds. No crashes—not even a rough landing, according to the pilots."

"Just a horse that went off the rails," she said, watching as Sun pawed at the dirt as if he were killing a snake.

"Yup." Richard hung his head. "The horse ain't right but Mr. Beaumont's convinced he can be fixed—a horse to build a stable on, he keeps saying. Spent some ungodly sum of money on him—he'd hate to lose his investment. Personally, I can't stand to see an animal suffer like that. But Mr. Beaumont won't let me put Sun out of his misery. I hired three other trainers before you and none of them lasted a week. You're the horse's last chance. You can't fix him, he'll have to be put down."

This had to be why Richard hadn't gone into specifics over email. He was afraid he'd scare Jo off. "Who'd you hire?"

The older man dug the tip of his boot into the grass. "Lansing, Hoffmire and Callet."

Jo snorted. Lansing was a fraud. Hoffmire was a former farm manager, respected in horse circles. Callet was old-school—and an asshole. He'd tracked her down once to tell her to stay the hell away from his clientele.

She would take particular joy in saving a horse he couldn't.

Moving slowly, she walked to the paddock gate, Betty trotting to keep up. She unhooked the latch on the gate and let it swing open about a foot and a half.

Sun stopped and watched her. Then he *really* began to pitch a fit. His legs flailed as he bucked and reared and slammed his hooves into the ground so hard she felt the shock waves through the dirt. *Hours of this*, Jo thought. *And no one knows why.*

She patted her leg, which was the signal for Betty to stay close. Then Jo stepped into the paddock.

"Miss—" Richard called out, terror in his voice when he realized what she was doing. "Logan, get the tranq gun!"

"Quiet, please." It came out gentle because she was doing her best to project calm.

She heard footsteps—probably Logan and the other

hands, ready to ride to her rescue. She held up a hand, motioning them to stop, and then closed the gate behind her and Betty.

The horse went absolutely wild. It hurt to see an animal so lost in its own hell that there didn't seem to be any way out.

She knew the feeling. It was a hard thing to see, harder to remember the years she'd lost to her own hell.

She'd found her way out. She'd hit bottom so hard it'd almost killed her but through the grace of God, Granny and Itty Bitty Betty, she'd fought her way back out.

She'd made it her life's work to help animals do the same. Even lost causes like Sun could be saved—*not* fixed, because there was no erasing the damage that had already been done. Scars were forever. But moving forward meant accepting the scars. It was that simple. She'd accepted hers.

Jo could stand here for hours listening to the world move, if that was what it took.

It didn't. After what was probably close to forty-five minutes, Sun stopped his frantic pacing. First, he stopped kicking, then he slowed from a run to a trot, then to a walk. Finally, he stood in the middle of the paddock, sides heaving and head down. For the first time, the horse was still.

She could almost hear him say, *I give up*.

It was a low place to be, when living hurt that much.

She understood. She couldn't fix this horse. No one could. But she could save him.

She patted her leg again and turned to walk out of the paddock. A group of seven men stood watching the show Sun had put on for her. Richard had a tranq gun in the hand he was resting on a bar of the paddock.

They were silent. No one shouted about her safety as she turned her back on Sun, no one talked about how the horse must be possessed. They watched her walk to the gate, open it, walk out, and shut it as if they were witnessing a miracle.

"I'll take the job."

Relief so intense it almost knocked her back a step broke over the ranch manager's face. The hired hands all grinned, obviously thankful that Sun was someone else's problem now.

"Provided," she went on, "my conditions are met."

Richard tried to look stern, but he didn't quite make it. "Yeah?"

"I need an on-site hookup for my trailer. That way, if Sun has a problem in the middle of the night, I'm here to deal with it."

"We've got the electric. I'll have Jerry rig up something for the sewer."

"Second, no one else deals with Sun. I feed him, I groom him, I move him. The rest of you stay clear."

"Done," Richard agreed without hesitation. The hands all nodded.

So far, so good. "We do this my way or we don't do it at all. No second-guessing from you, the hired hands or the owners. I won't rush the horse and I expect the same treatment. *And* I expect to be left alone. I don't date or hook up. Clear?"

She hated having to throw that out there because she knew it made her sound as if she thought men would be fighting over her. But she'd done enough harm by hooking up before. Even if she was sober this time, she couldn't risk another life.

Plus, she was a single woman, traveling alone in a trailer with a bed. Some men thought that was enough. Things worked better if everything was cut-and-dried up front.

Richard looked around at his crew. Some were blushing, a few looked bummed—but most of them were just happy that they wouldn't have to deal with Sun anymore.

Then Richard looked across the fields. A long, black limousine was heading toward them.

"Damn," one of the hands said, "the boss."

Everyone but Jo and Richard made themselves scarce. Sun found his second wind and began a full-fledged fit.

"This isn't going to be a problem, is it?" Jo asked Richard, who was busy dusting off his jeans and straightening his shirt.

"Shouldn't be." He did not sound convincing. "Mr. Beaumont wants the best for Sun."

The *but* on the end of that statement was as loud as if Richard had actually said the word. *But* Phillip Beaumont was a known womanizer who made headlines around the world for his conquests.

Richard turned his attention back to her. "You're hired. I'll do my level-best to make sure that Mr. Beaumont stays clear of you."

In other words, Richard had absolutely no control of the situation. A fact that became more apparent as the limo got closer. The older man stood at attention as the vehicle rolled to a stop in front of the barn.

Phillip Beaumont didn't scare her. Or intimidate her. She'd dealt with handsome, entitled men before and none of them had ever tempted her to fall back into her old ways. None of them made her forget the scars. This wouldn't be any different. She was just here for the job.

The limo door opened. A bare, female leg emerged from the limo at the same time as giggling filled the air. Behind her, Jo heard Sun kick it up a notch.

The first leg was followed by a second. Jo wasn't that surprised when a second set of female legs followed the first. By that time, the first woman had stepped clear of the limo's door and Jo could see that, while she was wearing clothing, the dress consisted of little more than a bikini's worth of black sequined material. The second woman stood up and pulled the red velvet material of her skirt down around her hips.

Beside her, Richard made a sound that was stuck somewhere between a sigh and a groan. Jo took that to mean that this wasn't the first time Phillip had shown up with women dressed like hookers.

Betty nickered in boredom and went back to cropping grass. Jo pretty much felt the same way. Of course this was how Phillip Beaumont rolled. Those headlines hadn't lied. The thing that had been less honest had been that interview in *Western Horseman*. That had probably been more about rehabilitating his brand image than about his actual love and respect for horses.

But on the bright side, if he'd brought his own entertainment to the ranch, he'd leave her to her work. That's what was important here—she had to save Sun, cement her reputation as a horse trainer and add this paycheck to the fund that she'd use to buy her own ranch. Adding Beaumont Farms to her résumé was worth putting up with the hassle of, well, *this*.

Then another set of legs appeared. Unlike the first sets, these legs were clad in what looked like expensive Italian leather shoes and fine-cut wool trousers. Phillip Beaumont himself stood and looked at his farm over the top of the limo, all blond hair and gleaming smile. He wore an odd look on his face. He almost looked *relieved*.

His gaze settled on her. As their eyes met across the drive, Jo felt…disoriented. Looking at Phillip Beaumont was one thing, but apparently being looked at by Phillip Beaumont?

Something else entirely.

Heat flushed her face as the corner of his mouth curved up into a smile, grabbed hold of her and refused to let her go. She couldn't pull away from his gaze—and she wasn't sure she wanted to. He looked as if he was glad to see her—which she knew wasn't possible. He had no idea who she was and couldn't have been expecting her. Besides, compared to his traveling companions, no one in their right mind would even notice her.

But that look.... Happy and hungry and *relieved*. Like he'd come all this way just to see her and now that she was here, the world would be right again.

No one had looked at her like that. *Ever*. Before, when she'd been a party girl, men looked at her with a wolfish hunger that had very little to do with her as a woman and everything to do with them wanting to get laid. And since the accident? Well, she wore her hair like this and dressed like she did specifically so she wouldn't invite people to look at her.

He saw right through her.

The women lost their balance and nearly tumbled to the ground, but Phillip caught them in his arms. He pulled them apart and settled one on his left side, the other on his right. The women giggled, as if this were nothing but hilarious.

It hurt to see them, like ghosts of her past come back to haunt her.

"Mr. Beaumont," Richard began in a warm, if desperate, tone as he went to meet his boss. "We weren't expecting you today."

"Dick," Phillip said, which caused his traveling companions to break out into renewed giggles. "I wanted to show my new friends—" He looked down at Blonde Number One.

"Katylynn," Number One giggled. Of course.

"Sailor," Number Two helpfully added.

Phillip's head swung up in a careful arc, another disarming smile already in place as he gave the girls a squeeze. "I wanted to show Sun to Katylynn and Sailor."

"Mr. Beaumont," Richard began again. Jo heard more anger in his voice this time. "Sun is not—"

"Wha's wrong with that horse?" Sailor took a step away from Phillip and pointed at Sun.

They all turned to look. Sun was now bucking with renewed vigor. *Damn stamina*, Jo thought as she watched him.

"Wha's making him do that?" Katylynn asked.

"You are," Jo informed the trio.

The women glared at her. "Who are you?" Sailor asked in a haughty tone.

"Yes, who are you?" Phillip Beaumont spoke slowly—carefully—as his eyes focused on her again.

Again, her face prickled with unfamiliar heat. *Get ahold of yourself*, she thought, forcibly breaking the eye contact. She wasn't the kind of woman who got drunk and got lost in a man's eyes. Not anymore. She'd left that life behind and no one—not even someone as handsome and rich as Phillip Beaumont—would tempt her back to it.

"Mr. Beaumont, this here is Jo Spears. She's the horse…" She almost heard *whisperer* sneak out through his teeth. "Trainer. The new trainer for Sun."

She gave Richard an appreciative smile. A quick study, that one.

Phillip detached himself from his companions, which led to them making whimpering noises of protest.

As Phillip closed the distance between him and Jo, that half-smile took hold of his mouth again. He stopped with two feet still between them. "You're the new trainer?"

She stared at his eyes. They were pale green with flecks of gold around the edges. *Nice eyes*.

Nice eyes that bounced. It wasn't a big movement, but Phillip's eyes were definitely moving of their own accord. She knew the signs of intoxication and that one was a dead giveaway. He was drunk.

She had to admire his control, though. Nothing else in his mannerisms or behaviors gave away that he was three sheets to the wind. Which really only meant one thing.

Being this drunk wasn't something new for him. He'd gotten very good at masking his state. That was something that took years of practice.

She'd gotten good at it, too—but it was so exhausting to keep up that false front of competency, to act normal when she wasn't. She'd hated being that person. She wasn't anymore.

She let this realization push down on the other part of her brain that was still admiring his lovely eyes. Phillip Beaumont represented every single one of her triggers wrapped up in one extremely attractive package. Everything she could never be again if she wanted to be a respected horse trainer, not an out-of-control alcoholic.

She *needed* this job, needed the prestige of retraining a horse like Sun on her résumé and the paycheck that went with it. She absolutely could not allow a handsome man who could hold his liquor to tempt her back into a life she'd long since given up.

She did not hook up. Not even with the likes of Phillip Beaumont.

"I'm just here for the horse," she told him.

He tilted his head in what looked like acknowledgement without breaking eye contact and without losing that smile.

Man, this was unnerving. Men who looked at her usually saw the bluntly cut, shoulder-length hair and the flannel shirts and the jeans and dismissed her out of hand. That was how she wanted it. It kept a safe distance between her and the rest of the world. That was just the way it had to be.

But this look was doing some very unusual things to her. Things she didn't like. Her cheeks got hot—was she blushing?—and a strange prickling started at the base of her neck and raced down her back.

She gritted her teeth but thankfully, he was the one who broke the eye contact first. He looked down at Betty, still blissfully cropping grass. "And who is this?"

Jo braced herself. "This is Itty Bitty Betty, my companion mini donkey."

Instead of the lame joke or snorting laughter, Phillip leaned down, held his hand out palm up and let Betty sniff his hand. "Well hello, Little Bitty Betty. Aren't you a good girl?"

Jo decided not to correct him on her name. It wasn't worth it. What was worth it, though, was the way Betty snuffled at his hand and then let him rub her ears.

That weird prickling sensation only got stronger as she watched Phillip Beaumont make friends with her donkey. "We've got nice grass," he told her, sounding for all the world as if he was talking to a toddler. "You'll like it here."

Jo realized she was staring at Phillip with her mouth open, which she quickly corrected. The people who hired her usually made a joke about Betty or stated they weren't paying extra for a donkey of any size. But Phillip?

Wearing a smile that bordered on cute he looked up at Jo as Betty went back to the grass. "She's a good companion, I can tell."

She couldn't help herself. "Can you?"

Richard had said his boss was a good judge of horses. He'd certainly sounded as if were true it in that interview. She wanted him to be a good judge of horses, to be a real person and not just a shallow, beer-peddling facade of a man. Even though she had no right to want that from him, she did.

His smile went from adorable to wicked in a heartbeat and damned if other parts of her body didn't start prickling at the sight. "I'm an *excellent* judge of character."

Right then, the party girls decided to speak up. "Philly, we want to go home," one cooed.

"With you," the other one added.

"Yes," Jo told him, casting a glare back at the women. "I can see that."

Sun made an unholy noise behind them. Richard shouted and the blondes screamed.

Jesus, Jo thought as Sun pawed at the ground and then charged the paddock fence, snot streaming out of his nose. If he hit the fence at that speed, there wouldn't be anything left to save.

Everyone else dove out of the way. Jo turned and ran toward the horse, throwing her hands up and shouting "Hi-yahh!" at the top of her lungs.

It worked with feet to spare. Sun spooked hard to the left and only hit the paddock fence with his hindquarters—which might be enough to bruise him but wouldn't do any other damage.

"Jesus," she said out loud as the horse returned to his bucking. Her chest heaved as the adrenaline pumped through her body.

"I'll tranq him," Richard said beside her, leveling the gun at Sun.

"No." She pushed the muzzle away before he could squeeze the trigger. "Leave him be. He started this, he's got to finish it."

Richard gave her a hell of a doubtful look. "We'll have to tranq him to get him back to his stall. I can't afford anymore workman's comp because of this horse."

She turned to give the ranch manager her meanest look. "We do this my way or we don't do it at all. That was the deal. I say you don't shoot him. Leave him in this paddock. Set out hay and water. No one else touches this horse. Do I make myself clear?"

"Do what she says," Phillip said behind her.

Jo turned back to the paddock to make sure that Sun hadn't decided to exit on the other side. Nope. Just more bucking circles. It'd almost been a horse's version of *shut the hell up*. She grinned at him. On that point, she had to agree.

She could feel her connection with Sun start to grow, which was a good thing. The more she could understand what he was thinking, the easier it would be to help him.

"Philly, we want to go," one of the blondes demanded with a full-on whine.

"Fine," Phillip snapped. "Ortiz, make sure the ladies get back to their homes."

A different male voice—probably the limo driver— said, "Yes sir, Mr. Beaumont." This announcement was met with cries of protest, which quickly turned to howls of fury.

Jo didn't watch. She kept her eye on Sun, who was still freaking out at all the commotion. If he made another bolt for the fence, she might have to let Richard tranq him and she really didn't want that to happen. Shots fired now would only make her job that much harder in the long run.

Finally, the limo doors shut and she heard the car drive off. Thank God. With the women gone, the odds that Sun would settle down were a lot better.

She heard footsteps behind her and tensed. She didn't want Phillip to touch her. She'd meant what she'd said to the hired hands earlier—she didn't hook up with anyone. Especially not men like Phillip Beaumont. She couldn't afford to have her professional reputation compromised, not when she'd finally gotten a top-tier client—and a horse no one else could save. She needed this job far more than she needed Phillip Beaumont to smile at her.

He came level with her and stopped. He was too close— more than close enough to touch.

She panicked. "I don't sleep with clients," she announced into the silence—and immediately felt stupid.

She was letting a little thing like prickling heat undermine her authority here. She was a horse trainer. That was all.

"I'll be sure to take that into consideration." He looked down at her and turned on the most seductive smile she'd ever seen.

Oh, what a smile. She struggled for a moment to remember why, exactly, she didn't need that smile in her life. How long had it been since she'd let herself smile back at a man? How long had it been since she'd allowed herself even a little bit of fun?

Years. But then the skin on the back of her neck pulled and she remembered the hospital and the pain. The scars. She hadn't gotten this job because she smiled at attractive men. She'd gotten this job because she was a horse trainer who could save a broken horse.

She was a professional, by God. When she'd made her announcement to the hired hands earlier, they'd all nodded and agreed. But Phillip?

He looked as if she'd issued a personal challenge. One that he was up to meeting.

Heat flushed her face as she fluttered—honest-to-God fluttered. One little smile—that wouldn't cost her too much, would it?

No.

She pushed back against whatever insanity was gripping her. She no longer fluttered. She did not fall for party boys. She did not sleep with men at the drop of a hat because they were cute or bought her drinks. She did not look for a human connection in a bar because the connections she'd always made there were never very human.

She would not be tempted by Phillip Beaumont. It didn't matter how tempting he was. She would not smile back because one smile would lead to another and she couldn't let that happen.

He notched up one eyebrow as if he were acknowledging how much he'd flustered her. But instead of saying something else, he walked past her and leaned heavily against the paddock fence, staring at Sun. His body language pulled at her in ways she didn't like. So few of the people who hired her to train horses actually cared about their animals. They looked at the horse and saw dollars—either in money spent, money yet to be made, or insurance payments. That's why she didn't get involved with her clients. She could count the exceptions on one hand, like Whitney Maddox, a horse breeder she'd stayed with a few months last winter. But those cases were few and far between and never involved men with reputations like Phillip Beaumont.

But the way Phillip was looking at his horse... There was a pain in his face that seemed to mirror what the horse was feeling. It was a hard thing to see.

No. She was not going to feel sorry for this poor little rich boy. She'd come from nothing, managed to nearly destroy her own life and actually managed to make good all by herself.

"He's a good horse—I know he is." Phillip didn't even glance in her direction. He sounded different now that the ladies were gone. It was almost as if she could see his mask slip. What was left was a man who was tired and worried. "I know Richard thinks he should be put out of his misery, but I can't do it. I can't—I can't give up on him. If he could just..." He scrubbed a hand through his hair, which, damn it, only made it look better. He turned to her. "Can you fix him?"

"No," she told him. What was left of his playboy mask fell completely away at this pronouncement.

In that moment, Jo saw something else in Phillip Beaumont's eyes—something that she didn't just recognize, but that she understood.

He was *so* lost. Just like she'd been once.

"I can't fix him—but I can save him."

He looked at her. "There's a difference?"

"Trust me—all the difference in the world."

Jo looked back at Sun, who was quickly working through his energy. Soon, he'd calm down. Maybe he'd even drink some water and sleep. That'd be good. She wanted to save him in a way that went beyond the satisfaction of a job well done or the fees that Phillip Beaumont could afford to pay her.

She wanted to save this horse because once, she'd hurt as much as he did right now. And no one—no horse—should hurt that much. Not when she could make it better.

She wasn't here for Phillip Beaumont. He might be a scarred man in a tempting package, but she'd avoided temptation before and she'd do it again.

"Don't give up on him," he said in a voice that she wasn't sure was meant for her.

"Don't worry," she told the horse as much as she told Phillip. "I won't."

She would *not* give up on the horse.

She wasn't sure she had such high hopes for the man.

Two

Light. Too much light.

God, his head.

Phillip rolled away from the sunlight but moving his head did not improve the situation. In fact, it only made things worse.

Finally, he sat up, which had the benefit of getting the light out of his face but also made his stomach roll. He managed to get his eyes cracked open. He wasn't in his downtown apartment and he wasn't in his bedroom at the Beaumont Mansion.

The walls of the room were rough-cut logs, the fireplace was stone and a massive painting showing a pair of Percherons pulling a covered wagon across the prairie hung over the mantle.

Ah. He was at the farm. Immediately, his stomach unclenched. There were a lot worse places to wake up. He knew that from experience. Back when his grandfather had built it, it'd been little more than a cabin set far away from the world of beer. John Beaumont hadn't wasted money on opulence where no one would see it. That's why the Beaumont Mansion was a work of art and the farm was…not.

Phillip liked it out here. Over the years, the original cabin had been expanded, but always with the rough-hewn logs. His room was a part he'd added himself, mostly because he wanted a view and a deck to look at it from. The hot tub outside didn't hurt, either, but unlike the hot tub at his bachelor pad, this one was mostly for soaking.

Mostly. He was Phillip Beaumont, after all.

Phillip sat in bed for a while, rubbing his temples and trying to sift through the random memories from the last few days. He knew he'd had an event in Las Vegas on… Thursday. That'd been a hell of a night.

He was pretty sure he'd had a club party in L.A. on Friday, hadn't he? No, that wasn't right. Beaumont Brewery had a big party tent at a music festival and Phillip had been there for the Friday festivities. Lots of music people. *Lots* of beer.

And Saturday…he'd been back in Denver for a private party for some guy's twenty-first birthday. But, no matter how hard he tried to remember the party, his brain wouldn't supply any details.

So, did that mean today was Sunday or Monday? Hell, he didn't know. That was the downside of his job. Phillip was vice president of Marketing in charge of special events for Beaumont Brewery, which loosely translated into making sure everyone had a good time at a Beaumont-sponsored event and talked about it on social media.

Phillip was very good at his job.

He found the clock. It was 11:49. He needed to get up. The sun was only getting brighter. Why didn't he have room-darkening blinds in here?

Oh, yeah. Because the windows opened up on to a beautiful vista, full of lush grass, tall trees and his horses. Damn his aesthetic demands.

He got his feet swung over the bed and under him. Each movement was like being hit with a meat cleaver right between the eyes. Yeah, that must have been one *hell* of a party.

He navigated a flight of stairs and two hallways to the kitchen, which was in the original building. He got the coffee going and then dug a sports drink out of the fridge. He popped some Tylenol and guzzled the sports drink.

Almost immediately, his head felt better. He finished the first bottle and cracked open a second. Food. He needed food. But he needed a shower first.

Phillip headed back to his bathroom. That was the other reason he'd built his own addition—the other bathroom held the antique claw-foot tub that couldn't hope to contain all six of his feet.

His bathroom had a walk-in shower, a separate tub big enough for two and a double sink that stretched out for over eight feet. He could sprawl out all over the place and still have room to spare.

He soaked his head in cool water, which got his blood pumping again. He'd always had a quick recovery time from a good party—today was no different.

Finally, he got dressed in his work clothes and went back to the kitchen. He made some eggs, which helped his stomach. The coffee was done, so he filled up a thermal mug and added a shot of whiskey. Hair of the dog.

Finally, food in his stomach and coffee in his hand, he found his phone and scrolled through it.

Ah. It was Monday. Which meant he had no recollection of Sunday. Damn.

He didn't dwell on that. Instead, he scrolled through his contacts list. Lots of new numbers. Not too many pictures. One he'd apparently already posted to Instagram of him and Drake on stage together? Cool. That was a dream-come-true kind of moment right there. He was thrilled someone had gotten a photo of it.

He scanned some of the gossip sites. There were mentions of the clubs, the festival—but nothing terrible. Mostly just who's-who tallies and some wild speculation about who went to bed with whom.

Phillip heaved a sigh of relief. He'd done his job well. He always did. People had a good time, drank a lot of Beaumont Beer and talked the company up to their friends. And they did that because Phillip brought all the elements together for them—the beer, the party, the celebrities.

It was just that sometimes, people talked about things that gave the PR department fits. No matter how many times Phillip tried to tell those suits who worked for his brother Chadwick that there was no such thing as bad PR, every time he made headlines for what they considered the "wrong" reasons, Chadwick felt the need to have a coming-to-Jesus moment with Phillip about how his behavior was damaging the brand name and costing the company money and blah, blah, blah.

Frankly, Phillip could do with less Chadwick in his life.

That wasn't going to happen this week, thank God. The initial summaries looked good—the Klout Score was up, the hits were high and on Saturday, the Beaumont party tent had been trending for about four hours on Twitter.

Phillip shut off his phone with a smile. That was a job well done in his book.

He felt human again. His head was clearing and the food in his stomach was working. *Hair of the dog always does the trick*, he thought as he refilled his mug and put on his boots. He felt good.

He was happy to be back on the farm in a way he couldn't quite put into words. He missed his horses—especially Sun. He hadn't seen Sun in what felt like weeks.

The last he knew, Richard had hired some trainer who'd promised to fix the horse. But that was a while ago. Maybe a month?

There it was again—that uneasy feeling that had nothing to do with the hangover or the breakfast. He didn't like that feeling, so he took an extra big swig of coffee to wash it away.

He had some time before the next round of events kicked off. There was a lull between now and Spring Break. That was fine by Phillip. He would get caught up with Richard, evaluate his horses, go for some long rides—hopefully on Sun—and ignore the world for a while. Then, by the time he was due to head south to help ensure that Beaumont Beers were the leading choice of college kids everywhere, he'd be good to go. Brand loyalty couldn't start early enough.

He grabbed his hat off the peg by the door and headed down to the barn. The half-mile walk did wonders for his head. The whole place was turning green as the last of the winter gave way to spring. Daffodils popped up in random spots and the pastures were so bright they hurt his eyes.

It felt good to be home. He needed a week or two to recover, that was all.

As he rounded the bend in the road that connected the house to the main barn, he saw that Sun was out in a paddock. That was a good sign. As best he could recall, Richard had said they couldn't move the horse out of his stall without risking life and limb. Phillip had nearly had his own head taken off by a flying hoof the one time he'd tried to put a halter on his own horse—something that Sun had let him do when they were at the stables in Turkmenistan.

God, he wished he knew where things had gone wrong. Sun had been a handful, that was for sure—but at his old stables, he'd been manageable. Phillip had even inquired into bringing his former owner out to the farm to see if the old man who spoke no English would be able to settle Sun down. The man had refused.

But if that last trainer had worked wonders, then Phillip could get on with his plan. The trainer's services had cost a fortune, but if he'd gotten Sun back on track, it was worth it. The horse's bloodlines could be traced back on paper to the 1880s and the former owner had transcribed an oral bloodline that went back to the 1600s. True, an oral bloodline didn't count much, but Philip knew Sun was a special horse. His ancestors had taken home gold, the Grand Prix de Dressage and too many long-distance races to count.

He needed to highlight Sun's confirmation and stamina—that was what would sell his lineage as a stud. Sun's line would live on for a long time to come. That stamina—and his name—was what breeders would pay top dollar for. But beyond that, there was something noble about the whole thing. The Akhal-Tekes were an ancient breed of horse—the founder of the modern lines of the Arabians and Thoroughbreds. It seemed a shame that almost no one had ever heard of them. They were amazing animals—almost unbreakable, especially compared to the delicate racing Thoroughbreds whose legs seemed to shatter with increasing frequency on the racetrack. A horse like Sun could reinvigorate lines—leading to stronger, faster racehorses.

Phillip felt lighter than he had in a while. Sun was a damned fine horse—the kind of stud upon which to found a line. He must be getting old because as fun as the parties obviously were—photos didn't lie—he was getting to the point where he just wanted to train his horses.

Of course he knew he couldn't hide out here forever. He had a job to do. Not that he needed the money, but working for the Beaumont Brewery wasn't just a family tradition. It was also a damned good way to keep Chadwick off his back. No matter what his older brother said, Phillip wasn't wasting the family fortune on horses and women. He was an important part of the Beaumont brand name—that *more* than offset his occasional forays into horses.

Phillip saw a massive trailer parked off to the side of the barn with what looked like a garden hose and—was that an extension cord?—running from the barn to the trailer. Odd. Had he invited someone out to the farm? Usually, when he had guests, they stayed at the house.

He took a swig of coffee. He didn't like that unsettling feeling of not knowing what was going on.

As he got closer, he saw that Sun wasn't grazing. He was running. That wasn't a good sign.

Sun wasn't better. He was the same. God, what a depressing thought.

Then Phillip saw her. It was obvious she was a *her*—tall, clad in snug jeans and a close-fit flannel shirt, he could see the curve of her hips at three hundred yards. Longish hair hung underneath a brown hat. She sure as hell didn't look like the kind of woman he brought home with him—not even to the farm. So what was she doing here?

Standing in the middle of the paddock while Sun ran in wild circles, that's what.

Phillip shook his head. This had to be a post-hangover hallucination. If Sun weren't better, why would *anyone* be in a paddock with him? The horse was too far gone. It wasn't safe. The horse had knocked a few of the hired hands out of commission for a while. The medical bills were another thing Chadwick rode his ass about.

Not only did the vision of this woman not disperse, but Phillip noticed something else that couldn't be real. Was that a donkey in there with her? He was pretty sure he'd remember buying a donkey that small.

He looked the woman over again, hoping for some sign of recognition. Nothing. He was sure he'd remember thighs and a backside like that. Maybe she'd look different up close.

He walked the rest of the way down to the paddock, his gaze never leaving her. No, she wasn't his type, but variety was the spice of life, wasn't it?

"Good morning," he said in a cheerful voice as he leaned against the fence.

Her back stiffened but she gave no other sign that she'd heard him. The small donkey craned its neck around to give him a look that could only be described as *doleful* as Sun went from a bucking trot to a rearing, snorting mess in seconds.

Jesus, that horse could kill her. But he tried not to let the panic creep into his voice. "Miss, I don't think it's safe to be in there right now." Sun made a sound that was closer to a scream than a whinny. Phillip winced at the noise.

The woman's head dropped in what looked like resignation. Then she patted the side of her leg as she turned and began a slow walk back to the gate. Betty followed close on her heels.

The donkey's name was Betty. How did he know that?

Oh, crap—he *did* know her. Had she been at the party? Had they slept together? He didn't remember seeing any signs of a female in his room or in the house.

He watched as she walked toward him. She was a cowgirl, that much was certain—and not one of those fake ones whose hats were covered in rhinestones and whose jeans had never seen a saddle. The brown hat fit low on her forehead, the flannel shirt was tucked in under a worn leather belt that had absolutely no adornment and her chest—

Phillip was positive he'd remember spending a little quality time with that chest. Despite the nearly unisex clothing, the flannel shirt did nothing to hide the generous breasts that swelled outward, begging him to notice them.

Which he did, of course. But he could control his baser

urges to ogle a woman. So, after a quick glance at what had to be perfection in breast form, he snapped his eyes up to her face. The movement made his head swim.

It'd be *so* nice if he could remember her, because she was certainly a memorable woman. Her face wasn't made up or altered. She had tanned skin, a light dusting of freckles and a nose that looked as if it might have been broken once. It should have made her look awkward, but he decided it was fitting. There was a certain beauty in the imperfect.

Then she raised her eyes to his and he felt rooted to the spot. Her eyes were clear and bright, a soft hazel. He could get lost in eyes like that.

Not that he got the chance. She scowled at him. The shock of someone other than Chadwick looking so displeased with him put Phillip on the defensive. Still, she was a woman and women were his specialty. So he waited until she'd made it out of the gate and closed it behind Betty.

Once the gate clicked, she didn't head for where he stood. Instead, she went back to ignoring him entirely as she propped a booted foot up on the gate and watched the show Sun was putting on for them.

What. The. Hell.

He was going to have to amend his previous statement—*most* women were his specialty.

Time to get back to basics. One compliment, coming right up. "I don't think I've ever seen anyone wear a pair of jeans like you do." That should do the trick.

Or it would have for any other woman. Instead, she dropped her forehead onto the top bar of the gate—a similar motion to the one she'd made out in the paddock moments ago. Then she turned her face to him. "Was it worth it?"

His generous smile faltered. "Was what worth it?"

Her soft eyes didn't seem so soft anymore. "The black-out. Was it worth it?"

"I have no idea what you're talking about."

That got a smirk out of her, just a small curve of her lips. It was gone in a flash. "That's the definition of a blackout, isn't it? You have no idea who I am or what I'm doing here, do you?"

Sun made that unholy noise again. Phillip tensed. The woman he didn't know looked at the horse and shook her head as if the screaming beast was a disappointment to her. Then she looked at Phillip and shook her head again.

Unfamiliar anger coursed through him, bringing a new clarity to his thoughts. Who the hell was this woman, any-way? "I know you shouldn't be climbing into the paddock with Sun. He's dangerous."

Another smirk. Was she challenging him?

"But he wasn't when you bought him, was he?"

How did she know about that? An idea began to take shape in his mind like a Polaroid developing. He shook his head, hoping the image would get clearer—fast. It didn't. "No."

She stared at him a moment longer. It shouldn't bother him that she knew who he was. Everyone knew who he was. That went with being the face of the Beaumont Brew-ery.

But she didn't look at him like everyone else did—with that gleam of delight that went with meeting a celebrity in the flesh. Instead, she just looked disappointed.

Well, she could just keep on looking disappointed. He turned his attention to the most receptive being here—the donkey. "How are you this morning, Betty?"

When the woman didn't correct him, he grinned. He'd gotten that part right, at least.

He rubbed the donkey behind the ears, which resulted

in her leaning against his legs and groaning in satisfaction. "Good girl, aren't you?" he whispered.

Maybe he'd have to get a little donkey like this. If Betty wasn't his already.

Maybe, a quiet voice in the back of his head whispered, that blackout *wasn't* worth it.

He took another swig of coffee.

He looked back at the woman. Her posture hadn't changed, but everything about her face had. Instead of a smirk, she was smiling at him—him and the donkey.

The donkey was hers, he realized. And since he already knew the donkey's name, he must have met the woman, too.

Double damn.

That's when he realized he was smiling back at her. What had been superior about her had softened into something that looked closer to delight.

He forgot about not knowing who she was, how she got here or what she was doing with his prize stallion. All he could think was that *now* things were about to get interesting. This was a dance he could do with his eyes closed—a beautiful woman, a welcoming smile—a good time soon to be had by all.

Genuine compliment, take two. "She's a real sweetie, isn't she? I've never seen a donkey this well-behaved." He took a risk. "You did an amazing job training her."

Oh, yeah, that worked much better than the jeans comment had. Her smile deepened as she tilted her head to one side. Soft morning light warmed her face and suddenly, she looked like a woman who wanted to be kissed.

Whoever she was, this woman was unlike anyone he'd ever met before. Different could be good. Hell, different could be great. She wasn't a woman who belonged at the clubs but then, he wasn't at the clubs. He was at his farm and this woman clearly fit in this world.

Maybe he'd enjoy this break from big-city living more than he'd thought he would. After all, his bed was more than large enough to accommodate two people. So was the hot tub.

Yes, the week was suddenly looking up.

But she still hadn't told him who the hell she was and that was becoming a problem. Kissing an anonymous woman in a dark club? No problem. Kissing a cowgirl who was inexplicably on his ranch in broad daylight?

Problem.

He had to bite the bullet and admit he didn't remember her name. So, still rubbing Betty's ears, he stuck out a hand. "We got off to a rough beginning." He could only assume that was true, as she'd opened with a blackout comment. "Let's start over. I'm Phillip Beaumont. And you are?"

Some of her softness faded, but she shook his hand with the kind of grip that made it clear she was used to working with her hands. "Jo Spears."

That didn't ring a single damned bell in his head.

It was only after she'd let go of his hand that she added, with a grin that bordered on cruel, "I'm here to retrain Sun."

Three

"*You're* the new trainer?"

Jo fought hard to keep the grin off her face. She wasn't entirely sure she succeeded. Even yesterday, when he'd been toasted, she hadn't been able to surprise Phillip Beaumont. But she'd caught him off guard this morning.

How bad was his hangover? It had to be killer. She could smell whiskey from where she stood. But she would have never guessed it just by looking at him. Hell, his eyes weren't even bloodshot. He had a three-day-old scruff on his cheeks that should have looked messy but, on him, made him look better—like a man who worked with his hands.

Other than that…she let her eyes drift over his body. The jeans weren't the fancy kind that he'd spent hundreds of dollars to make look old and broken in—they looked like the kind he'd broken in himself. The denim work shirt was much the same. Yes, his brown boots had probably cost a pretty penny once—but they were scuffed and scratched, not polished to a high shine. These were his work clothes and he was clearly comfortable in them.

The suit he'd had on yesterday had been the outfit of the Phillip Beaumont who went to parties and did commercials. But the Phillip Beaumont who was petting Betty's ears today?

This was a cowboy. A real one.

Heat flooded her body. She forced herself to ignore it. She would not develop a crush or an infatuation or even an *admiration* for Phillip Beaumont just because he looked good in jeans.

She'd been right about him. He had no memory of yesterday and he'd spiked his coffee this morning. He was everything she couldn't allow herself, all wrapped up in one attractive package. She had a job to do. And if she did it well, a reference from Phillip Beaumont would be worth its weight in gold. It'd be worth that smile of his.

"I believe," she said with a pointed tone that let him know he wasn't fooling anyone, "that we established our identities yesterday afternoon."

The change was impressive. It only took a matter of seconds for his confusion to be buried beneath a warm smile. "Forgive me." He managed to look appropriately contrite while also adding a bit of smolder to his eyes. The effect was almost heady. She was *not* falling for this. Not at all. "I'm just a little surprised. The other trainers have been…"

"Older? Male? Richard told me about his previous attempts." She turned her attention back to the horse to hide her confusion. She could not flutter. Too much was at risk here.

Sun did seem to be calming down. Which meant he hadn't made that screaming noise in a couple of minutes. He was still racing as if his life depended on it, though. "I think it's clear that Sun needs something else."

"And that's you?" He kept his tone light and conversational, but she could hear the doubt lurking below the surface.

The other three men had all been crusty old farts, men who'd been around horses their whole lives. Not like her. "Yup. That's me."

Phillip leaned against the paddock fence. Jo did not like how aware of his body she was. He kicked a foot up on the lowest railing and draped his arms over the top of the fence. It was all very casual—and close enough to touch.

"So what's your plan to fix him?"

She sighed. "As I told you yesterday, I don't fix horses. No one can fix him."

She managed to keep the crack about whether or not he'd remember this conversation tomorrow to herself. She was already pushing her luck with him and she knew it. He was still paying her and, given how big a mess Sun was, she might have enough to put a down payment on her own ranch after this.

Wouldn't that be the ultimate dream? A piece of land to call her own, where the Phillip Beaumonts of the world would bring her their messed-up horses. She wouldn't have to spend days driving across country and showering in a trailer. Betty could run wild and free on her own grass. Her own ranch would be safety and security and she wouldn't have to deal with people at all. Just horses. That's what this job could give to her.

That's why she needed to work extra hard on keeping her distance from the man who was *still* close enough to touch.

He ignored the first part of the statement. "Then what do you do?"

There was no way to sum up what she did. So she didn't. "Save him."

Because she was so aware of Phillip's body, she felt the

tension take hold of him. She turned her head just enough to look at him out of the corner of her eye. Phillip's gaze was trained on the half-crazed horse in the paddock. He looked stricken, as if her words had sliced right through all his charm and left nothing but a raw, broken man who owned a raw, broken horse.

Then he looked at her. His eyes—God, there was so much going on under the surface. She felt herself start to get lost in them, but Sun whinnied, pulling her back to herself.

She could not get lost in Phillip Beaumont. To do so would be to take that first slippery step back down the slope to lost nights and mornings in strangers' beds. And there would be no coming back from that this time.

So she said, in a low voice, "I *only* save horses."

"I don't need to be saved, thank you very much."

Again, the change was impressive. The warm smile that bordered on teasing snapped back onto his face and the honest pain she'd seen in his eyes was gone beneath a wink and twinkle.

She couldn't help it. She looked at his coffee mug. "If you say so."

His grip tightened on the handle, but that was the only sign he'd gotten her meaning. He probably thought the smell of the coffee masked the whiskey. Maybe it did for regular folks, but not for her.

"How are you going to *save* my horse then?" It came out in the same voice he might use to ask a woman on a date.

It was time to end this conversation before things went completely off the rails. "One day at a time."

Let's see if he catches that, she thought as she opened the gate and slowly walked back into the paddock, Betty trailing at her heels.

As she closed the gate behind her, she heard Richard come out of the barn. "Mr. Beaumont—you're up!"

Good. She wanted more time with Sun alone. The horse had almost calmed down before Phillip showed up. If she could get the animal to stay at a trot...

That wasn't happening now. Sun clearly did not like Richard, probably because the older man had been the one to tranquilize him and move him around the most. She was encouraged that, although the horse did freak out any time Phillip showed up, he had sort of settled down this morning as she and Phillip had talked in conversational tones. Sun didn't have any negative associations with Phillip— he just didn't like change. That was a good thing to know.

"Just getting to know the new trainer," Phillip said behind her. She had to give him credit, he managed not to make it sound dismissive.

"If you two are going to talk," she said in a low voice that carried a great distance, "please do so elsewhere. You're freaking out the horse."

There was a pause and she got the feeling that both men were looking at her. Then Richard said, "Now that you're here, I'd like you to see the new Percheron foals." That was followed by the sounds of footsteps leading away from the paddock.

But they weren't far away when she heard Phillip say, "Are you sure about her?"

Jo tensed.

Richard, bless his crusty old heart, came to her defense. As his voice trailed off, she heard him reply, "She came highly recommended. If anyone can fix Sun... She's our last chance."

She couldn't fix this horse. She couldn't fix the man, either, but she had no interest in trying. She would not be swayed by handsome faces, broken-in jeans or kind words for Betty.

She was just here for the horse.

She needed to remember that.

* * *

Phillip woke up early the next day and he knew why. He was hoping there'd be a woman with an attitude standing in a paddock this morning.

Jo Spears. She was not his type—not physically, not socially. Not even close. He sure as hell remembered her today. How could he have forgotten meeting her the day before? That didn't matter. What mattered now was that he was dying to see if she was still in that arena, just standing there.

He hurried through his shower while the coffee brewed. He added a shot of whiskey to keep the headache away and then got a mug for her. While he was at it, he grabbed a couple of carrots from the fridge for the donkey.

Would Jo still be standing in the middle of that paddock, watching Sun do whatever the hell it was Sun did? Because that's what she'd done all day yesterday—just stand there. Richard had gotten him up to speed on the farm's business and he'd spent some time haltering and walking the Percheron foals but he'd always been aware of the woman in the paddock.

She hadn't been watching him, which was a weird feeling. Women were always aware of what he was doing, waiting for their opportunity to strike up a conversation. He could make eye contact with a woman when he walked into a club and know that, six hours later, she'd be going back to his hotel with him. All he had to do was wait for the right time for her to make her move. She would come to him. Not the other way around.

But this horse trainer? He'd caught the way her hard glare had softened and she'd tilted her head when he'd complimented her little donkey. That was the kind of look a woman gave him when she was interested—when she was going to be in his bed later.

Not the kind of look a woman gave him when she proceeded to ignore him for the rest of the day. And night.

Phillip Beaumont was not used to being ignored. He was the life of the party. People not only paid attention to what he was doing, who he was doing it with, what he was wearing—hell, who he was tweeting about—but they paid good money to do all of that with him. It was his job, for God's sake. People always noticed him.

Except for her.

He should have been insulted yesterday. But he'd been so surprised by her attitude that he hadn't given a whole lot of thought to his wounded pride.

She was something else. A woman apart from others.

Variety is the spice of life, he thought as he strolled down to the barn. That had to be why he was so damned glad to see her and that donkey in the middle of the paddock again, Sun still doing laps around them both. But, Phillip noted, the horse was only trotting and making a few small bucks with his hind legs. Phillip wasn't sure he'd seen Sun this calm since…well, since Asia.

For a moment, he allowed himself to be hopeful. So three other trainers had failed. This Jo Spears might actually work. She might save his horse.

But then he had to go and ruin Sun's progress by saying, "Good morning."

At the sound of Phillip's voice, Sun lost it. He reared back, kicking his forelegs and whinnying with such terror that Phillip's hope immediately crumbled to dust. Betty looked at him and he swore the tiny thing rolled her eyes.

But almost immediately, Sun calmed down—or at least stopped making that God-awful noise and started running.

"You got that part right today," Jo said in that low voice of hers.

"It's good?" He looked her over—her legs spread shoulder-width apart, fingers hooked into her belt loops. Everything about her was relaxed but strong. He could imagine those legs and that backside riding high in the saddle.

And then, because he was Phillip Beaumont, he imagined those legs and that backside riding high in his bed.

Oh, yeah—it could be good. Might even be great.

"It's morning." She glanced over her shoulder at him and he saw the corner of her mouth curve up into a smile. "Yesterday when you said that, it was technically afternoon."

He couldn't help but grin at her. Boy, she was tough. When was the last time someone had tried to make him toe the line? Hell, when was the last time there'd even *been* a line?

And there was that smile. Okay, *half* a smile but still. Jo didn't strike him as the kind of woman who smiled at a man if she didn't actually want to. That smile told Phillip that she was interested in him. Or, at the very least, attracted to him. Wasn't that the same thing?

"Back at it again?"

She nodded.

Sun looped around the whole paddock, blowing past Phillip with a snort. His instinct was to step back from the fence, but he didn't want to project anything resembling fear—especially when she was actually inside the fence and he wasn't.

She pivoted, her eyes following the horse as he made another lap. Then, when he went back to running along the far side of the paddock again, she made that slow walk over to where Phillip stood.

Watching her walk was almost a holy experience. Instead of a practiced wiggle, Jo moved with a coiled grace that projected the same strength he'd felt in her handshake yesterday.

Did she give as good as she got? Obviously, in conversation the answer was *yes*. But did that apply to other areas?

She opened the gate and, Betty on her heels, walked out. When the gate closed behind her, she didn't come to him. She didn't even turn her head in his direction.

What would it take to get her to look at him? He could say something witty and crude. That would definitely get her attention. But instead of being scandalous and funny—which was how such comments went over when everyone was happily sloshed at a bar—he had a feeling that Jo might hit him for being an asshole.

Still, he was interested in that image of her riding him. He was the kind of man who was used to having female company every night. And he hadn't had any since he'd woken up at the farm.

He would enjoy spending time in Jo's company. He couldn't say why he liked the idea so much—she wouldn't make anything easy on him.

But that didn't bother him. In fact, he felt as if it was a personal challenge—one he was capable of meeting.

When was the last time he'd chased a woman? He tried to scroll through the jumbled memories but he wasn't coming up with anyone except…Suzie. Susanna Whaley, British socialite. She'd come from vulgar money—which was to say, by British definition, someone whose family had only gotten rich in the last century. She didn't care that Phillip was wealthy. She had enough money of her own. And she didn't care that he'd been famous. Before they'd met, she'd been dating some European prince. Phillip had been forced to work overtime just to get her phone number.

Something about that had been…well, it'd been *good*. He'd liked chasing her and she'd liked being chased. They'd dated internationally for almost a year. He'd looked at rings. He'd been twenty-six and convinced that *this* marriage would be different from his parents' marriage.

Then his father had died. Suzie had accompanied him to the funeral and met the entire Beaumont clan—his father's ex-wives, Phillip's half-siblings. All the bitter fighting and acrimonious drama that Phillip had tried so hard to get free of had been on full display. The police had gotten involved. Lawsuits had been filed.

So much for the Beaumont name.

The relationship had ended fairly quickly after that. He'd been upset, of course but deep down, he'd agreed with Suzie. His family—and, by extension, he himself—were too screwed up to have a shot at a happily-ever-after. They'd parted ways, she'd married that European prince and Phillip had gone right back to his womanizing ways. It was easier than thinking about what he'd almost had—and what he'd lost.

Still, he'd liked the chase. It'd been…different. Proof that it wasn't just his name or his money or even his famous face that a woman wanted. He'd had to prove his worth. That wasn't a bad thing.

Jo Spears clearly wasn't swayed by his name or his money. If she was as good a trainer as she claimed to be, she'd probably spent plenty of time in barns owned by equally rich, equally famous men and women. He didn't spend a lot of time with people who didn't want a piece of his name, his fortune—of him. The feeling was…odd.

He could stay out here for a few weeks. And he wouldn't mind having a little company.

He could chase Jo. It'd be fun.

"Coffee?" A thoughtful gesture was always a good place to begin.

She looked at the mugs in his hands and sniffed. "I don't drink."

He was going to have to switch brands of whiskey. Apparently Jack had a stronger smell than he remembered.

"Just coffee." When she gave him a look that could have peeled paint, he was forced to add, "In yours."

She took the mug, sniffed it several times and then took a tentative sip. "Thanks."

He stood there, feeling awkward, which was not normal. He wasn't awkward or unsure, not when it came to women. But every time he deployed one of his tried-and-true techniques on her, it backfired.

Oh yeah, this was going to be a challenge.

"How's it going?" he asked. Always good to focus on the basics.

That worked. She tilted her head in his direction, an appreciative smile on her face. "Not bad."

"I noticed," he continued, trying not to stare at that smile, "that you spend a lot of time standing in the paddock. With a donkey."

Her eyebrow curved up. "I do."

"Can I ask why, or are the mysteries of the horse whisperer secret?"

Damn, he lost her. Her warm smile went ice-cold in a heartbeat. "I do not *whisper*. I *train*."

Seducing her was going to prove harder than hell if he couldn't stop pissing her off. "Sensitive about that?"

Oh, that was a vicious look, one that let him know she'd loaded up both barrels and was about to open fire. "I'd explain my rules to you again, but what guarantee do I have that you'll remember them *this* time?"

Ouch. But he wasn't going to let her know how close to the quick she'd cut. He wouldn't back up in fear from his horse and he sure as hell wouldn't do it from a woman. He gave her his wicked smile, one that always worked. "I can be taught."

"I doubt it." Her posture changed. Instead of leaning toward him, she'd pulled away, her upper body angled in the direction of the barn.

Okay, he needed a different approach here, one that didn't leave his flank open to attack. Yesterday, when he hadn't remembered meeting her, she'd warmed up while he'd patted Betty. Time to put this theory to the test.

"Come here, girl," he said, crouching down and pulling the baggie of carrots out of his back pocket. "Do you like carrots?"

Betty came plodding over to him and snatched the carrot out of his hand. "That's a good girl."

"Did you bring one for Sun?"

"I did." He hadn't, but he'd brought enough. "But I don't think he likes me enough to let me give him one."

Then he looked up at her. Her light brown eyes were focused on his face with such intensity that it seemed she was seeing into him.

He fished another carrot out and looked at the horse that was still going in pointless circles around the paddock. Yeah, no getting close to *that* without getting trampled. "Like I said, I don't think he likes me."

"He doesn't *not* like you, though." She kept her gaze on the horse.

"How do you figure?" Betty snuffled at his hand, so he gave her the carrot he was holding. He still had two left. "Every time he sees me, he goes ballistic."

Jo sighed, which did some impressive things with her chest. "No, every time he sees you, it's something different. He doesn't like the different part. It has nothing to do with you. If you want to see what he does when he actively hates someone, you can call Richard out here."

"He hates Richard?" Although, now that he thought about it, Sun often did seem more agitated when the farm manager was around.

She nodded. "Richard and your hands are the ones who've shot him with the tranq gun, lassoed him in his stall and, from Sun's point of view, generally terrorized him. You don't have those negative associations in Sun's mind."

Everything she said made sense. He palmed another carrot, wondering if he should give it to the donkey or if he should try to walk into the paddock and give it to his horse. He'd be risking death, but it might be a positive thing the horse could associate with him. "He just doesn't like change?"

"Nope." She looked at his hand, then nodded to where there was a water bucket and a feed bucket hanging on the side of the paddock. "Put it in his bucket. But go slow."

"Okay." So it felt a little ridiculous to move at a snail's pace around the fence. But he noticed that Sun slowed to a trot and watched him.

Phillip held up the remaining two carrots so that Sun could see them and then dropped them over the fence and into the bucket. Then Phillip slowly worked his way back to where Jo was standing.

The approval on her face was something new. Something good. Wow, she could be pretty when she smiled.

"How was that?" He felt a little like a puppy begging for approval, but, for some reason, it was important to him.

Her smile deepened. "You *can* be taught."

"I'm a very quick study." He didn't walk over to her or run his hand down her arm—all things that worked wonders in a club—but he didn't need to. The blush that graced her cheeks was more than good enough to know that, no matter how icy or judgmental she could be, she was also a flesh-and-blood woman who responded to him.

Oh, yeah—the chase was *on*.

She looked away first. Aside from the blush and the smile, she gave no other sign of interest. She didn't lean in his direction, she didn't compliment him again. All she said was, "Watch," as she looked at Sun.

The horse was still trotting, but Phillip realized that each pass brought him closer to the buckets. Within a few minutes, he was making small loops back and forth right in front of the carrots.

He could probably smell them. Phillip hoped the horse would realize they were treats.

Sun slowed down enough that he was moving at a fast walk. He dipped his long nose into the bucket but before Phillip could allow himself to be hopeful, the horse knocked the whole thing off the fence, spilling the carrots and leftover grain on the ground. Then he was off again, running and bucking and throwing a hell of a fit.

"Damn."

"It's not you," Jo said again. "It's different. He's got to get used to someone leaving him a treat."

"And in the meantime?"

She shrugged. "We wait."

"Wait for what?"

"Wait for him to get tired."

He looked at her. "*This* is your grand plan to save him? Wait for him to get bored?" At his words, Sun began to rear up.

Jo sighed. "Don't you ever get tired?"

"Excuse me?"

"*Tired.*" She spoke the word carefully, as if she were pronouncing it for someone who didn't speak English. "Don't you get tired of the days and the nights blending together with no beginning and no end? Of waking up and not knowing who you are or where you are or most importantly of all, *what* you've done? Tired of realizing that you've done something horrible, something there's no good way to move on from, so you angle for that blackout again so you don't have to think about what you've become?"

She turned her face to him. Nothing about her was particularly lovely at this moment, but there was something in her eyes that wouldn't let him go.

"Doesn't it ever just wear you out?"

He did something he didn't usually allow himself to do—he glared at her. She couldn't know what she was talking about and, as far as he was concerned, she was not talking about him.

Still, her words cut into him like small, sharp knives and although it made no sense—she was wrong about him and that was *final*—he wanted to drink the rest of his coffee and let the whiskey in it take the edge off the inexplicable pain he felt, but she was watching him. Waiting to see if he'd buckle.

Well, she could just keep right on waiting. "I have no idea what you're talking about." His voice came out quieter than he'd meant it to. He almost sounded shaky to his own ears. He didn't like that. He didn't betray weakness, not to his family, not to anyone.

A shadow of sadness flickered across her face, but it was gone as she turned back to the paddock. "If that's what gets you through the night." She didn't wait for him to deny it. "Sun's been in this paddock for three straight days now. Sooner or later, he's going to get tired of doing the same thing over and over again. He'll want to do something different. Anything different, really, as long as it's not going mad. That's when I'll get him."

Going mad. Was that how she thought of the horse? Of him?

He needed to get the conversation onto firmer ground. Thus far, she'd responded best when he'd actively engaged her about horses and donkeys—not when the focus had been on him. "If he gets bored, won't he start cribbing or something? We've got collars that keep him from doing that, but I don't want to try and put one on him at this stage."

Cribbing happened when horses got bored. They bit down on the wood in their stalls or their rubber buckets and sucked in air. It seemed harmless at first, but it could lead to colic. And colic could be deadly.

Jo pivoted—not a sideways glance, but her whole body turned to him. He kept his eyes above her neck, and saw how she looked at him—confused, yes. But there was more to it than that.

"Really." The way she said it, it wasn't a question. More a wonderment.

He kept his voice casual. "You may not believe this, but I actually know a great deal about horses. My father had a racehorse back in 1987 that died of colic when the former farm manager hadn't realized the mare was cribbing. Yet another stumbling block in my father's eternal quest to win a Triple Crown."

That had been a bad year. Hardwick Beaumont had fired the entire staff at the farm and some of his employees at the Brewery and had been so unbearable to be around that he'd probably hastened his second divorce by at least two years.

Needless to say, it hadn't been much fun for Phillip. Even back then, the farm had been a sanctuary of sorts—a place to get away from half-siblings and step-parents. A place where Hardwick realized he *had* a second son, where they did things together. Even if those things were just leaning on a pasture fence and watching the trainers work the horses.

Hardwick had talked to Phillip during those times. Not Chadwick, not his new babies with his new wife. Just Phillip. The rest of the time, Hardwick had always been too busy running the Beaumont Brewery and having affairs to pay any attention to Phillip. But on the farm…

Phillip had cried that day. He'd cried for Maggie May, the horse who'd died, and he'd cried when the farm staff—the same grizzled old cowboys who'd always been happy to saddle up Phillip's pony and let him ride around the property—had been kicked out. Up until that day, he'd always thought the farm was a place safe from the real world, but all it had taken was one prize-winning mare's death to rip the veil from his eyes.

"Maggie May—that was the mare's name, right?"

Phillip snapped his attention back to the woman standing four feet from him. She was looking at Sun, who'd calmed down to an almost-mellow trot, but there was a sadness about her that, for once, didn't carry the weight of disappointment. It was almost as if she felt bad for the horse.

"You know about that?"

This time, she did give him the side-eye. "I'm also a quick study."

Electricity sparked between them. He felt it. She had to have felt it—why else did that pretty blush grace her cheeks again? "What else do you know about me?"

It was unusual to ask, more unusual to not know the answer. But she'd confounded him at every single turn thus far and, he realized, it was because she knew far more about him that he was anticipating.

She shrugged. "I always do my homework before I take a job. You're an easy man to find online."

But Maggie May—that horse wouldn't pop up in the first twenty pages of a web search. That sort of detail would be buried deep underneath an avalanche of Tumblr feeds and press releases. That was the sort of detail someone would really have to dig to come up with.

"Are you always this thorough, then?"

She didn't hesitate. "Always." Her blush deepened. "But how can I be sure that your reported horse sense is on the level?" She tried to give him a cutting look, but didn't quite make it.

So she was aware of the magnitude of his reputation. That certainly explained her disapproval of his high-flying lifestyle. But there was something underneath that, something deeper.

Something interested.

He recalled doing an interview in *Western Horseman*. He'd had a particularly bad month of headlines. Chadwick had been ready to kill him, so his half-brother Matthew had suggested setting up the interview to show people that there was more to Phillip Beaumont than just scandals.

The reporter had spent three days on the farm with Phillip, following him around as he evaluated his horses, worked with Richard, and generally projected a sane, in-control appearance. The write-up had been so well received that Chadwick had been almost charitable to him for months after that.

That had to be what she was talking about. She'd probably assumed that one main article about him being a real cowboy was a PR plant. And she hadn't been half wrong.

Except he was a real cowboy—at least, he was when he was on the farm. This was the only place where he fit—where he could be Phillip instead of Hardwick's forgotten second son. The horses never cared who he was. They just cared that he was a good man who looked out for them.

Was that what she needed—to know that the horses came first for him? "I guess I'll have to prove myself to you."

"I guess you will," she agreed.

Oh, yeah—the chase was *on*. Jo was unlike any woman he'd ever pursued before. Instead of being a turn-off, he was more and more intrigued by her. She refused to cut him a single bit of slack, but all the signals were there.

Maybe she was a good girl who was intrigued by his bad boy antics. Maybe she'd like a little walk on the wild side. But the things that got her attention weren't the bad boy things. She noticed his interactions with the horses more.

Bad boy with a healthy dash of cowboy—*that* was something he could pull off. If she needed to know that his horse sense, as she called it, was on the level, then he'd have no problem showing her exactly how much he really understood about horses.

Starting now. "I need to get to the foals," he said, leaning toward her just a tad. She didn't pull back. "I'll stop by later and see if Sun ate his carrots."

She did not turn those pretty eyes in his direction, but her grin was broad enough that he knew he'd said the right thing. "I'd like that," she said in a low voice. Then she seemed to remember herself. Her cheeks shot bright red. "I mean, that'd be good. For Sun." Then, before he could say anything else, she opened the gate and walked into the paddock, the tiny donkey at her heels.

Interesting. She might try to act as if she were a tough-as-nails woman, but underneath was someone softer—someone who was enjoying the chase.

Oh, yeah—it'd be good, all right.

Might even be great.

Four

What the hell was she doing?

Jo stood in the middle of the paddock as Sun wore down. At least he was finally wearing down after three days. He kept looping closer to where the carrots lay in the dirt near his bucket.

The horse was calming down, but Jo? She was beginning to spiral out of control.

She had absolutely no business flirting with Phillip Beaumont. None. The list of reasons why started and ended with whiskey. And vodka. And tequila. She'd always been partial to tequila—she thought. She couldn't really remember.

And that was exactly why she had no business encouraging him. *Really, Jo? Really? It'd be good if he stopped by later?*

She didn't want to look forward to seeing him again. She was not the least bit curious to know if he'd bring her more coffee or Betty and Sun some carrots. She didn't even want to know what he was doing with the Percheron foals.

She was not here for Phillip Beaumont.

Now if she could get that through her thick skull.

It was hard, though. No one brought her coffee. Everyone took her at her word when she said she didn't hook up and left her alone. Which was how she liked it.

Well, maybe she didn't like it. It was a lonely life, never letting herself get close to people.

She'd made friends with Whitney Maddox last winter because Whitney…understood. Whitney had been down the same path, after all. It was easy to be friends with someone else who only trusted animals.

But Phillip? Not only did he *not* leave her alone, he kept coming back for more. It was almost as if he enjoyed her refusal to kowtow to him.

She started to wonder why that was but stopped. She didn't care if he thought she was a hoot or a breath of fresh air or if he was silently mocking her every single move. She *didn't* care.

Not much, anyway.

She rubbed Betty's ears and focused on Sun. Her thoughts didn't often get away from her like this, not anymore. And when they did…

No. She wasn't going to have a bad night. She wasn't even going to have a bad day. She forced herself to breathe regularly. Just because Phillip Beaumont was handsome and tempting and got this smile on his face when he looked at her.…

Right. Not happening.

His reputation preceded him. He probably looked at every woman as if she were the one person he'd been waiting for. This had nothing to do with her and everything to do with the fact that she was the only woman on the ranch.

She knew all these things. The sheer logic of the situation should have defused her baser instincts. That's how it'd always worked before.

So why was she thinking about that smile? Or the way his hands would feel on her body? Or what his body would feel like against hers?

Jesus, this was getting out of control. She'd left men in her past with the tequila and the nights she couldn't remember. She would not be tempted by a man who was every one of her triggers wearing a pair of work jeans.

Work jeans that fit him really well.

Damn.

Betty leaned against her, anchoring Jo to reality. She let herself rub the back of her neck, her fingers tracing the scar tissue that she'd earned the hard way. This was not the first time she'd been tempted by a man. The first job she'd taken off her parents' ranch had featured a hot young cowboy named Cade who liked to raise hell on a Friday night. Yes, it'd been a year since the accident at that point, but Jo had healed. She'd been flattered to know that she hadn't managed to totally destroy her looks and, truthfully, she *had* been tempted.

Cade had been her idea of a good time for years. It would have been so easy to take him up on his offer for a little fun. So damned easy to get into his truck, not knowing where they were going and not knowing if she'd remember it in the morning.

But she was tired of not remembering. So she'd passed on Cade's offer and never forgotten him. Funny how that worked out.

Sun was calmer today. That was good. The carrots had provided him something to focus on.

Finally, after Jo spent an hour and a half trying not to think about Phillip's smile or his jeans while she waited for Sun to get tired, the horse slowed down to what looked

like an angry walk, as if he'd only stopped running as a
favor to her. He continued to pace near the carrots.

Jo waited. Would the horse actually eat one? That would
be making more progress than she'd hoped for. And if Sun
improved faster, the sooner she could pack up Betty into
the trailer and be on her way to the next job, far away from
the temptation named Phillip Beaumont.

Sun dipped his nose into the water bucket and took a
couple of deep drinks, then leaned down to sniff the carrots.

And pawed them into mush.

Close, she thought with a weary sigh.

She tried to focus on the positive here. Sun was, in fact,
getting bored with being out-of-control. Something as innocent as carrots hadn't sent him into spasms of panic. He
hadn't even destroyed them outright. He'd been curious—
so much so that his curiosity had distracted him from his
regularly scheduled pacing. This was all good news.

She heard hoofbeats coming up the drive. Sun heard
them too and, with a whinny that sounded closer to a horse
than a demon, resumed trotting and kicking.

Moving slowly, Jo turned to see a beautiful pair of Percherons hitched to a wagon loaded with hay and driven by
none other than Phillip Beaumont, who was sitting high
on a narrow bench. His coffee mug was nowhere in sight.
The wagon looked as though it was a hundred years old—
wooden wheels painted red and gray. The whole thing was
a scaled down version of the Beaumont Beer wagon that
the Percherons pulled in parades and commercials.

Phillip put both reins in one hand and honest-to-God
tipped his hat to her. Heat flushed her face.

"Did he eat the carrots?"

"He pulverized them." She pointed to the orange-
colored dirt.

"Damn." He looked a little disappointed, but not as if the world had ended. "I'll try again tomorrow."

He seemed so sincere about it—a man who was concerned about his horse.

She'd be lying if she said she didn't find it endearing. "That'd be good."

She was pretty sure this was flirting. Maybe she was being the ridiculous one, reading intent where there was none.

Her face got hotter.

"I can't help but notice," Phillip went on as if she weren't slowly turning into a tomato, "that you've spent at least two days standing in the middle of a paddock."

"This is true."

He jiggled the reins. "There's more to this farm than just that patch of dirt." The invitation sounded pretty casual, but then he turned that smile in her direction. That was a smile that promised all kinds of wicked fun. "Want to go for a ride?"

That was flirting. It had to be.

And she had no idea how to respond.

After a moment's pause, Phillip went on. "I'm getting Marge and Homer here used to pulling the wagon. I'm headed out to the other side of the ranch, where I keep the Appaloosas. Have you seen them?"

"No." She hadn't even really seen the Percherons—but she wanted to. Could she accept this ride at face value—a chance to see the rest of the storied Beaumont Farm and the collection of horses it contained? "You named your horses after *The Simpsons?*"

"Doesn't everyone?" Good lord, that grin was going to be her undoing. "I'd love to get your professional opinion on them and the Appaloosas."

There—now did that qualify as flirting or not? Dang it, she was *so* out of practice.

He must have sensed her hesitation. "I'm just going to drop off the hay. Twenty, thirty minutes tops."

Wait—a multi-millionaire like Phillip Beaumont moved his own hay? This she had to see for herself. "One condition—I want to drive."

For a moment, the good-time grin on his face cracked, but she was serious. Drunk driving—whether it was a team of Percherons or a Porsche—was a non-starter for her.

Then the grin was back. "Can you handle a team?" His voice had dropped a notch and was in danger of smoldering. If she hadn't seen the crack in his mask before, she might not have noticed it this time. He hid it well.

"I can see how you'd question my skills, what with me being an equestrian professional." He notched an eyebrow at her and she almost felt bad for being a smart-ass. So she added, "I was raised on a ranch. I can drive a team."

"Ever driven Percherons?"

"There's a first for everything."

That was flirting—for her, anyway. Phillip took it that way, too. "Then come on."

He waited while she exited the paddock, her donkey on her heels. "What about Betty?" she asked after she got the gate closed.

She couldn't leave Betty alone with Sun. But she didn't want Betty wandering around the farm. She was small enough that, if she really put her mind to it, she could fall down a hole or get stuck in a gap in the fences.

"I thought she might like to try out a new pasture, meet some of the not-crazy horses we have here," he replied, pointing to a gate about two hundred yards up the drive. Clearly, he'd been anticipating this question. There was a certain measure of thoughtfulness about him that was, she had to admit, appealing. "The grass is always greener on the other side."

She grinned up at him. "So it is. I'll follow the wagon up."

She gave Sun a final look. The horse was actually standing still, watching them with the kind of look that seemed to say that he was taking in everything they did and said. Would he freak out as they left him alone or would he watch them go?

Phillip gave her one of those old-fashioned nods of his head and clucked to his team. The wagon started and she followed, Betty on her heels.

This was just some professional consideration, right? Phillip was a noted horseman and she was an increasingly noted horse trainer. His asking her to look at other horses on the farm had nothing to do with any real or imagined interest on his part and everything to do with getting the most out of what he was paying her.

When they got to the gate at the pasture across the road, Phillip surprised her again by hopping down off the wagon and opening the gate for Betty. "There you go, girl. Enjoy the grass—we'll be back."

Betty gave him one of her looks as she plodded past him into the pasture. Phillip latched the gate behind her. "Have fun!" He turned to Jo, the goofiest grin she'd ever seen on his face.

"What?"

"I like Betty. Everything about her is hilarious. Here, let me help you."

Now, Jo was perfectly capable of climbing up onto the narrow seat of a rack wagon all by herself, but Phillip moved to her side and placed a hand on the small of her back. "Just step up on the wheel there...."

His touch sent licking flames of heat up and down her back. His hand was strong and confident against her. How long had it been since a man had touched her? Since...

Bad. Bad, bad, *bad*. She slammed the breaks on that line of thinking and shook him off before she did something insane like pretend to stumble so he'd be forced to catch her. "I have done this before, you know."

She didn't catch the double entendre until he said, "Have you, now?" low and close to her ear. His breath was warm and didn't smell like whiskey.

It had been a long time. Really long. Could she indulge herself, just this once, and not slide back down to rock bottom? She had needs. It'd be nice to have someone else help her meet them.

She looked over her shoulder at Phillip, who was less than two feet away, an expectant look on his face. But he didn't press the issue or find some excuse to keep touching her. He just waited for her response.

She swallowed and hefted herself into the seat. This was starting to look like a bad idea—all of it. She tried to refocus her thinking. She was at the Beaumont Farms because this job would make her reputation as a trainer. Phillip Beaumont was not just an attractive, attentive man with a reputation as one of the better lovers in the world, he was the client who'd hired her to save his horse.

And getting in the wagon to see the farm and his other horses was…was…a wise business decision. He might have another horse who needed retraining, which would mean more money for her, a better reference.

That was a stretch and she knew it, especially when Phillip swung up into the seat and managed to make it look smooth. He settled onto the bench next to her, their thighs touching, and handed her the reins. "Marge likes to go fast, Homer likes to go slow. Try to keep them together." Then he leaned back, slung one arm behind her on the bench and said, "Show me what you can do."

He wasn't touching her but she swore she could feel the heat from his arm anyway. She gathered the reins and flicked them. "Up!"

Phillip chuckled as the horses began to walk. "Up?"

"It's what we said at home. And," she couldn't help but point out, "it worked. What do you say?"

"I'm partial to 'Let's Go.' So you were raised on a ranch?"

She adjusted the reins in her hands until she had more tension on Marge's. "Yup." She felt as if she should say more, but small talk was not one of her strengths. Never had been. Maybe that's why parties had always been easier with a beer in her hand.

"Where's home?"

"Middle of nowhere, South Dakota. Nothing to do but stare at the grass."

"Oh? So you've been training horses your whole life?"

She shrugged. She didn't like talking about herself. She especially didn't like talking about the six or so years that were a total blur. So she skipped it entirely.

"Not like this. But I'd come back to the ranch after college—" That was the most diplomatic way to put it. "—and a neighbor's barn caught fire. He lost four horses, but one survived. Oaty was his name. That horse was a mess. The vet almost put him down twice but…"

"But you couldn't let him do that." Phillip's tone was more than sympathetic. He understood.

"Nope. I just watched him. For days. And the longer I watched him, the more I could understand him. He was terrified and I couldn't blame him."

"You waited for him to get bored?"

"More like to calm down. Took about a month before I could get close enough to brush him. He was scarred and his coat never did grow back right on his flank, but he's still out on my parents' ranch, munching grass and hanging out with the donkeys."

The day she'd saddled old Oaty up and ridden him across the ranch had been one of the best days of her life. For so long she'd felt lost and confused and hadn't known why, but saving Oaty had been saving herself. She hadn't given up on Oaty and she wouldn't give up on herself.

She was good at something—saving horses no one else could. She'd stayed on her parents' ranch for a few more years, driving around the state to other semi-local ranches to work with their horses, and as her successes had mounted, so had the demand for her services.

Besides, a woman could only live with her parents for so long. So she'd bought her trailer and hit the road, Betty in tow, determined to make a name for herself. It'd taken years, but she'd finally made it to a place like Beaumont Farms—the kind of place where money was no object.

"That must have been huge for you."

"Oaty was a tough case. Probably the toughest I've had up until now."

Phillip chuckled. "I'm honored to be the toughest case."

She couldn't help it. She turned to look at him. "It's not really an honor."

Their gazes met. There was something raw in his eyes, something…honest.

She did not fix people. She did not sleep with people. She didn't do anything involving alcohol anymore. She'd been clean and sober for ten years and had never crossed back over to the dark side. Apart from a long-ago cowboy named Cade, she'd never once been tempted by a man.

Until now.

She shouldn't be attracted to Phillip and most certainly not interested in him.

But she was. Against all known logic and common sense, she was.

"Here," she said, thrusting the reins at him. "You drive."

Five

"You really haul your own hay?" Jo asked as she watched him grab a bale.

The question struck him as funny, considering the woman was holding a bale at mid-chest without breaking a sweat.

"Of course. This is a working farm, after all."

"But *you* work?"

He shot her a smarmy look, but it felt differently on his face than it normally did. He picked up a bale, aware of how she was looking at his arms. "I work." Then he flexed.

She could be quite lovely when she blushed—as she was doing right now. She wasn't a traditionally beautiful woman, what with her strong jaw, dark hair that brushed her shoulders and her flannel shirt with only one button undone, but underneath that…

She wasn't his type. But he was having trouble remembering what he liked so much about all the women he normally kept company with. Compared to Jo, they all looked…the same.

"This way," he said, leading her back to the hay room.

Working in silence, they got the hay unloaded in a matter of minutes. He carried in the final bale and turned to get out of her way. But he didn't walk back out to the wagon. He stood there for a moment in the dim room, watching her heft her final bale on top of his. Then she turned and caught him staring at her.

A ripple of tension moved across her shoulders and he thought she was going to blow past him and rush for the open air. After all, they could do things in this hay room and no one would be the wiser. But she'd made her position pretty damned clear. If she stormed out of here, he wouldn't be the least bit surprised.

She didn't. Instead, she hooked her thumbs in her belt, leaned back against the hay bales and looked at him as if she was waiting for him to make his move. No overt come-on, no suggestive posturing. Just standing there, watching him watch her.

He knew what he wanted to do. He wanted to press her back against the bale and find out if she liked things soft and sweet and pretty like her blush or if she wanted it rough and tough.

But, as she stood there and waited, he *didn't* want to. Which didn't make any sense. Of course he wanted to kiss her, to touch her. But…

Something stopped him.

She was starting to unnerve him. Suddenly, he realized this must be what his horse felt like. She could stand here all day and wait for him to get bored.

So he did something. Something that bordered on being out of character for him. He did not ask her to dinner and he did not ask her if she'd like to soak in his hot tub with a view. "Would you like to see the Appaloosas?"

The corner of her mouth moved up into what might have been a pleased smile on someone else. It was almost as if that had been the thing she'd hoped he'd say. It was weird how good that little half-smile of approval made him feel. "I would."

He walked her through the barn to the nearby pasture where his Appaloosas were grazing. "I've got four breeding mares," he told her, pointing the spotted horses out to her. "We usually get two foals a year out of them. We have between six and nine on site at any given time."

"What do you do with them?"

"Sell them. They're good workhorses, but I sell a lot to Hollywood. I focus on the blanket-with-spots coloring, which is what producers want." He pointed to the nearest mare. "See? Black in the front, white flank with spots in the back."

She gave him that look again, the one that said he was making a fool of himself. "I know what a blanket Appaloosa is, you know."

He grinned at her. She did *not* cut him any slack. Why did he like it so much? "Sorry. The women I normally hang out with don't know much about horses."

"I'm not like other women."

He couldn't help it. He leaned toward where she was, his voice dropping an octave. "A fact I've become more aware of every day."

She let him wait a whole minute before she acknowledged what he'd said. "Are you hitting on me?"

"No." Even though she wasn't looking at him, he still saw the way her face twisted in disagreement, so he added, "By all agreed-upon Dude Law, this barely breaks the threshold for flirting."

She snorted in what he hoped was amusement. "Do you have an Appaloosa stallion?"

"No. I use different stock to keep the genetics clean."

"Smart," she said in the kind of voice that made it clear she hadn't expected a smart answer.

"I told you, I know a great deal about horses." He pointed out the yearling. "That's Snowflake. I've got a breeder who's interested in him out in New York if his coat fills in right."

"Why do you breed them?"

"I like them. They've got history. The story is that my great-grandfather, Phillipe Beaumont, drove a team of Percherons he'd brought over from France across the Great Plains after the Civil War and then traded one with the Nez Perce for one of their Appaloosas—he considered that a fair trade."

She looked at him again, those soft hazel eyes almost level with his. If this were any other woman in the world, he'd touch her. He was thinking about doing it anyway, but he didn't want to push his luck.

He'd basically promised that they were just here to look at the horses, so that's all they were going to do. He'd given his word. He wanted the woman, but he wanted her to want him, too.

And she just might, given the way she was looking at him, her full lips slightly parted and her head tilted to one side as if she really wouldn't mind a kiss. "You keep Appaloosas because your great-grandfather bought one a hundred and fifty years ago?"

"More like a hundred and thirty years. Of course, he only got the one Appaloosa, so my mares don't go back that far. But the Percherons do."

Man, he could get lost in her eyes. He could only guess at what she was thinking right now.

Because she didn't seem to be thinking about horses. "You spend a lot of time out here with them?"

"Always have. The farm is a more pleasant place to be than the Beaumont Mansion."

That was the understatement of the year. Growing up a Beaumont in the shadow of Hardwick's chosen son, Chadwick, had been an experience in privileged neglect. No one had paid a bit of attention to Phillip. His mother had divorced his father when he was five, but Hardwick had retained full custody of the boys for reasons that, as far as Phillip could tell, could only be called spiteful.

Hardwick had devoted all of his attention to Chadwick, grooming him to run the Beaumont Brewery. Phillip?

No one had cared. When his mother had lost the lengthy custody battles, she acted as if Phillip had purposefully chosen Hardwick just to punish her. Then Hardwick had gotten married again—and again, and again—and always paid more attention to his new wife and his new children. Because there were always new wives and new children.

Phillip had been all but invisible in his own home. He could come and go and do as he pleased and it just didn't matter. The freedom was heady. What had grades mattered to him? They hadn't. Teachers didn't dare make him toe the line because of his father's reputation. He'd discovered that, although no one cared a bit for him at home, people out in the world cared about his name a great deal—so much so that he could break every rule in the book and no one would stop him.

By the time he'd gotten to college, he had his pick of women. He had a well-deserved reputation as a man who would satisfy. Women were complicated. They liked to feel sexy and desirable and wanted. Most of them wanted to feel swept away, but some liked to call the shots. He'd learned that early.

Not much had changed since then. His reputation always preceded him. Women came to him, not the other way around. And his brother Chadwick only cared what he did when he thought Phillip had made a spectacle of the Beaumont name. Chadwick was the only person who ever tried to make Phillip toe the line, and Phillip made him pay for it.

No one stopped Phillip Beaumont. Except possibly a horse trainer named Jo Spears.

"That surprises me," she said in her quiet tone. "You seem more like a big-city kind of man."

That's what she said. What he heard was 'party guy.' And he couldn't blame her. Beaumont Farms wasn't exactly the social center of the world.

"The big city has its advantages, it's true. But sometimes it's good to take a break from the hustle and bustle and slow down."

He'd always come out to the farm to get away from the tension that was his family. Here, there were rules. If he wanted to ride his pony, he had to brush that pony and clean the stall. If he wanted to drive the team with a wagon, he had to learn how to hook up the harness. And if he wanted to gentle the foals and get them used to being haltered, he had to be able to hold on to a rearing animal.

When he'd been a kid, this had been the only place in his life where there were consequences for his actions. If he screwed up or only half-assed something, then he fell off the horse because the girth wasn't tight enough or got kicked for startling a horse from behind.

But it'd also been the place where he'd done things right and gotten rewarded for it. When he got his pony saddled all by himself, he'd gotten to go for a ride with his father. When he'd learned how to walk around horses without scaring them, he'd gotten to spend more time working with them. And when he learned how to ask a horse to do something the right way, he'd gotten to race and jump and have a hell of a good time.

He'd gotten the attention of his father. Hardwick Beaumont had been a horseman through and through. It came with the Beaumont name and Hardwick had lived up to it.

His horse obsessions had followed all the usual paths—expensive Thoroughbred horses in an attempt to win the Triple Crown, lavish show horses designed to win gold and the Percherons, of course.

Phillip had been too big to be a jockey, so he couldn't ride for the Crown. He'd been a good rider, but never great. But he could talk horses and help with the Percherons. When it'd been just the two of them out on the farm, his father had not only noticed him, but approved of him. He'd never won the Triple Crown, but his jockeys and trainers had won the Preakness three times and Churchill Downs twice.

Horses had been the only thing that had set Phillip apart from Chadwick. Phillip was good with horses. He understood the consequences—never understood it better than when Maggie May had died. Horses were valuable and, as the second son, it was his duty to keep that part of the Beaumont legacy alive.

The only time he missed his father was when he was on the farm.

"So, you work," Jo repeated, calling him back to himself.

She wasn't looking at him, but he felt as if he had her full attention. "Yes."

"Do you clean tack?"

The question would have been odd coming from any other woman. Somehow, he wasn't surprised she'd asked it. "I have on occasion."

He could only see half her face, but he didn't miss the quick smile. "Can you be in the paddock around eight tomorrow morning?" Then she angled her face in his direction. "Or is that too early for you?"

Hell, yeah it was early. But he wasn't going to let her know that. "I'll bring the coffee." Doubt—he recognized it now—flashed over her face. "You take yours black, right?"

She held his gaze for another long moment. Finally, she said, "Yup," and let it drop.

"You want to drive the team back to the barn?"

She brightened. "They're beautiful animals. I've never worked with them before."

He felt himself relax. He could talk horses, after all. As long as they came back to the horses, she wouldn't look at him as if she was disappointed in him. "Well, you've come to the right place. Have you seen any of the foals?"

Her eyes lit up. She really was striking. So very tough but underneath that… "Foals?" Then she sighed. "I need to get back to Sun."

"Maybe tomorrow afternoon?"

She dropped her chin and looked up at him through thick lashes. "I guess that depends on how well you clean tack."

There was that challenge again, writ large in both words and actions. Everything about her was a bet—one that he wanted to take. "I guess it does."

He could prove himself in the morning cleaning tack. It didn't matter why. He would show her that he knew his stuff and that he was good with his hands.

And then? He'd get out his carriage, the one with the roomy padded seat and the bonnet that provided a modicum of privacy. It was a big farm. Plenty of shady lanes hidden behind old-growth trees where a couple could have a picnic in private.

She was a challenge, all right. But he'd bet that he could win her over, even if he had to clean tack to do it.

Six

Phillip strolled up to the paddock at 7:58, two mugs in hand. "Good morning," he called out. "What are you doing?"

"Waiting for you," she replied, setting the cutter saddle down on the blanket she'd laid out in the middle of the paddock. Betty was nibbling the untrampled grass near the gate, but she looked up as Phillip approached and went to meet him.

Behind Jo, Sun whinnied. She turned in time to see him trot past his buckets. Checking for carrots? That was a good sign.

"I'm on time *and* under budget." His tone—light and teasing and promising good things—made her look up. Even though the dawning light of morning was just casting the farm in pinks and yellows, Phillip's smile was warm and bright. He reached through the gate to rub Betty's little head. "I even brought carrots."

Oh. He'd shaved today. The four-day growth he'd been

working on was gone and suddenly he looked more like the man in the commercials—the one to whom women flocked.

No flocking. She would not flock. This exercise in tack was not about spending time with Phillip Beaumont. This was about the fact that Phillip was Sun's owner. She was just encouraging the relationship between the horse and the man.

"Grab the saddle," she said, nodding toward the Trilogy English jumping saddle she'd set on top of the fence. The cutter saddle was by far the more complicated of the two saddles. Cleaning it would take her hours. If Phillip knew what he was doing, the jumping saddle would take him forty-five minutes. An hour, tops. And if he didn't know what he was doing...

Why did she want him to be able to clean a saddle so badly? It was just tack. True, both saddles were high-end. She felt bad about using them, but there hadn't been a lower-end option. She took some comfort in the fact that this wouldn't be a hardship for someone with the Beaumont name.

Phillip's brows jumped up. "And?"

"And open the gate, walk in slowly, and have a seat." She motioned to the blanket on the ground.

"What about the carrots?"

"Hang on to them. We might need them later."

"Okay." He grabbed the saddle and opened the gate.

Sun stopped trotting, stood still and watched Phillip—at least, until the gate was latched. Then he went into a round of bucking that would have won him first prize at any rodeo.

Phillip froze, just two steps inside the fence. Jo turned to watch Sun throw his fit. He'd been calming down for her quite nicely, but she couldn't say this was a surprise.

He didn't like change and another person in the paddock was a big change. Even if it was the person with the carrots.

"Should I leave?" Phillip asked. She had to admire the fact that he didn't sound as though he was quaking in his boots. If he could keep calm, Sun would chill out faster.

"Nope. Just walk toward me. Slowly."

She kept her eyes on Sun as Phillip made the long walk. Sun wasn't bucking as high as he had during the first days and he certainly wasn't working himself into a lather.

Phillip made it to the blanket, handed her a thermal mug and set the saddle down at his feet. Betty sniffed the saddle while Jo sniffed the coffee. "Thanks." Black, with no secret ingredients. Had he spiked his coffee again this morning? If so, he'd gone light. She didn't catch a hint of whiskey about him.

Instead, he smelled like…she leaned closer. Bay rum spice, warm and clean and tempting.

When he said, "Now what?" she almost jumped out of her skin.

Right. She had a job here, one that required her full attention. They couldn't sit down while Sun was bucking. The risk that he might charge was too great. But she was going to stop standing in this paddock today, by God. She could feel it. "We wait. Welcome to standing."

So they stood. Betty wandered back over to where the grass was greener, completely unconcerned with either Sun's antics or what the people were doing.

How long could Phillip do this? Thus far, he had not struck her as a man of inaction. Which was admirable, but there was something to be said for just watching. She was thinking he'd only last about five minutes before he started to get twitchy. Seven at the most.

After about ten minutes, Phillip asked, "How long is this going to take?"

She tried not to smile. *Not bad.* "As long as it takes."

Another five minutes passed. "Maybe I should give him the carrots? Would that help?"

"Nope."

"Why not?" Phillip was starting to sound exasperated. She wondered which one would crack first—the horse or the man.

"Because," she explained, "if you give him the carrots now, he'll associate carrots with temper tantrums. Wait until he's managed to be calm for at least ten minutes."

"Oh. Right."

They were silent for another five minutes as Sun continued to go through the motions.

"We're really just going to stand here?"

She couldn't help giving him a look. "Do you have a problem with silence?"

"No," he defended a little quicker than was necessary. Which was almost the same as a yes. "This just seems pointless."

This was not going how she'd thought it would. Yesterday, he'd seemed like a man who would understand what it took to retrain a horse. "Do you have something else you'd rather do than train your multi-million-dollar horse?"

That made him look a little more sheepish, which had the unfortunate side effect of making him look positively adorable. "No."

Sun reared up, which drew their attention. "See? He's a smart horse," she told Phillip. "He's picking up on your impatience. Just *be*, okay?"

"Okay."

She didn't think he could do it. Hell, the only reason she could do it was because she'd been in traction for a few months, physically incapable of doing anything but be still and quiet and painfully aware of her surroundings.

Months in traction, then almost another year out on her parents' ranch just sitting around while her body healed, watching the world. God, she'd been so bored in the beginning. She'd hurt and couldn't take any of the good painkillers and none of the nurses would bring her a beer. She'd tried watching television, but that had only made things worse.

Then her granny, Lina Throws Spears, had come to sit with her. Sometimes, Lina had told her old Lakota stories about trickster coyotes and spiders, but most of the time she'd just sat, looking out the window at the parking lot.

It'd almost driven Jo insane. Lina had always been weird, burning sage and drinking tea. But then Jo had started to actually see the world around her. People came with balloons and hopeful smiles for new babies. People left with tissues in their hands and tears in their eyes when someone died. They fought and sometimes met for quickies in the back of the parking lot. Some smoked. Some drank. Some talked on cell phones.

They did things for reasons. And, if you paid attention, those reasons weren't that hard to figure out.

When she'd finally been discharged and went home, she hadn't been good for much. So she sat on her parents' porch and watched the ranch.

It'd always been such a boring place—or so she'd thought. But then she'd actually sat still and paid attention.

She'd noticed things that she'd never seen before, like the snake that lived under the porch and the starlings that lived in the barn. The barn cat napped in the sun until the sun moved and then he went mousing.

There'd been something peaceful about it. She watched the wind blow through the pastures and storms blow in. She watched her dad saddle the horses and her mom bake pies.

The world had felt...okay. She'd felt okay in it. She'd never been able to say that before. And then, when Oaty had survived that fire, she'd watched him and figured out what he'd been trying to say.

But getting to the point where she could understand a horse as messed up as Oaty had taken her well over a year. It was ridiculous to think that a man like Phillip Beaumont—known for his wild ways—would be able to just stand here and pay attention because she asked him to half an hour ago.

And he couldn't. He was trying, that she could see, but within fifteen minutes, his fingers were tapping against his legs, beating out a staccato rhythm of impatience.

Not surprisingly, Sun picked up on this. His hoofbeats against the ground nearly matched Phillip's rhythm.

"Stop," she said, reaching over and pulling his hand away from his leg.

Which meant she was now holding his hand.

His fingers wrapped around hers. "Sorry." He didn't sound particularly sorry.

She stood *very* still. Aside from handshakes, she hadn't touched a man in so long. The feeling of something as simple as holding hands was...

It was a lot. Heat bloomed from where his skin touched hers, which set off a chain reaction across her body. Her nipples tightened. They went hard in a way she'd forgotten about. Her heart rate picked up and she knew she was blushing but she couldn't help it.

Skin on skin. It was only a light touch, but for the first time in a very long time, desire coursed through her.

Oh, no—this was bad.

She couldn't pull her hand away. The sensations flooding her body—the weight growing heavy between her legs, the heat clouding her thinking—left her unable to do anything but stand there and *keep* touching him.

As she spun out of control, both Phillip and Sun seemed

to be calming down. Instead of drumming his fingers against his leg, he went to…

To rubbing his thumb against her skin.

Jo's head swam as desire hit her hard. One of the most attractive, wealthy, available men in the country was stroking the back of her hand.

Once, it'd taken far less than this—coffee in the morning, horses in the afternoon, a light touch—to get her back to a room. Or into a car. Or even just up against a wall. Once, all a guy would have had to do was buy her a drink and maybe tell her she was hot. *Maybe*. That'd been all the reason she needed to go off with another man she didn't know, to wake up in a place she couldn't remember.

How was Phillip doing this to her? He hadn't pinned her against a wall or bitten her in that space between her neck and her shoulder or anything. He was just holding her hand! It shouldn't make her think of being pinned against walls and being bitten or touched. It just shouldn't.

In her confusion, she made the mistake of looking at him. He turned his head at almost the same time and smiled. That was it. Nothing but a nice, sexy, hot smile. For her.

Ten long years of no touching and no smiling caught up to Jo in milliseconds. She *wanted* him to pin her against the wall and bite that place on her neck. And a few other things. She wanted to feel his hands on a whole bunch of places. She wanted to know exactly how good this cowboy was.

This—this was exactly why she'd abstained from men. Something as small as a single touch having this much effect on her—it was like an alcoholic saying he could have one sip and be just fine.

Men, like drinking, were an all-or-nothing proposition for her. That's just the way it was. She was not going to fall off the wagon because Phillip Beaumont was gorgeous, thoughtful, rich and worried about his horse. She'd worked too hard to be the person she was now.

The look in his eyes got deeper. *Warmer.* And damn it all if it didn't make him look even hotter.

He was close enough that Jo could lean forward and kiss him.

Thank God, Sun saved her. He came to a halt in front of them, clearly trying to figure out what new thing the humans were doing.

Which made Phillip turn those beautiful eyes away from her. "Hey," he said in a quiet, strong voice that sent shivers racing down the back of her neck. "He stopped."

What's more than that, the horse didn't start back up when Phillip spoke. He just stood there. Then he *walked* over to where the buckets were. He stuck his nose into the food bucket and then looked back at Phillip. It was an amazing development.

"He wants a carrot," she told Phillip.

"Should I give him one?"

"Go ahead and put one in the bucket, but make sure he sees you've got more. After all, he did calm down and ask politely. He's earned a reward."

At this observation, Phillip turned a dazzling smile in her direction. "Do I get a reward, too?" he said in that same strong voice as the pad of his thumb moved over her hand again.

This time, the shivers were stronger.

His mouth settled from the dazzling smile into the grin that was so wicked she couldn't help but think about him scraping his teeth against her bare flesh as he pulled the snaps of her shirt apart....

"No," she gritted out, hoping she didn't sound as if she was about to start swooning.

She wasn't fooling him. She wasn't even fooling herself. He leaned forward, the air between them crystalizing into something so sharp it almost cut her. His grip on her hand tightened as he tried to pull her toward him. "Why not? I calmed down. I asked politely."

"You didn't do it on your own." She was desperate to stop touching him and completely unable to do so. "You have to earn a reward."

"And how do I do that?" Somehow, he managed to make it sound innocent and sensual all at the same time.

"Carrots for the horse. Then tack. Done right."

She jerked her hand out of his grasp, desperate.

He leaned forward, the air between them growing hot. He was going to kiss her and she was going to let him and if that happened, would she be able to control herself? Or would she be gone? Again?

His gaze searched hers. God, she probably looked like a deer in the headlights—blinded by his sheer sex appeal.

"One condition—I get to choose my own reward." His voice dropped to a dangerous level—silky and sensual and promising all sorts of good things. "I don't like carrots." Then he turned and began to walk to the bucket. Slowly.

Sun removed himself to the far side of the paddock and paced slowly. Jo knew she should be thrilled at this progress. The horse and the man were actually communicating.

So why did she feel so terrible? No, not terrible. *Weird*. Her skin felt hot and her knees had yet to stop shaking and her heart was pounding fast.

Then Phillip was walking back toward her.

Oh, God. She wasn't sure she was strong enough for this. She'd spent the last ten years convincing herself that she could get through the nights without a drink or a man or a man holding a drink.

Phillip Beaumont was going to be her undoing.

"So," he said when he reached her again. He waved at the saddles. "What are we doing with the tack?"

"Cleaning it."

Instead of looking as if he had her right where he wanted her, he looked more off-balance. Good. She shouldn't be the only one off-balance here. "It's…not dirty."

"Do you want to ride?" His eyes widened in surprise and she realized what she'd said. "I mean, the horse. Do you want to ride the horse? *Sun*."

Sweet merciful heavens, she could not be embarrassing herself more if she tried.

"Yes." But the way Phillip said it left the question of which kind of riding he was interested in doing wide open.

"Then you clean tack."

Seven

What did he want for a reward?

Phillip knew. He wanted to open his door tonight with a bottle of wine chilling on the table and then skip dinner entirely and head straight to the hot tub. He'd love to see how Jo's body filled out a bikini—or nothing at all. Nude was always fashionable.

He'd love his reward to go on for most of the evening. It'd been close to a week since he'd first woken up alone in his own bed and he missed having a woman to spend the evening with.

But that wasn't necessarily the reward he'd ask for.

He might ask for a kiss. That was a pretty big *might*. Her hand—warm and gentle but firm in his—had seemed to say that she was interested in a kiss. Combined with the entirely feminine blush that had pinked her cheeks? Yeah, a kiss would be good.

But he had to earn it first—by cleaning saddles, of all things. When was the last time he'd had to work so hard for something as simple as a kiss? He shouldn't be having fun. He should be frustrated that she was being so damned stubborn or insulted that his considerable charms were falling on mostly deaf ears.

But he wasn't. It struck him as beyond strange that he was actually enjoying the slow process of seducing Jo Spears.

So he cleaned a not-dirty saddle.

Normally, Phillip did not enjoy cleaning tack. It was his second least-favorite job on the farm, after shoveling stalls, the one he'd always had to do when he messed up.

But instead of feeling like a punishment, sitting on a blanket in the middle of a paddock taking apart a saddle and wiping it down—next to Jo—wasn't awful. In fact, it bordered on pleasant. The weather was beautifully sunny, with a bright breeze that ruffled the leaves on the trees.

As Phillip cleaned his saddle, he kept half an eye on the horse as he moved around the paddock. Sometimes he walked, sometimes he trotted, but he didn't race or buck or generally act like a horse that was out of control. That made Phillip feel pretty good.

But what made him feel better was the woman sitting next to him.

He had been patient and waited for her to touch him first. True, he hadn't been expecting her to grab his hand. He hadn't realized his hand had actually been moving. He'd been focused on not spooking Sun and trying to be still like she was. It'd taken a lot more energy than he'd anticipated. Who knew that standing still would be so hard?

Until she'd taken his hand. He realized she hadn't meant it as a come-on—but the way she'd reacted to his touch? The wall between them had busted wide open. She was attracted to him. He was interested in her.

Things were moving along nicely.

He kept cleaning the saddle until his feet started to fall

asleep. Boots were good for many things, but sitting on the ground wasn't one of them. "How long do we have to keep doing this?"

She leaned over to appraise his work. "Nice job."

"I had several years of practice."

"Really?" She stretched out her legs, which looked even longer and more muscular at this angle. What would it feel like to have legs that strong wrapped around his back? And how many saddles would he have to clean to find out? "How come?"

"Every time I did something wrong, I had to either clean tack or muck stalls. And when you're a hyper kid who's never had to follow rules before..." He shrugged. It was the truth, of course, but...he had never admitted that to another person.

He cleared his throat. "I cleaned a lot of tack. But it was good. I can harness the entire team of Percherons to the wagon myself."

She turned to look at him, an odd half-smile on her face. "What?"

"It's just that none of this," she replied, looking at the pile of polished leather they'd worked through, "fits with your public persona."

"There's more to me than just parties."

She grinned at him—a grin he was starting to recognize. She was about to give him some crap and she was going to enjoy doing it. He braced himself for the worst, but oddly, the fact that she was having fun made it not so bad.

"What would your lady friends say if they saw you sitting in the dirt?"

That's what she said. What he heard was superiority mixed in with a healthy dose of jealousy.

Jealous because she was interested.

Excellent. But he needed to move carefully here.

"I doubt they'd understand. Which is why they're not here." Only her. Before she could reload, he took control of the conversation. "Tell me about Betty."

Jo looked up, finding where her small donkey was now drinking from the bucket set at her height. "What do you want to know?"

"How long have you had her?" Yes, this was part of showing Jo there was more to him than a good time at a party or a family fortune. But he had to admit, he was curious.

"About ten years."

He supposed he shouldn't have been surprised by the short answer, but something in her tone indicated that perhaps not too many people had asked. "Where'd you get her?"

"My granny gave her to me." Jo sighed, as if the conversation were unavoidable and yet still painful. "I had…a rough patch. Granny thought I needed someone to keep me company. Most people would have gotten a puppy, but not Lina Throws Spears. She showed up with a donkey foal that only weighed twenty pounds." She grinned at the memory. "Itty Bitty Betty. We've been together ever since."

Phillip let that information sink in. There was a lot of it. How old was Jo? Given the faint lines around her eyes, he'd guess she wasn't in her twenties anymore.

What sort of rough patch had she had? Had someone broken her heart? That would certainly explain why she worked so hard at keeping that wall up between her and everyone else.

Letting Suzie go had hurt more than he'd expected—and that was before he'd read about her engagement to that prince. But to have a true broken heart, a man had to be in love.

After watching his parents and all of his stepparents and every horrid thing they did to each other in the name of love, Phillip would never do something as stupid as give his heart to anyone. Falling in love meant giving someone power to hurt you.

No love, no hurt. Just a long list of one-night stands that satisfied his needs quite well. Love was for the delusional. Lust was something honest and real and easily solved without risking hearts or family fortunes.

Also, what kind of name was Lina Throws Spears? Jo didn't look like an Indian—not like the ones in the movies, anyway. Her skin was tanned, but he'd always assumed that was because of the time she spent in the sun. She had a dusting of freckles across her nose and cheeks. Her hair was medium brown, not jet black.

Then there were her eyes. They were a pretty hazel color, light and soft in a woman who otherwise could appear hard.

On the other hand, there was that whole communing-with-the-animals thing she did. That certainly fit with his preconceived notions of American Indians.

"Yes?"

He quickly looked away. "What?"

Jo sighed again. "Go on. You know you're dying to ask."

"Throws Spears?"

"Granny—and my dad—are full-blooded Lakota Sioux. My mom's white. Any other questions?"

"You shortened your name?"

"My dad did."

Her tone brooked no warmth. Right. The topic of family was off-limits. He got that. His own family tree was so complicated that instead of a sturdy, upright oak it resembled a banyan tree that grew new trunks everywhere.

It was time to change the subject. "Where does Betty sleep?"

"If it's nice out, she stays in a pasture, but she's house trained," she said, nodding to the trailer.

"Really?"

That was a nice smile. "Really. I made a harness for her when we're driving. She sits up front. Likes to stick her nose out the window."

This bordered on the most ridiculous thing he had ever heard. "And you're sure she's a donkey and not a dog in disguise?"

"Very sure." She shot him a look that seemed to be the opposite of the hard tone she'd had when discussing her family. "Tomorrow, I'll saddle her up."

He looked at the small, fuzzy donkey. He couldn't quite imagine Betty with a saddle. "*Really?*" When Jo nodded, he added, "I…I look forward to seeing that."

She grinned. "Everyone does. Come on." Jo leaned back and stood, stretching her back. Which thrust out her chest.

From his angle, the view was amazing. His body responded with enthusiasm. Damn. This was going to make standing up even more difficult. "Where are we going?" It'd be nice if hot tubs or beds were the answer but somehow he knew it wouldn't be.

He managed to get to his feet, then leaned back down to grab his saddle. He'd spent close to an hour and a half getting the damned thing polished to a high shine.

"Leave it," Jo instructed.

"But I *cleaned* it."

"Leave it," she repeated in that no-nonsense tone. Then she began to walk to the gate.

"Better be a damn good reward," he muttered as he left all his hard work behind. He had a bad feeling about this.

Jo held the gate open for him, which meant it wasn't his fault that he had to pass close enough to her that he could count the freckles on her nose. She swung the gate behind him, but didn't step away. He didn't either. Close enough to touch, they both leaned against the now-closed gate. "Explain to me why we left the saddles in there? You know Sun is probably going to destroy them. Do you have any idea how much they cost?"

"You're already showing him you're not going to shoot him with a tranq gun or do anything else scary. Now you're going to show him that saddles and bridles are also not scary."

"But—"

"Shh." She had her eyes trained on the horse. "Just watch."

A damn good reward, he thought as he tried to rein in his irritation.

He watched. Trotting in looping circles, Sun looked at them, at the saddles and then at the bucket where Phillip had left the carrots.

Suddenly, Jo's fingers closed around his. "Be still," she said in that low voice again.

He hadn't realized he was moving, but did it matter? No, not with her fingers curling around his. Her touch did things to him—things that had nothing to do with being still and had everything to do with wanting to keep on moving—moving his lips over her fingers, her neck, her lips, his body moving over hers, with hers.

She must have felt it, too, because she turned her head toward him and favored him with one of those half-smiles.

He turned his hand over without letting go of her so they were palm-to-palm. He interlaced their fingers without looking away from Sun. After a moment, her hand relaxed into his.

It took everything he had to *not* lift her hand and press it to his lips, but he didn't. She'd made the first move and he'd countered with his own. Now it was her turn. If he skipped a turn, she might stop playing the game.

Then her fingers tightened on his. No mistaking it. They were holding hands in a way that had only the smallest of connections to what was happening in the paddock.

Not that the paddock wasn't interesting. Sun's loops were getting tighter and slower as he closed in on the bucket and carrots. Just when Phillip thought he would eat them, Sun spun and made straight for the saddles.

Oh, no. The horse hit the saddles with everything he had—and, considering he hadn't been bucking for hours on end, that was a lot. Phillip winced as Sun ground the saddles into the dirt.

The whole thing took less than five minutes. Betty stood off to the side, watching with an air of boredom. Then, head held high, Sun pranced over to the bucket and ate his carrots as if he'd planned it like that from the beginning.

"Some reward," Phillip muttered. He'd been upset about Sun before, but this was the first time he was out-and-out furious with the beast. That was an expensive saddle—and the one she'd been cleaning wasn't cheap, either. If his brother Chadwick knew that the horse trainer was letting Sun destroy several thousands of dollars of tack, he'd have her thrown off the premises. And possibly him, too.

"Stupid horse."

"Smart horse." Jo squeezed his hand, but that smile? That was for the horse.

"Why are you smiling? He ruined those saddles. *And* ate my carrots."

She notched an eyebrow as she cast him a sideways glance. The sudden burst of realization made him feel as if he'd been conned. "You *knew* he was going to do that?"

"Everyone's got to start somewhere," she replied, sounding lighthearted.

All that work for nothing. "Next time, he doesn't get carrots until he can behave himself." Even as he said the words, he knew they sounded ridiculous. Was he talking about a horse or a toddler? He glared at his multi-million dollar animal. "No rewards for that kind of attitude and that's final."

"Ah." Her voice—soft and, if he wasn't mistaken, nervous—snapped his attention back to where they were still palm-to-palm.

He had something coming to him, all the more so because she'd made him do all that work. He stroked his thumb along the length of her finger. He felt a light tremor, but she didn't pull away.

"Do I get my reward now? That saddle was very clean, right before it wasn't."

She tilted her head away, as if she were debating the merits of his argument. But he couldn't miss the way her lips were quirked into a barely contained smile.

"And I didn't even kill that horse when he trashed my tack," he reminded her as he leaned in.

She didn't lean away. "True." Her voice took on a sultry note, one that invited much more than holding hands. The pupils of her eyes widened; her gaze darted down to his lips. "Is this flirting?"

She was expecting him to kiss her, but something told him not to. Not yet. The longer he defied her expectations of him, the better the odds he'd wake up with her in his bed.

"It might be." He held her hand to his lips. A simple touch, skin against skin. Even though it about killed him not to take everything she was offering, he didn't.

Without breaking the contact between them, he raised his eyes to see Jo looking at him, her eyes wide with surprise and—he hoped—desire.

Raw need pumped through his blood. He almost threw his plans out the window and swept her into his arms. She was his, waiting for him to make his move....

She dropped her gaze. "What did you want for your reward?" The question could have been coy, but there was something else in her expression.

"All I wanted," he replied, not taking his eyes off her face, "was to see that beautiful blush on you."

Of course, that wasn't all he wanted. But it'd do for now. Then, to prove his point, he let her go and stepped back.

"That's...all?" The confusion that registered on her face was so worth it.

Clearly, not a lot of people had told her she was beautiful. What a crying shame. She had a striking look that was all her own. If that wasn't beautiful, he didn't know what was.

"Well..." He looked as innocent as he could. "I was supposed to clean a saddle. The saddle is, at this moment, quite dirty so I didn't really complete my task."

She blinked, managing to pull off coy in a cowboy hat. "Funny thing about that."

"What's funny?"

It shouldn't be right to find that little look of victory—one corner of her mouth quirked up into a smile, one eyebrow raised in challenge—so damned sexy, but he did. "Tomorrow morning—you, me and some saddles."

Phillip tried to stifle a groan, but he didn't manage it. "No."

"Yes." She paused, suddenly looking unsure of herself. "If you do a good job..."

He grinned on the inside but he kept his face calm. Oh, yeah—he had her right where he wanted her.

Almost, anyway.

Behind them, someone cleared his throat. Jo stiffened, a hard look wiping away anything sultry about her. She turned away and focused on Sun.

Phillip looked past her to see Richard standing a few feet away, hat in hands and an odd look on his face.

Damn. How long had he been standing there? Had he seen Phillip kiss her hand? It'd been easy to pretend that he and Jo were alone on the farm. The other hands steered well clear of her—probably because she'd told them to—and everyone more or less left him alone. The farm operated well enough without him.

But he and Jo weren't alone.

"I've got a farm to run," he said in a voice that was pitched just loud enough for Richard to hear. "I'll stop by later to see how you're getting on with Sun."

She nodded, looking as uninterested as physically possible.

She could hide the truth from Richard, but not from him.

Eight

Eight

Jo sat at the dinette table in her trailer that night, not seeing her email. She was supposed to be replying to horse owners who were looking for a miracle, but that's not what she was doing.

Phillip Beaumont had kissed her hand. And nothing more.

If that were her only problem, it would have been enough. But it wasn't. She wasn't sure how much Richard had seen.

For the first time in a very long time, Jo was…unsure of herself. One man who, by all accounts, was a spoiled party boy with more money than sense and she had apparently lost her damned mind.

She did not fool around with clients. Under any circumstances. Beyond being a temptation back into her old ways, it was bad for business. If word got around that she was open to affairs, people might stop hiring her.

What a mess. If flirting with Phillip Beaumont was

causing such a problem for her, why on God's green Earth was she letting it go on?

Because she'd seen the look on his face when she'd hinted that if he cleaned another saddle tomorrow morning, he'd get another reward.

She should have jerked her hand out of his when he kissed it. Hell, she shouldn't have touched him at all. She should have followed her own rules—rules she had in place for a variety of exceptionally good reasons—and steered well clear of Phillip Beaumont and his reputation.

If she didn't feel such a duty to Sun, she'd pack up and drive off to another, less tempting job tomorrow. Yes, it'd be a blow to her reputation to lose Beaumont Farms as a reference, but three other trainers had already failed. Bailing on this job wouldn't end her aspirations, not like having an affair with Phillip could.

But she wouldn't abandon the horse, not when they were making such progress. Richard had told her that if she couldn't save the horse, he'd have to be put down. True, Sun might have calmed to the point where another trainer could come in and finish the job, but she didn't know if she wanted to hope for the best and never look back. That's what the old her would have done. That's not what the woman she was now did.

Her only consolation was that she had rediscovered her restraint this afternoon when Phillip had driven past the paddock with a wagon full of hay to ask if she wanted to see his Thoroughbreds. Then he'd held the reins out to her.

She'd passed on his offer, saying she needed to keep an eye on Sun.

This would be so much easier if Phillip were a jerk. Some of the men—and women—who'd hired her were, in fact, total jerks. That's why she had that upfront policy of not hooking up or dating. That's why she kept her trailer door locked.

But Phillip wasn't a jerk. At least, not once he'd sobered up.

He cleaned tack because she asked him to. He tried to be still because it was important to Sun, even if he didn't totally succeed. He let her drive his Percheron team. Hell, he brought her coffee.

That wasn't jerkiness. That was thoughtfulness.

She had no idea how to respond to it.

Crap, she was in so much trouble.

This was a sign of how far she'd come. The old Jo would have embraced the trouble she was in and gone looking for more. She shouldn't beat herself up for encouraging Phillip, not really. She should be proud of the fact that she'd resisted his considerable charms and good looks thus far.

Now she just had to keep doing that.

In the midst of losing to herself in a debate, she heard something that sounded suspiciously like shouting. Loud, but muffled, shouting.

She scowled at the clock. That wasn't right. It was close to ten in the evening. The hired hands had all gone home before five. The whole farm was usually quiet at night, with the exception of the guards who checked the barns every other hour.

Not this evening. The shouting was louder now. She could make out two different voices.

Betty, she thought in a panic. The weather was supposed to be clear, so Jo had left the little donkey out in the pasture across the drive from Sun's paddock.

Moving fast, she slipped her jeans back on and shoved her feet into her boots. Thankfully, she hadn't taken her shirt off yet, so she didn't have to mess with the buttons. She left the trailer and grabbed her pistol from the glove box, tucking it into the back of her waistband. If someone was trying to take Betty or Sun or any other horse on this property, she wanted to catch them in the act. Then she could hold them until the guards came back around. She'd interrupted attempted robberies before. She knew how to handle her weapon.

She slipped along the side of her trailer and peeked out. A pair of headlights pointed into Sun's paddock and the horse was going nuts.

Two men were arguing in front of the headlights. She realized with a start that one of the men was Phillip. The other was slightly taller, slightly broader and had a slightly deeper voice but otherwise, he could have been Phillip's twin.

Chadwick Beaumont? Who else could it be?

Keeping to the shadows, she edged closer. They weren't trying to be quiet but she was having trouble making out what they were arguing about.

"...be insane!" Phillip yelled as he paced away then spun back to face his brother.

"The company—and, I might add, the family—cannot afford to keep standing idle while you throw good money after bad and you know it." Chadwick's voice was level, bordering on cruel. This was not a man who could be easily moved.

Phillip was anything but level. "The Percherons are not throwing money away," he shouted, flinging his hands around as if he were throwing money around. "They're our brand name!"

"Are they?" Chadwick sneered. "I thought *you* were our brand name. The face of Beaumont Beer. God knows you stick that face out enough."

Behind them, Sun made a noise that was closer to a scream than a whinny. Jo winced. How long would it take for the horse to calm down after this?

But the men didn't notice the horse. They were too lost in their argument.

Phillip threw up his hands. "Do you know what it'll do

to our public goodwill if we get rid of the Percherons? Do you have *any* idea?"

"This farm costs millions of dollars to operate," Chadwick countered so smoothly that Jo didn't have any doubt he'd anticipated this defense. "And all your pet projects cost several million more." At this, he threw a glance toward Sun, who was flat-out racing, just like he'd been the day Jo had shown up. The way Chadwick looked at the horse made Jo think that, if he'd been in charge, he would have let Richard put the animal down without hesitation. "To say nothing of all your little 'escapades.'"

As he paced, Phillip groaned. It was the sort of noise a man might make if he'd been punched in the kidneys. "Do you understand nothing about marketing? For God's sake, Chadwick—even Matthew—could explain how this works! People love the Percherons. *Love* them. And you want to just throw that all away?"

"Love," Chadwick intoned, "doesn't run a company."

Phillip whipped back to his brother, his fists balled. Jo flinched. If they started to brawl, she'd have to break them up. "You got that right, you heartless bastard. Can your bean-counting brain wrap itself around the damage you'll cost us with consumers? The Percherons are a part of this company, Chadwick. You can't sell them off any more than you can sell the company."

The silence that fell between the two men was so cold that Jo shivered.

"I already sold the company."

Jo's mouth dropped open, just as Phillip's had. "You… *what?*" Jo wasn't sure she'd ever heard Phillip sound so wounded. She couldn't blame him.

"I'm not going to work myself into an early grave so that I can pay for your failed horses or Frances's failed art or even Byron's failed romances," Chadwick said in a voice as hard as iron. "I've worked for ten years to keep the Beaumont family going and I'm sick of it. AllBev made an offer. The board accepted it. It's *done*. We'll announce when the lawyers give us the go-ahead."

Phillip gaped at him. "But…you…Dad…the company!"

"Hardwick Beaumont is dead, Phillip. He's been dead for years. I don't have to prove myself to him anymore and neither do you." Something in Chadwick's tone changed. For a moment, he sounded…kind. It was at such odds with the hard man she'd been listening to that Jo had to shake her head to make sure the same person was speaking. "I'm getting married."

"You're *what*? Aren't you already married?"

"My ex-wife is now just that—my ex. I'm starting over, Phillip. I'm going to be happy. You should do the same. Figure out who you are if you aren't Hardwick's second son."

Phillip's mouth open, closed, then opened again. "You can't sell the farm. You can't, Chadwick. Please. I need this place. I need the horses. Without them…"

Chadwick was unmoved. Anything that might have been understanding or brotherly was gone. "The new owners of the Brewery have no desire to take on the sinking money pit that is this farm. They do not want the Percherons and I can't afford them. I can't afford *you*."

Jo must have gasped or stepped on a twig or something because suddenly both men spun.

"Who's there?" they demanded in unison.

She stepped into the edge of the light. "It's me. Jo."

Phillip gave her something that might have been a smile. Chadwick only glared. "Who?" He turned his attention to Phillip. "Who's she?"

Phillip's shoulders slumped in defeat. "Jo Spears. The horse trainer who's saving Sun."

Jo nodded her head in appreciation. He'd gotten the saving part right.

Chadwick was not impressed. "Now you're keeping women on the farm?" He made a noise of disgust. "And how much is this costing?"

Jo bristled. Clearly, Chadwick Beaumont did not have his brother's way with words *or* women.

When Phillip didn't answer, Chadwick shook his head in disgust. He said, "I only came out here to warn you because we're family. If I were you, I'd start getting rid of the *excess*—" he looked at Sun, then at Jo "—as soon as possible on your own terms. Save yourself the embarrassment of a public auction." He walked back to his car. "If you don't, I will."

Then Chadwick Beaumont slammed the door shut, put the shiny little sports car in reverse, and peeled out.

Phillip dropped his head.

And stood absolutely still.

Chadwick was going to sell the horses. All of them. Not just Sun or the Appaloosas or even the Thoroughbreds, but *all* of them. The Beaumont Percherons—a self-sustaining herd of about a hundred horses that went back a hundred and twenty-three years—would be gone. The farm would be gone. The farmhouse that his great-grandfather had built as a refuge from the rest of the world—gone. And what would Phillip have once the horses and the farm were gone?

Nothing. Not a damned thing.

God, he needed a drink.

Sun made that unholy noise again, but Phillip couldn't even look. It was so tempting to blame Sun for this. The horse had cost seven million dollars. He'd never seen his brother so mad as when Phillip had told Chadwick about the horse. If only Sun hadn't cost so much....

But that was a cop-out and he knew it. Phillip was the one who'd bought the horse. And all the other horses. And the tack, the wagons, the carriages. He was the one who'd hired the farm hands. And Jo.

Jo.

Almost as if he'd called her, she came to stand next to him. Her hand slipped into his and her fingers intertwined with his. She felt…smaller than she had this afternoon.

He felt smaller.

"Come on," she said in that low voice that brooked no arguments. She gave his hand a gentle tug and he stumbled after her.

She led him to her trailer. Any other time, Phillip would have been excited about this development. But he couldn't even think about sex right now. Not when he was on the verge of losing everything he'd worked for.

She basically pulled him up the narrow trailer steps and then pushed him toward a small dinette table. "Have a seat."

He sat. Heavily. *Jesus.* He knew that the company was in trouble. But he had no idea that Chadwick would do this. That he'd even been considering selling the Brewery, much less the farm. He'd thought…Chadwick would win. That's what Chadwick did. He'd fight off the acquisition and save the company and everything would continue on as it had before.

But Chadwick hadn't. Wouldn't. He was going to get rid of the farm. Of Phillip.

This was…this was his home. Not the Beaumont family mansion, not the apartment in the city. The farm was where he'd always felt the most normal. *Been* the most normal. He'd been able to do something that had made him proud. Had made his father proud of him. Hardwick Beaumont had never had a second look for his second son out in the real world. But here, talking horses, his father had noticed him. Told him he'd done a good job. Been so proud of him.

And now it was going to be taken away from him.

Jo made some noise. Phillip looked up to see her filling an electric kettle, a small handgun set on the counter next to her. "What?"

"Making tea," she said in that same low and calming and ridiculously self-assured voice—the one she used when she was working with Sun.

He laughed, even though there was nothing funny about tea. "Got any whiskey to go with that? I could use a drink."

She paused while reaching into a cabinet. The pause lasted only a moment, but he felt the disapproval anyway.

He didn't care. He needed a drink. Several drinks. Maybe a fifth of drinks. He couldn't deal with losing the farm. With his horses. With Sun. Everything.

"I don't have any whiskey."

"I'll settle for vodka."

"I don't have anything but tea and a couple of cans of soda."

He laughed again. The universe seemed hell-bent on torturing him.

The kettle whistled—a noise that seemed to drive straight into his temple. Everything was too much right now—too much noise, too much light. Too much Jo sliding into the seat opposite him, looking at him with those big, pretty eyes of hers. His hands started to shake.

"Here." She slid a steaming mug toward him.

He looked at the tea. Insult to injury, that's what this was. It wasn't enough that he was about to lose everything he held dear. He had to have a horse trainer rub his nose in it.

The anger that peaked above the despair felt good. Well, not good—but better than the horrible darkness that was trying to swallow him inside out. "I've got whiskey at the house, you know. You're not stopping me from drinking."

She held her mug in her hands and blew on the tea, her

gaze never leaving his face. "No," she agreed, sounding too damned even, "I'm not."

"And I'm not some damned horse, either, so stop doing that whole calm-and-still bullshit," he snapped.

If she was offended, she didn't show it. Instead, she sipped the tea. "Does that help?"

"Jesus, you're doing it again. Does *what* help?"

"The blackout. Does that help?"

"It's a hell of a lot better than *this*." Logically, he knew he wasn't mad at her. She hadn't done anything but the job he'd hired her for.

But his world was ending and Chadwick was gone. Someone had to pay. And Jo was here.

"Don't you ever get tired of it?"

"You think you know me?" he said. Except it came out louder than he meant it to. "You don't know anything about me, so you can stop acting superior. You have no idea what my life is like."

"Any more than you have an idea of mine?"

He glared at her. "Fine. Just get it off your chest. Go ahead and tell me that I'm throwing my life away one drink at a time and alcohol never solved anything and blah, blah, blah."

She shrugged.

"I can stop whenever I want," he snapped.

"You just don't want to."

"I *want* a damn drink." Water pricked at his eyes. "You wouldn't understand."

"Yes," she said and this time he heard something different in her voice. "I would."

He looked up at her. She met his gaze without blinking and without deflecting. Her nose, he noticed again. It'd been broken. Without the shadows cast by her hat, it was easier to see the bump on the bridge that didn't match the rest of her.

She was beautiful. If she wasn't going to get him some whiskey, she could still sleep with him. Sex was always fine with him. He'd been chasing her for a week now with nothing more than a kiss on the hand to show for it. He could lose himself in this woman and it might make him feel better. At least for a little while.

She turned her head in one direction, then the other, giving him a better look at her nose. "I stopped."

The compliment he'd loaded up came to a screeching halt. "Stopped what?"

She set her mug down and slid out of her seat. "There was never a good reason. My parents are normal, happily married. No abuse, no alcoholism. I wasn't shy or awkward or even that rebellious." She stood and undid the top button on her shirt.

As her fingers undid the second button, his pulse began to pound. What the hell? He hadn't even busted out the compliment and she was undressing? All his hard work was paying off. He was about to get lucky. Thank God. Then he wouldn't have to think.

Except…this wasn't right. First off, there was far too much talking. But beyond that, Jo—just stripping? Jesus, he must be so messed up right now, because this wasn't how he wanted her. He didn't want her to give it up just to make him feel better. He wanted her to want him as much as he wanted her.

He didn't get the chance to tell her to wait. She went on, "Dad's Lakota, so I had my fair share of people who called me a half-breed, but doesn't everyone get teased for something?" Another button popped open.

Why was she telling him this? Even if she was trying to seduce him, this didn't seem like the proper way to go about it. But he could just see the swell of her breasts peek over the top of the shirt.

She undid another button. Unlike her nose, her breasts

were perfect. He opened his mouth to tell her just that, to try and get this seduction back on track, but he didn't get any further.

"I had my first drink in seventh grade at a Fourth of July party. A wine cooler I snagged. I opened it up and poured it into a cup and told everyone it was pink lemonade. It was good. I liked it. So I had another. And another."

She undid the last button and stood there. The curves of her breasts were tantalizingly at eye level, but she didn't move toward him, didn't shimmy or shake or anything a normal woman might have done. He leaned forward. If he could touch her, fill his hands with her soft skin and softer body, they could get to the part where they were both naked and he wasn't thinking about anything but sex. About her. That's what he wanted, wasn't it?

She turned her back to him. "By the time I was in high school, I was the resident party girl. I don't know how I graduated and I don't know how I didn't get pregnant. I have no idea how I got into college, but I did. I don't know if I ever went to a class sober. I don't remember going to that many classes."

The shirt began to slide down.

Phillip began to sweat. He tried to focus on what she was saying and not the body she was unwrapping for him, but it was a damned hard thing to attempt—a fact that was directly connected with other damned hard things happening to him right now.

"I'd wake up and not know where I was, who I was with. College guys, older guys—men I didn't know. I couldn't remember meeting them or going home with them." She shrugged, a bare shoulder going up and down. The movement pushed the shirt down even farther. "Couldn't remember the sex—couldn't remember if I wanted it or not."

Phillip tensed, torn between despair, desire and sheer confusion. Confusion won. Instead of a swath of smooth skin, Jo was revealing a back covered in puckers and ripples.

"I'd stumble back to my room and scan my phone for pictures or messages. For the memories, I told myself, but there were things I'd done…" She paused, but it was only the barest hint of emotion. "Facing them—no. It was easier to find another party and tell myself I was having a good time than it was to accept what I'd done. What I'd become."

The shirt fell off her right arm, revealing the true extent of the damage. Most of her back was scarred—horrible marks that went below the waistband of her pants. She tilted her head to the left and lifted her shoulder-length hair. Even her hairline was messed up—rough and uneven where the scars stole farther up. "The only reason I know his name is because my granny saved the article. Tony Holmes. He ran a red light, got T-boned so hard by a big SUV that it flipped the car. He wasn't buckled in. I was."

She tilted her body so he could see the contours of her back. Hidden among the mass of twisted skin were other scars—long, neat ones that looked surgical. "The car caught fire, but they got me out in time."

"Tony?"

For the first time in this dry recitation of facts, she seemed to feel something. "He wouldn't have felt the flames anyway."

Jesus. His stomach turned. This wasn't some crazy, "let's get in touch with our feelings" kind of talk. This was serious—life and death.

He didn't want to believe her—he'd never wanted to believe anything less in his life—but there was no arguing with the scars.

It could have been me, he thought. The realization made him dizzy. It *could* have been him—the wild party he didn't remember, the strange person buckled in next to him that he wouldn't have remembered, either. There was only one reason something like that hadn't happened. He wished to God that reason was because he was a responsible man.

But it wasn't. No, Ortiz—his driver—was the reason. His brothers Chadwick and Matthew had decreed that Phillip would have a driver whenever he was at a company-sponsored event. It was company policy.

A company policy that no one else in the company had to follow.

"My back was broken in two places. I shouldn't be able to walk. I shouldn't even be alive." She turned to the side to grab the shirt from where it hung off her left arm. Phillip caught a glimpse of her breast, full and heavy and his dick responded to the sight of her bare breast before she got ahold of her shirt and snapped the buttons back together.

But all he felt was cold and shaky. His head was pounding as if he had a hangover. He still wanted a drink. He dug the heels of his hands into his eyes, trying to block out the images she'd put there on purpose—images of her waking up with strangers, never really knowing what had happened. Of her trapped in a burning car next to a dead man. "I'm not like that."

"Because you don't drive?"

He nodded. He'd never been with anyone who'd died after a good party. He never did anything with anyone who didn't want it.

He felt the dinette shift as she sat back down at the table. It'd be safe to look at her. But he couldn't. He couldn't move.

"Between the back surgeries and the burn care, I was in traction in the hospital for months," she went on, as if he needed more torture. "It was a year before I could move without pain. And because I *am* an alcoholic, I never even got the good painkillers. I had to feel it all. Everything I'd done. Everything I was. I couldn't hide from it."

"How do you stand it?" Why did he have to sound as

though she was twisting the knife in his gut a quarter-turn at a time?

Because that's what she was doing. Twisting.

Except she wasn't, not really. More like she was holding up a mirror so he could see the knife he was twisting himself.

"I stopped. Stopped drinking, stopped sleeping around, stopped fighting it."

"What if…" He swallowed. *What if he couldn't stop*?

He heard the seat rustle as she leaned back. "Did you spike your coffee this morning?"

"No." But he was really wishing he had. Anything to numb the pain.

"What about yesterday?"

He shook his head. He'd thought he felt hopeless after Chadwick had driven off. But now?

He didn't know if he was coming or going.

"It's now…10:53. Another hour and seven minutes and you'll have made it through two days." She had the nerve to sound optimistic about this fact. "That's as good a place to start as any."

"Is this the part where I'm supposed to say 'One day at a time' and we sing 'Kumbaya' and then we talk about steps?"

"Nope."

"Good. Because I don't want to hear it."

"Our kind never does."

"We are not the same kind, Jo." But even as he said it, he knew it was a lie. The only difference was that she'd stopped and he hadn't.

"No," she agreed. "I have the scars to prove it."

"Does it…does it still hurt?" He didn't know if he was asking about the scars on her back or the other kind of scars.

"Not really. I have Betty now. She helps. It's only when…"

Something in her voice—something longing and wistful—made him pull his hands away from his face.

Jo was looking at him. That wasn't a surprise. The trailer was small and they were talking. But it was *how* she was looking at him. Gone was the unnatural calm.

Sitting across from him was a woman who wanted something that she would never allow herself to have.

Him.

She looked away first. "He wants you to give up," she told him as she studied the bottom of her mug.

Phillip was still trying to figure out that look, so her words took him completely off guard. "What?"

"Your brother. He expects you to run off and get so drunk that he can do whatever he wants with *your* farm and *your* animals and you won't be able to put up a fight." When she looked back up again, whatever longing he'd seen in her eyes was gone.

"What should I do?"

"That's not my place." She gave him a tight smile. "You have to decide for yourself. Fight or give up, it doesn't matter to me."

"It doesn't?" It hurt to hear that, but he wasn't sure why. "Not even a little?"

She gave him a long look. He got the feeling she wanted to say something else, but she didn't.

Finally, she said, "Can you live with yourself if you let the farm go without a fight?"

Phillip dropped his head into his hands again. This was the only place he'd ever been happy—where he was still happy, even though his father was dead and gone.

He didn't know who he was without the farm to come back to. The Phillip Beaumont that put on suits and went to parties—he didn't remember half of what that Phillip did.

He'd been telling himself that not remembering was the sign of a good time for how long? Years.

Decades.

Even if he fought for the farm, as she said, he wasn't sure he could live with himself.

"I need this place."

"Then fight for it."

He nodded, letting the words roll around in his head. They bounced off memories of Dad lifting him onto the back of a Percheron named Sally and leading him down the drive. Of piping up as Dad and his trainer argued over a Thoroughbred to say that Daddy should buy the horse because he ran fast—and having Dad pat him on the head with a smile as he said, "My Phillip's got a good head for horses."

Memories of buying his first Thoroughbred and watching it win its first race in the owner's box with Dad.

Of buying the Appaloosas over Dad's objections, then overhearing Dad tell the farm manager that the horses were better than he expected, but he should have known because Phillip always did have a good head for horses.

Of harnessing up the Percheron team himself for Dad's funeral and driving the team of ten in the procession over the objections of every single member of his family because that was how he chose to honor his father.

When he wasn't on the farm…he had nothing. Vague snippets of dancing and drinking and having sex with nameless, faceless women. Headaches and blackouts and checking his phone in a panic the next morning to see what he'd done.

"If I go back to the house, I'll get the whiskey."

Just saying it out loud was an admission of failure. It was also the truth. He didn't know which was worse.

He heard Jo take a deep breath. "If I make up a bed for

you, you understand that's not an invitation?" She exhaled. "It's not that I'm not…" her voice trailed off.

Interested.

She was interested. Here, in the safety of her trailer, with all their cards on the table, she wasn't going to hide it. "It has to be this way," she went on, sounding as hopeless as he'd ever heard her. "I gave up men when I gave up drinking."

He nodded even though he couldn't remember spending the night with a woman that didn't involve sex. "You'd let me stay? Why?"

The smile she gave him was sadder than anything he'd ever seen on her face. "Because," she said, leaning forward and placing her hand on top of his. "No one's past saving. Not even you."

But as quick as she'd touched him, she pulled away and was standing up. "I'll be right back."

He blinked up at her. "Where are you going?"

Jo stood. He didn't miss that she grabbed the gun off the counter and shoved it into her waistband. "I need to check on Sun and get Betty. She's good for nights like this."

He managed a small smile. "I'll be here."

No one was past saving. Not even him.

He didn't know if he should laugh or cry at that.

Jo stopped halfway down the steps and shot him that side-eye look. "Good," was all she said.

Then she was out the door.

Nine

Jo did not sleep.

She lay in her bed, listening to the sounds of Phillip also not sleeping. She could tell he wasn't sleeping by the way the trailer creaked with every toss and turn and also by the way that Betty would occasionally shake her head and exhale heavily.

Even without Betty's added exasperation, Jo would have been aware of every single one of Phillip's movements. She hadn't been this close to a man in, well…since before the accident.

She felt as if she'd walked into a bar and bellied up to the counter, only to nurse a Sprite. How was she supposed to make it through the night without falling back into her old ways?

Around two in the morning, Phillip shifted again. That noise was followed by the distinctive sound of the floors squeaking as he walked. Jo tensed. It wasn't a huge trailer. Where was he going?

Not here. Not to her. If he opened the sliding door and told her he couldn't get through the night and he needed her, she didn't think she'd be strong enough to direct him back to the dinette table that had converted into a too-small bed.

The footsteps stopped in the middle of the trailer, then she heard the fridge open up. Then the fridge door shut and his steps went back to the front of the trailer. She heard the cushions sag as he sat, then heard Betty shake her head.

She could see him sitting there, rubbing Betty's ears as he struggled. How many nights had she done the same thing?

She remembered when she'd finally been cleared to drive by herself. She'd made up some excuse to run to the grocery store, only to have her dad say, "Don't forget, Joey." Her mom had met her at the front door, car keys in hand. But instead of stopping her or announcing she was coming along, Mom had just wrapped Jo in a hug and said, "Don't forget, sweetie."

They hadn't stopped her. If they had, who knows—she might have tried harder to go around them. But they didn't. They made it clear it was her choice and hers alone.

So she'd stood there in the booze aisle at the convenience store and stared at the bottles of amber liquid. It would have been so easy to buy one can, slam it in the car and throw the can away. No one would have known.

Except...she would have known.

Jo had gone home empty-handed to find her granny, Lina, sitting on the front porch with a twenty-pound donkey on her lap. Lina had pulled Jo into a strong hug, taken a deep breath—to check for the smell of booze, no doubt—and asked, "Did you remember what you were looking for?"

"Yeah." She'd expected a greater sense of accomplishment. She'd stopped. She'd walked away. She was a stronger, better person now.

But all she'd felt was drained. How was she going to make the same choice every day for the rest of her life? She didn't think she could do it.

"This here is Itty Bitty Betty," Lina had said, plopping the donkey into Jo's lap. "She needs someone to look after her."

Jo sighed, doing some tossing and turning of her own. Betty was mellower now, less prone to taking corners too fast and crashing into walls. But she still had the same soft ears, the same understanding eyes. She kept Jo grounded.

Except that Betty was out there with Phillip—and Phillip was still not sleeping. Jo couldn't sleep if he didn't sleep.

She could open up the sliding screen that separated her bedroom from the rest of the camper and sit with him. She could wrap her hand around his and then he'd be still.

But she didn't. She didn't fix people and she couldn't save them and she sure as hell wasn't going to put herself in a position where she might kiss him because if she kissed him, she wasn't sure she could stop at just one kiss. She'd never been able to stop at just one.

And if she didn't stop at one kiss, what was to say she'd be able to stop at a couple of kisses? Or that she'd not run her hands over his body? That she wouldn't lean into his groan and tilt her head back, encouraging him to kiss her on that spot where her neck met her shoulders?

She kept the door firmly shut. And did not sleep.

At six, she heard him get up again. Groggy from lack of sleep, she wondered if she should make coffee for him. But before she could get her feet on the floor, the door opened and shut and the trailer was still.

Phillip was gone.

Somehow, she knew she'd be cleaning tack alone today.

* * *

Phillip was waiting at the door when Matthew drove up. "Took you long enough."

Matthew gave him a tired smile. "Something came up at work. I need a drink."

"Uh…"

Matthew turned. "Problem?"

"I don't have any alcohol in the house."

Matthew studied him, taking in everything from the boots to the jeans before finally staring him in the eye. "Either you drank everything you already had or…"

It wasn't the observation that hurt so much as the fact that it could have been true. "I had Richard come get all my booze and give it to the hands."

"You did?"

Phillip nodded. "I, uh, I'm trying to drink less. Or not at all."

"Is that so." It wasn't a question.

"Yeah…." Although a drink would be nice right now. When had it gotten so hard to talk to his brother? "A friend helped me realize if I wanted to keep the farm, I had to be sober to do it."

Matthew rubbed his eyes. "And when did this start?"

"Yesterday." Phillip swallowed.

"Good start." He almost sounded sincere. "I can't wait to meet this 'friend' of yours."

"She's down at the barn. With Sun."

Matthew rubbed his temples. "The seven-million dollar horse?"

"Yes."

There was a long pause. Phillip's stomach caved in. This was too much—he couldn't deal. What the hell had he been thinking? He couldn't even handle Matthew. He had to have been out of his mind to think he could confront Chadwick.

"She?"

Phillip nodded.

"You're going to screw up Chadwick's deal because you're trying to get *laid?*"

"I'm trying to save my farm," Phillip shot back. "Besides, correct me if I'm wrong, but aren't you about to lose your job if his deal goes through? I can't imagine that new owners would want a Beaumont vice president of whatever it is you do."

"Public relations," Matthew snapped, glaring at Phillip. "Which means I get to manage you whenever you go off the rails. Lucky freaking *me.*"

"I didn't go off the rails," Phillip promised. "Chadwick showed up here and said he was going to sell all my horses, the whole farm—what was I supposed to do? Go drink myself into oblivion? This is my life, Matthew. This is…" His voice caught. "This is the only part of me that's *real*. And you know it. I can't let it go."

"You're serious, aren't you?"

"Of course I'm serious. I need your help. Chadwick won't listen to me. I doubt he'll even listen to a poll with the tens of thousands of votes to keep the Percherons. You're the only one of us he trusts."

That was the right thing to say. Sure, Matthew raised an eyebrow as if he was certain Phillip were feeding him a line of bull, but the pissed-off look softened. "You really don't have anything to drink in the house?"

"I had my cleaning service go through my apartment, too."

Matthew nodded. "Okay. Tell me your plan. You do have one, right?"

Phillip took a deep breath. "I want to buy the farm from the company."

The hours he'd had to wait for Matthew had been filled

with frantic planning. Because if the farm stayed with the company, he'd still lose it. That was unacceptable.

But if he bought the farm, well, he could *lease* the Percherons back to the Brewery. The company would have all the marketing benefits of the Percheron team without having to carry the expense of the farm on the balance sheet.

It could work. Except for two little details. Matthew was staring at him, mouth open. Finally, he got himself under control. "Do you know how much that will cost? The land alone is probably worth five, ten million dollars."

"Eight. Eight million for three hundred acres, seven barns, twelve outbuildings and one house."

Matthew eyed him suspiciously. "And the horses?"

"About fifteen to twenty thousand a piece, just for the Percherons. I've got a hundred, so that's another one to two million. The total value of all the horses on the farm, including Kandar's Golden Sun and the Thoroughbreds, is between fifteen and twenty million. The hitches, tractors and other things are maybe another million, plus the ongoing cost of hired help, grain, and other overhead."

Phillip cleared his throat. So it wasn't such a little detail. "To buy the whole thing outright would be thirty million. To buy it piecemeal at auction might push it as high as fifty million. People would want a part of the Beaumont name."

For once in his life, Matthew did not have a snarky comeback to that. He shook his head before finally speaking. "You've done your homework. That worries me."

A sense of pride warmed the cockles of Phillip's heart. He'd managed to impress his younger brother. "The farm is mostly self-sustaining," he went on. "I sell a lot of horses. If I leased the Percherons back to the company, maybe started charging a nominal fee for parade appearances, that'd cover a lot of the cost. And Sun...well, the stud fees alone are going to earn back his purchase price."

That was all true. With some judicious management

and perhaps selling off some additional horses, the farm could break even.

Which still left one little problem.

"Do you have thirty million?" Matthew asked.

"Not exactly. I hoped Chadwick might cut me a deal, seeing as we're family."

Matthew gave him a look that didn't put much stock in brotherly love. "How much do you have?"

That little sticking point was stuck all right—in Phillip's throat. "I'd sell the apartment in the city and live here full time. Downsize my wardrobe, cars—everything. That'd bring in a million, maybe two."

"How much," Matthew said, carefully enunciating each word, "do you have?"

"Plus, I'd get my share of the company sale, right? I have executive benefits. How much is that worth?"

Matthew gave him a look better suited to their father. "You *might* get fifteen million. That's sixteen, seventeen million tops. I don't know if 'brotherly love' would cover the other twelve."

Phillip forced himself to breathe as Matthew scowled. "It's the best I can do."

"That's it?" Matthew said it in the kind of dismissive tone that made it sound as if they were talking about hundreds, not millions. "That's all you've got? You don't have any other assets? Stocks?"

Phillip shook his head.

"Property?" When Phillip shook his head again, Matthew groaned. "Nothing?"

"I drank it all."

His brother rubbed his temples again, as if that would provide the solution. "You realize Chadwick's still bitter about the seven-million-dollar horse?"

"Yeah, I realize."

"He's going to make you pay him back for that horse. You're aware of that."

"Yeah." This is what defeat tasted like. Bitter.

But, really, did he deserve any less? He'd spent most of a lifetime being a pain in Chadwick's ass.

When it came to horses, Phillip could finally beat his older brother. For a few hours a month, he was Hardwick's golden son. He'd done everything in his power to make sure that Chadwick never forgot it.

Even bought a horse named Kandar's Golden Sun. Just because he could. Because that's what Hardwick would have done.

But their father was dead and gone. Had been for years. Why had it only been in the last six days that Phillip had tried to figure out who he was if he wasn't Hardwick Beaumont's second son?

It'd been because of Jo, because she hadn't seen Hardwick's forgotten second child. She'd seen a man who had a good head for horses—a man who could be weak and stupid, yes, a man who drank too much and remembered too little. She hadn't seen a man she could fix.

She'd seen a man worth saving.

"Matthew," Phillip said, suddenly unsure of what he was going to say. "I'm sorry."

Matthew glared at him. "You should be. This is one hell of a mess."

"No," Phillip went on, trying to find some steel for his resolve. "I'm *not* sorry about trying to save the farm. I'll do anything to save this place. I'm…I'm sorry about everything else. I'm sorry your job is managing me when I go off the rails. I'm sorry I go off the rails sometimes—" Matthew shot him a mean look. "All the time. I'm sorry I don't remember half the stuff I've done because I blacked out."

"Phillip," Matthew said, sounding uncharacteristically nervous.

"No, let me finish." Finishing was suddenly important.
Phillip had been so mad at Chadwick, he'd never taken the
time to understand why the man was so mad at him. But
he could see it now, cleared of the haze of drinking. "I'm
sorry you were always in between me and Chadwick. *Are*
always in between us. I'm—I'm sorry I hated you when
you were a kid."

Matthew stared at him. "What?"

"I'm a terrible brother. I blamed you for my mother
going away but you were just a kid. It wasn't your fault
and it wasn't fair of me to blame you."

They stood there, staring at each other as Phillip's words
settled around them. He felt as if he should say something
else but he didn't know what. Of course, he hadn't known
he was going to say that, either.

"Why are you saying all of this?"

Phillip shrugged. Truthfully, he didn't know. Only…
he needed to. He couldn't live with himself if he didn't.

"I don't want to be the kind of guy who has to have
someone else clean up his messes anymore. I want to manage myself, my own life from here on out." He swallowed
again. "I'm sorry it took me this long to figure that out."

"You…" Matthew cleared his throat and straightened
his shoulders. "You were just a kid, too. It wasn't your
fault."

Phillip shook his head. "Maybe when we were six, but
we're not anymore. We're grown men and I've been—well,
I've been an asshole and I'm sorry."

Matthew walked away from him. He didn't go far,
maybe five paces before he stopped and dropped his head,
but in that moment, Phillip felt hopelessness clawing at
him. It'd seemed like a good idea. A *necessary* one. But….

"You can't hide out here forever. You're still contractu-
ally obligated to represent Beaumont Breweries at events.
If you have any hope of convincing Chadwick to go along

with your plan, you've got to hold up your end of the bargain. You're still the—what was it? The 'handsome face of the Beaumont Brewery'."

"I know." That was the other little detail that wasn't little. He knew that if he stayed out here on the farm where he could work with Sun, talk to Jo and pet Betty's ears, he could stay sober. It wasn't that hard.

Hell. He'd already asked Matthew to make the long drive down because he didn't trust himself to go into Denver and not hit a liquor store or a club. If he *had* to go to a club and spend several hours surrounded by alcohol and party people—how was he going to Just Say No? He'd wanted to crack open a fifth about three times in the last twenty minutes. And that was just talking to Matthew.

"That's why I need your help, Matthew. I don't know how to do this myself and you're the only one of us who Chadwick listens to."

"You're not just doing this for a woman?"

"She's not like that."

He needed Matthew's organization, his contacts, his ability to pacify Chadwick. Especially that.

Matthew sighed deeply. "I shouldn't."

"But you will?"

Matthew shot him a snarky look over his shoulder. "I must be nuts."

"Nope," Phillip said, unable to stop himself from grinning. He'd convinced Matthew. No matter what, that was a victory. One he knew he'd remember in the morning. "You're just a Beaumont."

Ten

Jo cleaned saddles, then Sun trashed them. The process repeated itself several times over the next three days. The only change of pace was when she paused to saddle up Betty. She'd clean a saddle again, wait for Sun to grind it into the dirt and then unsaddle Betty.

She never left Betty's saddle where Sun could get to it.

Jo felt awful and she wasn't sure why. She was not responsible for Phillip Beaumont. Never had been. She could not be the reason he drank or didn't drink. She couldn't fix him and it wasn't her responsibility to save him. Anything he did—*everything* he did—had to be a choice he made of his own free will.

However, all of that fine logic was subsumed beneath a gnawing sense of guilt. He'd been in a world of hurt and she couldn't help but feel as if she hadn't done enough. After all, she'd had a medical staff monitoring her for a couple of months. She'd moved back in with her parents and grandmother. She'd had Betty.

The fight to sobriety might have felt lonely, but she hadn't been alone.

Not like Phillip was. She didn't know what his relationship was like with the rest of his family, but she didn't think she was wrong about his brother waiting for Phillip to drink himself out of the picture.

She'd loaned him Betty for the night. And then he'd left.

She shouldn't care. Her guilt had nothing to do with the way he'd brought her coffee in the morning or kissed her hand after she made him clean saddles. It had nothing to do with how he'd looked at her as if she was the boat he could cling to in a storm.

But it did.

Jo focused on her work. What else could she do? If Phillip had given up, Sun would be sold. It hurt her to even think of that—the change would erase all the progress they'd made. But she had an obligation to make sure he was as manageable as possible, no matter who owned him.

She had a duty to herself, too—her reputation as a world-class trainer, and the reference she'd get from this job. That's where her focus had to be.

On the third day of cleaning saddles, Sun wandered over to where she'd left the jumping saddle and gave it a few half-hearted paws before he went to check on his bucket.

She didn't have any carrots. But Phillip would have.

She walked over to the saddle, dusted the hoof prints off of it, and walked away. Sun sniffed the saddle a few minutes later, but didn't trash it.

Finally, she thought. He'd gotten bored with this game they were playing. They could move on to the next phase— getting the clean saddle on the horse.

She didn't have any illusions that saddling Sun would be something she could accomplish in an afternoon. The process might take weeks—weeks she didn't know if she had.

She needed a break. For the first time, she was tired of standing in a paddock. Impatience pulled at her mind.

She gathered up the saddle and her cleaning supplies and slung them over the paddock fence. She'd leave them there so Sun would see them. Maybe Richard wouldn't mind if she borrowed one of the horses and went for a long ride. She'd love to give the Appaloosas a go.

She could call Granny. Just to check in, see how she was doing. Or she could go see a movie. Or something. Anything, really, as long as it didn't involve Beaumont Farms.

She unsaddled Betty and left the saddle next to Sun's. Jo didn't trust Sun enough yet to leave Betty alone with him, but the two animals had been co-existing better than she'd hoped. The little donkey was doing quite well in the pasture across the drive. That was another encouraging sign that should have put her in a good mood but didn't.

She was walking out of the paddock when she heard it—the sound of a car. She looked up to see a long, black limousine driving toward them.

Phillip. She glanced back at the barn, but Richard hadn't popped his head out yet.

Suddenly, Jo was nervous. One of the nice side effects of not getting involved with her clients' personal lives was that she never had to wonder how to act around them because she always acted the same—reserved. Concerned about the horses and not with their messy lives.

What if he was drunk, like he'd been the first time? It would mean he'd given up. She'd load up Betty and be gone by tonight. She wouldn't have to call Granny—she could just go home for a bit and get right with the world again.

Then she could keep doing what she'd done—traveling from ranch to farm, saving broken horses, building her business and never getting involved. She'd never have to see Phillip Beaumont again.

But what if…

The limo pulled up in front of her. Instead of the expensive Italian leather shoes and fine-cut wool trousers that he'd been wearing the first time she'd seen him get out of that limo, a pair of polished ostrich cowboy boots and artfully distressed jeans exited the vehicle.

Then Phillip stood and smiled at her over the door.

Oh God—Phillip.

Even at this distance she could see his eyes were clear and bright. His jaw was freshly shaven, his hair artfully messy.

She blinked at him as he leaned forward and thanked his driver. Then he shut the door and the limo drove off, leaving Phillip in the middle of the drive.

In addition to the jeans, he was wearing the kind of western shirt that hipsters wore—black with faint pinstripes and a whole lot of detailed embroidery on the shoulders and cuffs. He even had a rugged-looking leather-and-silver cuff on his arm.

Her breath caught as he walked toward her. He shouldn't—couldn't—look that good. She watched for his tells—the extra-slow, extra-careful movements, the jumping eyes—but found nothing.

Phillip Beaumont strode toward her with purpose. God, he looked *so* good. Better than she remembered. Although, to be fair, he had looked like hell the last time she'd seen him. He certainly didn't look like hell at the moment. In fact, she couldn't remember him looking as confident, as capable—as *sexy*—as he did right now.

Behind her, Sun snorted. Jo heard his hoofbeats, but they weren't frantic. Sun was just trotting around. His lack of overreaction might mean he not only recognized Phillip, but was also glad to see him.

As though she was glad to see him. "You're back."

"I am." He stopped less than two feet from her—more than far enough away to be considered a respectable distance but close enough that Jo could reach out and touch him if she wanted to.

Oh, how she wanted to. The man standing before her was a hybrid of the slick, handsome playboy in commercials and the cowboy who'd worked by her side for over a week.

A man should not look this good, she decided. It wasn't fair to everyone else. It wasn't fair to her.

She forced herself to breathe regularly. No gasping allowed. "What have you been up to?"

"Did you watch *Denver This Morning* this morning?"

She gave him a look. "No."

"Or *Good Morning America* yesterday?"

"No."

"No," he said with the kind of grin that did a variety of very interesting things to her. "I didn't figure you had."

She couldn't help herself. She leaned forward and took a deep breath, just as Granny had done once to her. Coffee, subtly blended with bay rum spice. Not a hint of alcohol on him.

"I've had a lot of coffee in the last five and a half days." He smelled warm and clean and tempting. Oh so tempting. "It's a good place to start, I've heard."

"As good as any," she agreed. Why was breathing so hard right now? She shouldn't care that he'd been sober for five days. She shouldn't care that he'd come back to the farm looking better than any man had a right to look.

"I hired a sober coach," he went on. "Big guy named Fred. He'll help me stay on the straight and narrow. I'm meeting with him tomorrow morning and he'll be accompanying me to all my required club appearances."

"You did...*what?*" She couldn't have heard him right.

"Sober coach. To help me stay sober. So I can save my farm." He lowered his head to look at her. "I wanted to thank you."

She blinked at him. Why was he telling her this? "For what?"

Before he could answer, Betty wandered over and leaned into his leg, demanding to be petted. "Hey, girl," he said in a bemused tone as he rubbed her head. "Been keeping an eye on Jo for me?"

He'd been thinking of her. "She missed you," Jo managed to say.

Phillip notched an eyebrow at her. Yeah, she wasn't fooling him any. How could she hope to fool herself?

You gave up men when you gave up drinking, she reminded herself as he pulled a device out of his back pocket. *You don't get to have this. Him.*

Phillip tapped on the screen a few times. "Here," he said, handing it to her.

The sun chose that moment to break through the clouds. The glare off the screen made it impossible to watch what he'd called up, but she heard a perky voice say, "...with us this morning is the handsome face of the Beaumont Brewery, Phillip Beaumont himself."

"I can't see," she told him.

"You need to get out of the sun."

She glanced back at her trailer. Suddenly, the distance of a couple hundred feet felt way too close and also too far away at the same time. "We could go to my trailer."

The moment she said it, she knew she'd meant something other than to just watch a video.

She turned her head back to Phillip. Her mind was swimming. Fifteen minutes ago, she'd written him off as a drunk who wasn't interested in saving himself. But now?

Their eyes met and a spark of something so intense it almost wasn't recognizable passed between them. She recognized it anyway. Sheer, unadulterated lust coursed through her, suddenly as vital as the blood that pounded through her heart.

This was the moment.

She could invite Phillip back to her trailer and pin him against the wall and kiss him as a reward for having had nothing but coffee for almost a week and no one would ever know.

Except she would.

And so would he.

"We could," Phillip said, his voice dropping down to something that would have been a whisper if the tone hadn't been so deep. "If that's what you want."

She wanted. She wanted the Phillip who wasn't afraid to grab a hay bale or clean a saddle, the Phillip who knew how to harness and drive a team. The Phillip who made her blush.

She wanted to kiss him.

Unable to come up with any words at all, she simply turned and walked to her trailer.

She opened the door and stepped up. But she didn't make a move toward the bed. She stopped at the top of the steps and turned.

Phillip stopped, too—one foot on the lowest step. He wasn't inside, but he wasn't out either.

"Here," he said, leaning forward to tap the screen a few more times. "Watch."

The video restarted. "Welcome back to *Good Morning, America*," a perky woman who looked vaguely familiar beamed into the camera. "With us this morning is the handsome face of the Beaumont Brewery, Phillip Beaumont himself."

The camera panned to Phillip sitting on a couch. His leg was crossed and his hands rested on his shin. He seemed quite comfortable on camera. He looked so good in his fancy western shirt—different than the one he was wearing now—and boots that were probably eel. He grinned at the perky woman—the same grin he'd given Jo the first time they'd met.

"The Beaumont Brewery is home to the world-famous Beaumont Percherons," the woman went on. "But there could be some changes underway and Phillip is here today with the details. Phillip?"

Phillip turned his attention to the camera. There he was, the sophisticated man-about-town. "Thanks, Julie. The Percherons have been a part of the Beaumont Brewery since 1868."

The screen cut away to a black-and-white commercial with the Percherons leading a wagon of beer. Phillip's voice over explained the history of the Brewery's Percheron team from the Colorado Territory to the present as decades of commercials played.

Besides the quality of the video, very little changed across the years. The horses were all nearly identical, the wagon the same—years of Beaumont Percherons anchoring the company to the public consciousness.

The camera refocused on Phillip and the woman. "Those are some classic commercials," the woman announced.

"They are," Phillip agreed. "But now the Beaumont Brewery is trying to decide whether to branch out from the Percherons or stick with tradition. So we've set up a poll for people to vote—should Beaumont Brewery keep the Percherons or not?"

"Fascinating," the woman said as she nodded eagerly. "How can people vote?"

"Visit the Facebook page we've set up for the poll," Phillip said as the web address popped up at the bottom of the screen. "We encourage people to leave a comment telling us what the Percherons mean to them."

Phillip and the woman engaged in a little more light banter before the segment ended.

Jo blinked at the screen. "You did that?"

"I'd show you the one from *Denver This Morning*, but it was basically the same thing," he said. Then he set his other foot on the step.

"We?" Because that interview had been a lot of *we*— *we* set up the poll, *we* made a Facebook page.

"My brother Matthew helped me," he corrected. "But they didn't know that Chadwick hadn't exactly signed off on this particular line of publicity." He smiled the wicked smile of a man who does whatever he wants and gets away with it. "We've already had over sixty thousand votes to keep the Percherons and four thousand comments in less than forty-eight hours. I dare Chadwick to ignore that— and I doubt the new Brewery owners will be able to ignore it, either."

"You," she whispered, staring at the screen as if it held all the answers.

He wasn't going to give up on Sun or the Percherons. Or himself. He wasn't going down without a damned good fight.

He lifted her hat off her head and set it in the seat next to the door. He wasn't touching her, not really, but licking flames danced over her skin, setting her on fire. "I did a lot of thinking that night," he said, low and close. So close she could kiss him. "About who I was and what I wanted. Who I wanted to be."

"I know you didn't sleep," she admitted. "Neither did I."

"I decided I needed to make some changes, so I called my cleaning service the next morning," he went on, brushing his fingertips over her cheek and pushing her hair back. "I had them get rid of all the alcohol in my apartment in the city. I also told Richard to get everything out of the house and give it to the hands. I talked to Matthew and hired a sober coach."

"You did all that?" Amazing, yes—but why? Because

no matter how impressive of a step it was, she couldn't be the reason. "Did you do this for me?"

He climbed the second step. The door swung shut behind him, closing them off from the rest of the world. They were the same height now, close enough she could feel the heat from his chest radiating through his shirt. He brought his other hand up, cupping her face. "If you were any other woman in the world, I'd say yes." He searched her eyes. "But…"

"But?" It was the most important *but* she'd ever said.

"But," he went on, a small, soft grin taking hold of his lips, "I didn't. Not really."

"Who did you do it for?"

"I did it for Sun and Marge and Homer and Snowflake and all the horses. I even did it for Richard, the old goat, because he's a good farm manager and he's too damn old to be unemployed."

"Yeah?" She couldn't help herself. She dropped the device on top of her hat and slid her arms around his waist. He was solid and warm and quite possibly the best thing she'd ever held.

"I did it for me," he told her.

It should have sounded like a selfish announcement from one of the most selfish men in the world, but it didn't. His voice was low and steady and he looked at her with such heated fervor that she knew the touch of his lips would scorch her and there'd be no turning back.

"Because I couldn't live with myself if I let it go."

"Oh," was all she could say. It seemed inadequate. So she surrendered to the pull he had on her and kissed him. She couldn't fight her attraction to him any longer and she was tired of trying.

It was a simple touch of her lips to his, but he sighed into her with such contentment that it demolished her reserves. *Skin on skin.* Desire burned through her. Her nipples went tight—so tight it almost hurt. Only his touch could ease the pain.

She was kissing Phillip Beaumont, really kissing him. She tilted her head for better access. He responded by opening his mouth for her. When she swept her tongue in to touch his, he groaned, "Jo." Then he kissed her back.

Any sense she had left evaporated. She ran her fingers up his back, feeling each muscle before she laced her fingers through his hair. Everything about her felt...odd. Different. Warm and hot and shivery all at the same time.

She wanted to see the body that was doing things to her—pooling heat low in her belly that demanded attention *right now*. The weight between her legs got so heavy so fast that she was suddenly having trouble standing.

And thinking? Yeah, that wasn't happening either. All she could think was how long it'd been. Years. Over a decade she'd denied that she needed this—to feel a man's arms around hers, to feel desirable.

She grabbed the front of his shirt. Snaps, not buttons. *Done*. The shirt gave and Phillip's chest was laid bare for her.

She had to look—had to—so she broke the kiss and let her fingertips trace the outline of his chest.

Carved of stone, that's what his muscles were. Smooth and hard but warm—almost hot to the touch. Or maybe that was just her. "Wow," she breathed as she traced his six-pack.

"Mmm," he said, pushing the hair away from the left side of her neck—the smooth side—and...and...

Years of pent-up sexual frustration unleashed themselves on her when he bit down on the space between her shoulder and her neck. Her hips tilted toward him, desperate for a release of the tightness that felt like a rubber band about to snap back on her. "*Phillip*."

"Too hard?" He kissed the spot he'd bitten. It was all the more tender compared to his bite.

This was it—the last possible moment she could back away from the edge before she went spiraling out of control.

Except she didn't want to back away. She wanted to throw herself forward without a look back.

"No," she said, grabbing at his belt buckle. The damned thing was far more complicated than the shirt had been. "Not hard enough."

He growled against her skin. "Bed?"

"Bed." Although she didn't exactly care at this moment where they wound up. Just so long as he kept doing what he was doing.

Then, to her surprise, Phillip picked her up. He held her against his chest as he mounted the last step. One arm around her waist, one under her bottom. The hand under her bottom squeezed her hard, making her squirm.

"You like it a little hard?" he asked.

"A little rough." Or, at least, she thought she did. A wave of insecurity almost froze her. "It's been so long...." Not only that, but she'd never done this with the scars. Even though the blinds were down, enough daylight suffused the bedroom that there was no way to hide.

He set her down and cupped her face again. "Then we better make sure it's worth the wait." As he kissed her, he unsnapped her shirt. "You about killed me the other night," he murmured against her skin before biting her shoulder as he pushed off her shirt.

She swallowed. "I did?"

The shirt hit the ground and then his fingers were tracing the swells of her breasts, barely contained by her bra. "Just a glimpse of you...." Then his mouth was moving lower as his hands went around her back. Over her scars. "I wanted a taste."

The bra gave and mercifully he brought his hands up to cup her breasts again. "Amazing," he whispered as his tongue lapped against her rock-hard nipple. "Simply amazing."

"I…"

He scraped his teeth down the side of her breast as he pulled her nipple into his mouth. "Yes?"

There was no mistaking the bulge in his jeans. "More," she gasped as he sucked hard.

"I love a woman who knows what she wants," he replied, smoothly undoing her belt and then her jeans.

He sat her down on the bed, where she kicked off her boots and jeans. Then she was in nothing but her panties.

Her pulse was racing so hard that she was having trouble focusing.

Which, admittedly, became a whole lot easier when Phillip undid his stubborn belt and shucked his jeans. His erection strained against the boxer-briefs he wore—red, of course—and those were gone, too.

Jo began to breathe so fast she was in danger of panting. She felt as if she should say something, but the problem was, she didn't know what. She was no shy, retiring virgin—but she had been celibate for the last decade.

She didn't know what she was doing.

Phillip stepped toward her. Jo sat up. Maybe he expected her to start with a little oral? Although—honestly—there wasn't much that was "little" about it.

He was, for lack of a better word, *huge*. She took him in hand, her fingers barely meeting as she encircled him. Once, twice, she moved her hand up and down.

"Jo," he groaned as his hands tangled in her hair.

When she leaned forward to take him in her mouth, he stopped her. "Wait."

"Wait?"

He pushed her back with enough force that she had to

lean on her elbows. She watched as he took a deep breath—
a man struggling to remain in control. Then he opened
his eyes—the green much darker with desire. "Saving the
farm," he said, the strain in his voice unmistakable, "isn't
about you."

Phillip crouched down to the ground and pulled a condom out of his back pocket. "But this," he said, dropping
the condom on the bed next to her, "this *is*."

Before she could process that, he'd kneeled between
her legs and was pulling her panties down. "It's really
been ten years?"

She couldn't even talk as his fingertips slid down her
thighs, over her knees, down her ankles. She bit her lip
and tried to nod, but her head felt as if it was in danger of
floating away.

His hands skimmed up her calves, flushing her with
heat as he sat on his heels and looked her over. For a
moment, she panicked. He was used to other kinds of
women—women with perfect bodies and flat stomachs
and smooth, soft skin. She hadn't even shaved her bikini
line recently. She hadn't planned on things getting this
far, this fast.

For a horrific moment, she wished she had a drink. A
shot of liquid courage to help her get out of her own head
and into the perfect man between her legs. And the moment she thought that, she almost told him to stop.

Like alcohol, men were a drug she'd already quit once.

Phillip leaned down and kissed…her knee. "Do you
want to remember this?"

"What?"

He kissed her other knee. "You said you didn't remember the sex before. Didn't remember if you wanted it or
not."

Good to know he'd been paying attention and all, but
she was pretty sure this wasn't a normal seduction.

He shifted to place a kiss on her hip bone. It shouldn't have felt good—just a regular old hip bone—but the tender way he was touching her focused her thoughts. Where would he kiss her next?

"Well?" Another kiss on the top of her thigh.

"I want to remember," she told him, knowing it was the truth. "I want to remember *you*."

Eleven

Yes. "That's what I want, too."

He leaned forward, letting his erection brush against her as he kissed the spot where he'd lost his head and bit down earlier. "Do you still want it a little rough? Or a little gentle?" Then he flicked his tongue over her earlobe.

She squirmed underneath him, which about drove him insane. "Both? Is that even an answer?" She tried to laugh it off as a joke, but he heard something else.

She was nervous. Well, he couldn't blame her. Ten years was a long time.

He grabbed her hands and pinned her down. Much more of her body moving under his and they wouldn't even make it to the memorable sex.

His arms began to shake under the strain of not plunging into her warm body. But he had to do this right for her.

"Both it is." Soft and tough—just like she was.

He bit down on the spot that had nearly broken her earlier. She sucked in a hot breath against his ear, her hips thrusting up against him. *Yes*, he thought again.

He moved to the other side—the side where she wore her scars like tattoos. She tried to tilt her head to hide herself but he had her pinned.

He kissed down her shoulder until he switched to her breast—full and heavy.

He licked her nipple, blowing air on the wet skin to see it tighten up. Her hips shimmied beneath his. Not yet. Too soon. He had to kneel back to break the contact.

He kissed the space between her breasts and then used his teeth to leave a mark on the inside of the left one. She sucked air again as her body strained against his hands. "Okay?" he asked, just to be sure.

"Yes." She nodded, but her eyes were closed.

"Then look at me," he ordered. When she didn't immediately open her eyes, he bit her again, his teeth skimming her nipple. "*Jo*. Look at what I'm doing to you."

Then he fastened onto her nipple and sucked hard until her eyes flew open. There—the anxiety that had lurked there earlier was gone, leaving nothing but need and want in its place.

He let his teeth scrape over her, putting a hint of pressure on her skin. Not enough to hurt her, but more than enough that she wouldn't forget this.

"Oh—Phillip," she gasped out, tilting her hips up—begging for his touch.

He didn't let go of her hands as he moved his mouth lower and lower. He pulled her with him until she was nearly sitting up. No way he was going to let her lie back.

"Keep your eyes open," he told her before he pressed a kiss against her sex.

"Why," she ground out through clenched teeth as he licked her, "why do you get to do this to me and I didn't get to do it to you?"

It was a fair enough question. "You've been a very good girl," he told her, keeping his mouth against her so she'd feel his voice more than she heard it. It worked, given the way she bucked against him, her body asking for more even if her mouth couldn't. He looked up the length of her body—she was watching him. *Good.* "You deserve a reward."

He filled his mouth with her, savoring her taste the way he'd savor a fine wine. Nothing was clouded by the haze of a wild night. This was just him and her and *nothing* in between them.

He was not gentle. It paid off. After only a few agonizing minutes of teasing her, Jo's back arched off the bed. She made a high-pitched noise in the back of her throat before collapsing back against the bed, panting hard.

He kissed her inner thigh, then turned his head and bit the other one. His dick throbbed, but in a good way. "Memorable?"

"Unforgettable," she said and this time, there was no hesitation in her voice at all. Nothing but a dreamy tone that spoke volumes about satisfaction.

"Good." He swallowed, the taste of her desire still on his lips. "Now roll over."

Jo froze. "What?"

She couldn't roll over. She absolutely could not have sex with a man—especially a man as physically perfect at Phillip Beaumont—where the only thing he could see would be the burn marks on her back.

He covered her body with his, the weight of his erection pressing hard against her. Her mind was in a state of confusion, but her body? Nothing confused there. That first orgasm had primed her pump, just as she knew it would. She needed more. She couldn't get enough of him.

He leaned over her and placed his teeth against her

neck. His hips flexed, putting him right against her. "Do you want this?"

She nodded.

He moved to the other side of her neck. The side with the scars that usually hid behind the collar of her shirts and her hair.

But she couldn't hide from him now. He wouldn't allow it.

"You can have it if you roll over," he whispered against her skin. He flexed again, his tip pushing against her. "Roll over for me, Jo. Don't hide who you really are."

"But I'm—it's—so ugly."

"Not to me." He let go of her and propped himself up on his hands so he could look her fully in the eyes. "It wasn't ugly when you stripped for me the other night. It was real and honest and true. That's what you are to me, Jo—the truth. No one else gives me a hard time like you do. No one else expects me to do anything—*be* anything. But you expect better of me. You make me want to be a better man."

They weren't the words of seduction, not even close. But that didn't change the fact that it was the sweetest thing anyone had ever said to her.

She took his face in her hands. "I can't be the reason." She wasn't fooling herself. When Sun was manageable, she and Betty would be gone and Phillip would be on his own again. The changes in his life couldn't be because of her.

That wicked grin would be her undoing. "You can be one of them. And a far more beautiful one than Richard's wrinkly old mug."

He leaned down to kiss her. The taste of coffee gone now; nothing but her and him mingled together. Her skin burned in the best possible way where he'd left marks on her body—pulling her into the here and now by brute force.

He flexed again, insistent in his need. "Let me see you, Jo. All of you."

She rolled, careful not to kick him.

Then she was exposed. Totally, utterly exposed to him. It left her feeling raw.

She didn't realize how tense she was until the first touch came. When his hands traced her shoulders, she jumped. "Sorry."

"Don't be." He smoothed her hair away and kissed the scar. His hands moved over her ribs, his fingertips tracing the sides of her breasts.

Then he was moving lower—kissing the surgical scars that ran alongside where her back had been broken. She'd been so broken.

She didn't feel broken right now. How could she, with Phillip lavishing such tender caresses on her?

He kissed the base of her back, just above her bottom. "You are so beautiful," he groaned—and then bit one of her cheeks.

Jo started against the bed. It felt good. It felt…as though she was alive. She grabbed the sheets and closed her eyes, letting her skin feel what she couldn't see—Phillip. She memorized every touch.

His hand grabbed her other cheek and squeezed, then a finger slipped inside of her. She clenched down. "More." She needed all of him.

His warmth left her. She turned her head to see him ripping open the condom wrapper, then rolling on the protection. Then he grabbed her hips, pulling her back to him with anything but gentleness.

Both. She'd asked for both because she didn't know what she wanted, not anymore. Just him.

Make it worth ten years of waiting, she thought.

He touched her again. "You're so ready for me." His tone was almost reverent. Then he was against her and, with a thrust, buried inside of her.

Jo's back arched as she groaned. "Oh, yes, *please*."

But he didn't. He stopped. The seconds dragged on for years before he grabbed her by the hips again, tilting her backside up. Then he grabbed her hair and wrapped it around his fist. "If this pulls at your back, you tell me, okay?"

Then he tugged her head back. Her neck lengthened and suddenly, his mouth was on her throat, biting at just the right spot.

Then he thrust. All Jo could do was groan at the wonderful agony of it all.

"Okay?"

"More." He tugged at her hair, popping her head up. "More, *please*."

He fell into a rhythm—long, steady strokes punctuated only by his teeth against her skin. Every bite, every thrust kept her in the here and now. Just her and Phillip.

It was freeing. She was free.

Jo came with a cry that she muffled against the mattress. Leaning back, Phillip let go of her hair and dug his fingertips into the flesh of her bottom, thrusting harder and harder until he let go with a low roar of pure satisfaction. Then he fell forward on her.

"Jo," he whispered in her ear in a voice that made him sound vulnerable.

She rolled again—not to hide her skin from him, but to face him.

Phillip smoothed her hair away from her cheeks and kissed her softly. "Beautiful," he sighed against her lips before he pulled her into a strong hug.

This was so much better than waking up with a sense of horror at feeling used and alone and knowing it was her own damned fault.

Her skin was still warm from Phillip's touch, her body weak from the orgasms. She wouldn't forget this. She wouldn't forget him.

And now that she had this moment, how was she supposed to not want it more? Already, she wanted him again.

Oh, no.

She couldn't believe she'd done this. She'd thrown away ten years of sticking to the straight and narrow and for what? For thirty minutes of sweet, heady freedom with Phillip Beaumont, a world-renowned womanizer with all of five days of sobriety under his belt?

How could she have been so stupid?

Then his phone rang.

Twelve

"Is that…the Darth Vader theme music?"

Phillip tensed at the sound of Chadwick's ring tone. "The 'Imperial March,' yes."

He pulled Jo into his arms and kissed her forehead. He didn't want to get up. He wanted to stay here and explore Jo some more. Yeah, he'd wanted to make that memorable but the truth was, he wasn't going to forget her.

It was a weird feeling to realize that he couldn't remember the face, much less the name, of the last woman he'd been with. It all ran together.

Everything about Jo stood out. The way her body had closed around his, the way she'd responded to his touch, his commands—he wanted to do that again, just to make sure it hadn't been some one-off fluke.

But Chadwick was calling. He'd gotten wind of what Phillip had been up to.

This was about to get ugly.

He forced himself to let go of her and sat up. "I need to leave."

"Oh."

He didn't like her quiet note. But before he could say anything else, his phone started singing again. He grabbed his pants off the floor.

She tried to slip past him, but he hadn't forgotten that vulnerable *Oh*. "Tonight," he said as he grabbed her arm.

"Tonight?" Anything vulnerable about her was gone and the tough cowgirl was back in place.

"Have dinner with me." His phone stopped marching, only to pick up the beat two seconds later. "Come up to the house."

She tilted her head toward him and waited. The power had shifted between them. She'd given him control over the sex, but she'd taken that back now.

"Please," he added as he curled his arm around her waist. He put his lips against the curve of her neck and whispered, "Please," against her skin.

She pulled away from him. "No."

Then she was gone, striding down the hall and out the trailer before he could process what she'd just said. *No?*

He stared at the empty hallway, then the bed they'd only just vacated. What happened? One minute they were having electric sex—her pleading for more, for the release he knew she couldn't have been faking. The best sex he could remember. And the next, she was *done* with him?

He started after her, but his damned phone began to march again. *Son of a...*

"What?" he demanded as he slammed the trailer door shut after him. Jo already had Betty and was shutting the paddock gate behind them both.

She couldn't have been clearer—she didn't want to talk to him.

"Have you lost your mind?" Chadwick thundered on the other end.

"And hello to you, too," Phillip said as he tried to figure out where he'd gone wrong. She'd wanted it both soft and rough. Hadn't he delivered?

"You are single-handedly jeopardizing this *entire* deal," Chadwick yelled in his ear. "Even by your standards, you've screwed this up."

"I've done nothing of the sort," Phillip replied, forcing himself to remain calm. Mostly because he knew he wouldn't win a shouting match with his older brother, but also because he knew it'd drive the jerk crazy. "I've merely reminded the future owners of our brewery that we mean more to our vast customer base than just a nice, cold beer."

Jo stood with her back to him as she haltered Betty. Sun was aware of him, though. The horse was making short strides back and forth in front of her, his head never pointing away from where Phillip was pacing.

"...pissed off Harper and the entire board," Chadwick was yelling. "Do you know what that man will do to us if this deal falls through?"

"To hell with Harper," Phillip said, only half paying attention. Maybe he should have asked Jo if he could come back to her trailer instead of inviting her up to the house? "I can't stand the guy. And he hates us."

"I always thought you had a brain somewhere in that head of yours and that you *chose* not to use it," Chadwick fumed. "I can see now that I was wrong. For your information, Phillip, Harper will sue us into last *century*. And any hope that you're keeping the farm with this PR gambit will go down the drain in legal fees."

"Oh," Phillip said, Chadwick's words registering for the first time. "I hadn't thought about that."

"What a surprise—you didn't think something through. You *never* think things through, do you?" Chadwick made a noise of disgust in the back of his throat. "All you care about is where the next party is."

"That's not true," Phillip snapped. His head began to throb. This would be the time in his conversation with Chadwick where he'd normally tuck the phone under his chin and start opening cabinets to see if he had any whiskey. He hated it when his older brother talked down to him.

Even though Phillip knew he wasn't going to drink, the habit had him looking around for a cabinet.

Damn, this was going to be harder than he thought.

"Isn't it?" Chadwick's tone made it clear that he was sneering. "The next party, the next drink, the next woman. You've never cared for anything else in your entire, selfish life."

Phillip's pride stung, mostly because it was a somewhat accurate statement. But not entirely, and he clung to that *not* with everything he had.

If Chadwick wanted to hit below the belt, fine. Phillip would just hit right back. "You know who you sound like right now?" he said in his most calm voice, "Dad."

There was a hideous screeching noise and then the call ended. If he had to guess, Phillip would say Chadwick had thrown his phone at a wall. Good. That meant the asshole wouldn't be calling back anytime soon.

He glared at the phone, then the silent woman who, not twenty feet away from him, was leading Betty around the paddock. She might as well have been on a different continent. Any good buzz he'd had earlier from his media coup and seduction of Jo was dead.

He'd had a plan—show Chadwick and the new Brewery owners that the Percherons were too valuable to auction off.

That plan wasn't dead, he realized. He'd just finished Phase One. Now he needed to start Phase Two—getting control of this farm away from Chadwick.

Which meant he needed a new plan.

He looked at the paddock again. The cold shoulder from Jo was about to give him frostbite.

One-night stands were his specialty. He loved them when they were there, forgot about them when they were gone. So what if Jo was ignoring him? No big deal, right? He'd had his fun, just as he always did. Now was as good a time as any to move on.

But he didn't want to move on.

It must be the chase. She was exceptionally hard to get—that had to be what still called to him.

Fine. She wanted to be chased? He'd chase.

Time for Phase Two.

Thirteen

Jo needed to go in. A breeze had picked up as dusk approached and, given the clouds that were scuttling across the spring sky, they were in for some rain. She hoped it was a gentle rain and not Mother Nature throwing a fit, but she wasn't going to hold her breath.

Besides, her legs ached. Okay, so it wasn't the standing and walking that had them aching. That was more to do with the *unusual* strain of the afternoon.

She shoved back that thought and focused on the tasks at hand. If it was going to rain, she wanted to brush Betty before the donkey could track any more dirt into the trailer. And Sun—a gentle rain wouldn't kill the horse, but a storm with crashing thunder and lightning might push him over the edge. She couldn't risk him trying to bust through the fences. She needed to get him haltered and into the barn.

She needed not to get killed doing it. There wasn't anyone else around at this point—everyone else had driven off about half an hour ago.

She was not going to ask Phillip for help. She didn't need it. She wouldn't need *him*.

Jo was so focused on her work that the effort was physically exhausting. But it was still better than thinking about what she'd just done. With Phillip.

So she didn't think about it. She thought about the horse.

Sun was, by all reasonable measurements, quite calm. She haltered Betty again and led the patient donkey around the paddock again. This time, she walked within five feet of Sun. The horse didn't skitter away.

No, she was not thinking about the way Phillip had picked her up and carried her back to bed. She was also not thinking about the way he'd made her watch as he went down on her. And she was certainly not thinking about the way every molecule in her body had been pulling her into his arms when he'd whispered "Please" against her skin.

How she'd wanted to say *yes*. Just…let herself be at his beck and call. Be in his bed when he wanted, how he wanted. Let him mark her skin and fill her body and make her come so hard. It'd be easy—for as long as she was here, she could have him.

He could have her.

But then what? She was going to throw herself at him—because, God, she *wanted* to throw herself at him—and then quit him cold turkey in a week, or two weeks or however long she had left to train Sun?

And if she went to his house, went to his bed—word would get out. People would notice. People would *talk*. Her reputation as a professional horse trainer who could take on the toughest cases would be shot to hell and back. People would think she'd gotten this job because she was sleeping with Phillip.

She knew what kind of man he was. He'd move on, just as he always did.

Just as she used to do. One man was the same as another, after all.

But he'd made her remember what she liked about men in the first place. The warm bodies, soft and hard at the same time. The way orgasms felt different in someone else's arms compared to when she did them herself. The feeling, for a fleeting moment, of being complete.

That was the part she'd blindly run after. She'd always confused being *wanted* with being *had*, though. But now she knew. Wanting and having were not the same.

She'd wanted Phillip. Now she'd had him. But, unlike all those men from long ago, she wanted him again. Not just *a* man, but Phillip.

God, she was so mad at herself. She knew she couldn't have him and just let him go any more than she could have one drink and not have any more. She *knew* that. What had she been thinking?

That was the problem. She didn't know what to think anymore.

So she un-haltered Betty. And re-haltered her. Again.

This time, she walked up to Sun and stopped right in front of him. The horse's head popped up and he stared at her, his ears pointed at her as he chewed grass.

This was good. She wished she felt more excited about the victory.

"See?" she said in a soft voice. Sun's head jerked back, but he didn't bolt. "It's not so bad. Betty doesn't mind it, do you girl?"

She rubbed Betty's head between her ears. *It's not so bad*, she silently repeated to herself. She'd had Phillip once. She could back away from the brink of self-destruction again. She'd already said no to him a second time, right? Right. *Not so bad.*

Out of the corner of her eye, she saw movement. Then, unexpectedly, Sun's nose touched Betty's. It was a brief thing, lasting only two seconds, tops. Then Sun backed up and trotted off, looking as if he'd just won the horse lottery.

Jo grinned at his retreating form as she un-haltered Betty. So her mental state was all out of whack. The horse, however, was doing fine and dandy. She watched as Betty trotted after Sun. It looked like a little sister chasing after her big brother. Jo could almost hear Betty saying, "*Wait for me!*"

Jo walked back over to the gate and picked up Sun's halter and lead rope. Maybe… "Betty," she called. "Come on."

Betty exhaled in what was clearly donkey frustration. She only had so much patience for non-stop haltering. But after a moment, she plodded toward Jo.

Sun followed.

Jo moved slowly, demonstrating on Betty how the halter went over the nose and then the ears, then how the lead rope clipped on. She knew he'd been haltered before, but a refresher never hurt anyone.

She held the halter up for Sun to sniff just as a distant rumble echoed from the clouds. Sun whipped his head around, trying to find the source of the noise—then he took off at a jumpy trot. Crap. This whole process needed to happen sooner rather than later. She didn't want to spend a night standing in a downpour just to make sure Sun didn't accidentally kill himself.

Just then, Sun's ears whipped back and he blew past her to rush to the edge of the paddock. Seconds later, she heard it, too—the sound of whistling.

Yes, she was mad at herself and yes, she knew that it wasn't healthy to take her anger out on anyone else but *damn* it was tempting to light into Phillip. Everything had been going fine until he'd arrived on the farm. She'd been a well-respected horse trainer that never, ever gave in to temptation, no matter how long or lonely the nights were.

She wanted to go back to being in control, removed from the messy lives of her clients.

She also wanted to stomp over to that gate, throw it open and demand to know what the hell he was thinking, but she didn't get that far.

Phillip came forward, looking at the halter in her hands. "Any luck?"

Then he had the damned nerve to wink at her.

She wanted to tell him to shove his luck where the sun didn't shine but she didn't. "I *was* making progress. A storm's coming in. I need to move him to the barn without setting him off again."

Phillip looked at her with such intensity that it made her sweat. "I know what he needs," he replied in a voice that was too casual to be anything *but* a double entendre.

She glared at him. She was not going to lose her head again. She was not going to give in to her addictions. One and done. That was final.

He reached into his shirt pocket and pulled out a small baggie of carrots. "Oh," she said, feeling stupid. "Okay."

Phillip opened the gate and walked in. He took out a carrot and stood remarkably still, the carrot held out on the flat of his palm.

Betty came up to him, her lead rope trailing behind her as she snuffled for the treat. "Go ahead," Jo said when Phillip looked to her for approval.

Sun looped around the paddock a few times, each circle tightening on where Phillip stood, another carrot at the ready. This wasn't how she wanted to do this. They were forcing something that she normally would have worked on for a week, maybe more.

But the sky was starting to roil as the clouds built and moved. So she stood next to Phillip, ready to halter a horse.

They waited. For once, Phillip had all the patience in the

paddock. Jo was the one who kept glancing at the menacing clouds as if she could keep them at bay by sheer will.

"Come on, Sun," Phillip said in a low voice that sent a tremor down Jo's back. "It'll be okay, you'll see."

Miraculously, Sun came. Head down, he walked toward them as if he agreed to be haltered every day.

Jo held her breath as the horse sniffed the carrot in the man's palm. Then Sun's big teeth scraped the carrot off Phillip's hand.

"Good, huh?" Phillip said, lifting his hand to rub Sun's nose. "I have more if you let Jo put the halter on you."

Sun shook his head and walked away. But he didn't go far.

A few days ago, Phillip might have whined about how long this was taking. But not today. He merely got another carrot out and waited.

Betty leaned against his legs, so he broke the carrot in half and gave her the smaller part. That got Sun's attention, fast. He came back over to Phillip.

"Carrots," Phillip said, letting Sun take the remaining half, "are *that* good, aren't they?"

He started to fish out another carrot—and Sun was waiting for it—but Jo stopped him. "Let me try to get the halter on, then give him another one if he cooperates."

Sun gave her a baleful look. Clearly, he was too smart for his own good.

"You heard the lady," Phillip said in a teasing tone to his horse. "No more without the halter."

Sun shook his head again. Thunder rumbled again, closer this time.

"You don't want to spend the night in the rain, do you?" Sun blew snot on the ground. "No," Phillip went on, "I didn't think so." He held out another carrot so Sun could smell it.

Jo stepped forward as quickly as she could and slipped

the halter over Sun's nose. He shook her off and reached for the carrot, but Phillip pulled back. "No halter, no carrot."

Sun dropped his head in resignation. Jo slipped the lead rope over his neck and handed the ends to Phillip. Then she leaned forward and slipped the halter over his nose, then over his ears. She clipped the throat latch.

Victory. She knew it, Phillip knew it—hell, even Betty seemed to know it. She clipped the lead rope on the halter. Phillip gave Sun another carrot.

"Now we have to get him to the barn," she said. "Can you lead him?"

Phillip gave her the kind of smile that didn't so much chip away at her defenses as blow them up. Nope. Not working on her today. Or any other day.

She was not that girl anymore. She would not throw herself at a man. Not even Phillip Beaumont.

"I can honestly say I've done this before. Plus," he added with that grin, "I'm the one with the carrots."

She steeled her resolve. Sun hadn't been indoors in almost two weeks. This could go south on them. Maybe she should leave Betty in the stall next to Sun for the night? It couldn't hurt. "Fine. Betty and I will lead the way."

Why did she have a sinking feeling that things were about to get interesting?

Phillip had a death grip on the lead rope. The odds that Sun would freak out were maybe 50/50. He couldn't do anything about bucking except stay out of the way, but if Sun tried to bolt, he'd have to spin the horse in a small, tight circle before he could build up a head of steam. And if he reared...

Damn, Phillip wished he had on some gloves. If Sun reared, Phillip just might get rope burn on both palms. He tightened his grip.

He followed Jo and Betty into the barn. The lights came

on overhead, which made Sun start, but he didn't bolt. Jo led her donkey past Sun's stall and then paused. "This stall is empty," she said in a gentle voice. "I'll put Betty in."

"Okay." The situation made him nervous. Leading a mostly-calm Sun down a wide hallway was one thing. Being in a stall with him was a whole different thing.

"Easy does it," Jo said. For the first time since she'd walked away from him that afternoon, he heard something soft in her voice.

Phillip nodded as he walked into the stall with Sun. Then Jo was standing next to him, unclipping the throat latch and sliding the halter from Sun's head.

The three of them stood there for a moment, humans and horse, wondering if they'd just accomplished that without shouting, ropes or guns. Sun shook his head and pawed at the ground, but didn't freak out. Hell, he didn't do anything even remotely Sun-like. He just stood there.

"Carrot?" Jo said in her quiet voice.

"Carrot," Phillip agreed, fishing the rest out of his pocket and holding them out to the horse.

His horse.

The wind gusted. He gave Jo a sideways smile that was absolutely not working. "It's going to storm."

"I know."

"We're under a tornado watch until eleven p.m.," he told her. "You should come up to the house—the trailer may not be safe."

Of all the sneaky, underhanded things... "I'll sleep in the barn with the horses."

"*Jo.*" He was forced to shout as the wind gusted up. "Come to the house, damn it. This isn't about seduction, this is about safety."

She hesitated. "I'm not sleeping with you tonight."

He stared at her. "First off, I have a fully stocked guest room. Second off…" He stepped toward her. "I'm sorry."

"For what?"

He ducked his head, looking sheepish. "Well, that's part of the problem. I'm not sure for what. But I've clearly done something you didn't like and it's put me in an odd position."

She stared at him as he studied the tips of his toes. Was this actual sincerity? "What position is that?"

"I want to make it up to you, but I don't have the first idea how. I mean, normally, I wouldn't even care if I'd been a jerk and if I did, I'd throw some roses or diamonds at the problem and be done with it. But I know that won't work. And I don't want to be done with it. With you."

Oh, God. This was sincerity. She considered bolting from the barn, but there was no guarantee he wouldn't follow her. "What do you want from me, Phillip?"

"I want…" He turned away as he ran his hands through his hair. "I want to understand what it is about you that makes me want to do…things. Stay home on the farm. Stay sober. Not—" He paused.

Jo leaned forward, suddenly very interested in that *not*. "Yes?"

He let out a short, sharp laugh. "Is it always this hard?"

"No. Sometimes it's harder." Although, frankly, this was pretty damned hard. She hadn't been faced with this level of emotion—involvement—in so long. She didn't know what to do.

It'd be easy to think he was feeding her a line of bull.

She watched as the muscles in his jaw twitched. He really thought he'd screwed up. Damn.

"If I say it's not you, it's me—will you laugh?" she asked.

That got her a rueful grin. "I haven't heard that line in a long time."

"I had given up men, remember?" She wanted to touch him, but she didn't want to. Life was so much simpler when she followed her own rules.

But there'd been that moment in his arms, watching him bring her to orgasm....

Simpler was not always better.

"You said that."

"I always mixed up the two. Men and alcohol. There was no way to separate them in my mind. They were two wagons that were hitched together and I couldn't fall off of one without falling off the other."

He nodded. "I can see that."

"Then you come along and you're...all my triggers wrapped up in one gorgeous smile. And I—" Jo swallowed, wishing this were easier. But it wasn't. It wouldn't ever be. "I wasn't strong enough to say no to you. Not the first time."

Phillip spun to face her fully. She could see him trying to understand, trying to make the connection. "You think that sleeping with me will lead to drinking?"

She nodded. "Don't get me wrong. The sex—you were amazing. I'd...I'd forgotten how good it could be. How much I liked it."

"That's a relief." He grinned, but instead of his normal, confident grin, this one seemed a little more unsure. "I thought I'd done something you didn't like."

"Yeah, no—*amazing*." She shuddered at the memory of his teeth moving against her skin. "But in my mind, I'd fallen off one wagon. I can't afford to fall off the other. What if I lose control? Because then I'll lose everything I've worked for. *Everything*."

"I understand. Weirdly enough."

She looked at him in surprise. "You do?"

"Look, my six days isn't much on your decade, but... this is *so* much harder than I thought."

She knew that feeling—that the mountain was insurmountable and failure was guaranteed. "*This*," she said, unable to keep the grin off her face, "is the part where I say 'one day at a time.'"

"I don't have to sing 'Kumbaya,' do I?"

She laughed. "God, no."

He came to her then, his arms slipping around her waist. She hugged him back. She couldn't fight this attraction. "Stay with me, Jo. Wake up with me."

"For how long? Sun's getting better. He won't need me much longer."

Phillip stroked his thumb over her cheek. "For as long as you want. Betty loves it here. And I have other horses, if you're worried about missing a job."

A job? No, she wasn't worried about that. She set her own schedule and that schedule could be rearranged. But would she still *get* jobs, if word got around? "I don't want people to know about this. About us. No tweeting or press releases or pictures."

His eyebrows shot up. She kept going before she lost her nerve. "I am a professional. I can't have this compromise my reputation as a trainer."

He nodded. "This has nothing to do with Sun. You've done an amazing job with him. This is between us and us alone."

She swallowed. "What about your club appearances?"

"That's why I hired Fred. He'll be with me any time I have to leave the farm." He stroked the edge of his thumb over her cheek.

They were standing on the edge again, but it felt less like falling off a cliff and more like…falling in love. Which was ridiculous. She'd never been in love. She had no plans to start now. "I thought you weren't seducing me."

He brushed his lips across her forehead. "You can stay in the guest room tonight if you want."

She gave him a look then pulled away from him so she could get her thoughts in order. "I can't put myself at risk for you. If you want to be with me, you have to stay sober." She cupped his face in her hands. "I *cannot* kiss you and taste whiskey. I just can't. It's a deal breaker."

His eyes searched hers. Gone was the haunted, raw pain she'd seen a few days ago. His eyes were clear and bright and filled with a different kind of need. "I'm *done* drinking, Jo."

He kissed her then, rough and gentle at the same time.

She'd already fallen off the man wagon. But that didn't have to mean she'd fall right back into drinking. As long as she kept a hard line between her time with Phillip and alcohol—and they kept a hard wall between what happened in the paddock and what happened in the bedroom—she could indulge in some great safe sex and enjoy herself without repercussions.

She hoped.

Thunder cracked around them. Sun whinnied, but he didn't freak out. "Come up to the house," Phillip murmured as his teeth scraped over the skin where her neck and shoulder joined. "Wake up with me."

Her remaining resolve crumbled. How could she say no to that?

She couldn't.

So she didn't.

Fourteen

The next three weeks were something far outside of Jo's experience. Suddenly, she was living with Phillip Beaumont. She'd never lived with anyone besides her parents and a few unfortunate college roommates.

But this? Waking up with Phillip's arms wrapped around her waist? Making sweet love in the morning, then having breakfast together? Spending the day working with Sun—sometimes with Phillip, sometimes without—then heading back up to the house after the hired help had gone home for the night to have dinner with him? Falling into bed with him at night where he was both rough and gentle in the best possible ways?

It was easy. What's more, it was good. Well, of course the sex was good. But her time with Phillip went well beyond that. Yes, they had sex at least once a day—usually twice. But she got up the next morning, kissed Phillip, and did what she always did—worked with Sun.

After a week, he would come to her to be haltered. After

two, he consented to be tied to the fence so she could brush him. He really was golden, a shimmering color that she'd never seen on a horse before.

She even had Richard walk by a few times while Jo led the horse around the paddock. Sun wasn't happy, but he also wasn't insane with fear.

A new sense of calm filled her. After ten damned long years, she'd managed to unhook the men wagon from the drinking wagon. The realization that she could enjoy Phillip and still be the same woman was—well, it was freeing.

Phillip left the farm after a week and a half. His sober coach showed up at the farm the afternoon Phillip was to leave. Jo stayed with Sun, but she knew that Phillip, Fred and Ortiz were discussing ways they would keep Phillip in control. No drinking, no hook-ups—Phillip had promised—and no blackouts. That was the plan.

Phillip would text her at regular intervals. She could also follow along at home via Twitter, where he'd be posting to his account.

Jo stayed in her trailer, Betty bedded down next to her as she toggled between texts and Twitter, where Phillip shared his Instagram photos. "Can't believe how stupid some people are drunk," he texted her with a photo of a public sex act between two women and one guy.

She smiled at her phone. "Doing okay?"

"Miss you & Betty," was the response. "Home soon."

Later that night, her phone buzzed her out of a dream. It was a photo of Fred in one of two double beds in a hotel room. "Not alone tonight," the text read. "Just me & Fred. He's no Betty, but he'll do. J Miss you."

"Miss you too." She was shocked by how much.

Phillip was back in the paddock by four Sunday afternoon. He'd made it through three events in two days without a drop of liquor. They'd been doing really well about not displaying their affection in front of the hired help, but she didn't stop him when he kissed her for what felt like a good five minutes. When the kiss broke, they realized Sun was watching them.

"Later," she'd giggled. Actually giggled.

"You can bet on it."

"Later" couldn't come fast enough but finally they made it to the bedroom without even eating dinner. After amazing sex where Phillip held her down and left bite marks on her breasts, he said, "I did it," as he lay in her arms, both of them panting and satisfied.

She knew he wasn't talking about the two orgasms that had her body humming. "You did. I knew you could."

He propped himself up on his elbows to look down at her. "You did?"

"No one's past saving."

He lowered himself down onto her. "Who knew being saved could be so good?"

She didn't get a chance to reply.

Phillip was home for another week before he had to go again. This time, he headed to a music festival where Beaumont Brewery had sponsored a party tent. Jo was nervous for him—this wasn't a few hours at a party, but a solid weekend of temptation. But he had Fred and he knew he could do it. So she sent him off with a kiss and the reminder, "Don't forget." She wanted to say more. But she didn't.

"I won't," he promised her. And she believed him.

That Saturday, she had to fight the temptation to check her phone constantly. She'd made it a policy not to check her phone while she was in the paddock with Sun—the horse was smart enough to know when her focus was elsewhere. Distractions were how trainers got hurt. So she left her phone in the trailer. That way, it wouldn't tempt her.

She checked her messages at lunch. Only one text that

read, "Gonna be a long day. Wish I was home with you," that he'd sent at ten that morning. Nothing since.

She swallowed, feeling a kind of anxiety she hadn't felt in a long time—a futility that she couldn't change things so why bother? That'd been the way she used to think when she'd wake up and be confronted with what she'd done. Changing seemed so hard, so impossible—why even try?

Expecting Phillip to change, just like that?

No, wait. No need to jump to conclusions. Phillip had just realized that she'd be working in the paddock all day, that was all. And he was busy doing…party things.

She sent a text—"I know you can do this, babe." Then, she sent another—"Don't forget."

Don't forget me, she wanted to add, but didn't. Instead, she took a quick photo of Sun and sent it.

She didn't get a reply.

What could she do? Nothing. It was not as if she could go to him. He was in Texas. This was up to him. She couldn't make the choice for him, any more than her parents could have kept her from driving to that convenience store.

So she pushed her worry from her mind. She wanted to try and saddle Sun and that required her full attention. But the work didn't stop her from praying that Phillip remembered. Or, at the very least, that Fred forcibly reminded Phillip what was on the line.

Because what was on the line was the farm. The horses. This was about Sun and the Appaloosas and all the Perseverons—Beaumont Farms. Not her. What she needed to remember was that she was here for the reference, the paycheck—the prestige of having saved a horse no one else could.

She had to keep up the wall between what happened in the paddock and the bedroom.

But he'd promised her. And she so desperately wanted him to keep that promise.

She didn't get Sun saddled. The horse must have picked up on her nerves because he refused to stand still long enough for her to brush him. She did get him back into his stall. She left Betty in the stall next to him—hopefully that would help him mellow out more.

Then, dread building in her stomach, she went to her trailer and got her phone. No new text messages.

She sat there, her fingers on the buttons. She shouldn't be afraid to look, right? He had Fred. He had a clear head. He wouldn't forget. He wouldn't forget *her*. She was making a mountain out of a molehill. He was working, no doubt. She needed to get a grip.

Fortified by these completely logical thoughts, she toggled over to Twitter—and her stomach immediately fell in. Oh, *no*. He'd posted pictures almost every half hour of him with famous people she recognized and a lot of people she didn't. A lot of women.

The women were concerning—but not nearly as worrisome as the look in Phillip's eyes. As she scrolled through the feed, his eyes got blearier. Each smile stayed the same—infectious and fun-loving—but his eyes? They were flatter and flatter.

What had he done?

Then she saw it. The bottle of Beaumont Beer in his hand, almost hidden behind the waist of a curvaceous redhead. Open.

The next photo, the bottle was less hidden. She needed to stop scrolling, but she couldn't help herself. How far had he fallen? How much had he forgotten?

Everything. The women in the pictures got more outrageous, more hands-on. The beer got more obvious. And the look in Phillip's eyes? He wouldn't remember any of this.

And she knew that she'd never forget it.

Each picture after that was worse until she got to the photos he'd posted about an hour ago. She knew the guys in the photo were some famous band, but she didn't know which one. All she knew was that they were surrounding Phillip on stage and they were toasting with their beer bottles. Phillip toasted with them.

After that, she shut her phone off and sat there, staring at the dinette tabletop. This *feeling* of hopelessness, helplessness—this was exactly why she'd held herself back. She'd always told herself it was to keep people safe, like Tony, the guy who'd died in a car next to her. She couldn't get involved with people because it would end badly for them. And there was no question that this would end badly for Phillip.

But he'd made his choice. He could drink away his pain.

She couldn't. That hard wall she'd demanded between men and alcohol—between Phillip and whiskey—she had to cling to that wall.

She never should have slept with him. Cared about him. Fallen for him.

Because now she was going to hurt. And just like the pain she'd had to feel when she'd been coming out of surgeries and physical therapy, she'd have to feel all of this.

She didn't want to. God, she didn't want to hurt, to know she'd broken her own rules and now she was going to pay the price for it.

Her mind spun, trying to find something that would allow her to sidestep around the heartache. Okay, Phillip had fallen off the wagon. Everyone did, right? Obviously, there'd been a problem with the sober coach because he hadn't been in any of the pictures. Fred had screwed up. They'd fire Fred, wherever he was, and hire another sober coach. Someone who wouldn't bail on Phillip in high-pressure situations. This could be fixed. This could be…

Against her will, she picked up her phone. A new picture popped up. Phillip, with his arms around two women who could have been the same two he'd brought to the ranch a month ago. He had a bottle in each hand. His lips were pressed against the cheek of one of the women.

No, it couldn't be fixed. She was making excuses for him and she knew it. They'd had a deal. She couldn't be with him if he wasn't sober. She couldn't kiss him and taste whiskey.

Whatever Fred did or did not do, it still came down to Phillip. It was his call. He'd gone to this event just like she'd driven herself to that gas station all those years ago. He'd been faced with a beer tent, just like she'd stood in front of the walls of cans.

She'd walked away from beer. She'd stayed on the wagon.

He hadn't.

Phillip was an alcoholic. And he was, at this very moment, drunk and probably getting drunker. She'd told him she couldn't be the reason he chose to stay sober. She'd meant it every single time she'd said it.

It shouldn't have hurt so much. But it did. God, it did.

She couldn't save Phillip if he didn't want her to. And to stay around him when he had whiskey on his breath.... He'd tempt her.

Could she really stop kissing him? Could she really stop loving him?

She couldn't. It was all or nothing with her. Always had been. And once she tasted that whiskey...

She rubbed at the skin on the back of her neck. The deal was broken. In so many ways.

What did that leave her with? Besides a broken heart?

It was time to go. She'd done her job. Sun could be haltered, moved and brushed without causing harm to himself or anyone else. The horse, at least, was on the road to recovery.

She *had* to leave before Phillip took her down with him.

She'd left jobs before. Leaving shouldn't be the hard part. Except...she'd started to think of the Beaumont Farms as home. Betty loved it here. Betty and Sun were friends.

She just...she needed another job. Something new to focus on. Something to remind her who she was and what she wanted. She was a horse trainer. One of the best. She didn't need friends or...love.

It just caused pain and since she was an alcoholic, she couldn't ever take anything to numb it. The high wasn't worth it. It wasn't worth *this*.

The only thing she had was her work and her rules. Rules she wouldn't bend, much less break, ever again.

She opened her laptop and blindly scrolled through emails about damaged horses, only to find herself typing a message to her parents. "*Coming home,*" she wrote. "*I didn't forget.*"

It was only then that she realized she was crying.

Fifteen

Everything moved, including Phillip's stomach. *Urgh*.

Jo. He needed Jo. Jo would make this better.

He was moving. Why was he moving? He tried to open his eyes, but it didn't work, so he patted around with his hands.

God, his head. Why did it hurt so badly? Combined with the moving…his stomach was going to make him pay.

He hit something cool and round and long. A bottle. Why was there a bottle next to him on the seat?

Everything shifted to the right and the bottle rolled away. It made the dull clanking noise of glass bouncing off glass. The noise did horrible things to his head.

But he managed to get his eyes open. He was in his limo. He thought. Except…there were bottles everywhere. His fingers closed around something soft and lacy. He held up a scrap of fabric and stared at it for a minute before he realized that it was a pair of red panties. Not the kind Jo wore.

Oh, *shit*. He dropped them as if they were poison and stared around the limo. There were beer bottles all over the place and a few other scraps of clothing. And a woman's shoe. And some questionable stains. God, the *smell*. What had happened?

Oh, no. *No*.

He needed fresh air right now. He fumbled for the knobs on the door. His window went down, which let in way too much light. What time was it?

When was it?

He didn't know. He didn't know where he was or where Jo was and he didn't know what he'd done. But the limo— the limo was full of answers. The wrong ones.

That realization made him want to throw up.

He reached for his phone, but it wasn't there. He tried the knobs again and this time, the divider between the front and the back of the limo slid down.

"Mr. Beaumont? Is everything all right?"

"Uh…" He tried to think, but damn his head. "Ortiz?"

"Yes, Mr. Beaumont?"

"Where are we?"

"We'll be at the farm in ten minutes, Mr. Beaumont."

The farm. Jo. He needed her. Oh, God, she was going to be so mad. "What…time is it?"

"Four. In the afternoon," Ortiz helpfully added.

"Sunday?"

"Sunday."

That meant he hadn't missed that day. Just…Phillip rubbed his head, which did not help. Did he remember Saturday?

"What happened to Fred?"

"He was arrested."

That sounded bad. "Why?"

"He punched Pitbull—you know, the rapper?" Ortiz waited for some sign of recognition, but Phillip had nothing. Ortiz sighed. "There was a fight and Fred got arrested."

"I don't..." *I don't remember.* But that was probably obvious at this point. "Is he still in jail?"

Ortiz shook his head, which somehow made Phillip dizzy. "Your brother Mr. Matthew Beaumont bailed him out."

"Oh." That wasn't his fault, was it? If Fred got arrested and left him all alone, that wasn't his doing, right? He needed to send a message to Jo. He needed to tell her he hadn't done it on purpose. Any of it. It'd just been...it'd been a mistake. Everyone made them. He patted his pocket for his phone, but it still wasn't there. "Where's my phone?"

"It got...flushed. At least, that's what you told me." Ortiz looked at him in the rearview mirror.

"Oh. Right. I remember," he lied. Bad. Very bad.

He really was going to be sick.

Just then, they drove through the massive gates at the edge of Beaumont Farms. His heart tried to feel light—he loved coming back to this place—but there was no lightness in his soul.

He'd messed up. The blackout wasn't worth it.

But it wasn't his fault! Fred was supposed to be his sober coach and he'd gotten in a fight with a rapper and gotten hauled off to jail.

He just had to explain it to Jo, that was all. This was an accident.

He hadn't meant to drink. Bits and pieces filtered back into his consciousness. Fred had disappeared. Phillip had been onstage. Someone had put a beer in his hand. But he wasn't going to drink it. He remembered that clearly now. He wasn't going to drink that beer. He'd promised. He'd hold it, because that was his job. He wanted everyone else to drink Beaumont Beer and have fun. He did a good job. He always did.

But the beer…it'd smelled good. And some woman had kissed him, rubbing her body against his. Because he was Phillip Beaumont and that's what women did. And he *knew* that the picture would wind up online. And that Jo would see it. She'd see this strange woman who meant nothing to him kissing him and the beer bottle in his hand and Jo would think he'd failed her. She'd leave him.

Suddenly, he'd felt the same way he'd felt when Chadwick had said he was selling the farm and the horses—hopeless. He'd been good for three weeks, with Jo, but the moment things went wrong, he wound up with a beer in his hand and woman in his arms. Because it would never change. He would never change.

And the woman tasted like beer and he'd liked it. *Needed* it. Needed not to think about how Jo would look at him, the disappointment all over her.

There'd been a bottle in his hand….

And he'd stopped thinking. Stopped feeling.

"Mr. Beaumont, you want to go to the house?"

What had he done? He *needed* Jo. He needed that silly little donkey. He needed someone to tell him that it would be okay, that he could sleep it off and tomorrow they'd go back to normal. The farm. The horses. Sun. Tomorrow, this would all be a bad dream.

He needed to see her and know that she forgave him. That he hadn't disappointed her. That he hadn't forgotten her, not really.

"The white barn." Yeah, he probably looked like hell and smelled worse, but he had to talk to Jo *now*.

They drove through the perfect pastures. His horses trotted in the fields. It was perfect.

Except for the big trailer hitched to a truck out front. No, no, *no*. He'd gotten here just in time. She couldn't leave. She couldn't leave *him*.

Ortiz pulled off a few feet opposite the trailer. Phillip

tried to open the door but he missed the handle the first time. Then the door swung open and Ortiz was hauling him out. "You sure you want to do this, boss?"

Phillip winced at the sound. "Gotta talk to her." He tried to pull free, but the world started rolling, so he let Ortiz hold him up.

They awkwardly started toward her trailer. He didn't need Ortiz. He could walk. He stopped and straightened up, but his feet wouldn't cooperate. He stumbled and went down to one knee.

"Mr. Beaumont," Ortiz said. "Please."

Phillip heard noises but he couldn't make out what they were. Then he was on his feet again. His head rolled to one side and he saw that Richard was under his left side. "Dick?"

"Don't know if you realize this, sir, but you only call me Dick when you're drunk."

"Wasn't my fault," Phillip tried.

"Sure it wasn't. Let's get you to the house."

"No—need Jo. Betty?"

"*Sir*," Richard said in a voice that was too loud for everything. Then they started moving. Away from the barn. Away from the trailer.

"Wait," came a different voice. A female voice.

Jo.

Somehow, Phillip got himself turned around and found himself facing Jo. This turned out not to be a good thing.

The woman he'd spent weeks chasing? Gone. The chase was over. He could see it in her eyes—hard and cold.

Next to her stood Betty, her small body wrapped up in something that had to be a harness.

"No." It came out shaky. Weak. He tried to clear his throat and start again. "Don't go. I'm sorry."

"Sun," Jo said, "is manageable. He can be haltered and

walked from the stall to the paddock. He can be brushed. He's doing much better."

That statement hung in the air. Phillip was pretty sure he heard someone else whisper "unlike you" but every time he tried to move his head, he had to fight off nausea.

"I didn't—Fred—*Jo*," he begged. Why weren't the words there? Why couldn't he say the right things to make her stay? "Don't go. I'm sorry. I'll do better. I'll *be* better. For you."

Jo looked at the men on either side of Phillip. Both of them stepped back and, miracle of miracles, Phillip's legs held. He stood before her. It was all he could do.

"No. Not *for* me." She took a step toward him. "We had a deal, you and I." This time, her voice was softer. Sadder.

"It won't happen again. Don't leave me. I can't do this without you."

She reached up, her palm warm and soft against his cheek. He leaned into her touch so much he almost lost his balance.

"I can't kiss you and taste whiskey. I can't be the reason you drink or don't drink. I never could. I can't…" She swallowed then, closing her eyes as if she was digging deep for something. "I can't love you more than you love the bottle. So I won't."

Love. That was a good word. The best one he had. "I love you, Jo. Don't go."

Her smile wasn't one, not really. Not when tears spilled down her cheeks. "I won't forget our time together, Phillip." She leaned in close, her breath warming his cheek. "I won't forget you. I just wish…I wish you could say the same."

He tried to put his arms around her and hold onto her until she stopped saying she was leaving, but she was gone—away from him, picking up Betty off the ground and cradling her in her arms.

"No," he tried, but his voice didn't seem to be working so well. "Don't." He tried to chase after her, but he tripped and went down to his knees again. "*Don't*."

Then people were holding him back—or up, or both— he didn't know. All he knew was that she walked away from him.

She carried Betty to her truck. She got in. The door shut. She drove away.

After that, he didn't remember anything else.

He didn't want to.

Sixteen

Jo dusted off her chaps as she climbed back to her feet. Precious was not in the mood to run barrels right now. Jo sighed. If a horse could be passive aggressive, Precious was. She'd let Jo saddle her and mount up as if they were old friends and then *boom*. Jo was on the ground and Precious was on the other side of the paddock, munching grass.

Jo glared as she walked over to the horse. "Here's the bad news," she said as she grabbed the reins and wiped the sweat from her eyes. Late summer sun beat down on her head. Not for the first time, she missed the cool greenness of Beaumont Farms, even as she tried to tell herself that it was summer there, too. "That worked for about twelve seconds. Now we're going to do it again and again until you get tired of it."

Precious shook her head and tried to back up.

Oh, no—Jo wasn't having any of that. She swung into the saddle before the horse could get very far. This time, Jo was ready for her and managed to stay in the saddle when Precious went sideways. "Ha!" she said as she guided the horse around the makeshift barrel run she'd set up in her parents' paddock. "Again."

They ran the barrels several more times, Precious trying to buck her off at the same spot each time. Jo held on. The less fun the horse could have bucking her off, the more likely she'd stop doing it.

In the two months since she'd come home, Jo had continued to train horses. She'd given up the road—for the time being, at least. She was back in her room and her mom was back to grumbling about a donkey sliding around on the hallway rugs.

It'd taken a few days, but Jo had finally told her granny what had happened as they'd rocked on the porch swing.

"Be thankful for the rain," Lina had said after Jo had cried on her shoulder. Which was a very Lina thing to say. "Nothing grows, nothing moves forward without a little rain now and then."

Which was all well and good, except Jo didn't feel as if she'd grown much at all. She was still living with her parents, though that was her choice. She'd billed Beaumont Farms for the time she'd spent with Sun and received a check signed by Matthew Beaumont.

The check alone was enough for a down payment on a piece of land. She could have her pick of properties anywhere she wanted to stake her claim.

But she hadn't pulled the trigger on anything yet. It'd been a relief to come home, to be surrounded by people who loved her no matter what. People who didn't think she'd done the stupid thing by walking away from Phillip Beaumont, but the smart thing.

Plus, after a few months at Beaumont Farms, nothing seemed quite good enough.

She told herself that she was just taking some time off,

but that wasn't true, either. She'd had five horses delivered to her on the ranch, including Precious.

At least she was still getting jobs. Because Phillip had so spectacularly come apart, her leaving the job as she did—crying—had not come back to bite her on the butt. She didn't know what people might be saying about her and Phillip, but it hadn't impacted her work. She was still, first and foremost, a horse trainer who used "nontraditional" methods. Desperate horse owners still wanted her to save their horses. That was a good thing. It paid the bills.

She could be back on the road anytime she wanted to go. And now, she knew she would not have moments of weakness, moments of need. The walls she'd built up—for her own good—would stay up. No more Phillip. No more men. She'd gotten used to it once. She'd get used to it again.

She needed to get used to waking up alone, to going to sleep the same way. To frustrated sexual desire that she was having trouble burying like she used to.

She'd made it years without a man. It'd just take a little while to work Phillip out of her system, that was all. Once she was sure she could do fine on her own again, she'd load up her trailer and hit the road. She'd start looking for a place then.

She spent another hour with Precious, managing to stay in the saddle the whole time. Jo was about to call it a day when she saw a plume of dust kicking up down the road.

She looked back at the house. No one had mentioned they were expecting company today and Precious's owner wasn't due back until this weekend. Who would be driving this far out to the middle of nowhere?

As the car got closer, she saw it was an extended-cab, dual-wheeled truck—a lot like the one she used to haul her trailer. Must be a fellow rancher coming to talk to Dad, she reasoned as she pulled the saddle off Precious and began rubbing the horse down.

She heard the truck stop behind her, heard boots on gravel. "Dad's in the house," she called over her shoulder.

Then she heard Betty braying in the way she did when she was excited about something.

"Hey, Betty—you remember me? That's a good girl."

Jo froze, brush hovering over Precious's back. She knew that voice.

Phillip.

She turned slowly. Phillip Beaumont stood halfway between the truck and the paddock. He was wearing broken-in jeans and a button up shirt that walked the fine line between cowboy and hipster. The tips of brown boots were barely visible in the dirt.

He was rubbing Betty's ears. The donkey leaned into his legs as if the two of them had never been apart.

Something in Jo's chest clenched. He was here. It'd been almost two months, but he was here *now*.

Then he looked up at her. His eyes were brighter, the green in them greener. He looked good. Better than good. He looked right, like the true version of himself.

She was *so* glad to see him. She didn't want to be— she was getting him out of her system—but she was. God, she was.

Behind him, a small man wearing wire-rim glasses stepped out from the other side of the truck.

Phillip nodded his head to the man. "This is Dale," he said with no other introduction. "He's been my sober companion since I got out of rehab."

She should not be this glad to see him. It didn't matter to her one way or the other what he did or why he did it. But still… "You were in rehab?"

"Twenty-eight days in Malibu. I've been sober for fifty-three days now." He gave her a crooked grin, as if this statistic was something that he was both proud of and embarrassed by.

"You have?" She stared at him—and got hip-checked by Precious. She stumbled forward and turned to glare at the horse. "One second," she told Phillip and Dale.

She untied Precious's lead from the fence and opened the paddock gate. It didn't take longer than a minute or two to lead the horse to a pasture, but it felt as if it took a week. She felt Phillip's eyes on her the entire time and, just as it had that first time, it made her want to flutter.

She wanted to throw herself in his arms and tell him how damn much she'd missed him—missed working horses with him, missed waking up with him.

Things she couldn't miss. Things she *wouldn't* miss.

He was just a temptation, that was all. And she'd gotten very good at resisting temptations. Was this any different than standing in front of the beer coolers in a convenience store?

No. She was strong enough to resist.

Once the horse was turned loose, she faced Phillip again. "You finished rehab and have been sober for almost two months?"

"I knew you might not believe me." But instead of being put out by her doubt, Phillip's eyes focused on hers as if no one else in the world existed. "That's why I brought Dale. He can vouch for me."

She looked at Dale, who nodded. "He's followed his plan perfectly."

"You have a plan?" They'd had a plan before and that hadn't worked out so well. "What happened?"

Phillip took a step toward her. The confident grin was gone and he looked earnest. She wanted to believe him. Oh, how she wanted to believe him.

"I believe the correct phrase is 'hit bottom.' Matthew took me to rehab three days after you left. It wasn't exactly fun, but after my head cleared, I knew I could do it because I'd already done it with you."

Three days was a long time to bounce around at rock bottom. "And after that? Did you lose the farm?"

He took another step toward her. She wanted to reach out and touch him, to know that he was really here and whole and sober.

"The Beaumont Brewery has been sold. The deal closed. I was able to buy the horses with my share of the sale."

"Just the horses? But the farm…" The farm was his home.

For such a short time, the farm had felt like *her* home.

Another step forward. "Chadwick kept it."

"Oh."

Another step closer. He reached out and brushed his thumb over her cheek. "I no longer work for Beaumont Brewery," Phillip said, cupping her cheek in his hand. "After that last festival, well, we mutually agreed to part company. I have a new job."

"Doing what?"

This step brought him close enough that she could wrap her arms around his waist and hold on to him. She almost did, too. But she couldn't. She *wouldn't*.

"I'm the head of Beaumont Farms."

She blinked up at him. "You're *what?*"

"It turns out that the new owners of the Beaumont Brewery have decided that the Percheron draft team is too valuable to the brand to give up. They're leasing the Percherons from the Beaumont family. Chadwick got them to sign a ten-year non-exclusive contract."

"It worked? Going on the morning shows? The Facebook poll?"

He nodded. "It did. Plus, it turns out that Chadwick is keeping the Percheron Drafts craft beer brand for himself—he's going to use the Percherons, too. The Brewery had exclusive use of the Beaumont wagons and harnesses, but I've been working with Chadwick and Matthew on a marketing plan that will make the best use of the horses while differentiating between the companies."

"Wow. But—Percheron Drafts is still a beer company."

"I don't work for Percheron Drafts. I work for Beaumont Farms. Chadwick incorporated the land as a separate entity. Right now, I *choose* not to visit the new brewery. Chadwick and Matthew have been coming out to the farmhouse for our meetings. They're being extremely supportive."

"Even Chadwick?"

His smile—God, that was going to be her undoing. "Even Chadwick. It turns out that we get along a lot better when I'm not drunk and he's not a jerk."

He leaned down closer—too close. She pulled back, away from his sure hands and intent gaze. "That's really good. I'm happy for you. But why are you here?"

The space she'd put between them wasn't enough to stop the corner of his mouth from curving into a smile that wasn't quite predatory but came damned close. "Because I learned the hard way the blackouts weren't worth it. They weren't worth losing the farm and the horses and they most especially weren't worth losing you. I had a good month where you showed me that my life could be what I wanted it to be. I almost threw it all away. The choice was mine and so was the blame."

She shook her head. He was saying all the right things, all the things she needed to hear. But...

"I can't be the reason, Phillip."

For the first time, she saw doubt in his eyes. "I know. But it turns out, I couldn't live with myself for letting you go."

"You couldn't?"

"No." He took a deep breath. "I'm sorry that I broke my promise to you. I know I hurt you."

"You did. And worse, you made me doubt myself." He

nodded. No lame excuses, no blaming others. He took full responsibility. "But," she went on, "you also showed me that I was stronger than I gave myself credit for."

"Got your wagons unhitched now?"

She couldn't help herself. She smiled at him and was rewarded with a smile of his own. It wasn't fair for a man to look that good. It just wasn't. "Yup."

"Let me make it up to you, Jo. I want to make things right between us."

She eyed him. "How?"

There was that grin again—sharp and confident, a man who always got what he wanted. Even if he had to go through rehab to get it.

"As the manager of Beaumont Farms, I'm looking for ways to make Beaumont the premiere name in the horse world. I happen to have a well-trained stallion that's going to command huge stud fees, but I want to branch out."

Was he calling Sun well-trained? Her face grew hot. "Yeah?"

He nodded, warming to his subject. "I decided having a professional on-site trainer, someone who specializes in rehabilitating broken horses, would add a lot of validity to the brand."

Her mouth dropped open in shock. "You decided *that?*"

He cupped her face in his hands. "Come home to the farm, Jo. I want you. I don't want to lose you again. And I don't want to stay sober *because* of you. I want to do it *for* you. To show you that I'm the man who's not perfect, but perfect for you. Because with you, I'm the man I always wanted to be."

"I can't be with you if you drink. I can't kiss you and taste whiskey. Not now, not ever."

He leaned down, his lips brushing over hers. She was powerless to stop him, powerless to do anything but wrap her arms around his waist and pull him in tight.

"I will never drink again, Jo—because more than the horses, more than the land, I can't lose you. You make me chase you. You never pull your punches with me. I'm not a Beaumont when I'm with you. I'm just Phillip."

"You've always been more than a Beaumont to me," she told him. Her voice came out shaky, but she didn't care.

"I don't want to forget you," he whispered. "I *never* want to forget you."

She crushed her lips against his. His teeth scraped over her lip—rough, but gentle. Just the way she wanted it. Just the way she wanted *him*.

He rested his forehead against hers. Her hat fell off, but she didn't care.

"Don't give up on us. I can't fix what I did, but what we have is worth saving. Marry me, Jo. Come home."

Home. With Phillip. A piece of land she could call her own—*their* own. Everything she'd ever wanted.

"I couldn't forget you, either. I tried. I kept telling myself I just had to get you out of my system, but…"

He grinned, satisfied and hungry all at the same time. One of his fingers traced the spot where her neck met her shoulder. Her body ached for his touch, his bite. "Marry me. We'll remember the days—*and* the nights—together."

How could she say no to that?

She couldn't.

So she didn't.

* * * * *

A BEAUMONT CHRISTMAS WEDDING

BY
SARAH M. ANDERSON

To Fiona Marsden, Kelli Bruns and Jenn Hoopes—
three of the nicest Twitter friends around.
Thanks, ladies! You guys rock!

One

Matthew Beaumont looked at his email in amazement. The sharks were circling. He'd known they would be, but still, the sheer volume of messages clamoring for more information was impressive. There were emails from *TMZ, Perez Hilton* and PageSix.com, all sent in the past twenty minutes.

They all wanted the same thing. Who on earth was Jo Spears, the lucky woman who was marrying into the Beaumont family and fortune? And why had playboy Phillip Beaumont, Matthew's brother, chosen her—a woman no one had ever heard of before—when he could have had his pick of supermodels and Hollywood starlets?

Matthew rubbed his temples. The truth was actually quite boring—Jo Spears was a horse trainer who'd spent the past ten years training some of the most expensive horses in the world. There wasn't much there that would satisfy the gossip sites.

But if the press dug deeper and made the connection between Jo Spears, horse trainer, and Joanna Spears, they might dig up the news reports about a drunk-driving accident a decade ago in which Joanna was the passenger—and the driver died. They might turn up a lot of people who'd partied with Joanna.

They might turn this wedding into a circus.

His email pinged. *Vanity Fair* had gotten back to him. He scanned the email. Excellent. They would send a photographer if he invited their reporter as a guest.

Matthew knew the only way to keep this Beaumont wedding—planned for Christmas Eve—from becoming a circus was to control the message. He had to fight fire with fire and if that meant embedding the press into the wedding itself, then so be it.

Yes, it was great that Phillip was getting married. For the first time in his life, Matthew was hopeful his brother was going to be all right. But for Matthew, this wedding meant so much more than just the bonds of holy matrimony for his closest brother.

This wedding was the PR opportunity of a lifetime. Matthew had to show the world that the Beaumont family wasn't falling apart or flaming out.

God knew there'd been enough rumors to that effect after Chadwick Beaumont had sold the Beaumont Brewery and married his secretary, which had been about the same time that Phillip had very publically fallen off the wagon and wound up in rehab. And that didn't even include what his stepmothers and half siblings were doing.

It had been common knowledge that the Beaumonts, once the preeminent family of Denver, had fallen so far down that they'd never get back up.

To hell with common knowledge.

This was Matthew's chance to prove himself—not just in the eyes of the press but in his family's eyes, too. He'd show them once and for all that he wasn't the illegitimate child who was too little, too late a Beaumont. He was one of them, and this was his chance to erase the unfortunate circumstances of his birth from everyone's mind.

A perfectly orchestrated wedding and reception would show the world that instead of crumbling, the Beaumonts were stronger than ever. And it was up to Matthew, the former vice president of Public Relations for the Beaumont Brewery and the current chief marketing officer of Percheron Drafts Beer, to make that happen.

Building buzz was what Matthew did best. He was the only one in the family who had the media contacts and the PR savvy to pull this off.

Control the press, control the world—that's how a Beaumont handles it.

Hardwick Beaumont's words came back to him. When Matthew had managed yet another scandal, his father had said that to him. It'd been one of the few times Hardwick had ever complimented his forgotten third son. One of the few times Hardwick had ever made Matthew feel as if he *was* a Beaumont, not the bastard he'd once been.

Controlling the press was something that Matthew had gotten exceptionally good at. And he wasn't about to drop the ball now. This wedding would prove not only that the Beaumonts still had a place in this world but that Matthew had a place in the family.

He could save the Beaumont reputation. He could save the Beaumonts. And in doing so, he could redeem himself.

He'd hired the best wedding planner in Denver. They'd booked the chapel on the Colorado Heights University campus and had invited two hundred guests to the wedding. The reception would be at the Mile High Station, with dinner for six hundred, and a team of Percherons would pull the happy couple in either a carriage or a sleigh, weather depending. They had the menu set, the cake ordered, the favors ready and the photographer on standby. Matthew had his family—all four of his father's ex-wives and all nine of his half brothers and sisters—promising to be on their best behavior.

The only thing he didn't have under his control was the bride and her maid of honor, a woman named Whitney Maddox.

Jo had said that Whitney was a horse breeder who lived

a quiet life in California, so Matthew didn't anticipate too much trouble from her. She was coming two weeks before the wedding and staying at the farm with Jo and Phillip. That way she could do all the maid-of-honor things—dress fittings and bachelorette parties, the lot of it. All of which had been preplanned by Matthew and the wedding planner, of course. There was no room for error.

The wedding had to be perfect. What mattered was showing the world that the Beaumonts were still a family. A *successful* family.

What mattered was Matthew proving that he was a legitimate Beaumont.

He opened a clean document and began to write his press release as if his livelihood depended on it.

Because it did.

Whitney pulled up in front of the building that looked as if it was three different houses stuck together. She would not be nervous about this—not about the two weeks away from her horses, about staying in a stranger's house for said two weeks or about the press that went with being in a Beaumont Christmas wedding. Especially that.

Of course, she knew who Phillip Beaumont was—didn't everyone? He was the handsome face of Beaumont Brewery—or had been, right up until his family had sold out. And Jo Spears was a dear friend—practically the best friend Whitney had. The only friend, really. Jo knew all about Whitney's past and just didn't care. And in exchange for that unconditional friendship, the least Whitney could do was suck it up and be Jo's maid of honor.

In the high-society wedding of the year. With hundreds of guests. And photographers. And the press. And...

Jo came out to greet her.

"You haven't changed a bit!" Whitney called as she shut her door. She shivered. December in Denver was an entirely different beast from December in California. "Except you're not wearing your hat!"

"I didn't wear the hat when we watched movies in your house, did I?" Jo wore a wide smile as she gave Whitney a brief hug. "How was the drive?"

"Long," Whitney admitted. "That's why I didn't bring anyone with me. I thought about bringing the horses, but it's just too cold up here for them to be in a trailer that long, and none of my dogs do well in the car."

She'd desperately wanted to bring Fifi, her retired greyhound, or Gater, the little mutt that was pug and…something. Those two were her indoor dogs, the ones that curled up next to her on the couch or on her lap and kept her company. But Fifi did not travel well and Gater didn't like to leave Fifi.

Animals didn't care who you were. They never read the headlines. It didn't matter to them if you'd accidentally flashed the paparazzi when you were nineteen or how many times you'd been arrested for driving while intoxicated. All that mattered to animals was that you fed them and rubbed their ears.

Besides, Whitney was on vacation. A vacation with a wedding in it, but still. She was going to see the sights in Denver and get her nails done and all sorts of fun things. It didn't seem fair to bring the dogs only to leave them in a bedroom most of the time.

Jo nodded as Whitney got her bags out of the truck. "Who's watching them?"

"Donald—you remember him, right? From the next ranch over?"

"The crusty old fart who doesn't watch TV?"

Jo and Whitney shared a look. In that moment, Whitney was glad she'd come. Jo understood her as no one else did.

Everyone else in the world thought Donald was borderline insane—a holdover hippie from the 1960s who'd done too much acid back in the day. He lived off the grid, talked about animals as if they were his brothers and discussed Mother Earth as if she were coming to dinner next week.

But that meant Donald wasn't tuned in to pop culture. Which also meant he didn't know who Whitney was—who she'd been. Donald just thought Whitney was the neighbor who really should install more solar panels on her barn roof. And if she had to occasionally listen to a lecture on composting toilets, well, that was a trade-off she was willing to make.

She was going to miss her animals, but knowing Donald, he was probably sitting on the ground in the paddock, telling her horses bedtime stories.

Besides, being part of her best friend's wedding was an opportunity even she couldn't pass up. "What's this I hear about you and Phillip Beaumont?"

Jo smiled. "Come on," she said, grabbing one of Whitney's bags. "Dinner will be in about an hour. I'll get you caught up."

She led Whitney inside. The whole house was festooned—there was no other word for it—with red bows and pine boughs. A massive tree, blinking with red-and-white lights, the biggest star Whitney had ever seen perched on top, stood in a bay window. The whole place had such a rustic Christmas charm that Whitney felt herself grinning. This would be a perfect way to spend Christmas, instead of watching *It's a Wonderful Life* on the couch at home.

A small brown animal with extremely long ears clomped up to her and sniffed. "Well, hello again, Betty," Whitney said as she crouched down onto her heels. "You remember me? You spent a few months sitting on my couch last winter."

The miniature donkey sniffed Whitney's hair and brayed before rubbing her head into Whitney's hands.

"If I recall correctly," Jo said, setting down Whitney's bag, "your pups didn't particularly care for a donkey in the house."

"Not particularly," Whitney agreed. Fifi hadn't minded

as long as Betty stayed off her bed, but Gater had taken it as a personal insult that Whitney had allowed a hoofed animal into the house. As far as Gater was concerned, hoofed animals belonged in the barn.

She stood. Betty leaned against her legs so that Whitney could stroke her long ears.

"You're not going to believe this," Jo said as she moved Whitney's other bag, "but Matthew wants her to walk down the aisle. He's rigged up a basket so she can carry the flower petals and it's got a pillow attached on top so she can carry the rings. The flower girl will walk beside her and throw the petals. He says it'll be an amazing visual."

Whitney blinked. "Wait—Matthew? I thought you were marrying Phillip?"

"She is." A blindingly handsome man strode into the room—tall and blond and instantly recognizable. "Hello," he said with a grin as he walked up to Whitney. He leaned forward, his eyes fastened on hers, and stuck out a hand. "I'm Phillip Beaumont."

The Phillip Beaumont. Having formerly been someone famous, Whitney was not prone to getting starstruck. But Phillip was looking at her so intently that for a moment, she forgot her own name.

"And you must be Whitney Maddox," he went on, effortlessly filling the silence. "Jo's told me about the months she spent with you last winter. She said you raise some of the most beautiful Trakehners she's ever worked with."

"Oh. Yes!" Whitney shook her head. Phillip was a famous horseman and her Trakehner horses were a remarkably safe subject. "Joy was mine—Pride and Joy."

"The stallion who took gold in the World Equestrian Games?" Phillip smiled down at her and she realized he still had her hand. "I don't have any Trakehners. Clearly that's something I need to rectify."

She looked at Jo, feeling helpless and more than a little

guilty that Jo's intended was making her blush. But Jo just laughed.

"Too much," Jo said to Phillip as she looped her arm through his. "Whitney's not used to that much charm." She looked at Whitney. "Sorry about that. Phillip, this is Whitney. Whitney, this is Phillip."

Whitney nodded, trying to remember the correct social interaction. "It's a pleasure. Congratulations on getting married."

Phillip grinned at her, but then he thankfully focused that full-wattage smile on Jo. "Thanks."

They stared at each other for a moment, the adoration obvious. Whitney looked away.

It'd been a long time since a man had looked at her like that. And, honestly, she couldn't be sure that Drako Evans had ever looked at her quite like that. Their short-lived engagement hadn't been about love. It had been about pissing off their parents. And it had worked. The headlines had been spectacular. Maybe that was why those headlines still haunted her.

As she rubbed Betty's ears, Whitney noticed the dinner table was set for four. For the first time since she'd arrived, she smelled food cooking. Lasagna and baking bread. Her stomach rumbled.

"So," Phillip said into the silence. His piercing blue eyes turned back to her. "Matthew will be here in about forty minutes for dinner."

Which did nothing to answer the question she'd asked Jo earlier. "Matthew is…who?"

This time, Phillip's grin was a little less charming, a little sharper. "Matthew Beaumont. My best man and younger brother."

Whitney blinked. "Oh?"

"He's organizing the wedding," Phillip went on as if that were no big deal.

"He's convinced that this is the PR event of the year," Jo said. "I told him I'd be happy getting married by a judge—"

"Or running off to Vegas," Phillip added, wrapping his arm around Jo's waist and pulling her into a tight embrace.

"But he insists this big wedding is the Beaumont way. And since I'm going to be a Beaumont now..." Jo sighed. "He's taken control of this and turned it into a spectacle."

Whitney stared at Jo and Phillip, unsure what to say. The Jo she knew wouldn't let anyone steamroll her into a grandiose wedding.

"But," Jo went on, softening into a smile that could almost be described as shy, "it's going to be amazing. The chapel is beautiful and we'll have a team of Percherons pulling a carriage from there to the reception. The photographer is experienced and the dress..." She got a dreamy look in her eyes. "Well, you'll see tomorrow. We have a dress fitting at ten."

"It sounds like it's going to be perfect," Whitney said. And she meant it—a Christmas Eve ceremony? Horse-drawn carriages? Gowns? It had all the trappings of a true storybook wedding.

"It better be." Phillip chuckled.

"Let me show you to your room," Jo said, grabbing a bag.

That sounded good to Whitney. She needed a moment to sort through everything. She lived a quiet life now, one where she didn't have to navigate family relations or PR events masquerading as weddings. As long as she didn't leave her ranch, all she worried about was catching Donald when he was on a soapbox.

Jo led her through the house, pointing out which parts were original, which wasn't much, and which parts had been added later, which was most of it. She showed Whitney the part that Phillip had added, the master suite with a hot tub on the deck.

Then the hall turned again and they were in a different part, built in the 1970s. This was the guest quarters, Jo told her. Whitney had a private bath and was far enough removed from the rest of the house that she wouldn't hear anything else.

Jo opened a door and flipped on the light. Whitney had half expected vintage '70s decor, but the room was done in cozy green-and-red plaids that made it look Christmassy. A bouquet of fresh pine and holly was arranged on the mantel over a small fireplace.

Jo walked over to it and flipped a switch. Flames jumped to life in the grate. "Phillip had automatic switches installed a few years ago," she explained. On the other side of the bed was a dresser. Jo said, "Extra blankets are in there. It's going to be a lot colder here than it is at your ranch."

"Good to know." Whitney set her bag down at the foot of the bed. The only other furniture in the room was a small table with an armchair next to it. The room looked like a great place to spend the winter. She felt herself relax a little bit. "So...you and Phillip?"

"Me and Phillip," Jo agreed, sounding as though she didn't quite believe it herself. "He's—well, you've seen him in action. He has a way of just looking at a woman that's... *suggestive*."

"So I wasn't imagining that?"

Jo laughed. "Nope. That's just how he is."

This did nothing to explain how, exactly, Jo had wound up with Phillip. Of all the men in the world, Whitney would have put "playboy bachelor" pretty low on the list of possible husbands for Jo. But Whitney had no idea how to ask the question without it coming out wrong.

It could be that the Phillip in the kitchen wasn't the same as the Phillip in the headlines. Maybe things had been twisted and turned until nothing but the name was the same. More than anyone, Whitney knew how that worked.

"He has a horse," Jo explained, looking sheepish. "Sun— Kandar's Golden Sun."

Whitney goggled at her. "Wait—I've heard of that horse. Didn't he sell for seven million dollars?"

"Yup. And he was a hot mess at any price," she added with a chuckle. "Took me a week before he'd just stand still, you know?"

Whitney nodded, trying to picture a horse *that* screwed up. When Jo had come out to Whitney's ranch to deal with Sterling, the horse of hers that had developed an irrational fear of water, it'd taken her only a few hours in the paddock before the horse was rubbing his head against Jo. "A whole week?"

"Any other horse would have died of sheer exhaustion, but that's what makes Sun special. I can take you down to see him after dinner. He's an amazing stud—one to build a stable on."

"So the horse brought you together?"

Jo nodded. "I know Phillip's got a reputation—that's part of why Matthew insists we have this big wedding, to show the world that Phillip's making a commitment. But he's been sober for seven months now. We'll have a sober coach on hand at the reception." A hint of a blush crept over Jo's face. "If you'd like…"

Whitney nodded. She wasn't the only one who was having trouble voicing her concerns. "I don't think there's going to be a problem. I've been clean for almost eleven years." She swallowed. "Does Phillip know who I am?"

"Sure." Jo's eyebrow notched up in challenge. "You're Whitney Maddox, the well-known horse breeder."

"No, not that. I mean—well, you know what I mean."

"He knows," Jo said, giving Whitney the look that she'd seen Jo give Donald the hippie when he gave her a lecture on how she should switch to biodiesel. "But we understand that the past is just that—the past."

"Oh." Air rushed out of her so fast she actually sagged

in relief. "That's good. That's *great*. I just don't want to be a distraction—this is your big day."

"It won't be a problem," Jo said in a reassuring voice. "And you're right—the day will be very big!"

They laughed. It felt good to laugh with Jo again. She hadn't had to stay a whole two months with Whitney last year—Sterling hadn't been that difficult to handle—but the two of them had gotten along because they understood that the past was just that. So Jo had stayed through the slow part of the year and taught Whitney some of her training techniques. It'd been a good two months. For the first time in her adult life, Whitney hadn't felt quite so...alone.

And now she'd get that feeling again for two weeks.

"And you're happy?" That was the important question.

Jo's features softened. "I am. He's a good man who had an interesting life—to say the least. He's learned how to deal with his family with all that charm. He wasn't hitting on you—that's just how he copes with situations that make him nervous."

"Really? He must have an, um, unusual family."

Jo laughed again. "I'll just say this—they're a lot to handle, but on the whole, they're not bad people. Like Matthew. He can be a little controlling, but he really does want what's best for the family and for us." She stood. "I'll let you get freshened up. Matthew should be here in a few."

"Sounds good."

Jo shut the door on her way out, leaving Whitney alone with her thoughts. She was glad she'd come.

This was what she wanted—to feel normal. To *be* normal. To be able to walk into a room and not be concerned with what people thought they knew about her. Instead, to have people, like Phillip, take her at face value and make her feel welcome.

And he had a brother who was coming to dinner.

What did Matthew Beaumont look like? More to the

point, what did he act like? Brothers could like a lot of the same things, right?

What if Matthew Beaumont looked at her the way his brother did, without caring about who she'd been in the past? What if he talked to her about horses instead of headlines? What if—? What if he wasn't involved with anyone?

Whitney didn't hook up. That part of her life was dead and buried. But…a little Christmas romance between the maid of honor and the best man wouldn't be such a bad thing, would it? It could be fun.

She hurried to the bathroom, daring to hope that this Matthew Beaumont was single. He was coming to dinner tonight and it sounded as if he would be involved with a lot of the planned activities. She was here for two weeks. Perhaps the built-in time limit was a good thing. That way, if things didn't go well, she had an out—she could go home.

Although…it had been eleven years since she'd attempted anything involving the opposite sex. Making a pass at the best man might not be the smartest thing she could do.

She washed her face. A potential flirtation with Matthew Beaumont called for eyeliner, at the very least. Whitney made up her face and decided to put on a fresh top. She dug out the black silk before putting it aside. Jo was in jeans and flannel, after all. This was not a fancy dinner. Whitney decided to go with the red V-neck cashmere sweater—soft but not ostentatious. The kind of top that maybe a single, handsome man would accidentally brush with his fingers. Perfect.

Would Matthew be blond, like Phillip? Would he have the same smile, the same blue eyes? She was brushing out her short hair when, from deep inside the house, a bell chimed.

She slicked on a little lip gloss and headed out. She tried to retrace her steps, but she got confused. The house had a bunch of hallways that went in different directions. She tried one set of stairs but found a door that was locked at the bottom. That wasn't right—Jo hadn't led her through a door.

She backtracked, trying not to panic. Hopefully, everyone wasn't downstairs waiting on her.

She found another stairwell, but it didn't seem any more familiar than the first one had. It ended in a darkened room. Whitney decided to go back rather than stumble around in the dark. God, she shouldn't have spent so much time getting ready. She should have gone back down with Jo. Or gotten written directions. Getting lost was embarrassing.

She found her room again, which had to count for something. She went the opposite direction and was relieved when she passed the master suite. Finally. She picked up the pace. Maybe she wasn't too late.

She could hear voices now—Jo's and Phillip's and another voice, deep and strong. Matthew.

She hurried down the steps, then remembered she was trying to make a good impression. It wouldn't do to come rushing in like a tardy teenager. She needed to slow down to make a proper entrance.

She slammed on the brakes in the middle of a step near the bottom and stumbled. Hard. She tripped down the last two steps and all but fell into the living room. She was going down, damn it! She braced for the impact.

It didn't come. Instead of hitting the floor or running into a piece of furniture, she fell into a pair of strong arms and against a firm, warm chest.

"Oof," the voice that went with that chest said.

Whitney looked up into a pair of eyes that were a deep blue. He smiled down at her and this time, she didn't feel as if she were going to forget her own name. She felt as if she'd never forget this moment.

"I've got you."

Not blond, she realized. Auburn hair. A deep red that seemed just right on him. And he did have her. His arms were around her waist and he was lifting her up. She felt secure. The feeling was *wonderful*.

Then, without warning, everything changed. His warm smile froze as his eyes went hard. The strong arms became iron bars around her and the next thing she knew, she was being pushed not up but away.

Matthew Beaumont set her back on her feet and stepped clear of her. With a glare that could only be described as ferocious, he turned to Phillip and Jo.

"What," he said in the meanest voice Whitney had heard in a long time, "is Whitney Wildz doing here?"

Two

Matthew waited for an answer. It'd better be a damn good one, too. What possible explanation could there be for former teen star Whitney Wildz to be in Phillip's house?

"Matthew," Jo said in an icy tone, "I'd like you to meet my maid of honor, Whitney Maddox."

"Try to stop being an ass," Phillip said under his breath.

"Whitney," Jo went on, as if Phillip hadn't spoke, "this is Matthew Beaumont, Phillip's brother and best man."

"Maddox?" He turned back to the woman who looked as though she'd been stepped on by a Percheron. At least they could all agree her first name was Whitney. Maybe there was a mistake? But no. There was no missing that white streak in her hair or those huge pale eyes set against her alabaster skin. "You're Whitney Wildz. I'd recognize you anywhere."

Her eyes closed and her head jerked to the side as if he'd slapped her.

Someone grabbed him. "Try *harder*," Phillip growled in his ear. Then, louder, Phillip said, "Dinner's ready. Whitney, is iced tea all right?"

Whitney Wildz—Matthew had no doubt that was who she was—opened her eyes. A wave of pain washed over him when she looked up at him. Then she drew herself up.

"Thank you," she said in that breathy way of hers. Then she stepped around him.

Memories came back to him. He'd watched her show, *Growing Up Wildz*, all the time with his younger siblings Frances and Byron. Because Matthew was a good brother—the best—he'd watched it with them. He'd even scored VIP tickets to the *Growing Up Wildz* concert tour when it came through Denver and taken the twins, since their father couldn't be bothered to remember that it was their fifteenth birthday. Matthew was a good brother just taking care of his siblings. That was what he told everyone else.

But that wasn't, strictly, the truth.

He'd watched it for Whitney.

And now Whitney was here.

This was *bad*. This was quite possibly the worst thing that could have happened to this wedding—to him. It would have been easier if Phillip were screwing her. That sort of thing was easy to hush up—God knew Matthew had enough practice covering for his father's indiscretions.

But to have Whitney Wildz herself standing up at the altar, in front of the press and the photographers—not to mention the guests?

He tried to remember the last time she'd been in the news. She'd stumbled her way up on stage and then tripped into the podium, knocking it off the dais and into a table. The debate hadn't been about *if* she'd been on something, just *what*—drugs? Alcohol? Both?

And then tonight she'd basically fallen down the stairs and into his arms. He hadn't minded catching a beautiful woman at the time. The force of her fall had pressed her body against his and what had happened to him was some sort of primal response that had taken control of his body before he'd realized it.

Mine, was the only coherent thought he'd managed to produce as he'd kept her on her feet. Hell, yeah, he'd responded. He was a man, after all.

But then he'd recognized her.

What was she on? And what would happen if she stumbled her way down the aisle?

This was a disaster of epic PR proportions. This woman was going to mess up all of his plans. And if he couldn't pull off this wedding, would he ever be able to truly call himself a Beaumont?

Phillip jerked him toward the table. "For the love of everything holy," he hissed in Matthew's ear, "be a gentleman."

Matthew shook him off. He had a few things he'd like to say to his brother and his future sister-in-law. "Why didn't you tell me?" he half whispered back at Phillip. "Do you know what this *means* for the wedding?"

On the other side of the room, Jo was at the fridge, getting the iced tea. Whitney stood next to her, head down and arms tucked around her slender waist.

For a second, he felt bad. Horrible, actually. The woman who stood thirty feet away from where he and Phillip were didn't look much like Whitney Wildz. Yes, she had Whitney's delicate bone structure and sweetheart face and yes, she had the jet-black hair with the telltale white streak in it. But her hair was cut into a neat pixie—no teased perm with blue and pink streaks. Her jeans and sweater fit her well and were quite tasteful—nothing like the ripped jeans and punk-rock T-shirts she'd always worn on the show. And she certainly wasn't acting strung out.

If it hadn't been for her face—and those pale green eyes, like polished jade, and that hair—he might not have recognized her.

But he did. Everything about him did.

"It means," Phillip whispered back, "that Jo's friend is here for the wedding. Whitney Maddox—she's a respected horse breeder. You will knock this crap off now or I'll—"

"You'll *what*? You haven't been able to beat me up since we were eight and you know it." Matthew tensed. He had a scant half inch on Phillip but he'd long ago learned to make the most of it.

Phillip grinned at him. It was not a kind thing on his face. "I'll turn Jo loose on you and trust me, buddy, that's a fate worse than death. Now knock it off and act like a decent human being."

There was something wrong about this. For so long, Matthew had been the one who scolded Phillip to straighten up and fly right. Phillip had been the one who didn't know how to act in polite company, who'd always found the most embarrassing thing to say and then said it. And it'd been Matthew who'd followed behind, cleaning up the messes, dealing with the headlines and soothing the ruffled feathers. That was what he did.

Briefly, Matthew wanted to be proud of his brother. He'd finally grown up.

But as wonderful as that was, it didn't change the fact that Whitney Wildz was not only going to be sitting down for dinner with them tonight, but she was also going to be in the Beaumont wedding.

He would have to rethink his entire strategy.

"Dinner," Jo called out. She sounded unnaturally perky about it. There was something odd about Jo being perky. It did nothing to help his mood.

"I really wish you had some beer in the house," he muttered to Phillip.

"Tough. Welcome to sobriety." Phillip led the way back to the table.

Matthew followed, trying to come up with a new game plan. He had a couple of options that he could see right off the bat. He could go with denial, just as Phillip and Jo seemed to be doing. This was Whitney Maddox. He had no knowledge of Whitney Wildz.

But that wasn't a good plan and he knew it. He'd recognized her, after all. Someone else was bound to do the same and the moment that someone did, it'd be all over. Yes, the list of celebrities who were attending this wedding was long but someone as scandalous as Whitney Wildz would create a stir no matter what she did.

He could go on the offensive. Send out a press release announcing that Whitney Wildz was the maid of honor. Hit the criticism head-on. If he did it early enough, he might defuse the situation—make it a nonissue by the big day. It could work.

Or it could blow up in his face. This wedding was about showing the world that the Beaumonts were above scandal— that they were stronger than ever. How was that going to happen now? Everything Whitney Wildz did was a scandal.

He took his seat. Whitney sat to his left, Phillip to his right. Jo's ridiculous little donkey sat on the floor in between him and Whitney. Good. Fine. At least he didn't have to look at Whitney, he reasoned. Just at Jo.

Who was not exactly thrilled with him. Phillip was right—Matthew was in no mood to have Jo turned loose on him. So he forced his best fake smile—the one he used when he was defusing some ticking time bomb created by one of his siblings. It always worked when he was talking to reporters.

He glanced at Phillip and then at Jo. Damn. The smile wasn't working on them.

He could *feel* Whitney sitting next to him. He didn't like that. He didn't want to be aware of her like that. He wasn't some teenager anymore, crushing in secret. He was a grown man with real problems.

Her.

But Phillip was staring daggers at him, and Jo looked as though she was going to stab him with the butter knife. So Matthew dug deep. He could be a gentleman. He could put on the Beaumont face no matter what. Being able to talk to a woman was part of the Beaumont legacy—a legacy he'd worked too hard to make his own. He wasn't about to let an unexpected blast from his past undermine everything he'd worked for. This wedding was about proving his legitimacy and that was that.

Phillip glared at him. Right. The wedding was about Phillip and Jo, too. And now their maid of honor.

God, what a mess.

"So, Whitney," Matthew began. She flinched when he said her name. He kept his voice pleasant and level. "What are you doing these days?"

Jo notched an eyebrow at him as she served the lasagna. *Hey*, he wanted to tell her. *I'm trying.*

Whitney smiled, but it didn't reach her eyes. "I raise horses." She took a piece of bread and passed the basket to him. She made sure not to touch him when she did it.

"Ah." That wasn't exactly a lot to go on, but it did explain how she and Jo knew each other, he guessed.

When Whitney didn't offer any other information, he asked, "What kind of horses?"

"Trakehners."

Matthew waited, but she didn't elaborate.

"One of her horses won gold in the World Equestrian Games," Phillip said. He followed up this observation with a swift kick to Matthew's shin.

Ow. Matthew grunted in pain but he managed not to curse out loud. "That's interesting."

"It's amazing," Phillip said. "Not even Dad could breed or buy a horse that took home gold." He leaned forward, turned on the Beaumont smile and aimed it squarely at Whitney.

Something flared in Matthew. He didn't like it when Phillip smiled at her like that.

"Trust me," Phillip continued, "he tried. Not winning

gold was one of his few failures as a horseman. That and not winning a Triple Crown."

Whitney cut Matthew a look out of the corner of her eye that hit him funny. Then she turned her attention to Phillip. "No one's perfect, right?"

"Not even Hardwick Beaumont," he agreed with a twinkle in his eye. "It turns out there are just some things money can't buy."

Whitney grinned. Suddenly, Matthew wanted to punch his brother—hard. This was normal enough—this was how Phillip talked to women. But seeing Whitney warm to him?

Phillip glanced at Matthew. *Be a gentleman*, he seemed to be saying. "Whitney's Trakehners are beautiful, highly trained animals. She's quite well-known in horse circles."

Whitney Wildz was well-known in horse circles? Matthew didn't remember any mention of that from the last article he'd read about her. Only that she'd made a spectacle of herself.

"How long have you been raising horses?"

"I bought my ranch eleven years ago." She focused her attention on her food. "After I left Hollywood."

So she really was Whitney Wildz. But…eleven years? That didn't seem right. It couldn't have been more than two years since the last headline.

"Where is your ranch?"

If Matthew had known who she really was, he would have done more digging. Be Prepared wasn't just a good Boy Scout motto—it was vital to succeeding in public relations.

One thing was abundantly clear. Matthew was not prepared for Whitney, whatever her last name was.

"Not too far from Bakersfield. It's very…quiet there."

Then she gazed up at him again. The look in her eyes stunned him—desperate for approval. He knew that look—he saw it in the mirror every morning.

Why would she want his approval? She was Whitney

Wildz, for crying out loud. She'd always done what she wanted, when she wanted—consequences be damned.

Except…nothing about her said she was out of control—except for the way she'd fallen into his arms.

His first instinct had been to hold her—to protect her. To claim her as his. What if…?

No.

There was no "what if" about this. His first duty was to his family—to making sure this wedding went off without a hitch. To making sure everyone knew that the Beaumonts were still in a position of power. To making sure he proved himself worthy of his father's legacy.

At the very least, he could be a gentleman about it.

"That's beautiful country," he said. Compliments were an important part of setting a woman at ease. If he were smart, he would have remembered that in the first place. "Your ranch must be lovely."

A touch of color brightened her cheeks. His stomach tensed. *She* was beautiful, he realized. Not the punk-rock hot she'd been back when he'd watched her show, but something delicate and ethereal.

Mine.

The word kept popping up in his head, completely unbidden. Which was ridiculous because the only thing Whitney was to him was a roadblock.

Phillip kicked him again. *Stop staring*, he mouthed at Matthew.

Matthew shook his head. He hadn't realized he was staring.

"Matthew, maybe we should discuss some of the wedding plans?" Jo said it nicely enough but there was no mistaking that question for an order.

"Of course," he agreed. The wedding. He needed to stay on track here. "We have an appointment with the seamstress tomorrow at ten. Jo, it's your final fitting. Whitney, we ordered your dress according to the measurements you sent in, but we've blocked out some additional time in case it requires additional fittings."

"That sounds fine," she said in a voice that almost sounded casual.

"Saturday night is the bachelorette party. I have a list of places that would be an appropriate location for you to choose from."

"I see," she said. She brushed her hand through her hair. He fought the urge to do the same.

What was wrong with him? Seriously—*what* was wrong with him? He went from attracted to her to furious at everyone in the room and now he wanted to, what—stroke her hair? Claim her? Jesus, these were exactly the sort of impulses he'd always figured had ruled Phillip. The ones that had ruled their father. See a beautiful woman, act on the urge to sweep her off her feet. To hell with anything else.

Matthew needed to regain control of the situation—of himself—and fast.

"We'll need to get the shoes and jewelry squared away. We need to get you in to the stylist before then to decide how to deal with your hair, so we'll do that after the dress fitting." He waited, but she didn't say anything.

So he went on. "The rehearsal dinner is Tuesday night. Then the wedding is Christmas Eve, of course." A week and a half—that didn't leave him much time to deal with the disruption of Whitney Wildz. "The ladies will get manicures that morning before they get their hair done. Then we'll start with the photographs."

Whitney cleared her throat—but she still didn't meet his gaze. "Who else is in the wedding party?"

He wanted her to look at him—he wanted to get lost in her eyes. "Our older brother Chadwick will be walking with his wife, Serena. Frances and Byron will be walking together—they're twins, five years younger than I am." For a second,

Matthew had almost said *we*—as in he and Phillip. Because he and Phillip were only six months apart.

But he didn't want to bring his father's infidelity into this conversation, because that meant Whitney would know that he was the second choice, the child his father had never really loved. Or even acknowledged, for that matter. So he said *I*.

"That just leaves the two of us," he added, suddenly very interested in his plate. How was he going to keep this primal urge to haul her off under control if they were paired up for the wedding?

He could not let her distract him from his goals, no matter how much he wanted to. He had to pull this off—to prove that he was a legitimate Beaumont. Ravishing the maid of honor did not fall anywhere on his to-do list.

"Ah." He looked up when he heard her chair scrape against the floor. She stood and, without looking at him, said, "I'm a little tired from the drive. If you'll excuse me." Jo started to stand, but Whitney waved her off. "I think I can find my way."

Then she was gone, walking in a way that he could only describe as graceful. She didn't stumble and she didn't fall. She walked in a straight line for the stairs.

Several moments passed after she disappeared up the stairs. No one seemed willing to break the tense silence. Finally, Matthew couldn't take it anymore.

"What the *hell*? Why is Whitney Wildz your maid of honor and why didn't either of you see fit to tell me in advance? Jesus, if I'd known, I would have done things differently. Do you have any idea what the press will do when they find out?"

It was easier to focus on how this was going to screw up the wedding than on how his desire was on the verge of driving him mad.

"Gosh, I don't know. You think they'll make a big deal out of stuff that happened years ago and make Whitney feel like crap?" Phillip shot back. "You're right. That would really suck."

"Hey—this is not my fault. You guys sprung this on me."

"I believe," Jo said in a voice so icy it brought the temperature of the room down several degrees, "I told you I was asking Whitney Maddox to be my maid of honor. Whitney Wildz is a fictional character in a show that was canceled almost thirteen years ago. If you can't tell the difference between a real woman and a fictional teenager, then that's *your* problem, not hers."

"It *is* my problem," he got out through gritted teeth. "You can't tell me that's all in the past. What about the headlines?"

Phillip rolled his eyes. "Because everything the press prints is one hundred percent accurate, huh? I thought you, of all people, would know how the headlines can be manipulated."

"She's a normal person," Jo said. Instead of icy, though, she was almost pleading. "I retrained one of her horses and we got to spend time together last winter. She's a little bit of a klutz when she gets nervous but that's it. She's going to be fine."

"If *you* can treat her like a normal person," Phillip added. "Man—I thought you were this expert at reading people and telling them what they wanted to hear. What happened? Hit your head this morning or something?"

Matthew sat there, feeling stupid. Hell, he wasn't just feeling stupid—he *was* stupid. His first instinct had been to protect her. He should have stuck with it. He could do that without giving in to his desire to claim her, right?

Right. He was in control of his emotions. He could keep up a wall between the rest of the world and himself. He was good at it.

Then he made the mistake of glancing at that silly donkey, who gave him a baleful look of reproach. Great. Even the donkey was mad at him.

"I should apologize to her."

Phillip snorted. "You think?"

Damn it, he felt like a jerk. It didn't come naturally to him. Chadwick was the one who could be a royal pain simply because he wasn't clued in to the fact that most people had actual feelings. Phillip used to be an ass all the time because he was constantly drunk and horny. Matthew was the one who smoothed ruffled feathers and calmed everyone down.

Phillip was right. Matthew hadn't been reading the woman next to him. He'd been too busy thinking about old headlines and new lust to realize that she might want his approval.

"Which room is she in?"

Jo and Phillip shared a look before Phillip said, "Yours."

Three

Whitney found her room on the first try and shut the door behind her.

Well. So much for her little fantasy about a Christmas romance. She doubted that Matthew would have been less happy to see her if she'd thrown up on his shoes.

She flopped down on her bed and decided that she would not cry. Even though it was really tempting, she wouldn't. She'd learned long ago this was how it went, after all. People would treat her just fine until they recognized her and then? All bets were off. Once she'd been outed as Whitney Wildz, she might as well give up on normal. There was no going back.

She'd thought for a moment there she might get to do something ordinary—have a little Christmas romance between the maid of honor and the best man. But every time she got it in her foolish little head that she could be whoever she wanted to be…well, this was what would happen.

The thing was, she didn't even blame Matthew. Since he recognized her so quickly, that could only mean that he'd read some of the more recent headlines. Like the last time she'd tried to redeem Whitney Wildz by lending her notoriety to the Bakersfield Animal Shelter's annual fund-raising gala dinner. She'd been the keynote speaker—or would have been if she hadn't gotten the fancy Stuart Weitzman shoes she'd bought just for the occasion tangled up in the microphone cords on her way up to the podium.

The headlines had been unforgiving.

Whitney shivered. Boy, this was going to be a long, *cold* two weeks.

As she was getting up to turn her fireplace back on, she heard it—a firm knock.

Her brain diverted all energy from her legs to the question of who was on the other side of that door—Jo or a Beaumont?—and she tripped into the door with an audible *whump*.

Oh, for the love of everything holy. Just once—once!—she'd like to be able to walk and chew gum at the same time. She could sing and play the guitar simultaneously. She could do complicated dressage moves on the back of a one-ton animal. Why couldn't she put one foot in front of the other?

She forced herself to take a deep breath just as a male voice on the other side of the door said, "Is everything all right in there, Miss…uh…Ms. Maddox?"

Matthew. Great. How could this get worse? Let her count the ways. Had he come to ask her to drop out of the wedding? Or just threaten her to be on her best behavior?

She decided she would not cower. Jo had asked her to be in the wedding. If Jo asked her to drop out, she would. Otherwise, she was in. She collected her thoughts and opened the door a crack. "Yes, fine. Thanks."

Then she made the mistake of looking at him. God, it wasn't fair. It just *wasn't*.

Matthew Beaumont was, physically, the perfect man to have a Christmas romance with. He had to be about six foot one, broad chested, and that chin? Those eyes? Even his deep red hair made him look distinctive. Striking.

Gorgeous.

Too darned bad he was an ass.

"Can I help you?" she asked, determined to be polite if it killed her. She would not throw a diva fit and prove him right. Even if there would be a certain amount of satisfaction in slamming the door in his face.

He gave her a grin that walked the fine line between awkward and cute. He might be even better-looking than his brother, but he appeared to possess none of the charm. "Look, Ms. Maddox—"

"Whitney."

"Oh. Okay. Whitney. We got off on the wrong foot and—" She winced.

He paused. "*I* got off on the wrong foot. And I want to apologize to you." His voice was strong, exuding confidence. It made everything about him that much sexier.

She blinked at him. "What?"

"I jumped to conclusions when I realized who you were and I apologize for that." He waited for her to say something but she had nothing.

Was he serious? He looked serious. He wasn't biting back laughter or— She glanced down at his hands. They were tucked into the pockets of his gray wool trousers. No, he wasn't about to snap an awful photo of her to post online, either.

He pulled his hands from his pockets and held them at waist level, open palms up, as if he knew what she was thinking. "It's just that this wedding is incredibly important for rebuilding the public image of the Beaumont family and it's my job to make sure everyone stays on message."

"The…public image?" She leaned against the door, staring up at him. Maybe he wasn't a real man—far too handsome to be one. And he was certainly talking like a space alien. "I thought this was about Jo and Phillip getting married."

"That, too," he hurried to agree. This time, his smile was a little more charming, like something a politician might pull out when he needed to win an argument. "I just— Look. I just want to make sure that we don't make headlines for the wrong reason."

Embarrassment flamed down the back of her neck. She looked away. He was trying to be nice by saying *we* but they both knew that he meant *her*.

"I know you don't believe this, but I have absolutely no desire to make headlines. At all. Ever. If no one else recognized me for the rest of my life, that'd be super."

There was a moment of silence that was in danger of becoming painful. "Whitney…"

The way he said her name—soft and tender and almost reverent—dragged her eyes up to his. The look in his eyes hit her like a bolt out of, well, the blue. He had the most amazing eyes…

For that sparkling moment, it almost felt as if…as if he was going to say something that could be construed as romantic. Something that didn't make her feel as though the weight of this entire event were being carried on her shoulders.

She wanted to hear something that made her feel like Whitney Maddox—that being Whitney Maddox was a good thing. A great thing. And she wanted to hear that something come out of Matthew's mouth, in that voice that could melt away the chilly winter air. Desire seemed to fill the space between them.

She leaned toward him. She couldn't help it. At the same time, his mouth opened as one of his hands moved. Then, just as soon as the motion had started, it stopped. His mouth closed and he appeared to shake himself. "I'll meet you at the dress fitting tomorrow. To make sure everything's—"

"On message?"

He notched up an eyebrow. She couldn't tell if she'd offended him or amused him. Or both. "Perfect," he corrected. "I just want it to be perfect."

"Right." There would be no sweet words. If there was one thing she wasn't, it was perfect. "Will it just be you?"

He gave her a look that was surprisingly wounded. She couldn't help but grin at him, which earned her a smile that looked more…real, somehow. As though what had just passed between them was almost…flirting.

"No. The wedding planner will be joining us—and the seamstress and her assistants, of course."

"Of course." She leaned against the door. Were they flirting? Or was he charming her because that was what all Beaumonts did?

God, he was *so* handsome. He exuded raw power. She had no doubt that whatever he said went.

A man like him would be hard to resist.

"Tomorrow, then," she said.

"I look forward to it." He gave her a tight smile before he turned away. Just as she was shutting the door, he turned back. "Whitney," he said again in that same deep, confident and—she hoped—sincere voice. "It truly is a pleasure to meet you."

Then he was gone.

She shut the door.

Heavens. It was going to be a *very* interesting two weeks.

"So," Whitney began as they passed streetlights decorated like candy canes. The drive had, thus far, been quiet. "Who's on the guest list again?"

"The Beaumonts," Jo said with a sigh. "Hardwick Beaumont's four ex-wives—"

"Four?"

Jo nodded as she tapped on the steering wheel. "All nine of Phillip's siblings and half siblings will be there, although only the four he actually grew up with are in the wedding— Chadwick, Matthew, Frances and Byron."

Whitney whistled. "That's a *lot* of kids." Part of why she'd loved doing the show was that, for the first time, she'd felt as though she'd had a family, one with brothers and sisters and parents who cared about her. Even if it were all just pretend, it was still better than being the only child Jade Maddox focused on with a laserlike intensity.

But ten kids? *Dang.*

"And that doesn't count the illegitimate ones," Jo said in a conspiratorial tone. "Phillip says they know of three, but there could be more. The youngest is…nineteen, I think."

As much as she hated gossip… "Seriously? Did that man not know about condoms?"

"Didn't care," Jo said. "Between you and me, Hardwick Beaumont was an old-fashioned misogynist. Women were solely there for his entertainment. Anything else that happened was their problem, not his."

"Sounds like a real jerk."

"I understand he was a hell of a businessman, but…yeah. On the whole, his kids aren't that bad. Chadwick's a tough nut to crack, but his wife, Serena, balances him out really well. Phillip's… Well, Phillip's Phillip." She grinned one of those private grins that made Whitney blush. "Matthew can come on a bit strong but really, he's a good guy. He's just wound a bit tight. Very concerned with the family's image. It's like…he wants everything to be perfect."

"I noticed." Whitney knew she was talking about the coming-on-strong part, but her brain immediately veered back to when she'd stumbled into his arms. His strong arms.

And then there was the conversation they'd had—the private one. The one that could have been flirting. And the way he'd said her name…

"We're really sorry about last night," Jo repeated for about the fifteenth time.

"No worries," Whitney hurried to say. "He apologized."

"Matthew is…very good at what he does. He just needs to lighten up a little bit. Have some fun."

She wondered at that. Would fun be a part of this? The dinner had said no. But the conversation after? She had no idea. If only she weren't so woefully out of practice at flirting.

"I can still drop out," she said. "If that'll make it simpler."

Jo laughed—not an awkward sound, but one that was

truly humorous. "You're kidding, right? Did I mention the ex-wives? You know who else is going to be here?"

"No…"

"The crown prince of Belgravitas."

"You're kidding, right?" God, she hoped Jo was kidding. She didn't want to make a fool of herself in front of honest-to-God royalty.

"Nope. His wife, the princess Susanna, used to date Phillip."

"Get *out.*"

"I'm serious. Drake—the rapper—will be there, as well. He and Phillip are friends. Jay Z and Beyoncé had a scheduling conflict, but—"

"Seriously?" It wasn't as though she didn't know that Phillip Beaumont was a famous guy—all those commercials, all those stories about parties he hosted at music festivals—but this was crazy.

"If you drop out," Jo went on, "who on earth am I going to get to replace you? Out of the two hundred people who'll be at the wedding and the six hundred who'll be at the reception, you know how many I invited? My parents, my grandma Lina, my uncle Larry and aunt Penny, and my parents' neighbors. Eleven people. That's it. That's all I have. And you."

Whitney didn't know what to say. She didn't want to do this, not after last night. But Jo was one of her few friends. Someone who didn't care about Whitney Wildz or *Growing Up Wildz* or even that horrible Christmas album she'd put out, *Whitney Wildz Sings Christmas, Yo.*

She didn't want to disappoint her friend.

"Honestly," Jo said, "there's going to be so many egos on display that I doubt people will even realize who you are. Don't take that the wrong way."

"I won't," Whitney said with a smile. She could do this. She could pull off normal for a few weeks. She couldn't compete with that guest list. She was just the maid of honor. Who would notice her, anyway? Besides Matthew, that was…

"And you're right. It won't be like that last fund-raiser."

"Exactly," Jo said, sounding encouraging. "You were the headliner there—of course people were watching you. Matthew only acted like he did because he's a perfectionist. I truly believe you'll be fine." She pulled into a parking lot. "It'll be fine."

"All right," Whitney agreed. She didn't quite believe the sentiment but she couldn't disappoint Jo. "It will be fine."

"Good."

They got out. Whitney stared at the facade of the Bridal Collection. This was it. Once she was in the dress, there was no backing out.

Oh, who was she kidding? There was no backing out anyway. Jo was right. They were the kind of people who didn't have huge social circles or celebrities on speed dial. They were horse people. She and Jo got along only because they both loved animals and they both had changed their ways.

"You're really having a wedding with Grammy winners and crown princes?"

"Yup," Jo said, shaking her head. "Honestly, though, it's not the over-the-top wedding that matters. It's the marriage. Besides," she added as they went inside, "David Guetta is going to be doing the music for the reception. How cool is that?"

"Pretty cool," Whitney agreed. She didn't recognize the name, but then, why would she? She wasn't famous anymore.

Maybe Jo was right. No one would care about her. She'd managed to stay out of the headlines for almost three years, after all—that was a lifetime in today's 24/7 news cycle. In that time, there'd been other former teen stars who'd grabbed much bigger headlines for much more scandalous reasons.

They walked into the boutique to find Matthew pacing between rows of frothy white dresses and decorations that were probably supposed to be Christmas trees but really looked more as though someone had dipped pipe cleaners in glitter. The whole place was so bright it made her eyes hurt.

Matthew—wearing dark gray trousers and a button-up shirt with a red tie under his deep green sweater—was so out of place that she couldn't *not* look at him. She wouldn't have thought it possible, but he looked even better today than he had the other night. As she appreciated all the goodness that was Matthew Beaumont, he looked up from his phone.

Their eyes met, and her breath caught in her throat. The warmth in his eyes, the curve to his lips, the arch in his eyebrow—heat flooded Whitney's cheeks. Was he happy to see her? Or was she misreading the signals?

Then he glanced at Jo. "Ladies," he said in that confident tone of his. It should have seemed wholly out of place in the midst of this many wedding gowns, but on him? "I was just about to call. Jo, they're waiting for you."

"Where's the wedding planner?" Whitney asked. If the planner wasn't here, then she and Jo weren't late. Late was being the last one in.

"Getting Jo's dress ready."

Dang. Whitney tried to give her friend a smile that was more confident than she actually felt. Jo threaded her way back through racks of dresses and disappeared into a room.

Then Whitney and Matthew were alone. Were they still almost flirting? Or were they back to where they'd been at dinner? If only she hadn't fallen into him. If only he hadn't recognized her. If only...

"Is there someone else who can help me try my dress on?"

"Jo's dress requires several people to get her into it," he said. Then he bowed and pointed the way. "Your things are in here."

"Thanks." She held her head high as she walked past him.

"You're welcome." His voice trickled over her skin like a cool stream of water on a too-hot day.

She stepped into a dressing room—thankfully, one with a door. Once she had that door shut, she sagged against it. That voice, that face were even better today than they'd been last night. Last night, he'd been trying to cover his surprise and anger. Today? Today he just looked happy to see her.

She looked at the room she'd essentially locked herself in. It was big enough for a small love seat and a padded ottoman. A raised dais stood in front of a three-way mirror.

And there, next to the mirrors, hung a dress. It was a beautiful dove-gray silk gown—floor length, of course. Sleeveless, with sheer gathered silk forming one strap on the left side. The hemline was flared so that it would flow when she walked down the aisle, no doubt.

It was stunning. Even back when she'd walked the red carpet, she'd never worn a dress as sophisticated as this. When she was still working on *Growing Up Wildz*, she'd had to dress modestly—no strapless, no deep necklines. And when she'd broken free of all the restrictions that had hemmed her in for years, well, "classic" hadn't been on her to-do list. She'd gone for shock value. Short skirts. Shorter skirts. Black. Torn shirts that flashed her chest. Offensive slogans. Safety pins holding things together. Anything she could come up with to show that she wasn't a squeaky-clean kid anymore.

And it'd worked. Maybe too well.

She ran her hands over the silk. It was cool, smooth. If a dress could feel beautiful, this did. A flicker of excitement started to build. Once, before it'd been a chore, she'd liked to play dress-up. Maybe this would be fun. She hoped.

Several pairs of shoes dyed to match were lined up next to the dress—some with four-inch heels. Whitney swallowed hard. There'd be no way she could walk down the aisle in those beauties and not fall flat on her face.

Might as well get this over with. She stripped off her parka and sweater, then the boots and jeans. She caught a glimpse of herself in the three-way mirror—hard not to with those angles. Ugh. The socks had to go. And…

Her bra had straps. The dress did not.

She shucked the socks and, before she could think better about it, the bra. Then she hurried into the dress, trying not to pull on the zipper as the silk slipped over her head with a shushing sound.

The fabric puddled at her feet as she tried to get the zipper pulled up, but her arms wouldn't bend in that direction. "I need help," she called out, praying that an employee or a seamstress or anyone besides Matthew Beaumont was out there.

"Is it safe to come in?" Matthew asked from the other side of the door.

Oh, no. Whitney made another grab at the zipper, but nothing happened except her elbow popped. *Ow.* She checked her appearance. Her breasts were covered. It was just the zipper.…

"Yes."

The door opened and Matthew walked in. To his credit, he didn't enter as if he owned the place. He came in with his eyes cast down before he took a cautious glance around. When he spotted her mostly covered, the strangest smile tried to crack his face. "Ah, there you are."

"Here I am," she agreed, wondering where else on earth he thought she could have gotten off to in the ten minutes she'd been in here. "I can't get the zipper up all the way."

She really didn't know what to expect at this point. The majority of her interactions with Matthew ranged from outright rude to surly. But then, just when she was about to write him off as a jerk and nothing more, he'd do something that set her head spinning again.

Like right now. He walked up to her and held out his hand, as if he were asking her to dance.

Even in the cramped dressing room, he was impossibly

handsome. But he'd already muddled her thoughts—mean one moment, sincere the next. She didn't want to let anything physical between them confuse her even further.

When she didn't put her hand in his, he said, "Just to step up on the dais," as if he could read her thoughts.

She took his hand. It was warm and strong, just as his arms had been. He guided her up the small step and then to the middle. "Ah, shoes," he said. Then he let her go.

"No—just the zipper," she told him, but he was already back by the shoes, looking at them.

Lord. She knew what was about to happen. She was all of five-four on a good day. He would pick the four-inch heels in an attempt to get her closer to Jo's height. And then she'd either have to swallow her pride and tell him she couldn't walk in them or risk tripping down the aisle on the big day.

"These should work," he said, picking up the pair of peep-toed shoes with the stacked heel only two inches high. "Try these on."

"If you could just zip me up first. *Please*." The last thing she wanted to do was wobble in those shoes and lose the grip she had on the front of her dress.

He carried the shoes over to her and set them on the ground. Then he stood.

This time, when his gaze traveled over her, it didn't feel as if he were dismissing her, as he had the first time. Far from it. Instead, this time it was almost as if he was appreciating what he saw.

Maybe.

She felt him grab the edges of the dress and pull them together. Something about this felt…intimate. Almost too intimate. It blew way past possible flirting. She closed her eyes. Then, slowly, the zipper clicked up tooth by tooth.

Heat radiated down her back, warming her from the inside out. She breathed in, then out, feeling the silk move over her bare flesh. Matthew was so close she could smell his cologne—something light, with notes of sandalwood. Heat built low in her back—warm, luxurious heat that made her want to slowly turn in his arms and stop caring whether or not the dress zipped at all.

She could do it. She could hit on the best man and find out what had been behind that little conversation they'd had in private last night. And this time, she wouldn't trip.

Except...except for his first reaction to her—if she hit on him, he might assume she was out to ruin his perfect wedding or something. So she did nothing. Matthew zipped the dress all the way up. Then she felt his hands smoothing down the pleats in the back, then adjusting the sheer shoulder strap.

She stopped breathing as his hands skimmed over her.

This had to be nothing. This was only a control freak obsessively making sure every detail, every single pleat, was perfect. His touch had nothing to do with *her*.

She felt him step around her until he was standing by her side. "Aren't you going to look?" he asked, his voice warm and, if she didn't know any better, inviting.

She could feel him waiting right next to her, the heat from his body contrasting with the cool temperature of the room. So she opened her eyes. What else could she do?

The sight that greeted her caused her to gasp. An elegant, sophisticated woman stood next to a handsome, powerful man. She knew that was her reflection in the mirror, but it didn't look like her.

"Almost perfect," Matthew all but sighed in satisfaction.

Almost. What a horrible word.

"It's amazing." She fought the urge to twirl. Someone as buttoned-up as Matthew probably wouldn't appreciate a good twirl.

The man in the reflection grinned at her—a real grin, one that crinkled the edges of his eyes. "It's too long on you. Let's try the shoes." Then, to her amazement, he knelt down and held out a shoe for her, as if this were some backward version of *Cinderella*.

Whitney lifted up her skirt and gingerly stepped into the shoe. It felt solid and stable—not like the last pair of fancy shoes she'd tried to walk in.

She stepped into the other shoe, trying not to think about how Matthew was essentially face-to-knee or how she was in significant danger of snagging these pretty shoes on the edge of the dais and going down in a blaze of glory.

When she had both shoes firmly on, Matthew sat back. "How do those feel?"

"Not bad," she admitted. She took a preliminary step back. "Pretty good, actually."

"Can you walk in them? Or do you need a ballerina flat?"

She gaped at him. Of all the things he might have asked her, that wasn't even on the list. Then it hit her. "Jo told you I was a klutz, right?"

He grinned again. It did some amazing things to his face, which, in turn, did some amazing things to the way a lazy sort of heat coiled around the base of her spine and began to pulse.

"She might have mentioned it."

Whitney shouldn't have been embarrassed, and if she was, it shouldn't have bothered her anymore. Embarrassment was second nature for her now, as ordinary as breathing oxygen.

But it did. "Because you thought I was drunk."

His Adam's apple bobbed, but he didn't come back with the silky smile he'd pulled out on her last night, the one that made her feel as if she was being managed.

"In the interest of transparency, I also considered the option that you might have been stoned."

Four

Whitney blinked down at him, her delicate features pulled tight. Then, without another word, she turned back to the mirror.

What happened? Matthew stood, letting his gaze travel over her. She was, for lack of a better word, stunning. "The color suits you," he said, hoping a compliment would help.

It didn't. She rolled her eyes.

Transparency had always worked before. He'd thought that his little admission would come out as an ironic joke, something they could both chuckle over while he covertly admired the figure she cut in that dress.

What was it about this woman that had him sticking his foot in his mouth at every available turn?

It was just because she wasn't what he'd been expecting, that was all. He'd been up late last night, digging into the not-sordid-at-all history of Whitney Maddox, trying to get his feet out of his mouth and back under his legs. She *was* a respected horse breeder. Her horses *were* beautiful animals and that one *had* won a gold medal. But there weren't any pictures of Whitney Maddox anywhere—not on her ranch's website, not on any social media. Whitney Maddox was like a ghost—there but not there.

Except the woman before him was very much here. His hands still tingled from zipping her into that dress, from the glimpse of her panties right where the zipper had ended. How he itched to unzip it, to expose the bare skin he'd seen but not touched—slip those panties off her hips.

He needed to focus on what was important here, and that was making sure that this woman—no matter what name she went by—did not pull this wedding off message. That she did not pull *him* off message. That was what he had to think about. Not the way the dress skimmed over her curves or the way her dark hair made her stand out.

Before he knew what he was doing, he said, "You look beautiful in that dress."

This time, she didn't roll her eyes. She gave him the kind of look that made it clear she didn't believe him.

"You can see that, right? You're stunning."

She stared at him for a moment longer. "You're confusing me," she said.

She had a sweet smell to her, something with warm vanilla notes overlaying a deeper spice. Good enough to eat, he thought, suddenly fascinated with the curve of her neck. He could press his lips against her skin and watch her reaction in the mirror. Would she blush? Pull away? Or lean into his touch?

She looked away. "I could change my hair."

"What?"

"I could try to dye it all blond, although," she said with a rueful smile, "it didn't turn out so well the last time I tried it. The white streak won't take dye, for some reason. God knows I've tried to color it over, but it doesn't work. It's blond or nothing."

"Why on God's green earth would you want to dye your hair?"

He couldn't see her as a blonde. It would be wrong on so many levels. It'd take everything that was fine and delicate about her and make it washed-out, like a painting left out in the rain.

"If I'm blonde, no one will recognize me. No one would ever guess that Whitney Wildz is standing up there. That way, if I trip in the shoes or drop my bouquet, people will just think I'm a klutz and not assume I'm stoned. Like they always do."

Shame sucker punched him in the gut. "Don't change your hair." He reached out and brushed the edge of her bangs away from her face.

She didn't lean away from him, but she didn't lean into him, either. He didn't know if that was a good thing or not.

"But…" She swallowed and tried to look tough. She didn't make it. "I look like me. People will *recognize* me. I thought you didn't want that to happen."

"You say that as if looking like yourself is a bad thing."

In the mirror's reflection, her gaze cut to him. "Isn't it?"

He took a step closer to her, close enough that he could slide his fingers from the fringe of her hair down her neck, down her arm. He couldn't help it, which was something outside of his experience entirely. He'd *always* been able to help himself. He'd never allowed himself to get swept up in something as temporary, as fleeting, as emotional attraction. He'd witnessed firsthand what acting on attraction could do, how it could ruin marriages, leave bastard babies behind—leave children forgotten.

With the specter of his father hovering around him, Matthew managed to find some of the restraint that normally came so easy to him. He didn't slide his hand down her bare arm or pull her into his chest. Instead, he held himself to arranging the shoulder of the dress. She watched him in the mirror, her eyes wide. "You are *beautiful*," he said. It came out like something Phillip would say—low and seductive. It didn't sound like Matthew talking at all.

She sucked in a deep breath, which, from his angle, did

enticing things to her chest. He wanted to sweep her into his arms. He wanted to tell her he'd had a crush on her back in the day. He wanted to get her out of that dress and into his bed.

He did none of those things.

Focus, damn it.

He took a step back and tried his hardest to look at her objectively. The heels helped, but the hem of the dress still puddled around her. She'd need it hemmed, but they had to settle on the shoes first.

"Let's see how you walk in those." There. That was something that wasn't a come-on and wasn't a condemnation. Footwear was a safe choice at this point.

She stood for a moment, as if she was trying to decide what his motivations were. So he held out his arm for her. He could do that. She'd walk back down the aisle on his arm after the ceremony. Best they get used to it now.

After a brief pause, she slipped her hand around his elbow and, after gathering her skirts in one hand, stepped off the dais. They moved toward the door, where he opened it for her.

She walked ahead of him, the dress billowing around her legs just as he'd wanted it to. The salon had a bouquet of artificial flowers on a nearby table. He handed them to her. "Slow steps, big smile."

"Right," she said, an odd grin pulling up at the corners of her mouth. "No skipping. Got it."

She walked down the aisle, then turned and came back toward him with a big fake smile on her face. Then, just as she almost reached him, the toe of her shoe caught in the too-long hem of the dress and she stumbled. The bouquet went flying.

He caught her. He had to, right? It wasn't about pulling her into his arms. This was a matter of personal safety.

He had her by her upper arms. "Sorry," she muttered as he pulled her back onto her feet.

"Don't worry about it."

She gave him a hard look, her body rigid under his hands. "I had to worry about it yesterday. You're sure I'm not on anything today?"

Okay, yes, he deserved that. That didn't make it any less sucky to have it thrown back in his face.

Without letting go of her, he leaned down and inhaled deeply. "No trace of alcohol on your breath," he said, staring at her lips.

She gasped.

Then he removed one of his hands from her arm and used it to tilt her head back until she had no choice but to look him in the eyes.

Years of dealing with Phillip while he was drunk had taught Matthew what the signs were. "You're not on anything."

"You...can tell?"

He should let her go. She had her balance back. She didn't need him to hold her up and she certainly didn't need him to keep a hand under her chin.

But he didn't. Instead, he let his fingers glide over her smooth skin. "When you become a Beaumont, you develop certain skills to help you survive."

She blinked at him. "When you *become* a Beaumont? What does that mean? Aren't you a Beaumont?"

Matthew froze. Had he really said that? Out loud? He *never* drew attention to his place in the family, *never* said anything that would cast doubt on his legitimacy. Hell, his whole life had been about proving to the whole world that he was a Beaumont through and through.

What was it about this woman that made him stick his foot into his mouth?

Whitney stared at him. "You're confusing me again,"

she repeated, her voice a whisper that managed to move his heart rate up several notches. Her lips parted as she ever so slightly leaned into his hand.

"You're the one who's confusing me," he whispered back as he stroked his fingertips against her skin. For a woman who was neither here nor there, she was warm and solid and so, *so* soft under his hands.

"Then I guess we're even?" She looked up at him with those pale green eyes. He was going to kiss her. Long. Hard. He was going to taste her sweetness, feel her body as it pressed against his and—

"Whitney? Matthew?"

Jo's voice cut through the insanity he'd been on the brink of committing. He let go of Whitney, only to grab her immediately when she took a step back and stepped on her hem again.

"I've got you," he told her.

"Repeatedly," she said. He couldn't tell if she was amused or not.

Then Jo came around the corner, seamstresses and salon employees trailing her. She pulled up short when she saw the two of them and said, "I need to go," as the wedding planner started unfastening the back of her dress.

"What?" Matthew said.

"Why?" Whitney said at the same time.

"A mare I'm training out on the farm is having a meltdown and Richard is afraid she's going to hurt herself." She looked over her shoulder at the small army of women who were attempting to get her out of her dress. "Can you go any faster?"

There were murmurs of protest from the seamstresses as the wedding planner said, "We can't risk tearing the dress, Ms. Spears."

Jo sighed heavily.

Whitney and Matthew took advantage of the distraction

to separate. "I'll come with you," Whitney said. "I can help. You taught me what to do."

"No, you won't," he said.

It must have come out a little harsher than he meant it to, because every woman in the room—all six of them—stopped and looked at him. "I mean," he added, softening his tone, "we have too much to do. We have to get your dress hemmed, we have an appointment with the stylist this afternoon— everyone is set except you. We *must* keep your schedule."

There was a moment of silence, broken only by the sound of Jo's dress rustling as the seamstresses worked to free her from the elaborate confines.

Whitney wasn't looking at him. She was looking at Jo. She'd do whatever Jo said, he realized. Not what he said. He wasn't used to having his orders questioned. Everyone else in the family had long ago realized that Matthew was always right.

"Matthew is right," Jo said. "Besides, having a new person show up will only freak out Rapunzel. I need to do this alone."

"Oh," Whitney said as if Jo had just condemned her to swing from the gallows. "All right."

"Your dress is amazing," Jo said, clearly trying to smooth over the ruffled feathers.

"Yours, too," Whitney replied. Jo's compliment must have helped, because Whitney already sounded better.

That was another thing Matthew wasn't expecting from Whitney Wildz. A willingness to work? A complete lack of interest in throwing a diva fit when things didn't go her way?

She confused him, all right. He'd never met a woman who turned his head around as fast and as often as Whitney did. Not even the celebrities and socialites he'd known made him dizzy the way she did. Sure, such women made plays for him—he was a Beaumont and a good-looking man. But none of them distracted him from his goal. None of them got him off message.

He tried telling himself it was just because he'd liked her so many years ago. This was merely the lingering effects of a crush run amok. His teenage self was screwing with his adult self. That was all. It didn't matter that Whitney today was a vision in that dress—far more beautiful than anything he'd ever imagined back in the day. He had a job to do—a wedding to pull off, a family image to rescue, his rightful place to secure. His adult self was in charge here.

No matter what the Beaumonts put their minds to, they would always come out on top. That'd been the way Hardwick Beaumont had run his business and his family. He'd amassed a huge personal fortune and a legacy that had permanently reshaped Denver—and, one could argue, America. He expected perfection and got it—or else.

Even though Chadwick had sold the Beaumont Brewery, even though Phillip had crashed and burned in public, Matthew was still standing tall. He'd weathered those storms and he would pull this wedding off.

"There," one of the seamstresses said. "Mind the edge..."

Jo clutched at the front of the dress. "Matthew, if you don't mind."

Right. He turned his back to her so she could step out of the $15,000 dress they'd chosen because it made Jo, the tomboy cowgirl, look like a movie-star goddess, complete with the fishtail bodice and ten-foot-long train. The Beaumonts were about glamour and power. Every single detail of this wedding had to reflect that. Then no one would ever question his place in the family again.

Not even the maid of honor.

He looked down at Whitney out of the corner of his eye. She was right. With her fine bone structure, jet-black hair with the white stripe and those large eyes, he could dress her in a burlap sack and she'd still be instantly recognizable. The dress only made her features stand out that much more.

So why hadn't he agreed that a drastic change to her hair was a good idea?

It'd be like painting pouty ruby-red lips on the *Mona Lisa.* It'd just be wrong.

Still, he felt as if he'd done very little but insult her in the past twenty-four hours, and no matter what his personal feelings about Whitney were, constantly berating a member of the wedding party was not the way to ensure things stayed on message.

"I'll take you to lunch," he offered. "We'll make a day of it."

She gave him the side eye. "You normally spend your day styling women for weddings?"

"No," he said with a grin. "Far from it. I'm just making sure everything is—"

"Perfect."

"Exactly."

She tilted her head to one side and touched her cheek with a single fingertip. "Aren't you going to miss work?"

"This is my job." Again, he got the side eye, so he added, "I do the PR for Percheron Drafts, the beer company Chadwick started after he sold the Beaumont Brewery." He'd convinced Chadwick that the wedding needed to be a showcase event first. It hadn't been that hard. His older brother had learned to trust his instincts in the business world, and Matthew's instincts told him that marrying former playboy bachelor Phillip Beaumont off in a high-profile high-society wedding would pay for itself in good publicity.

Convincing Phillip and Jo that their wedding was going to be over-the-top in every possible regard, however, had been another matter entirely.

"I see," she said in a way that made it pretty clear she

didn't. Then she cleared her throat. "Won't your girlfriend be upset if you take me out to lunch?"

That was what she said. What she meant, though, was something entirely different. To his ears, it sure sounded as though she'd asked if he had really been about to kiss her earlier and whether he might try it again.

He leaned toward her, close enough he caught the scent of vanilla again. "I'm not involved with anyone," he said. What he meant?

Yeah, he might try kissing her again. Preferably someplace where seamstresses wouldn't bust in on them.

He watched the blush warm her skin. Again, his fingers itched to unzip that dress—to touch her. But... "You?"

His web searches last night hadn't turned up anything that suggested she was in a relationship.

She looked down at the floor. "I find it's best if I keep to myself. Less trouble that way."

"Then lunch won't be a problem."

"Are you sure? Or will you need to search my bag for illegal contraband?"

Ouch. Her dig stung all the more because he'd earned it. Really, there was only one way to save face here—throw himself on his sword. If he were lucky, she'd have mercy on him. "I'm sure. I'm done being an ass about things."

She jolted, her mouth curving into a smile that, no matter how hard she tried, she couldn't repress. "Can I have that in writing?"

"I could even get it notarized, if that's what it'd take for you to forgive me."

She looked at him then, her eyes full of wonder. "You already apologized last night. You don't have to do it again."

"Yes, I do. I keep confusing you. It's ungentlemanly."

Her eyebrows jumped up as her mouth opened but behind them, someone cleared her throat. "Mr. Beaumont? We're ready to start on Ms. Maddox's dress."

Whitney's mouth snapped shut as that blush crept over her cheeks. Matthew looked around. Jo and her dress were nowhere to be seen. He and Whitney had been standing by themselves in the middle of the salon for God knows how long, chatting. Flirting.

Right. They had work to do here.

But he was looking forward to lunch.

Five

"I'm sorry, sir, but the only seats we have are the window seats," the hostess said.

Matthew turned to look at Whitney. He hadn't expected Table 6 to be this crowded. He'd thought he was taking her to a quiet restaurant where they could talk. Where he could look at her over a table with only the bare minimum interruption.

But the place was hopping with Christmas shoppers taking a break. Shopping bags crowded the aisle, and there were more than a few people wearing elf hats and reindeer antlers. The hum of conversation was so loud he almost couldn't hear Bing Crosby crooning Christmas carols on the sound system.

"We can go someplace else," he offered to Whitney.

She pulled down her sunglasses and shot him a look, as if he'd dared her to throw a diva fit. "This is fine."

Matthew glanced around the restaurant again. He really didn't want to sit at a bar-high counter next to her. On the other hand, then he could maybe brush against her arm, her thigh.

They took the only two spots left in the whole place. A shaft of sunlight warmed their faces. Whitney took off her sunglasses and her knit hat and turned her face to the light.

She exhaled, a look of serene joy radiating from her. She was so beautiful, so unassuming, that she simply took his breath away.

Then it stopped. She shook back to herself and gave him an embarrassed look. "Sorry," she said, patting her hair back into place. "It's a lot colder here than it is in California. I miss the sun."

"Don't apologize." Her cheeks colored under his gaze. "Let's order. Then tell me about California." She notched a delicate eyebrow at him in challenge. "And I mean more than the basics. I want to know about *you*."

The corners of her mouth curved up as she nodded. But the waitress came, so they turned their attention to the daily specials. She ordered the soup and salad. He picked the steak sandwich. The process seemed relatively painless.

But Matthew noticed the way the waitress's eyes had widened as Whitney had asked about the soup du jour. *Oh, no*, he thought. The woman had recognized her.

Maybe it wouldn't be a problem. The restaurant was busy, after all. The staff had better things to do than wonder why Whitney Wildz had suddenly appeared at the counter, right?

He turned his attention back to Whitney. Which was not easy to do, crammed into the two seats in this window. But he managed to pull it off. "Now," he said, fixing her with what he really hoped wasn't a wolfish gaze, "tell me about you."

She shrugged.

The waitress came back with some waters and their coffee. "Anything else?" she asked with an ultraperky smile.

"No," Matthew said forcefully. "Thank you."

The woman's eyes cut back to Whitney again and she grinned in disbelief as she walked away. Oh, hell.

But Whitney hadn't noticed. She'd unwrapped her straw and was now wrapping the paper around her fingers, over and over.

Matthew got caught up in watching her long fingers bend the wrapper again and again and forgot about the waitress.

"You're confusing me," she said, staring hard at her scrap of paper. "Again."

"How?" She gave him the side eye. "No, seriously—please tell me. It's not my job here to confuse you."

She seemed to deflate, just a little. But it didn't last. "You're looking at me like that."

He forced his attention to his own straw. Hopefully, that would give her the space she needed. "Like how?"

The silence stretched between them like a string pulling tight. He was afraid he might snap. And he never snapped. He was unsnappable, for God's sake.

But then his mind flashed back to the bare skin of her back, how the zipper had ended just at the waistband of her panties. All he'd seen was a pretty edge of lace. Now he couldn't get his mind off it.

"I can't decide if you think I'm the biggest pain in the neck of your life or if you're— If you—" She exhaled, the words coming out in a rush. "If you like me. And when you look at me like that, it just…makes it worse."

"I can't help it," he admitted. It was easier to say that without looking at her. Maybe this counter seating wasn't all bad.

Her hands stilled. "Why not?" There was something else in her voice. That something seemed to match the look she'd given him last night, the one that craved his approval.

He couldn't tell her why not. Not without telling her… what? That he'd nursed a boyhood crush on her long after he'd left boyhood behind? That he'd followed her in the news? That this very afternoon, she'd been the most beautiful woman he'd ever seen?

"Tell me about you," he said, praying that she'd go along with the subject change. "Tell me about your life."

He felt her gaze on him. Now it was his turn to blush. "If I do, will you tell me about you?"

He nodded.

"Okay," she agreed. He expected her to begin twisting her paper again, but she didn't. She dug out her phone. "This is Pride and Joy," she said, showing him a horse and rider holding a gold medal.

The picture was her phone's wallpaper. Her pride and joy, indeed. "That was the Games, right?"

"Right." Her tone brightened considerably at his memory. "I'd been getting close to that level but…I wanted him to win, you know? Having bred a horse that could win at that level made me feel legitimate. Real. I wasn't some crazy actress, not anymore. I was a real horse breeder."

She spoke calmly—no hysterics, no bravado. Just someone determined to prove her worth.

Yeah, he knew that feeling, too. Better than he wanted to.

"There are people in this world who don't know about that show," she said, staring at her phone. "People who only know me as Whitney Maddox, the breeder of Pride and Joy. You have no idea how *huge* that is."

"I'm starting to get one." He lifted the phone from her hand and studied the horse. He'd seen a similar shot to this one online. But she wasn't in either one.

She slid her fingertip over the screen and another horse came up. Even he could tell this was a younger one, gangly and awkward looking. "This is Joy's daughter, Ode to Joy. I own her mother, Prettier Than a Picture—Pretty for short. She was a world-champion dressage horse, but her owner got indicted and she was sold at auction. I was able to get her relatively cheap. She's turned out some amazing foals." The love in her voice was unmistakable. Pretty might have been a good business decision, but it was clear that the horse meant much more to Whitney than just a piece of property. "Ode's already been purchased," she went on. "I could keep studding Joy to Pretty for the rest of my life and find buyers."

"Sounds like job security."

"In another year, I'll deliver Ode," she went on. "She's only one right now." She flicked at her screen and another photo came up. "That's Fifi," she told him. "My rescued greyhound."

The sleek dog was sprawled out on a massive cushion on the floor, giving the camera a don't-bother-me look. "A greyhound?"

"I was fostering her and just decided to keep her," Whitney replied. "She'd run and run when she was younger and then suddenly her life stopped. I thought—and I know this sounds silly because she's just a dog—but I thought she understood me in a way that most other living creatures don't."

"Ah." He didn't know what else to say to that. He'd never felt much kinship with animals, not the way Phillip did with his horses. His father had never really loved the horses he'd bought, after all. They'd been only investments for him—investments that might pay off in money or prestige. "You foster dogs?"

She nodded enthusiastically. "The no-kill shelter in Bakersfield never has enough room." Her face darkened briefly. "At first they wouldn't let me take any animals but…" Her slim shoulders moved up and down. Then the cloud over her face was gone. "There's always another animal that needs a place to stay."

He stared at her. It could have been a naked play for pity—poor little celebrity, too notorious to be entrusted with animals no one else wanted. But that was not how it came out. "How many animals have you fostered?"

She shrugged again. "I've lost count." She flicked the screen again and a strange-looking animal appeared.

He held the phone up so he could get a better look, but the squished black-and-white face stayed the same. "What is *that*?"

"That," she replied with a giggle that drew his gaze to her face, "is Gater. He's a pug-terrier-something."

Hands down, that was the ugliest mutt Matthew had ever seen. "How long have you had him?"

"Just over two years. He thinks he rules the house. Oh, you should have seen him when Jo and Betty stayed with me. He was furious!" She laughed again, a sweet, carefree sound that did more to warm him than the sun ever could.

"What happened?"

"He bit Betty on the ankle, and she kicked him halfway across the living room. No broken bones or skin," she hurried to add. "Just a pissed-off dog and donkey. Gater thinks he's the boss, and Fifi doesn't care as long as Gater stays off her cushion."

Whitney leaned over and ran her fingers over the screen again. A photo of some cats popped up, but that was not what held Matthew's attention. Instead, it was the way she was almost leaning her head against his shoulder, almost pressing her body against his arm.

"That's Frankie and Valley, my barn cats."

"Frankie and Valley? Like Frankie Valli, the singer?"

"Yup." Without leaning away, she turned her face up toward his. Inches separated them. "Frankie was a…stray." Her words trailed off as she stared at Matthew's face, his lips. Her eyes sparkled as the blush spread over her cheeks like the sunrise after a long, cold night.

He could lean forward and kiss her. It'd be easy. For years, he'd thought about kissing Whitney Wildz. He'd been young and hormonal and trying so, *so* hard to be the Beaumont that his father wanted him to be. Fantasies about Whitney Wildz were a simple, no-mess way to escape the constant effort to be the son Hardwick Beaumont wanted.

Except he didn't want to kiss that fantasy girl anymore. He wanted to kiss the flesh-and-blood woman sitting next to him. She shouldn't attract him as she did. He should see nothing but a headache to be managed when he looked at her. But he didn't, damn it. He didn't.

Matthew couldn't help himself. He lifted the hand that

wasn't holding her phone and let the tips of his fingers trail down the side of her cheek.

Her breath caught, but she didn't turn away—didn't look away. Her skin was soft and warmed by the sun. He spread his fingers out until the whole of his palm cradled her cheek.

"I didn't realize you were such a fan of Frankie Valli," she said in a breathy voice. Her pupils widened as she took another deep breath. As if she was waiting for him to make his move.

"I'm not." The problem was, Matthew didn't have a move to make. Phillip might have once moved in on a pretty woman without a care in the world about who saw them or how it'd look in the media.

But Matthew cared. He had to. It was how he'd made a place for himself in this family. And he couldn't risk all of that just because he wanted to kiss Whitney Maddox.

So, as much as it hurt, he dropped his hand away from her face and looked back at the screen. Yes. There were cats on the screen. Named after an aging former pop idol.

He could still feel Whitney's skin under his touch, still see her bare back...

Something outside the window caught his eye. He looked up to see two women in their mid-twenties standing on the sidewalk in front of the restaurant. One had her phone pointed in their general direction. When they saw that he'd noticed them, they hurried along, giggling behind their hands.

Dread filled him. Okay, yes, Whitney was recognizable— but she wasn't the only woman in the world with an unusual hair color, for crying out loud. This had to be...a coincidence.

He turned his attention back to the phone, but pictures of cats and dogs and horses barely held his attention. He wanted their food to come so they could eat and get the hell out of here. He wanted to get Whitney to a place where even if people did recognize her, they had the decency not to make a huge deal out of it.

She flicked to the last photo, which was surprisingly *not* of an animal. Instead, it was of a cowgirl wearing a straw hat and tight jeans, one foot kicked up on a fence slat. The sun was angled so that the woman in the picture was bathed in a golden glow—alone. Perfect.

Whitney tried to grab the phone from him, but he held on to it, lifting it just out of her reach. "Is this...you?"

"May I have that back, please?" She sounded tense.

"It *is* you." He studied the photo a little more. "Who took it?"

"Jo did, when she was out last winter." She leaned into him, reaching for the phone. "Please."

He did as the lady asked. "So that's the real Whitney Maddox, then."

She froze, her fingertip hovering over the button that would turn the screen off. She looked down at the picture, a sense of vulnerability on her face. "Yes," she said in a quiet voice. "That's the real me." The screen went black.

He cleared his throat. "I think I like the real you."

Even then she didn't look at him, but he saw the smile that curved up her lips. "So," she said in a bright voice, "your turn."

Hell. What was he supposed to say? He looked away—and right at the same two women he'd seen earlier. Except now there were four of them. "Uh..."

"Oh, don't play coy with me," she said as she slipped her phone back into her jacket pocket. Then she nudged him with her shoulder. "The real you. Go."

This time, when the women outside caught him looking, they didn't hurry off and they sure didn't stop pointing their cameras. One was on her phone.

It was then that he noticed the noise. The restaurant had gone from humming to a hushed whisper. The carols over the sound system were loud and clear. He looked over his shoulder and was stunned to find that a good part of the restaurant was staring at them with wide eyes. Cell phones were out. People were snapping pictures, recording videos.

Oh, hell. This was about to become a PR nightmare. Worse—if people figured out who he was? And put two and two together? Nightmare didn't begin to cut what this was about to become.

"We need to leave."

The women outside were headed inside.

"Are you trying to get…out…?" Whitney saw the women, then glanced around. "Oh." Shame flooded her cheeks. She grabbed her sunglasses out of her bag and shoved them back onto her face. "Yes."

Sadly, the glasses did little to hide who she was. In fact, they gave her an even more glamorous air, totally befitting a big-name star.

Matthew fished a fifty out of his wallet and threw it on the counter, even though they weren't going to eat anything they'd ordered.

As they stood, the small group of women approached. "It's really you," one of the woman said. "It's really Whitney Wildz!"

The quiet bubble that had been building over the restaurant burst and suddenly people were out of their seats, crowding around him and Whitney and shoving camera phones in their faces.

"Is this your boyfriend?" someone demanded.

"Are you pregnant?" someone else shouted.

"Are you ever going to clean up your act?" That insult was shouted by a man.

Matthew was unexpectedly forced into the role of bouncer. He used his long arms to push people out of Whitney's way as they tried to walk the twelve feet to the door. It took several minutes before they were outside, but the crowd moved with them.

He had his arm around her shoulders, trying to shield her as he rushed for his car. With his long legs, he could have left half of these idiots behind, but Whitney was much shorter than he was. He was forced to go slow.

Someone grabbed Whitney's arm, shouting, "Why did you break Drako's heart?"

Matthew shoved and shoved hard. They were at his car, but people were pushing so much that he had trouble getting the passenger door open. "Get back," he snarled as he hip-checked a man trying to grab a lot more than Whitney's arm. "Back off."

He got the door open and basically shoved her inside, away from what had rapidly become a mob. He slammed the door shut, catching someone's finger. There was howling. He was feeling cruel enough that he was tempted to leave the finger in there, but that would be the worst sort of headline—Beaumont Heir Breaks Beer Drinker's Hand. So he opened the door just enough to pull the offending digit out and then slammed it shut again.

Whitney sat in the passenger seat, already buckled up. She stared straight ahead. She'd gotten her hat back on, but it was too late for that. The parts of her face that were visible were tight and blank.

Matthew stormed around to the driver's side. No one grabbed him, but several people were recording him. Great. Just freaking great.

He got in, fired up the engine on his Corvette Stingray and roared off. He was furious with the waitress—she'd probably called her girlfriends to tell them that Whitney Wildz was at her table. He was furious with the rest of the idiots, who'd descended into a mob in mere minutes.

And he was furious with himself. He was the Beaumont who always, always handled the press and the public. Image was everything and he'd just blown his image to hell and back. If those people hadn't recognized him from the get-go, it wouldn't take much online searching before they figured it out.

This was exactly what he hadn't wanted to happen—Whitney Wildz would turn this wedding and his message into a circus of epic proportions. Yeah, he'd been a jerk to her about it last night, but he'd also been right.

Even if she was a cowgirl who fostered puppies and adopted greyhounds, even if she was a respected horse breeder, even if she was *nothing* he'd expected in the best possible ways, it didn't change the perception. The perception was that Whitney Wildz was going to ruin this wedding.

And he wouldn't be able to control it. Any of it. Not the wedding, not the message—and not himself.

He was screwed.

Six

They drove in silence. Matthew took corners as if he were punishing them. Or her. She wasn't sure.

She wished she had the capacity to be surprised by what had happened at the restaurant, but she didn't. Not anymore. That exact scene had played out time and time again, and she couldn't even feel bad about it anymore.

Instead, all she felt was resigned. She'd known this was going to happen, after all. And if she was disappointed by how Matthew had reacted, well, that was merely the by-product of him confusing her.

She'd allowed herself to feel hopeful because, at least some of the time, Matthew liked her.

The real her.

She thought.

She had no idea where they were, where they were going, or if they were going there in a straight line. He might be taking the long way just in case any of those fans had managed to follow them.

"Are you all right?" he growled out as he pointed his sleek car toward what she thought was downtown Denver.

She wouldn't flinch at his angry tone. She'd learned a long time ago that a reaction—any reaction—would be twisted around. Best to be a placid statue. Although that hadn't always worked so well, either.

"I'm fine."

"Are you sure? That one guy—he *grabbed* you."

"Yes." Had that been the same man whose hand had gotten crushed in the door?

Even though she had her gaze locked forward, out of the corner of her eye she could see him turn and give her a look of disbelief. "And that doesn't piss you off?"

This time, she did wince. "No."

"Why the hell not? It pissed me off. People can't grab you like that."

Whitney exhaled carefully through her nose. This was the sort of thing that someone who had never been on the receiving end of the paparazzi might say. Normal people had personal space, personal boundaries that the rest of humanity agreed not to cross. You don't grab my butt, I won't have you arrested.

Those rules hadn't applied to her since the days after her show had been canceled. The day she'd bolted away from her mother's overprotective control.

"It's fine," she insisted again. "It's normal. I'm used to it."

"It's bullshit," he snapped. "And I won't stand by while a bunch of idiots take liberties with you. You're not some plaything for them to grope or insult."

She did turn to look at him then. He had a white-knuckle grip on the steering wheel as he glared at the traffic he was speeding around. He was serious.

She couldn't remember the last time someone hadn't just stood by and watched the media circus take her down.

Like the time she'd flashed the cameras. She hadn't had on any panties because the dress made no allowances for anything, the designer had said. Yeah, she'd been high at the time, but had anyone said, "Gee, Whitney, you might want to close your legs"? Had anyone tried to shield her from the cameras, as Matthew had just done, until she could get her skirt pulled down?

No. Not a single person had said anything. They'd just kept snapping pictures. And that next morning? One of the worst in her life.

He took another corner with squealing tires into a parking spot in front of a tall building. "We're here."

"Are you on my side?" she asked.

He slammed the car into Park, causing her to jerk forward. "What kind of question is that?"

"I mean…" Was he the kind of guy who would have told her she was flashing the cameras? Or the kind who would have gotten out of the way of the shot? "No one's ever tried to defend me from the crowds before."

Now it was his turn to look at her as if she were nuts. "No one?"

This wasn't coming out well. "Look, like you said—in the interest of transparency, I need to know if you're on my side or not. I'm not trying to mess up your message. I mean, you saw how it was." Suddenly, she was pleading. She didn't just want him on her side, watching her back—she *needed* him there. "All I did was take off my hat."

He gave her the strangest look. She didn't have a hope in heck of trying to guess what was going on behind his deep blue eyes.

"That's just the way it is," she told him, her voice dropping to a whisper. Every time she let her guard down—every time she thought she might be able to do something normal people did, like go out to lunch with a man who confused her in the best possible ways—this was always what would happen. "I—I wish it wasn't."

He didn't respond.

She couldn't look at him anymore. Really, she didn't expect anything else of him. He'd made his position clear. His duty was to his family and this wedding. She could respect that. She was nothing but a distraction.

A distraction he'd almost kissed in a crowded restaurant.

So when he reached over and cupped her face in his hand,

lifting it until she had no choice but to look at him, she was completely taken off guard. "I refuse to accept that this is 'just the way it is.' I *refuse* to." His voice—strong and confident and so close—did things to her that she barely recognized. "And you should, too."

Once, she'd tried to fight back, to reclaim her name and her life. She'd tried to lend her celebrity status to animal shelters. It'd gotten her nothing but years of horrible headlines paired with worse pictures. She hadn't done anything public since the last incident, over two years ago.

She looked into his eyes. If only he were on her side… "What I do doesn't matter and we both know it."

He gave her another one of those looks that walked the fine line between anger and disgust. "So what are you going to do about it?"

She glared at him. She couldn't get mad at those people—but him? She could release a little rage on him. After all, he'd been barely better than those people last night. "I'm not going to sit around and fume and mope about how I'm nothing but a *commodity* to people. I'm not going to sit around and feel bad that once upon a time I was young and stupid and crazy. And I'm not going to let anyone else sit around and feel bad for me. I'm not an object of your pity *or* derision. Because that's not who I am anymore."

If he was insulted by her mini tirade, he didn't show it. He didn't even let go of her. Instead, one corner of his mouth curled up into an amused grin.

"Derision, huh?" He was close now, leaning in.

"Yes."

That'd been last night. Right after she'd first fallen into his arms. After she'd dared to hope she might have a little Christmas romance. The memory made her even madder.

"So if you're going to ask me to drop out, just get on with it so I can tell you I already told Jo I would and she begged me not to because *you* invited a bunch of strangers to her wedding and she wants one friend standing next to her. Now, are you on my side or not?"

Because if he wasn't, he needed to stop touching her. She was tired of not knowing where she stood with him.

He blinked. "I won't let anyone treat you like that."

"Because it's bad for your message?"

His fingers pulled against her skin, lifting her face up. Closer to him. "Because you are *not* a commodity to me."

The air seemed to freeze in her lungs, making breathing impossible. He was going to kiss her. God, she wanted him to. Just as she'd wanted him to kiss her in the restaurant.

And see what had happened? She could still feel that man's hand on her butt.

As much as she wanted to kiss Matthew—to be kissed for the real her, not the fake one—she couldn't.

"I'm going to ruin the wedding." It was a simple statement of an unavoidable fact.

It worked. A shadow clouded his face, and he dropped his hand and looked away. "We're going to be late."

"Right." She didn't want to do this anymore, didn't want to be the reason the wedding went off script. She wanted to go back to her ranch—back where dogs and cats and horses and even Donald, the crazy old coot, didn't have any expectations about Whitney Wildz.

Matthew opened her door and held out his hand for her. She'd promised Jo. Until Jo told her she could quit, she couldn't. She wouldn't. That was that.

So she sucked it up, put her hand in Matthew's and stood.

He didn't let go of her, didn't step back. Instead, he held on tighter. "Are you sure you're okay?"

She put on a smile for him. She wouldn't be okay until she was safely back home, acres of land between her and the nearest human. Then she'd put her head down and get back to work. In a while—a few weeks, a few months—this wedding would be superseded by another celebrity or royal doing something "newsworthy." This would pass. She knew that now. She hadn't always known it, though.

"I'm fine," she lied. Then, because she couldn't lie and look at him, she stared up at the white building. "Where are we?" Because the sign said Hotel Monaco.

"The Veda spa is inside the hotel."

He still didn't let her go. He tucked her hand into the crook of his elbow, as if they'd walked out of 1908 or something. When she shot him a look, he said, "Practice."

Ah, yes. That whole walking-down-the-aisle thing.

So she put on her biggest, happiest smile and held an imaginary bouquet in front of her. She'd been an actress once, after all. She could fake it until she made it.

He chuckled in appreciation. "That's the spirit," he said, which made her feel immensely better. He handed his keys to a valet and they strode through the hotel lobby as if they owned the place.

"Mr. Beaumont! How wonderful to see you again." The receptionist at the front desk greeted them with a warm smile. Her gaze flicked over Whitney. "How can I help you today?"

"We're here for the spa, Janice," he said. "Thank you." As he guided Whitney down a hallway, she gave him a look. "What?"

Jealousy spiked through her. "You check into a hotel in your hometown in the middle of the day often? So often they know you by name?"

He pulled up right outside the salon door. "The Beaumonts have been using the hotel for a variety of purposes for years. The staff is exceedingly discreet. Chadwick used it for board meetings, but our father was...fond of using it for other purposes." Then he blushed. The pink color seemed out of place on his cheeks.

Ah—the father who sired countless numbers of children. She bit her tongue and said, "Yes?"

"Nothing," he said with more force than she expected. "The Beaumonts have a long business relationship with the hotel, that's all. I personally do not check into the rooms."

He opened the door to the spa. Another receptionist stood to greet them. "Mr. Beaumont," she said with a deferential bow of the head. "And this is—" she checked a tablet "—Ms. Maddox, correct?"

"Yes," Whitney said, feeling her shoulders straighten a bit more. If she could get through this as Ms. Maddox, that'd be great.

"This way. Rachel is ready for you."

They went back to a private room. Whitney hadn't been in a private salon room in a long time. "This is nice," she said as Matthew held the door open for her.

"And it better stay that way. Rachel," he said to the stylist with every color of red in her hair, "can you give me a moment? I have something I need to attend to."

"Of course, Mr. Beaumont." Rachel turned to face her. "Ms. Maddox, it's a delight to meet you."

Whitney tried not to giggle. A delight? Really? Still, this was a good test of her small-talk skills. At the wedding, she would be meeting a lot of people, after all. "A pleasure," she agreed.

She sat in the chair, and Rachel fluffed her hair several times. "Obviously, the bride will have her hair up," Rachel said. "Ms. Frances Beaumont has requested Veronica Lake waves, which will look amazing. Ms. Serena Beaumont will have a classic twist. You…" Her voice trailed off as she fingered Whitney's home-cut pixie.

"Don't have a lot to work with," Whitney said. "I know. I was thinking. Maybe we should take it blond."

Rachel gasped in horror. "What? Why?"

"She's not taking it blond," Matthew announced from the door as he strode in. He didn't look at Whitney—he was too busy scowling at his phone. But the order was explicit.

"Of course not," Rachel hurriedly agreed. "That would be the worst possible thing." She continued fluffing. "We could add in volume and extensions. Blond is out but colored strands are very hot right now."

Whitney cringed. Extensions? Volume? Colored streaks?

Why not just put her in a torn T-shirt emblazoned with the *Growing Up Wildz* logo and parade her down the street?

"Absolutely not," Matthew snapped. "We're going for a glamorous, classic look here."

If the stylist was offended by his attitude, she didn't show it. "Well," she said, working her fingers through Whitney's hair, "I can clean up the cut and then we can look at clips? Something bejeweled that matches the dresses?"

"Perfect," Matthew agreed.

"People will recognize me," Whitney reminded him, just because she felt as if she should have some say in her appearance. She glanced at the stylist, who had the decency to not stare. "Just like they did at the restaurant. If you won't let her dye it, at least get me a wig."

"No." But that was all he said as he continued to scowl at his phone.

"Why the heck *not*?"

He looked up at her, his eyes full of nothing but challenge. "Because you are beautiful the way you are. Don't let anyone take that away from you." Then his phone buzzed and he said, "Excuse me," and was gone.

Whitney sat there, stunned, as Rachel cleaned up her pixie cut.

Beautiful?

Was that how he thought of her?

Seven

This was going south on him. Fast. Matthew struggled to keep his cool. He'd learned a long time ago that losing his temper didn't solve anything. But he was getting close to losing it right now.

When the photo of him and Whitney, taken from the sidewalk while they sat inside the restaurant, had popped up on Instagram with the caption OMG WHITNEY WILDZ IN DENVER!?! he'd excused himself from the stylist's room so that he could be mad without upsetting Whitney. She'd had enough of that already.

He'd already reported the photo, but he knew this was just the beginning. And after years of cleaning up the messes his siblings and stepmothers had left behind, he also knew there was no way to stop it.

He was going to make an effort, though. Containment was half the battle. The other half? Distraction.

If he could bury the lead on Whitney under some other scandal…

He scanned the gossip sites, hoping that someone somewhere had done something so spectacularly stupid that no one would care about a former teen star having lunch.

Nothing. Of all the weeks for the rest of the world to be on its best behavior.

In the days of old—when he'd found himself faced with a crowd of paparazzi outside his apartment, demanding a reaction about his second stepmother's accusation that she'd caught Hardwick Beaumont in bed with his mistress in this very hotel—Matthew had relied on distraction.

He'd called Phillip, told him to make a scene and waited for the press to scamper off. It'd worked, too. Bailing Phillip out was worth it when Hardwick had called Matthew into his office and told him he'd done a nice job handling the situation.

"You're not mad at Phillip? Or…me?" Matthew had asked, so nervous he'd been on the verge of barfing. The only other times Hardwick had called Matthew into his office had been to demand to know why he couldn't be more like Chadwick.

Hardwick had gotten up and come around his desk to put his hands on Matthew's shoulders. Hardwick had been older then, less than five years from dying in the middle of a board meeting.

"Son," Hardwick had said with a look that could have been described only as fatherly on his face. It'd looked so unnatural on him. "When you control the press, you rule the world—that's how a Beaumont handles it."

Son. Matthew could count on both hands the number of times that Hardwick had used that term of affection. Matthew had finally, *finally* done something the old man had noticed. For the first time in his life, he'd felt like a Beaumont.

"You just keep looking out for the family," Hardwick had said. "Remember—control the press, rule the world."

Matthew had gotten very good at controlling the press—the traditional press. It was the one thing that *made* him a Beaumont.

But social media was a different beast, a many-headed hydra. You cut off one Instagram photo, another five popped up.

He couldn't rely on Phillip to cause a scene anymore, now that the man was clean and sober. Chadwick was out, as well—he didn't deal with the press beyond the controlled environment of interviews that Matthew prescreened for him.

Matthew stared at his phone. He could call his sister Frances, but she'd want to know why and how and details before she did anything. And once she found out that her former childhood idol Whitney Wildz was involved...

That left him one choice. He dialed his younger brother Byron.

"What'd I do now?" Byron said. He yawned, as if Matthew had woken him up at two in the afternoon.

"Nothing. Yet." There was silence on the other end of the line. "You *are* in Denver, right?"

"Got in this morning." Byron yawned again. "Hope you appreciate this. It's a damn long flight from Madrid."

"I need a favor."

"You mean beyond flying halfway around the world to watch Phillip marry some horse trainer?" Byron laughed.

Matthew gritted his teeth. Byron sounded just like Dad. "Yes. I need you to be newsworthy today."

"What'd Phillip do this time? I thought he was getting married."

"It's not Phillip."

Byron whistled. "What'd you get into?"

Matthew thought back to the photo he'd already reported. Whitney—sitting right next to him. Those people hadn't known who he was, but it wouldn't take long for someone to figure out that Whitney Wildz was "with" a Beaumont. "I just need a distraction. Can you help me out or not?"

This was wrong. All wrong. He was trying to prove that the Beaumont family was back on track, above scandal. He was trying to prove that he had complete control over the situation. And what was he doing?

Asking his brother to make a mess only days before the wedding...to protect Whitney.

What was he thinking?

He was thinking about the way her face had closed down the moment she realized people were staring, the way she sat in his car as if he were driving her to the gallows instead of a posh salon.

He was thinking about the way she kept offering to change her hair—to drop out—so that he could stay on message.

He was thinking how close he'd come to kissing her at that lunch counter.

"How big a distraction?"

"Don't kill anyone."

"Damn," Byron said with a good-natured chuckle. "You'll bail me out?"

"Yeah."

There was a pause that made Matthew worry. "Hey—did you invite Harper to the wedding?"

"Leon Harper, the banker who forced Chadwick to sell the Brewery?"

"Yeah," was the uninformative response. But then Byron added, "Did you invite him?"

"No, I didn't invite the man who hated Dad so much he took it out on all of us. Why?"

"I'll only help you out if you invite the whole Harper family."

"He has a *family*?" Matthew had had the displeasure of meeting Harper only a few times, at board meetings or other official Brewery functions. The man was a shark—no, that was unfair to sharks everywhere. The man was an eel, slippery and slimy and uglier than sin.

Plus, there was that whole thing about hating the Beaumonts enough to force the sale of the family business

"Are you serious? Why on God's green earth would you want Harper there?"

"Do you want me to make headlines for you or not?" Byron snapped.

"They can't come to the wedding—there's no room in the chapel. But I'll invite them to the reception." There would be plenty of room for a few extra people at the Mile High Station. And in a crowd of six hundred guests—many of whom were extremely famous—the odds of Harper running into a Beaumont, much less picking a fight with one, were slim. Matthew could risk it.

"Done. Don't worry, big brother—I've got a bone or two to pick now that I'm Stateside." Byron chuckled. "Can't believe you want me to stir up trouble. You, of all people."

"I have my reasons. Just try not to get a black eye," Matthew told him. "It'll look bad in the photos."

"Yeah? This reason got a name?"

The back of Matthew's neck burned. "Sure. And does the reason you ran off to Europe for a year have a name?"

"I was working," Byron snapped.

"That's what I'm doing here. Don't kill anyone."

"And no black eyes. Got it." Byron hung up.

Matthew sagged in relief. Byron had been in Europe for over a year. He claimed he'd been working in restaurants, but really—who could tell? All that Matthew knew was that Byron had caused one hell of a scene at a restaurant before winding up in Europe. There he'd kept his head down long enough to stay the heck out of the headlines. That'd been good enough for Matthew. One less mess he had to clean up.

This would work. He'd send out a short, boring press release announcing that Whitney Maddox, former star of *Growing Up Wildz* and close friend of the bride, was in Denver for the Beaumont wedding. The Beaumonts were pleased she would be in the wedding party. He'd leave it at that.

Then tonight Byron would go off the rails. Matthew was reasonably sure that his little brother wouldn't actually kill anyone, but he'd put the odds of a black eye at two to one. Either way, he was confident that Byron would do something that washed Whitney right out of the press's mind. Who cared about a former child star when the prodigal Beaumont had returned to raise hell at his brother's wedding?

"Mr. Beaumont?" Rachel, the stylist, opened the door and popped her head out. "We're ready for the big reveal."

"How'd she turn out?" Now that he had his distraction lined up, he could turn his attention back to Whitney. *All* of his attention.

Rachel winked at him. "I think you'll be pleased with the results."

Matthew walked into the private room. Whitney's back was to him. Her hair wasn't noticeably shorter, but it was shaped and sleek and soft-looking. A large rhinestone clip was fastened on one side, right over her white streak. He walked around to the front. Her eyes were closed. She hadn't seen yet.

God, she was beautiful. *Stunning.* The makeup artist had played up her porcelain complexion by going easy on the blush and heavy on the red lips. Instead of the smoky eye that Frances and Serena were going to wear, the artist had gone with a cat's-eye look.

"Whoa," he heard himself say. How could people look at this woman and only see Whitney Wildz?

Because the woman sitting in the chair in front of him was so much *more* than Whitney Wildz had ever been.

Whitney's nose wrinkled at him, but there was no missing the sweet little smile that curved up the corners of her mouth.

He was *going* to kiss her. Just as soon as they didn't have hairstylists and makeup artists hanging around, he was going to muss up that hair and smudge that lipstick and he wasn't going to feel bad about it at all.

"Ready, Ms. Maddox?" Rachel said. She spun Whitney's chair around and said, "Ta-da!"

Whitney blinked at her reflection, her pale eyes wide with shock.

Rachel's smile tensed. "Of course, it'll look better with the dress. And if you don't like it…"

"No, it's perfect," Matthew interrupted. "Exactly how I want her to look. Great job."

Whitney swallowed. "Perfect?" It came out as a whisper. He noticed her chest was rising and falling with increasing speed.

He knew what was happening. His sister Frances had always done the same thing when she'd been busted for sneaking around with the hired help. The shallow, fast breathing meant only one thing.

Whitney was about to freak out.

"If you could give us a moment," he said to the stylist.

"Is everything—?" Rachel asked, throwing a worried look back at Whitney as Matthew hurried the woman out of the room.

"It's perfect," Matthew reassured her as he shut the door in her face. Then he turned back to Whitney.

She'd come up out of the chair and was leaning into the mirror now. His mind put her back in her dress. "You're going to look amazing."

She started, as if she'd forgotten he was still there. Meeting his gaze in the mirror's reflection, she gave him a nervous grin. "I don't look like...*her* too much?"

Like Whitney Wildz.

He couldn't see anything of that ghost of the past in the woman before him—anything beyond a distinctive hair color. She *wasn't* Whitney Wildz—not to him. She was someone else—someone better.

Someone he liked.

Someone he'd defend, no matter what the cost.

He couldn't help it. He closed the distance between them and brushed the careful edge of her hairstyle away from her cheek. Then he tilted her head back to face him.

"You look like *you*," he assured her.

Her gaze searched his. The desperation was undisguised this time. He wanted to make her feel better, to let her know that he'd take care of her. He wouldn't throw her to the wolves or leave her hanging.

His lips brushed hers. Just a simple, reassuring kiss. A friendly kiss.

Yeah, right.

Except…she didn't close her eyes. He knew this because he didn't, either. She watched him kiss her. She didn't throw her arms around his neck and she didn't kiss him back. She just…watched.

So he stopped.

She was even paler now, practically a ghost with red lips as she stared at him with those huge eyes of hers.

Damn it. For once he'd let his emotions do the thinking for him and he'd screwed up.

"Whitney…"

"Knock-knock!" Rachel said in a perky voice as the door opened. "What did we decide?"

He ran the back of his hand over his mouth and then looked at Whitney. "I think she's perfect."

Eight

Matthew had been right. The staff at the hotel and spa were exceedingly discreet. There were no cameras or phones pointed at her when she walked out of the hotel. No one yelled her name as the valet pulled up with Matthew's car. Not a single person tried to grab her while the doorman opened her door and waited for her to get seated.

But Matthew had kissed her. Somehow, that made everything worse. And better.

She didn't know which. All she knew was that when he'd touched her—when he'd looked at her—and said she looked like herself, she'd wanted to kiss him and not kiss him and demand to know which "you" she looked like.

Which Whitney he thought he was kissing.

God, her brain was a muddled mess. She knew what to expect from the crowd at the restaurant. She did not know what to expect from Matthew Beaumont.

Except that he was probably going to keep confusing her.

Which he did almost immediately.

"I have the situation under control," he told her as they drove off for what she hoped was Jo and Phillip's farm. She couldn't take any more of this gadding about town. "I've done a press release announcing your involvement in the wedding."

"You're *announcing* I'm here? I thought that's what you wanted to avoid." She was feeling better now. Ridiculous, yes. But the sight of her in that mirror, looking like…well, like a Hollywood movie star, but a classic one, had short-circuited her brain. And then he'd kissed her.

"Trust me—after what happened at the restaurant, everyone knows you're here. There's no putting that genie back in the bottle."

"This does not make me feel better." She ran her hand over her hair. It felt much smoother than normal. She didn't feel normal right now.

"As I was saying," Matthew went on with a tense voice, "I've sent out a short, hopefully boring press release announcing that we're happy you're here. Then tonight my younger brother Byron will do something excessive and highly Beaumont-like."

"Wait, what?"

He didn't look at her—traffic was picking up—but his grin was hard to miss. "Byron's going to bury the lead. That's you."

"I—I don't understand. I thought you wanted the Beaumonts to stay *out* of the headlines." She was sure that he'd said something to that effect yesterday.

"I do. Byron was going to be newsworthy anyway. He flew off to Europe over a year ago and even I don't know why. This is just…building on that buzz."

She gave him a look. Was he serious?

He was.

"And it's the kind of situation I'm used to dealing with," he went on. "I can control this kind of press. I'm not going to let people manhandle you." He said it in such a serious tone that she was momentarily stunned.

"Why?"

"Why what?"

She swallowed, hoping she wouldn't trip over her words.

At least she was safely buckled in a car. The chances of her tripping over her feet were almost zero. "Why are you doing this for me?"

"Because it's the right thing to do."

She wanted to believe that. Desperately. But... "You're going to throw a Beaumont under the bus for me? You don't even know me."

"That's not true. And it's not throwing Byron under the bus if he willingly agrees. The situation is under control," he said again, as if it was a mantra.

She wasn't sure she believed that, no matter how many times he said it. "You don't even *know* me," she repeated. "Yesterday you wouldn't have just thrown me under the bus to stay on message—you would have backed the bus over me a few times for good measure."

"I know you breed award-winning horses, rescue dogs, name your cats after aging pop singers and will do anything for your friends, even if it puts you in the line of fire." He glanced over at her. "I know you prefer jeans and boots but that you can wear a dress as well as any woman I've ever seen. I know that once you were a rock star but now you're not."

Her cheeks warmed at the compliments, but then she realized what he'd said. Rock star? She'd played a rock star on television. Most people considered her an actress first—if they considered her a musician at all.

Unless... There was something going on here, something that she had to figure out right now. "You recognized me. Right away."

He didn't respond immediately, but she saw him grip the steering wheel even tighter. "Everyone recognizes you. You saw what happened at lunch today."

"Women recognize me," she clarified. "Who watched the show when they were kids."

"I'm sure they do." Did he sound tense? He did.

She was getting closer to that *something*. "Did you watch my show?"

"Frances did." He sounded as if he was talking through gritted teeth. "My younger sister."

"Did you watch it with her?"

The moment stretched long enough that he really didn't have to answer. He used to watch the show. He used to watch *her*. "Did you see me in concert? Is that why you called me a rock star?"

In response, he honked the horn and jerked the car across two lanes. "Stupid drivers," he muttered.

Normally, she wouldn't want to know. She didn't want people's version of her past to project onto her present. But she needed to know—was this the reason why he'd run so hot and cold with her?

"Matthew."

"Yes, okay? I used to watch your show with Frances and Byron. Frances, especially, was a huge fan. We never missed an episode. It was the only time when I could *make* time for them, make sure they didn't feel forgotten by the family. Our father had already moved on to another wife, another set of new children and another mistress. He never had time for them, for any of us. And I didn't want my brother and sister to grow up like I had. So I watched the show with them. Every single one of them. And then your concert tour came through Denver the week before their fifteenth birthday, so I got them front-row tickets and took them. Our father had forgotten it was their birthday, but I didn't."

She sat there, flabbergasted. Jo had said Hardwick Beaumont was a bastard of a man, but to not even remember your own kids' birthdays?

"And...and you were amazing, all right? I'd always wondered if you really did the singing and guitar on the show or if it was dubbed. But it was all you up on that stage. You put on a hell of a show." His voice trailed off, as if he was lost in the memory, impressed with her musical talents all over again. "I'd always..." He sighed heavily.

"What? You'd always *what*?"

"I'd always had a crush on you." His voice was quiet, as if he couldn't believe he was saying the words out loud. "Seeing you in person—seeing how talented you really were—only made it worse. But then the show got canceled and you went off the rails and I felt...stupid. Like I'd fallen for a lie. I'd let myself be tricked because you were so pretty and talented. I was in college by then—it really wasn't cool to crush on a teen star. And the headlines—every time you made headlines, I felt tricked all over again."

Okay, so how was she supposed to reply to *that*? *Gosh, I'm sorry I destroyed a part of your childhood? That I never had a childhood?*

She'd had people tell her they loved her before—had it shouted at her on sidewalks. Love letters that came through her agent—he forwarded them to her with the quarterly royalty checks. And she'd had more than a few people tell her how disappointed they were that she wasn't a proper role model, that she wasn't really a squeaky-clean rock star.

That she wasn't what they wanted her to be.

"You weren't— Last night...you weren't mad at me?"

He chuckled. It was not a happy sound. "No. I was mad at myself."

Why hadn't she seen it earlier? He'd had a crush on her. He might have even fancied himself in love with her.

No, not with her. With Whitney Wildz.

"But *you* kissed *me*."

True, it hadn't been a let's-get-naked kind of kiss, but that didn't change the basic facts. He'd told her she was beautiful at several important points throughout the day, gone out of his way to reassure her, listened to her talk about her pets and...kissed her anyway.

He scrubbed a hand through his hair, then took an exit off

the highway. It was several minutes before he spoke. "I did." He said it as though he still didn't believe it. "My apologies."

"You're apologizing? For the kiss? Was it that bad?"

Yeah, he'd sort of taken her by surprise—she'd been in a state of shock about her face—but that wasn't going to be *it*, was it? One strike and she was out of luck?

"You didn't kiss me back."

"Because I didn't know who you thought you were kissing." Point of fact, despite all the illuminating personal details he'd just revealed, she *still* didn't know who he'd thought he was kissing.

"You," he said simply. "I was kissing you."

She opened her mouth to ask, *Who?*

This was not the time for ambiguous personal pronouns. This was the time for clarity, by God. Because if he still thought he was kissing a rock star or an actress, she couldn't kiss him back. She just couldn't.

But if he was kissing a klutz who rescued puppies…

She didn't get the chance to ask for that vital clarification, because suddenly they were at the guard gate for Beaumont Farms. "Mr. Beaumont, Ms. Maddox," the guard said, waving them through.

Matthew took the road back to the house at what felt like a reckless speed. They whipped around corners so fast she had to hold on to the door handle. Then they were screeching to a halt in front of Phillip and Jo's house. The place was dark.

Whitney's head was spinning from more than just his driving. She couldn't look at him, so she stared at the empty-looking house. "Who am I? Who am I to you?"

Out of the corner of her eye, she saw his hands flex around the steering wheel. After today she wouldn't be surprised if he'd permanently bent it out of shape, what with all the white-knuckle gripping he'd been doing.

He didn't answer the question. Instead, he said, "Can I walk you inside?"

"All right."

They got out of the car. Matthew opened the door to the house for her and then stood to the side so she could enter first. She had to stop—it was dark and she didn't know where the light switches were located.

"Here." Matthew's voice was close to her ear as he reached around her. She stepped back—back into the wall.

He flipped the light on but he didn't move away from her. Instead, he stood there, staring down at her with something that looked a heck of a lot like hunger.

What did people do in this situation?

To hell with what other people did. What did *she* want to do?

She still wanted the same thing she'd wanted when she'd shown up here—a little Christmas fling to dip her toes back into the water of dating and relationships. She still wanted to feel sexy and pretty and, yes, graceful.

But the way that Matthew was looking down at her...there was something else there, something more than just a casual attraction that might lead to some really nice casual sex.

It scared her.

"I don't think they're home," he said, his voice husky.

"That's a shame," she replied. He'd made her feel pretty today, but right now? That hunger in his eyes?

She felt sexy. Desirable.

He wanted her.

She wanted to be wanted.

Just a Christmas fling. The maid of honor and the best man. Something that'd be short and sweet and so, *so* satisfying.

He hesitated. "Is it?"

"No." She turned until her back was against the wall.

His other arm came up beside her, trapping her in between them. "I'll stop. If you want me to."

She touched one of his cheeks. His eyelashes fluttered. But he hadn't answered her question.

He seemed to realize it. "I don't know what you are to me," he told her, the words coming out almost harsh. He leaned down and touched his forehead to hers. "But I know *who* you are."

This time, she knew the kiss wouldn't be the soft, gentle thing he'd pressed against her lips before. This time, it would be a kiss that consumed her.

She wanted to be consumed.

But he hadn't clarified anything, damn it. She put her hands on his chest and pushed just hard enough to stop him. Not hard enough to push him away. "Tell me, Matthew. Tell me who you're going to kiss."

Now both of his hands were cradling her face—pulling her up to him. "Whitney," he whispered. The length of his body pressed her back against the wall, strong and hard and everything she wanted it to be. "Whitney Maddox."

She didn't wait for him to kiss her. She kissed him first. She dug her fingers into the front of his sweater and hauled him down so she could take possession of his mouth, so she could offer up her own for him.

He groaned into her as she nipped at his lower lip. Then he took control of the kiss. His tongue swept into hers as his hands trailed down her cheeks, onto her neck and down her shoulders. Then he picked her up. The sudden change in altitude caused her to gasp.

"You need to be taller," he told her as he kissed along her cheek to her neck, her ear. His hands were flat against her bottom, boosting her to make up for the eight-inch height difference between them. Then he squeezed.

She had no choice. Her legs went around his waist, pulling him into her. She could feel his erection straining against his pants, pressing against her. She trembled, suddenly filled with a longing she couldn't ignore for a single second more.

Then his hips moved, rocking into hers. The pressure was intense—*he* was intense. Even though she had on jeans, she could feel the pads of his fingertips through the denim, squeezing her, pulling her apart.

His body rocked against hers, hitting the spot that sent the pressure spiraling up. She wanted to touch him, wanted to feel all the muscles that were holding her up as if she weighed nothing at all, but suddenly she had to hold on to him for dear life as he ground against her.

Her head fell back and bounced off the wall, but she didn't care—and she cared a whole lot less when Matthew started nipping at her neck, her collarbone. His hips flexed, driving him against her center again and again.

"Oh," she gasped. "Oh, Matthew."

"Do you like it," he growled against her chest.

"Yes."

"Louder." He thrust harder.

"Yes—*Oh!*" She gasped again—he was— She was going to—

He rocked against her again, in time with his teeth finding the spot between her shoulder and neck. He bit down and rubbed and—and—

"Oh yes, oh yes, *oh yes!*" she cried out as he pinned her back against the wall and held her up as she climaxed.

"Kiss me back," he told her, his forehead resting against hers. He was still cupping her bottom in his hands, but instead of the possessive squeezing, he was now massaging her. The sensation was just right. *He* was just right. "Always kiss me back."

So she kissed him, even as the climax ebbed and her body sagged in his arms. She kissed him with everything she had, everything she wanted.

Because she wanted everything. Especially a man who put her first.

"Tell me what you want," he said. Already his hips were

moving again, the pressure between her legs building. "I want this to be perfect for you. Tell me everything you want."

She cupped his cheeks in her hands. "Perfect?"

He gave her a look that started out as embarrassed but quickly became wicked. "Do you doubt me?"

After that orgasm? For heaven's sake, they were still fully clothed! What was he capable of when they were naked?

She grinned at him, feeling wicked in her own right. "Prove it."

Nine

"Oh, I'll prove it," Matthew told her. He hefted her up again. Then they were moving. He carried her through the house. He knew where they were going—his old room. If he didn't get all these clothes off them and bury himself in her body soon, he might just explode.

She wasn't helping. True, she didn't weigh very much and, since he was carrying her, she didn't trip or stumble into him. But the way she busied herself by scraping her teeth over his earlobe? He was going to lose it. Him, who was always in control of the situation. Of himself.

She'd stripped that control away from him the moment she'd walked into his life.

"This is my old room," he told her when they got to her door. He managed to get the door open. Then he kicked it shut.

Then he laid her out on the bed. Normally, he took his time with women. He was able to keep a part of himself back—keep a certain distance from what he was doing, what they were trying to do to him. Oh, they enjoyed it—he did, as well—but that level of emotional detachment was important somehow. He didn't know why. It just was.

Besides, being detached made it easier to make sure the women he was with were getting what they wanted from him.

But seeing Whitney on his old bed? Her hair was mussed now, her red lipstick smudged. She was no longer the perfect beauty he'd tentatively—yes, detachedly—kissed in the salon.

She was, however, his. His for right now. And he couldn't hold back.

He stripped off his coat while she tried to wriggle out of her jeans. Then, just as he had his sweater over his head, she kicked him in the stomach.

"Oof," he got out through clenched teeth. He stepped out of range and jerked the sweater the rest of the way off.

"Sorry! Oh, my gosh, I'm so sorry." Whitney lay on her back. She had one leg halfway out of her jeans, the other stuck around the ankle. "I didn't— I wasn't trying to— Oh, *damn*."

He caught the jeans, now practically inside out, and yanked them off her. Then he climbed onto the bed. Her blush was anything but pale or demure. An embarrassing red scorched her cheeks.

"I'm sorry," she whispered, looking as if she might start crying.

He straddled her bare legs as he pinned her wrists by her head. "None of that," he scolded her. "Nervous?"

She dropped her gaze and gave him a noncommittal shrug.

"Look at me," he told her. "Do you still want to do this?"

She didn't look. "I'm such a klutz. I'm sorry I kicked you."

"*Look* at me, Whitney," he ordered. When she didn't, he slid her wrists over her head so he could hold them with one hand and then he took her by the jaw and turned her face to his.

There was so much going on under the surface. She was trying to hide it by not looking at him, but he wasn't having any of it. "Apology accepted. Now forget it happened."

"But—"

He cut her off with a kiss, his hand sliding down her neck. "One of the things I like about you is that you get clumsy when you're nervous. It's cute."

Defiance flashed over her face. Good. "I don't want to be cute."

"What do you want?"

She sucked in a tiny breath—and was silent.

Oh, no, you don't, he thought. He snaked his hand down her front and then up under her sweater until he found her breast.

God, what a breast. Full and heavy and warm—and so responsive. Even through her bra, her nipple went to a stiff point as he teased her. "Is that what you want?"

She didn't answer. Not in words. But her breathing was faster now, and she'd tucked her lower lip into her mouth.

What control he had regained when she'd kicked him started to fray like a rope. He rolled her nipple between his finger and thumb. Her back arched into him, so he did it again, harder. "Is that what you want?"

She nodded.

"Say it," he told her. "Say it or I will tie you to this bed and *make* you say it."

The moment the words left his mouth, he wondered where they'd come from. He didn't just randomly tie people up. He wasn't into that kinky stuff. And when he'd dreamed of making it with Whitney Wildz, well, hell, back then, he hadn't even known people did that sort of thing.

But she didn't reply. Her eyes got huge and she was practically panting, but she didn't utter a word.

Then she licked her lips. And he lost his head.

Challenge accepted.

He let go of her breast and pulled her up, then peeled her sweater off her. The bra followed. She said nothing as he tore her clothes off, but when he kissed the side of her breast, when he let his tongue trace over her now-bare shoulder, she shuddered into him.

He couldn't stop whatever this was he'd started. He'd made her cry out in the entry hall. He'd make her do it again. He wrenched his tie off, then looped it around her wrists. Not tight—he didn't want to hurt her. But knowing her, she'd hit him in the nose with her elbow and nothing ruined some really hot sex like a bloody nose.

The tie secure around her wrists, he loosely knotted it to the headboard. Then he got off the bed.

Whitney Maddox was nude except for a thin pair of pale pink panties that looked so good against her skin. Her breasts were amazing—he wanted to bury his face in them and lick them until she cried his name over and over.

And she was tied to his bed.

Because she'd let him do that. Because she'd *wanted* him to do that.

He'd never been so excited in his life.

He stripped fast, pausing only long enough to get the condom out of his wallet. He rolled it on and then went to her. "I want to see all of you," he said, pulling her panties down. She started to lift her legs so he could get them off her ankles, but he held her feet down. "I'm in charge here, Whitney."

He trailed a finger down between her breasts, watching her shiver at his touch. Finally, *finally*, she spoke.

"I expect perfection."

"And that's what you'll get."

He climbed between her legs and stroked her body. She moaned, her head thrashing from side to side as he touched her.

He couldn't wait much longer. "You okay?" he asked. He wanted to be sure. They could play this little game about making her say it, but he also didn't want to hurt her. "If it's not okay, you tell me."

"This is okay. This is…" She tried to shift her hips closer to his dick. "Am I…am I sexy?"

"Oh, babe," he said. But he couldn't answer her, not in words. So he fit his body to hers and thrust in.

"Matthew!" she gasped in the same breathless way she'd cried his name in the hall.

"Yeah, louder," he ground out as he drove in harder.

"Matthew!" she cried again. Her legs tried to come off the bed, and she almost kneed him in the ribs.

"Oh, no, you don't," he told her as he grabbed her legs and tucked them up under his arms. Then he leaned down into her.

She was completely open to him, and he took advantage of that in every way he knew how—and a few he didn't even know he knew.

"Is this what you want?" he demanded over and over.

"Yes." Always, she said yes.

"Say it louder," he ordered her, riding her harder.

"Yes! Oh, Matthew—*yes!*"

There was nothing else but the moment between when he slid out of her body and drove back in. No thoughts of family or message or public image. Nothing but the woman beneath him, crying out his name again and again.

Suddenly her body tensed up around his. "Kiss me," she demanded. "Kiss me!"

"Kiss me back," he told her before he lowered his lips to hers.

Everything about her went tight as she kissed him. Then she fell back, panting heavily.

Matthew surrendered himself to her body. He couldn't fight it anymore.

Then he collapsed onto her chest. Her legs slid down his, holding him close. He knew he needed to get up—he didn't want to lose the condom—but there was something about holding her after what he'd done to her...

Jesus—had he really tied her up? Made her cry out his name? That was...something his father would have done.

"Can you untie me now?" she asked, sounding breathless and happy.

Focus, he told himself. So he sat back and undid the tie from the headboard. He'd really liked that tie, too, but he doubted it'd ever be the same.

He started to get out of bed to get cleaned up and dressed, but she sat up and tackle-hugged him so hard it almost hurt. But not quite. After he got over his momentary shock, he wrapped his arms around her.

"Thank you," she whispered. "It was…"

"Perfect?" He hoped so, for her sake.

At that, she leaned back and gave him the most suggestive smile he'd ever seen. He could take her again. He had another condom. He could loop his demolished tie back through the headboard and…

"I'm not sure. We might have to do it again later. Just to have a point of comparison, you understand." Then a shadow of doubt crossed her face. "If you wanted to," she hurried to add.

He pulled her back into his arms. "I'd like that. I'd like that a lot. You were amazing. Except for the kicking part."

She giggled, her chin tucked in the crook of his neck. He grabbed one of her wrists and kissed where he'd had it bound.

Then, from the floor, his phone chimed Phillip's text message chime.

And the weight of what he was supposed to be doing came crushing back down on him.

Why was he lolling away the afternoon in bed with Whitney? This was not the time to be tying people up, for crying out loud. He had a wedding to pull off—a family image to save.

An image that was going to be a whole hell of a lot harder to save when Byron got done with it.

Matthew had to keep the wheels from falling off. He had

to take care of the family. He had to prove he was one of them. A Beaumont.

Then Whitney kissed his jaw. "Do you need to go?"

"Yeah."

He didn't want to. He wanted to stay here, wrapped up with her. He wanted to say to hell with the wedding, the message—he didn't care. He'd done the best he could.

He cared about Whitney. He shouldn't—her old image was going to keep making headaches for him and it'd been only twenty-four hours since he'd met her.

But that didn't change things.

And yet it changed everything.

The phone chimed again. And again. Different chimes. It sounded as though Byron had pulled his stunt.

"I've got to go bail out Byron," he told her. "But I'll see you soon." He got off the bed, trashed the condom and got dressed as fast as he could. By now his phone sounded like a bell choir.

"When?" She sat on the bed, her knees tucked up under her chin. Except for the part where she was completely nude—or maybe because of it—there was an air of vulnerability about her.

"Lunch, tomorrow. You've got to choose where you want to have the bachelorette party. I'll take you to all the places I've scouted out." He picked up his phone. Jeez, that was a lot of messages in less than five minutes. "What a mess," he muttered at his phone. "I'll get you at eleven—that'll give you time with Jo and it'll give me time to fix this."

He leaned down and gave her a quick, hard kiss. Then he was out the door.

He knew he shouldn't be surprised that Phillip was standing in the living room—this was his house, after all—but the last thing Matthew needed right now was to be confronted by his brother.

Phillip looked at him with a raised eyebrow. But instead

of asking about Whitney, he said, "Byron got picked up. He said to tell you he's sorry, but the black eye was unavoidable."

Matthew's shoulders sagged. His little brother had done exactly what he wanted him to—but damned if it didn't feel as though Matthew was suddenly right back at the bottom of the very big mountain he was doomed to be constantly climbing—Mount Beaumont. "What'd he do?"

"He went to a restaurant, ordered dinner, asked to see the chef and proceeded to get into a fistfight with the man."

Matthew rubbed the bridge of his nose. "And?"

"The media is reporting he ordered the salmon."

"Ha-ha. Very funny. I'll get him."

He was halfway to the door when Phillip said, "Everything okay with Whitney?"

"Fine," he shot back as he picked up the pace. He had to get out of here, fast.

But Phillip was faster. He caught up to Matthew at the door. "Better than yesterday?"

"Yes. Now, if you'll excuse me..."

Phillip grinned. "Never thought you had it in you, man. You always went for such...boring women."

"I don't know what you're talking about."

Denial—whether it was to the press or his family—came easily to Matthew. He had years of practice, after all.

"Right, right." He gave Matthew the smile that Matthew had long ago learned to hate—the one that said *I'm better than you are*. "Just a tip, though—from one Beaumont to another—always wipe the lipstick off *before* you leave the bedroom."

Matthew froze. Then he scrubbed the back of his hand across his mouth. It came away bright red.

Whitney's lipstick.

"Uh...this isn't what it looks like."

"Really? Because it looks like you spent the afternoon sleeping with the maid of honor." Matthew's fists curled, but

Phillip threw up his hands in self-defense. "Whatever, man. I'm not about to throw stones at your glass house. Say," he went on in a too-casual voice, "this wouldn't have anything to do with Byron telling me he'd done what you asked him to, would it? Except for the black eye, of course."

Matthew moved before he realized what he was doing. He grabbed Phillip by the front of his shirt. "Do. Not. Give. Her. Crap."

"Dude!" Phillip said, trying to peel Matthew's hands away from his shirt. "Down, boy—down!"

"Promise me, Phillip. After all the messes I cleaned up for you—all the times I saved your ass—*promise me* that you won't torture that woman. Or Byron won't be the only one with a black eye at this wedding."

"Easy, man—I'm not going to do anything."

Matthew let go of his brother. "Sorry."

"No, you're not. Go." Phillip pushed him toward the door. "Bail Byron out so we can all line up for your perfect family wedding. That's what you want, isn't it?"

As Matthew drove off, his mind was a jumble of wedding stuff and family stuff and Whitney. Zipping Whitney into the bridesmaid dress. Stripping her out of her clothes. Admiring her perfectly done hair. Messing her hair up.

He had to pull this wedding off. He had to stay on message. He had to prove he belonged up there with the other Beaumonts, standing by Phillip's side.

That was what Matthew wanted.

Wasn't it?

Ten

She checked her watch. Three to eleven. She'd gotten up at her regular time and gone out with Jo to look at the young mare she was working with. Jo hadn't pressed her about Matthew, except to say, "You and Matthew…" there'd been a rather long pause, but Whitney hadn't jumped into the breach "…do all right yesterday?" Jo had finally finished.

"Yeah. I think you were right about him—he seems like a good guy who's wound a bit too tight."

Which *had* to be the explanation as to why he'd tied her to the bed with a necktie.

Which did nothing to explain why she'd let him do it and explained even less why she'd enjoyed it.

And now? Now she was going to spend the afternoon with him again. Which was great—because it'd been so long since she'd had sex with another person and Matthew wasn't just up to the task—he was easily the best lover she'd ever had.

But it was also nerve-racking. After all, he'd tied her to the bed and made her climax several times. How was she supposed to look him in the eye after that? Yes, she'd slept around a lot when she'd been an out-of-control teenager trying to prove she was an adult. Yes, she'd had some crazy sex. The gossips never let her forget that.

But she'd never had that kind of sex clean and sober. She'd never had any kind of sex sober. She'd never looked a lover in the eye without some sort of chemical aid to cover up her anxiety at what she'd done, what she might still do.

And now, as she adjusted her hat and sunglasses, she was going to have to do just that. She had no idea what to do next. At least she had Betty—the small donkey's ears were soft, and rubbing them helped Whitney keep some sort of hold on her anxiety. It would be fine, she kept telling herself as she petted Betty. *It* will *be fine*.

At exactly eleven, Matthew walked through the door at Phillip and Jo's house, cupped her face in his hands and made her forget everything except the way she'd felt beneath his hands, his body. Beautiful. Sexy.

Alive.

"Hi," he breathed as he rested his forehead against hers.

Maybe this wouldn't be complicated. It hadn't seemed complicated when he'd pinned her to the wall yesterday. Maybe it would be…easy. She grinned, slipping her arms around his waist. "Hi." Then she looked at him. "You're wearing a tie?"

Color touched his cheeks, but he didn't look embarrassed. If anything, he looked the way he had yesterday—hungry for more. Hungry for her.

"I usually wear ties." Heat flushed down her back and pooled low. But instead of pulling that tie off, he added, "Are you ready?"

She nodded, unable to push back against the anxiety. This time, at least, it didn't have anything to do with him. "We have to go, right?"

He leaned back and adjusted her hat, making sure her hair was fully tucked under it. "We'll just look at the places. And after yesterday, I cut a couple of the other options off the list, so it's only four places. We'll park, go in, look at the menu and come back out. Okay?"

"What about lunch?" Because the going-in part hadn't been the problem yesterday.

"I decided we'll have lunch at my apartment."

She looked at him in surprise. "You decided, huh?"

Thus far, she hadn't actually managed to successfully make it through a meal with him. If they were alone at his place, would they eat or...?

He ran his thumb over her lower lip. "I did." Then Betty butted against his legs, demanding that he pet her, too. "You getting ready to walk down the aisle, girl?" he asked as he checked his phone. "We need to get going."

Despite the kiss that followed this statement—how was she going to make it to lunch without ripping his clothes off?—by the time they got into the car and were heading off the farm, she was back to feeling uneasy. She didn't normally fall into bed with a man she'd known for a day. Not since she'd started over.

Matthew had said he knew she was Whitney Maddox... but had he, really? He'd admitted having a huge crush on her back in the day.

"You're nervous," he announced when they were back on the highway, heading toward Denver.

She couldn't deny it. At least she'd made it into the car without stepping on him or anything. But she couldn't bring herself to admit that she was nervous about him. So she went with the other thing that was bothering her. "How's your brother—Byron?"

Matthew exhaled heavily. "He's fine. I got him bailed out. Our lawyers are working to get the charges dropped. But his black eye won't be gone by the wedding, so I had to add him to the makeup artist's list."

"Oh." He sounded extremely put out by this situation, but she was pretty sure he'd told his brother to do something dramatic. To bury her lead. She couldn't help but feel that, at the heart of it, this was her fault.

"The media took the bait, though. You didn't even make the website for the *Denver Post*. Who could pass up the chance to dig up dirt on the Beaumont Prodigal Son Returned? That's the headline the *Post* went with this morning. It's already been picked up by *Gawker* and *TMZ*."

She felt even worse. That wasn't the message Matthew wanted. She was sure that this was exactly what he'd wanted to avoid.

"You're quiet again," he said. He reached over and rubbed her thigh. "This isn't your fault."

The touch was reassuring. "But you're off message. Byron getting arrested isn't rehabilitating the Beaumont family image."

"I know." He exhaled heavily again. "But I can fix this. It's what I do. There's no such thing as bad PR."

Okay, that was another question that she didn't have an answer to. "Why? Why is *that* what you do?"

Matthew pulled his hand back and started drumming his fingers against the steering wheel. "How much do you know about the Beaumonts?"

"Um…well, you guys were a family beer company until recently. And Jo told me your father had a bunch of different children with four different wives and he had a lot of mistresses. And he forgot about your sister and brother's birthday."

"Did Jo say anything else?"

"Just that you'd threatened all the ex-wives to be on their best behavior."

"I did, you know." He chuckled again, but there was at least a little humor in it this time. "I told them if they caused a scene, I'd make an example out of them. No one's hands are clean in this family. I've buried too many scandals." He shot her an all-knowing grin. "They won't risk pissing me off. They know what I could do to them."

She let that series of ominous statements sink in. Suddenly, she felt as if she was facing the man who'd caught her the first night—the man who'd bury her if he got the chance.

But that wasn't the man who'd made love to her last night—was it? Had he offered his brother up as bait to protect her…or because that was still an easier mess to clean up than the one she'd make?

"Are your hands clean?"

"What?"

"You said no one's hands in your family are clean. Does that include you?"

His jaw tensed, and he looked at her again. He didn't say it, but she could tell what he was thinking. Not anymore. Not since he tied her to the bed.

Just then his phone chimed. He glanced down at the screen before announcing, "We need to keep to the schedule."

Right. They weren't going to talk about him right now.

He obviously knew a great deal about her past, but what did she know about him? He was a Beaumont, but he was behind the scenes, keeping everyone on message and burying leads.

"We're here," he announced after a few more minutes of driving. She nodded and braced herself for the worst.

The restaurant seemed overdone—white walls, white chairs, white carpet and what was probably supposed to be avant-garde art done in shades of black on the wall. A white tree with white ornaments stood near the front. It was the most depressing Christmas tree Whitney had ever seen. If a restaurant was capable of trying too hard, this one was. Whitney knew that Jo would be miserable in a place like this.

"Seriously?" she whispered to Matthew after reading the menu. Most of it was in French. She had no idea what kind of food they served here, only that it would be snooty.

"One of the best restaurants in the state," he assured her.

Then they went to a smaller restaurant with only six tables

that had a menu full of locally grown microgreens and other items that Whitney wasn't entirely sure qualified as food. Honest to God, one of the items touted a kind of tree bark.

"How well do you even know Jo?" she asked Matthew as they sped away from the hipster spot. "I mean, really. She's a cowgirl, for crying out loud. She likes burgers and fries."

"It's a nice restaurant," he defended. "I've taken dates there."

"Oh? And you're still seeing those women, are you?"

Matthew shot her a comically mean look.

She giggled at him. This was nice. Comfortable. Plus, she hadn't had to take her hat or sunglasses off, so no one had even looked twice at her. "Gosh, maybe it was your pretentious taste in dining, huh?"

"Careful," he said, trying to sound serious. The grin, however, completely undermined him. "Or I'll get my revenge on you later."

All that glorious heat wrapped around the base of her spine, radiating outward. What was he offering? And more to the point—would she take him up on it this time?

Still, she didn't want to come off as naive. "Promises, promises. Do either of the remaining places serve real food?"

"One." His phone chimed again. "Hang on." He answered it. "Yes? Yes, we're on our way. Yes. That's correct. Thanks."

"*We're* on our way?"

That got her another grin, but this one was less humorous, hungrier. "You'll see."

After a few more minutes, they arrived at their destination. It wasn't so much a restaurant but a pub. Actually, that was its name—the Pub. Instead of the prissiness of the first two places, this was all warm wood and polished brass. "A bar?"

"A pub," he corrected her. "I know Jo doesn't drink, so I was trying to avoid places that had a bar feel to them. But if I left it up to Frances, she'd have you all down at a male strip club, shoving twenties into G-strings."

Realization smacked her upside the head. This wasn't about her or even Jo—this whole search for a place to have a bachelorette party was about managing his sister's image. "You were trying to put us in places that would look good in the society page."

His mouth opened, but then he shut it with a sheepish look. "You're right."

The hostess came forward. "Mr. Beaumont, one moment and I'll get your order."

"Wait, what?"

He turned to her and grinned. "I promised you lunch." He handed her a menu. "Here you go."

"But...you already ordered."

"For the bachelorette party," he said, tipping the menu toward her.

She looked it over. There were a few oddities—microgreens, again!—but although the burgers were touted as being locally raised and organic, they were still burgers. With fries.

"In the back," Matthew explained while they were waiting, "they have a more private room." He leaned down so that his mouth was right by her ear. "It's perfect, don't you think?"

Heat flushed her neck. She certainly hadn't expected Denver at Christmas to be this...warming. "You knew I was going to pick this place, didn't you?"

"Actually, I reserved rooms in all four restaurants. There'll be people looking to stalk the wedding party no matter what. And since we've been seen going over the menu at three of the places, they won't know where to start. This will throw them off the trail."

She gaped at him. *That* was what covering your bases looked like. She'd never been able to plan like that. Which was why she was never ready for the press.

"Really? I can't decide if that's the most paranoid thing I've ever heard or the most brilliant."

He grinned, brushing his fingers over her cheek. "You can't be too careful."

He was going to kiss her. In public. She, more than anyone, knew what a bad idea that was. But she was powerless to stop him, to pull away. Something about this man destroyed her common sense.

The hostess saved Whitney from herself. "Your order, Mr. Beaumont."

"Thank you. And we have the private room for Friday night?"

"Yes, Mr. Beaumont."

Matthew grabbed the bagged food. "Come on. My place isn't too far away."

Matthew pulled into the underground parking lot at the Acoma apartments. He'd guessed right about the Pub, which was a good feeling. And after Whitney's observations about burgers and fries, he felt even better about ordering her that for lunch.

But best of all was the feeling of taking Whitney to his apartment. He didn't bring women home very often. He'd had a couple of dates that turned out to be looking for a story to tell—and sell. Keeping his address private was an excellent way to make sure that he wouldn't get up in the morning and find paparazzi parked outside the building, ready to catch his date leaving his place in the same outfit she'd had on the night before.

He wasn't worried about that happening with Whitney. First off, he had no plans of keeping her here all night long—although that realization left him feeling strangely disappointed. But second?

As far as he could tell, no one had made him as the man sitting next to Whitney Wildz the other day. Frankly, he couldn't believe it—it wasn't as if he were an unknown quantity. He talked to the press and his face was more than recognizable as a Beaumont.

Still, it was a bit of grace he was willing to use as he led Whitney to the elevator that went up to the penthouse apartment.

Inside, he pressed her back against the wall and kissed her hungrily. Lunch could wait, right?

Then she moaned into his mouth, and his body responded. He'd wanted to do this since he'd walked into Phillip's house this morning—show her that he could be spontaneous, that he could give her more than just one afternoon. He wanted to show her that there was more to him than the Beaumont name.

Even as the thought crossed his mind, the unfamiliarity of it struck him as…wrong. Hadn't it *always* been about the Beaumont name?

"Oh, Matthew," she whispered against his skin.

Yeah, lunch could wait.

Then the doors opened. "Come on," he said, pulling her out of the elevator and into his penthouse.

He wanted to go directly to the bedroom—but Whitney pulled up short. "Wow. This is…perfect."

"Thanks." He let go of her long enough to set the lunch bag down on a counter. But before he could wrap his arms around her again, she'd walked farther in—not toward the floor-to-ceiling windows but toward the far side of the sitting room.

The one with his pictures.

As Whitney stared at the Wall of Accomplishments, as he thought of it, something Phillip had said last night came back to him. *You always went for such boring women.*

They hadn't been boring. They'd been *safe*. On paper, at least, they'd been perfect. Businesswomen who had no interest in marrying into the Beaumont fortune because they had their own money. Quiet women who had no interest in scoring an invite to the latest Beaumont Brewery blowout because they didn't drink beer.

Women who wouldn't make a splash in the society pages.

Whitney? She was already making waves in his life—waves he couldn't control. And he was enjoying it. Craving more. Craving *her*.

"This..." Whitney said, leaning up on her tiptoes to look at the large framed photo that was at the center of the Wall of Accomplishments. "This is a wedding photo."

Eleven

"Yes. That's my parents' wedding."

The tension in his voice was unmistakable.

"But you're in the picture. That's you, right? And the boy you're standing next to—that's Phillip? Is the other one Chadwick?" The confusion pushed back at the desire that was licking through her veins. She couldn't make sense out of what she was looking at.

"That's correct." He sounded as if he were confirming a news story.

"But…you're, like, five or something? You're a kid!"

A tight silence followed this statement. She might have crossed some line, but she didn't care. She was busy staring at the photo.

A man—Hardwick Beaumont—was in a very nice tuxedo. He stood next to a woman in an exceptionally poofy white dress that practically dripped crystals and pearls. She had giant teased red hair that wasn't contained at all by the headband that came to a V-point in the middle of her forehead. The look spoke volumes about the high style of the early '80s.

In front of them stood three boys, all in matching tuxedos. Hardwick had his hand on Chadwick's shoulder. Next to Chadwick stood a smaller boy with blond hair. He wore a wicked grin, like a sprite out to stir up trouble. And standing in front of the woman was Matthew. She had her hand on his shoulder as she beamed at the camera, but Matthew looked as though someone were jabbing him with a hatpin.

When he did speak, he asked, "You didn't know that I wasn't born a Beaumont?"

She turned to stare at him. "What? No—what does that mean?"

He nodded, nearly the same look on his face now that little-kid Matthew had worn for that picture. "Phillip is only six months older than I am."

"Really?"

He came to stand next to her, one arm around her waist. She leaned into him, enjoying this comfortable touch. Enjoying that he wasn't holding himself apart from her.

"It was a huge scandal at the time—even by Beaumont standards. My mother was his mistress while he was still married to Eliza—that's Phillip and Chadwick's mother." He paused, as if he were steeling himself to the truth. "Eliza didn't divorce him for another four years. I was born Matthew Billings."

"Wait—you didn't grow up with your dad?"

"Not until I was almost five. Eliza found out about me and divorced Hardwick. He kept custody of Chadwick and Phillip, married my mom and moved us into the Beaumont mansion."

She stared at him, then back at the small boy in the photo. *Matthew Billings.* "But you and Phillip seem so close. You're planning his wedding. I just thought…"

"That we'd grown up together? No." He laughed, a joyless noise. "I remember her telling me how I'd have my daddy and he'd love me, and I'd have some brothers who'd play with me, so I shouldn't be sad that we were leaving everything behind. She told me it was going to be perfect. Just…perfect."

The way he said it made it pretty clear that it wasn't. Was this why everything had to be *just so*? He'd spent his life chasing a dream of perfection?

"What happened?"

He snorted. "What do you think? Chadwick hated me—deeply and completely. Sometimes Phillip was nice to me because he was lonely, too." He pointed at the wedding photo. "Sometimes he and Chadwick would gang up on me because I wasn't a real Beaumont. Plus, my mom got pregnant with Frances and Byron almost immediately and once they were born...well, they were Beaumonts without question." He sighed.

His dad had forgotten about him. That was basically what Jo had said Hardwick Beaumont did—all those wives, mistresses and so many children that they didn't even know how many there were. What a legacy. "So how did you wind up as the one who takes care of everyone else?"

He moved, stepping back and wrapping both arms around her. "I had to prove I belonged—that I was a legitimate Beaumont, not a Billings." He lowered his head so that his lips rested against the base of her neck.

She would not let him distract her with something as simple, as perfect, as a kiss. Not when the key to understanding *why* was right in front of her.

"How did you do that?"

His arms were strong and warm around her as they pulled her back into his chest. All of his muscles pressed against her. and for a moment she wondered if he was going to push her against the wall and make her cry out his name again, just to avoid answering the question.

But then he said, "I copied Chadwick. I got all As, just like Chadwick did. I went to the same college, got the same MBA. I got a job at the Brewery, just like Chadwick. He was the perfect Beaumont—still is, in a lot of ways. I thought—It sounds stupid now, but I thought if I could just *be* the perfect Beaumont, my mom would stop crying in her closet and we'd be a happy family."

"Did it work?" Although she already knew the answer to that one.

"Not really." His arms tightened around her, and he splayed his fingers over her ribs in an intimate touch. She leaned into him, as if she could tell him that she was here for him. That he didn't have to be perfect for her.

"When Frances and Byron were four, my parents got divorced. Mom tried to get custody of us, but without Beaumont money, she had nothing and Hardwick's lawyers were ruthless. I was ten."

"Do you still see her?"

"Of course. She's my mother, after all. She works in a library now. It doesn't pay all of her bills, but she enjoys it. I take care of everything else." He sighed against her skin, his hands skimming over her waist. "She apologized once. Said she was sorry she'd ruined my life by marrying my father."

"Do you feel the same way?"

He made a big show of looking around his stunning apartment. "I don't really think this qualifies as 'ruined,' do you?"

"It looks perfect," she agreed. But then, so did the wedding photo. One big happy family.

"Yeah, well, if there's one thing being a Beaumont has taught me, it's that looks are everything. Like when a jealous husband caught Dad with his wife. There was a scene—well, that's putting it mildly. I was in college and walked out of my apartment one morning and into this throng of reporters and photographers and they were demanding a good reaction quote from me—they wanted something juicy, you know?"

"I know." God, it was like reliving her own personal hell all over again. She could see the paparazzi jostling for position, shouting horrible things.

"I didn't know anything about what had happened, so I just started…making stuff up." He sounded as if he still didn't believe he'd done that. "The photos had been doctored. People would do anything for attention, including lay a trap for the richest man in Denver—and we would be suing for libel. The family would support Hardwick because he was right. And the press—they took the bait. Swallowed it hook, line and sinker. I saved his image." His voice trailed off. "He was proud of me. He told me, 'That's how a Beaumont handles it.' Told me to keep taking care of the family and it'd be just fine."

"Was it?"

"Of course not. His third wife left him—but he bought her off. He always bought them off and kept custody of the kids because it was good for his image as a devoted family man who just had really lousy luck when it came to women. But I'd handled myself so well that when a position in the Brewery public relations department opened up, I got the job."

He'd gone to work for his brother after that unhappy childhood. She wasn't sure she could be that big of a person. "Do your brothers still hate you?"

He laughed. "Hell, no. I'm too valuable to them. I've gotten Phillip out of more trouble than he even remembers and Chadwick counts me as one of his most trusted advisors. I'm…" He swallowed. "I'm one of them now. A legitimate Beaumont—the brother of honor at the wedding, even. Not a bastard that married into the family five years too late." He nuzzled at the base of her neck. "I just… I wish I'd known it would all work out when I was a kid, you know?"

She knew. She still wished she knew it would all work out. Somehow. "You know what I was doing when I was five?"

"What?"

"Auditions. My mother was dragging me to tryouts for commercials," she whispered into the silence. "I didn't care about acting. I just wanted to ride horses and color, but she wanted me to be famous. *She* wanted to be famous."

She'd never understood what Jade Maddox got out of it,

putting Whitney in front of all those people so she could pretend she was someone else. Hadn't just being herself been enough for her mother?

But the answer had been no. Always no. "My first real part was on *Larry the Llama*—remember that show? I was Lulu."

Behind her, Matthew stilled. Then, suddenly, he was laughing. The joy spilled out of him and surrounded her, making her smile with him. "You were on the llama show? That show was terrible!"

"Oh, I know it. Llamas are *weird*. Apparently everyone agreed because it was canceled about six months later. I'd hoped that was the end of my mother's ambitions. But it wasn't. I *dreamed* about having brothers or sisters. I didn't even meet my dad until I became famous, and then he just asked for money. Jade's the one who pushed me to audition for *Growing Up Wildz*, who pushed them to make the character's name Whitney."

His eyebrows jumped. "It wasn't supposed to be Whitney?"

"Wendy." She gave him a little grin. "It was supposed to be Wendy Wildz."

"Wow. That's just..." he chuckled. "That's just wrong. Sorry."

"It is. And I went along with it. I thought it'd be cool to have the same name as the character. I had no idea then it'd be the biggest mistake of my life—that I'd never be able to get away from Whitney Wildz."

He spun her around and gazed into her eyes. "That's not who you are to me. You know that, right?"

She did know. She was pretty sure, anyway. "Yes."

But then his mouth crooked back into a smile. "But... Lulu?"

"Hey, it was a great show about a talking llama!" she shot

back, unable to fight back the giggle. "Are you criticizing quality children's programming written by adults on drugs?"

"What was it ol' Larry used to say? 'It's Llama Time!' And then he'd spit?" He tried to tickle her.

She grabbed his hands. "Are you mocking llamas? They're majestic animals!"

He tested her grip, but she didn't let go. Suddenly, he wasn't laughing anymore and she wasn't, either.

She found herself staring at his tie. It was light purple today, with lime-green paisley amoebas swimming around on it. Somehow, it looked good with the bright blue shirt he was wearing. Maybe that was because he was wearing it.

He leaned down, letting his lips brush over her forehead, her cheek. "What are you going to do?" he asked, his voice husky. "Tie me up? For making fun of a llama?"

Could she *do* that? It'd been one thing to let him bind her wrists in a silk necktie yesterday. He'd been in control then—because she'd wanted him to be. She'd wanted him to make the decisions. She'd wanted to be consumed.

But today was different. She didn't want to be consumed. She wanted to do the consuming.

She pushed him back and grabbed his tie, then hauled his face down to hers. "I won't stand for you disparaging llamas."

"We could sit." He nodded toward a huge dining-room table, complete with twelve very available chairs surrounding it. The chairs had high backs and latticed slats. But he didn't pull his tie away from her hand, didn't try to touch her. "If you want to."

"Oh, I want to, mister. No one gets away with trash-talking *Larry the Llama*." She jerked on his tie and led him toward the closest chair.

"Larry was ridiculous," Matthew said as she pushed him down.

"You're going to regret saying that." She yanked his tie

off. It still had the knot in it, but she didn't want to stop to undo it. She didn't want to stop and think about what she was doing.

"Will I?" He held his hands behind his back.

"Oh, you will." She had no idea how to tie a man up in the best of times. So she looped the tie around his wrists and tried to tie it to the slat that was at the correct height. "There. That'll teach you."

"Will it?" Matthew replied. "Llamas look like they borrowed their necks from gira—"

She kissed him, hard. He shifted, as if he wanted to touch her, but she'd tied him to a chair.

She could do whatever she wanted, and he couldn't stop her.

Sexy. Beautiful. Desirable. That was what she wanted.

She stepped away from him and began to strip. Not like yesterday, when she'd been trying to get out of her clothes so fast she'd kicked him. No, this time—at a safe distance—she began to remove her clothing slowly.

First she peeled her sweater over her head, then she started undoing the buttons on her denim shirt—slowly. One at a time.

Matthew didn't say anything, not even to disparage llamas.

Instead, Matthew's gaze was fastened to Whitney's fingertips as one button after another gave.

A look of disappointment blotted out the desire when he saw the plain white tank top underneath.

"It's cold here," she told him. "You're supposed to dress in layers when it's cold."

"Did the llamas tell you that? They lie. You should be naked. Right now."

She was halfway through removing her tank top when he said that. She went ahead and pulled it the rest of the way off, but said, "Just for that, I'm not going to get naked."

His eyes widened in shock. "What?"

She stuck her hands on her hips, which had the handy effect of thrusting her breasts forward. "And you can't touch me, because you're tied up." Just saying it out loud gave her a little thrill of power.

For too damn long, she'd felt powerless. The only way she'd been able to control her own life was to become a hermit, basically—just her and the animals and crazy Donald up the valley. People took what they wanted from her—including deciding who she was—and they never gave her any say in the matter.

Not Matthew. He'd let her do whatever she wanted—be whoever she wanted.

She could be herself—klutzy and concerned about her animals—and he still looked at her with that hunger in his eyes.

She kicked off her boots and undid her jeans. Miracle of miracles, she managed to slide them off without tipping over and falling onto the floor.

Matthew's eyes lit up with want. With *need*. She could see him breathing faster now, leaning forward as if he could touch her. Heat flooded her body—almost enough to make up for the near-nudity. She felt sexy. Except for the socks.

Well, she'd already told him she wasn't going to get naked. Although she was having a little trouble remembering why, exactly.

Plus, he was sitting there fully clothed. And she didn't know where any condoms were. "Condoms?" They were required. She'd been accused of being falsely pregnant far too many times to actually risk a real pregnancy. The last thing she needed in her life were more headlines asking, Wildz Baby Daddy?

"Wallet." The tension in his voice set her pulse racing. "Left side."

"You just want me to touch you, don't you?"

He grinned. "That is the general idea. Since you won't let me touch you."

"I stand for llama solidarity," she replied as she walked toward him. "And until you can see reason…"

"Oh, I can't. No reason at all. Llamas are nature's mistake."

"Then you'll just have to stay tied up." She straddled him, but she didn't rest her weight on his obvious erection. Instead, she slid her hands over his waist and down around to his backside until she felt his wallet. She fished it out, dropped it onto the table and then ran her hands over him again. "I didn't really get to feel all of this last time," she told him.

"You were a little tied up."

She ran her hands over his shoulders, down his pecs, feeling the muscles that were barely contained by the button-down shirt and cashmere sweater. Then she leaned back so she could slide her hands down and feel what was behind those tweed slacks.

Matthew sucked in a breath so hot she felt it scorch her cheek as she touched the length of his erection. He leaned forward and tried to kiss her, but she pulled away, keeping just out of his reach. "Llama hater," she hissed at him.

"You're killing me," he ground out as he tried to thrust against her hand.

"Ah-ah-ah," she scolded. This was…*amazing*. She knew that, if he wanted to, he could probably get out of the tie and wrap her in his arms and take what she was teasing him with. And she'd let him because, all silliness aside, she wanted him *so* much.

But he wasn't. He wouldn't, because she was in control. She had all the power here.

Tension coiled around the base of her spine, tightening her muscles beyond a level that was comfortable. She let her body fall against his, let the contact between them grow.

"Woman," Matthew groaned.

She tsked him as she slid off. "You act like you've never been tied up before."

"I haven't." His gaze was fastened to her body again. She felt bold enough to strike a pose, which drew another low groan from him.

"You...haven't?"

"No. Never tied anyone up before, either." He managed to drag his gaze up to her face. "Have you?"

"No." She looked at him, trying to keep her cool. He hadn't done this before? But he'd seemed so sure of himself last night. It wasn't as though she expected a man as hot and skilled as he was to be virginal, but there was something about being the first woman he'd wrapped his necktie around—something about her being the first woman he'd let tie him to a chair—that changed things.

No. No! This was just a little fling! Just her dipping her sexual toes back in the sexy waters! This was not about developing new, deeper feelings for Matthew Beaumont!

She snagged the condom off the table. "I demand an apology on behalf of Larry the Llama and llamas everywhere." Then—just because she could—she dropped the condom and bent over to pick it up.

He sucked in another breath at the sight she was giving him. "I beg of your forgiveness, Ms. Maddox." She shifted. *"Please,"* he added, sounding desperate. "Please forgive me. I'll never impugn the honor of llamas again."

Ms. Maddox.

She needed him. Now.

She slid her panties off but kept the bra on. She undid his trousers and got them down far enough that she could roll the condom on. Then, unable to wait any longer, she let her body fall onto his.

She grabbed his face and held it so she could look into his eyes. "Matthew..."

But he was driving up into her and she was grinding down onto him and there wasn't time for more words. They had so very little time to begin with.

"Want to…kiss you," Matthew got out, each word punctuated with another thrust.

His clothing was rubbing against her, warming her bare skin. Warming everything. "Kiss me back?" she asked, knowing what the answer would be.

"Always," he replied as she lowered her lips to his. "Always."

Always. Not just right now but always.

She came apart when their lips met, and he came with her.

She lay on top of him, feeling the climax ebb from her body. It was then that she wished she hadn't tied him up, because she wanted him to hold her.

"I had no idea that llamas got you so worked up," he told her as his lips trailed over her bare shoulder. "I'll make a mental note of it."

She leaned back and grinned at him. "Was that okay? I didn't hurt you or anything—? Oh! I should untie you!"

"Uh—wait—" he said, but she was already at the back of the chair.

The tie lay in a heap on the ground. Not around his wrists. Not tied to the chair. She blinked at the puddle of bright fabric. Confusion swamped her. "When— Wait—if you weren't tied up, why didn't you touch me?"

He stood and adjusted his pants before turning around. He was, for all intents and purposes, the same as he'd been before, minus one necktie. And she was standing here in her socks and a bra. She couldn't even tie a man up.

"Why didn't you touch me?" she asked again.

He came to her then, wrapping his arms around her and holding her tight to him. "Because," he said, his lips pressing against her forehead, "you tied me up. It was kind of like…making a promise, that you were in charge. I keep my promises."

"Oh," she breathed. People didn't often keep promises, not to her. Her mother hadn't protected her, hadn't managed

her money. Her former fiancé hadn't kept a single promise to her.

She had crazy Donald, who didn't know who she was, and…Jo, who'd promised that she wouldn't tell anyone about the months she'd spent with Whitney, wouldn't tell a living soul where Whitney lived.

And now Matthew was promising to follow her wishes.

She didn't know what to make of this.

From somewhere far away, his phone chimed. "Our lunch is probably ice-cold," he said without letting her go or answering his phone.

At the mention of the word *cold*, she shivered. She was mostly naked, after all. "We haven't had a successful meal yet."

The phone chimed again. It seemed louder—more insistent. "I need to deal with some things. But if you want to hang out for a bit, I can take you home and we can try to have dinner out at the farm?"

"I'd like that."

"Yeah," he agreed, brushing his lips over hers as his phone chimed again and again. "So would I."

Twelve

It was a hell of a mess. And what made it worse was that it was self-inflicted. He'd made this bed. Now he had to lie in it.

Matthew tried to focus on defusing the situation—which wasn't easy, given that Whitney was exploring his apartment. Normally, he didn't mind showing off his place. It was opulent by any normal standard—truly befitting a Beaumont.

But now? What would she see when she looked at his custom decorating scheme? Would she see the very best that money could buy or...would she see something else?

None of the other women he'd brought back here had ever focused on his parents' wedding picture. They might have made a passing comment about how cute he was as a kid, but the other women always wanted to know what it was like being Phillip's brother or meeting this actor or that singer. They wanted to know how awesome it was to be one of the famous Beaumont men.

Not Whitney. She already knew what fame felt like. And she'd walked away from it. She didn't need it. She didn't need other people's approval.

What must she think of him, that he *did* need it? That he had to have the trappings of wealth and power—that he had to prove he was not just *a* Beaumont but the best one?

Focus. He had a job to do—a job that paid for the apartment and the cars and, yes, the ties. Matthew didn't know why Byron had gone after that chef. His gut told him there was a history there, but he didn't know what it was and Byron wasn't talking.

So Matthew did what he always did. He massaged the truth.

He lied.

The other guy had swung first. All Byron had done was complain about an underdone salmon steak, and the chef took it personally. Byron was merely defending himself. So what if that wasn't what the police report said? As long as Matthew kept repeating his version of events—and questioning the motives of anyone who disagreed with him—sooner or later, his reality would replace the true events.

"What's in here?" Whitney called out. Normally, he didn't like people in general and women in particular to explore his space on their own. He kept his apartment spotless, so it wasn't that. He liked to explain how he'd decided on the decorating scheme, why the Italian marble was really the only choice, how a television that large was really worth it. He liked to manage the message of his apartment.

He liked to manage the people in his apartment.

However, Whitney was being so damned adorable he couldn't help but smile.

"Where?" he shouted back.

"Here— Oh! That's a *really* big TV!"

He chuckled. "You're in the theater room!"

"Wow…" Her voice trailed off.

He knew that in another five minutes they'd have almost the exact same conversation all over again.

Matthew realized he was humming as he gave his official Beaumont response to the "unfortunate" situation again and again. Byron was merely noting his displeasure with an undercooked dish. The Beaumonts were glad the cops were called so they could get this mess straightened out. They would have their day in court.

Then a new email popped up—this one wasn't from a journalist but from Harper, his father's nemesis.

"Thank you for inviting us to the reception of Phillip Beaumont and bride at the last second, but sadly, no one in the Harper family has the least interest in celebrating such an occasion."

The old goat hadn't even bothered to sign the kiss-off. Nice.

Normally, it would have bothered Matthew. Maybe it did, a little. But then Whitney called out, "You have your own gym? Really?"

And just like that, Matthew didn't care about Harper.

"Really!" he called back. He sent off a short reply stating how very much Harper would be missed—Hardwick Beaumont had always counted him as a friend. Which was another bold-faced lie—the two men had hated each other from the moment Hardwick had seduced Harper's first wife less than a month after Harper had married her. But Harper wasn't the only one who could write a kiss-off.

Speaking of kissing…Matthew checked the weather, closed his computer and went looking for Whitney. She was standing in his bathroom, of all places, staring at the wide-open shower and the in-set tub. "It's just you, right? Even the bathroom is monster huge!"

"Just me. You need to make a decision."

Her eyes grew wide. "About what?"

He brushed his fingers through her hair. It'd gotten mussed up when she'd stripped for him. He liked it better that way. "The weather might turn later tonight. If you want to go back to the farm, we'll need to leave soon."

One corner of her mouth curved up. "*If*? What's the other option?"

"You are more than welcome to stay here with me." He looked around his bathroom. "I have plenty of room. And

then I could show you how the shower works. And the bath."
He'd like to see that—her body wet as he soaped her up.

She gave him a look that was part innocence, part sheer
seduction. A look that said she might like to be soaped up—
but the thought scared her, as well. "I don't have any of my
things…"

He nodded in agreement. Besides, he tried to reason with
himself, just because there hadn't been paparazzi waiting for
them when they got to the building didn't mean that there
wouldn't be people out there in the morning. And the last
thing he needed right now was someone to see him and the
former Whitney Wildz doing the walk of shame.

"Besides," she went on, looking surprisingly stern, "it's
Christmas—almost, anyway—and you don't even have a
tree. Why don't you have a tree? I mean, this place is amazing—but no tree? Not a single decoration? Really?"

He brushed his fingertips over her cheeks again. He didn't
normally celebrate Christmas here. "I spend Christmas night
with my mom. If they're in town, Frances and Byron come
by. She always has stockings filled with cheesy gifts like
yo-yos and mixes for party dips. She has a small tree and
a roasted turkey breast and boxed mashed potatoes—not
high cuisine by any stretch." He wouldn't dare admit that
to anyone else.

Christmas night was the one night of the year when he
didn't feel like Matthew Beaumont. Back in Mom's small
apartment, cluttered with photos of him and her and Frances and Byron—but never Hardwick Beaumont—Matthew
felt almost as if he were still Matthew Billings.

It was a glimpse into the past—one that he occasionally let himself get nostalgic about, but it never lasted very
long. Then, after he gave his mother the present he'd picked
out for her—something that she could use but a nicer version than she could afford herself—he'd kiss her goodbye
and come back to this world. His world. The world where
he would never admit to being Matthew Billings. Not even
for an afternoon.

Except he'd just admitted it to Whitney. And instead of the clawing defensiveness he usually felt whenever anyone brought up the Billings name, he felt…lighter.

Whitney gave him a scolding look. "It sounds lovely. I watch *It's a Wonderful Life* and share a ham with Gater and Fifi. I usually bring carrots to the horses, that sort of thing." She sighed, leaning into his arms. "I miss having someone to celebrate with. That's why I came to this wedding. I mean, I came for Jo, but…"

"Tell you what—we'll head back to the farm now, because it looks all Christmassy, and then—" his mouth was moving before he realized what he was saying "—then after the wedding, maybe we can spend part of Christmas together before you go home?"

"I'd like that." Her cheeks flushed with warmth. "But I don't have a present for you."

He couldn't resist. "You are the only present I want. Maybe even tied up with a bow…." He gathered her into his arms and pressed her back against the tiled wall with a rather heated kiss.

Several minutes passed before she was able to ask, "Are you done with your work?"

"For now, yes." Later he'd have to log back in and launch another round of damage control. But he could take a few hours to focus on Whitney. "Let me take you home."

She giggled. "I don't think I have much of a choice in that, do I? My truck's still out on the farm." A look of concern crossed her face. "Can you drive your car in the snow?"

"I'm a Beaumont," he said, his words echoing off the tiled walls of the bathroom. "I have more than one vehicle."

After a comfortable drive out to the farm in his Jeep, Whitney asked him if he'd stay for dinner. Jo had already set a place for him at the table and Phillip said, "Hang out, dude."

So, after a quick check of his messages to make sure that

nothing else had blown up, Matthew sat down to dinner—homemade fried chicken and mashed potatoes. Finally, over easy conversation about horses and celebrities, he and Whitney managed to successfully eat a meal together.

Then Jo said, "We're going to watch *Elf*, if you want to join us."

"I auditioned for that movie," Whitney said, leaning into him. "But I was, um, under the influence at the time and blew it pretty badly, so Zooey Deschanel got the part. It's still a really funny movie. I watch it every year."

Matthew looked at Phillip, who was pointedly not smiling at the way Matthew had wrapped his arm around Whitney's waist. "Sure," Matthew heard himself say. "It sounds like fun."

As the women popped popcorn and made hot chocolate, of all things, Phillip pulled him aside under the pretense of discussing the sound for the movie. "Who are you," he said under his breath, "and what have you done with my brother Matthew?"

"Shove it," Matthew whispered back. He didn't want to have this conversation. Not even with Phillip.

His brother did no such shoving. "Correct me if I'm wrong," he went on, "but weren't you on the verge of personally throwing her out of the wedding a few nights ago?"

"Shove. It."

"And yesterday—well, she's an attractive woman. I can't fault you for sleeping with her. But today?" Phillip shook his head, clearly enjoying himself. "Man, I don't think I've ever seen you be so…lovey-dovey."

Matthew sighed. He wanted to deck Phillip so badly, but the wedding was in a matter of days. "Lovey-dovey?"

"Affectionate. I can't remember the last time I've seen you touch a woman, outside of handshakes and photo ops. And you *never* just sit around and watch a movie. You're always working."

"I'll have to log back on in a few hours. I'm still working."

Phillip looked at him out of the corner of his eye. "You can't keep your hands off her."

Matthew shrugged, hoping he looked noncommittal. He touched women. He took lovers. He was a Beaumont—having affairs was his birthright.

Boring women, he remembered Phillip calling them yesterday. Women he took to stuffy restaurants and to their own place to bed them so no one would see that he'd had a guest overnight.

It wasn't that he wasn't affectionate. It was that he was careful. He had to be.

He wished Jo and Whitney would hurry the hell up with that popcorn. "I like her."

"Which her? The fallen star or the horse breeder?"

"The horse breeder. I like her."

Phillip clapped him on the shoulder. "Good answer, man. Good answer. The movie is ready, ladies," he added as Jo and Whitney made their way over to them.

Matthew hurried to take the full mugs of cocoa—complete with marshmallows—from Whitney. Then Jo produced blankets. She and Phillip curled up on one couch with the donkey sitting at their feet as they munched popcorn and laughed at the movie.

Which left him and Whitney with the other couch. He didn't give a rat's ass for the popcorn. He set his cocoa down where he could reach it, then patted the couch next to him. Whitney curled up against his side and pulled the blankets over them.

"Do you watch a lot of movies?" he asked in a quiet voice, his mouth against her ear.

"I do. I get up really early when it's warm—farmer's hours—and I'm pretty tired at night. Sometimes I read—I like romances." He could see the blush over her face when she said that, as if he'd begrudge her a happy ending. "It took a while before I could watch things like this and not think a bunch of what-ifs, you know?"

He wrapped his arms around her waist and lifted her onto his lap. Maybe Phillip was right. Maybe he wasn't normally affectionate with the women who came into his life. But he *had* to touch Whitney.

They watched the movie. Whitney and Jo had clearly watched it together before. They laughed and quoted the lines at each other and had little inside jokes. Matthew's phone buzzed a few times during the show, but he ignored it.

Phillip was right about one thing—when was the last time he'd taken a night off and just hung out? It'd been a while. Matthew tried to think—had he planned on taking a couple of days off after the wedding? No, not really. The wedding was the unofficial launch of Percheron Drafts, Chadwick's new craft beer. Matthew had a 30 percent stake in the company. They were building up to a big launch just in time for the Big Game in February. The push was going to be hard.

He'd made plans to have dinner with his mother. That was all the time he'd originally allotted for the holiday. But now? He could take a few days off. He didn't know when Whitney was heading back to California, but if she wanted to stick around, he would make time for her.

By the time the movie ended, he and Whitney were lying down, spooning under their blankets. He hadn't had any popcorn, and the cocoa was cold, but he didn't care. With her backside pressed against him, he was having a hard time thinking. Other things were also getting hard.

But there was a closeness that he hadn't anticipated. He liked just holding her.

"I should go," he said in her ear.

She sighed. "I wish you didn't have to."

Phillip and Jo managed to get untangled from their covers first. "Uh, Matthew?"

"Yeah?" He managed to push himself up into a sitting position without dumping Whitney on the floor.

"Icy."

"You see what?"

"No, icy—as in ice. On your car. And the driveways."

"Damn, really?" He waited long enough for Whitney to sit up. Then he walked to a window. Phillip was right. A glaze of ice coated everything. "The weather said snow. Not ice. Damn. I should have…"

"You're stuck out here, man." Phillip gave him a playful punch in the shoulder. "I know it'll be a real hardship, but you can't drive home on ice."

Matthew looked at Whitney. She'd come to stand next to him. "Ice…wow," she said in the same tone she'd used when she'd been exploring his apartment. "We don't get ice out in California. Not like this!" She slipped her hand into his and squeezed.

He could stay the night. One night wrapped up in Whitney and then he could fall asleep with her in his arms. Wake up with her there, too. He didn't do that often. Okay, he didn't ever do that.

Only one problem. "I didn't bring anything."

"We have guest supplies," Jo called out.

Phillip stood up straight and looked Matthew over. "Yeah, we probably still wear the same size."

"Stay," Whitney said in a voice that was meant only for him. "Stay with me. Just for the night. Call it…an early Christmas present."

It really wasn't an argument. He couldn't drive home on ice and honestly? He didn't want to. Suddenly he understood why Phillip had always preferred the farmhouse. It was warm and lived-in. If Matthew went back to his apartment—monster huge, as Whitney had noted, and completely devoid of holiday cheer—and Whitney wasn't there with him, the place would feel…empty.

Lonely.

It'd never bothered him before. But tonight he knew it would.

"I'll need to log on," he told everyone. "We still have a wedding to deal with."

"Of course," Jo said. She was smiling, but not at him. At Whitney. "You do what you need to do."

Matthew spent an hour answering the messages he'd ignored. Whitney had gone up to read so she wouldn't distract him from his work. He knew he was rushing, but the thought of her in his room again—well, that was enough to make a man hurry the hell up.

When he opened his door, the fire was blazing in the hearth, and Whitney was in bed. She looked...perfect. He couldn't even see Whitney Wildz when he looked at her anymore. She was just Whitney.

The woman he wanted. "I was waiting for you," she told him.

"I'll make it worth the wait." Then she lifted up the covers and he saw that she was nude.

Thank God for ice.

Thirteen

The day of the bachelorette party came fast. Whitney got to stay on the farm for a couple of days, which should have made her happy. She was able to work with Jo and some of the many horses on the farm—Appaloosas, Percherons and Sun, the Akhal-Teke. Phillip treated her like a close friend and the staff on the farm was the definition of discreet and polite at all times. They made cookies and watched holiday shows. Even the farm manager, an old hand named Richard, took to calling her Whit.

By all rights, it should have been everything she wanted. Quiet. Peaceful. Just her and a few friends and a bunch of horses. No cameras, no gossips, no anything having to do with Whitney Wildz. Except…

She missed Matthew.

And that wasn't like her. She didn't miss people. She didn't get close enough to people to miss them when they went.

Well, that wasn't true. She'd missed the easy friendship with Jo when Jo had hitched her trailer back up to her truck and driven on to the next job.

But now, after only two days without him, she missed Matthew. And she shouldn't. She just shouldn't. So he'd made love to her that night, rolling her onto her stomach to do things to her that *still* made her shiver with desire when she thought about them. And so she'd woken up in his arms the next morning and they'd made love so sweetly that she still couldn't believe she hadn't dreamed the whole thing.

How long had it been since she'd woken up with a man in bed? A long time. Even longer since the man in question had made love to her. Told her how beautiful she was, how good she was. How glad he was that he'd stayed with her.

It was a problem. A huge one. This was still a temporary thing, a Christmas fling that would end with the toss of the bridal bouquet. If she were lucky, she'd get Christmas morning with him. And that'd be it. If she missed Matthew now, after just a couple of good days, how bad off would she be when she went home? When she wouldn't have to wait another day to see him?

How much would she miss him when she wasn't going to see him again?

It'd hurt to watch him get into his car and slowly drive away. He'd offered to let her come with him, but she'd refused. She was here for Jo and, anyway, Matthew had things he needed to do. Weddings to manage, PR debacles to control. Just another reminder of how far apart their lives really were.

To her credit, Jo hadn't said much about the sudden relationship. Just, "Are you having a good time with Matthew?"

"I am," Whitney had said truthfully. Although *fun* seemed as if it wasn't strong enough of a word. Fun was a lovely day at an amusement park. Being with Matthew? It was amazing. That was all there was to it. He was *amazing*.

"Good." That was all Jo said about it.

Now, however, Whitney and Jo were driving in to the Pub to meet the other women in the wedding party. Matthew would be out with Phillip and all their brothers—bowling, of all things. Although Whitney wasn't sure if that was one of those fake activities Matthew had planned to keep the paparazzi guessing.

Whitney kept her hat on as the hostess showed them back to the private room. There were already several other women there, as well as a small buffet laid out with salads, burgers and fries. *Matthew*, Whitney thought with a smile as she took off her hat and sunglasses. Maybe he did know Jo better than she thought.

"Hi, all," Jo said. "Let me introduce—"

"*Oh, my God*, it's really you! You're Whitney Wildz!" A young woman with bright red hair came rushing up to Whitney. In the brief second before she grabbed Whitney by the shoulders, Whitney could see the unmistakable resemblance to both Matthew and Phillip—but especially Matthew. The red hair helped.

"You really *are* here! And you know Jo! *How* do you know Jo? I'm Frances Beaumont, by the way."

"Hi," Whitney tried out. She'd known this was going to happen—and today was certainly a more controlled situation than normal. She had Jo and there were only a few women in the room. But she'd never really mastered the proper response to rabid fans.

"Yes, as I was saying," Jo said in a firm voice as she pried Frances's hands off Whitney's shoulders, "this is Whitney Maddox. She's a horse breeder. I know her because we've worked horses together." She tried to steer Frances away from Whitney, but it didn't work.

"You're really *here*. Oh, my God, I know you probably have this happen all the time, but I was your *biggest* fan. I loved your show *so* much and one time Matthew took me to see you in concert." Before Whitney could dodge out of the way, Frances threw her arms around her and pulled Whitney into a massive hug. "I'm *so* glad to meet you. You have no idea."

"Um…" was all Whitney could get out as her lungs were crushed. Frances was surprisingly strong for her size. "I'm getting one."

"Frances," Jo said, the warning in her voice unmistakable. "Could you at least let Whitney get her coat off before you embarrass yourself and go all fangirl?"

"Right, right! Sorry!" Frances finally let go. "I'm just so excited!" She pulled out her cell phone. "Can I get a picture? Please?"

"Um…" Whitney looked around, but she found no help. Jo looked pissed and the other women were waiting for her to make a decision. She was on her own here. What would Matthew do? He'd manage the message.

"If you promise not to post it on social media until after the wedding." She smiled at how in control that sounded.

"Of course! I don't have to post it at all—this is just for me. You have *no* idea how awesome this is." She slung her arm around Whitney's shoulders and held the camera up overhead before snapping the selfie. "That is so awesome," she repeated as she approved the picture. "Can I send it to Byron and Matthew? We always used to watch your show together."

"I've already met him. Matthew, that is." Suddenly, she was blushing in an entirely different way. And there was no hiding from it, since everyone in the room was staring at her.

Another woman stood up. "You'll have to excuse Frannie," this woman said with a warm smile. She looked nothing like a Beaumont, but beyond that, she was holding a small baby that couldn't be more than a month old. "She's easily excitable. I'm Serena Beaumont, Chadwick's wife. It's delightful to meet you." She shifted the baby onto her shoulder and held out a hand.

"Whitney." She didn't have a lot of experience dealing with babies, but it had to be safer than another hug attack from Frances. "How old is your baby?"

"Six weeks." Serena smiled. She turned so that Jo and Whitney could see the tiny baby's face. "This is Catherine Beaumont."

"She's adorable." She was actually kind of wrinkly and still asleep, but Whitney had no other points of reference, so the baby was adorable by default.

"Her being pregnant made getting the bridesmaids' dresses a mess," Frances said with a dramatic roll of her eyes. "Such a pain."

"Said the woman who is not now, nor has ever been, pregnant," Serena said. But instead of backbiting, the whole conversation was one of gentle teasing. The women were clearly comfortable with each other.

Whitney was introduced to the rest of the women in attendance. There was Lucy Beaumont, a young woman with white-blond hair who did not seem exactly thrilled to be at the party. She left shortly after the introductions, claiming she had a migraine.

Whitney also met Toni Beaumont, who seemed almost as nervous as Whitney felt. "Toni's going to be singing a song at the wedding," Jo explained. "She's got a beautiful voice."

Toni blushed, looking even more awkward. She was considerably younger than the other Beaumonts Whitney had met. Whitney had to wonder if she was one of Hardwick Beaumont's last children? If so, did that make her…maybe twenty? She didn't get the chance to find out. Toni, too, bailed on the proceedings pretty quickly.

Then it was just Jo, Frances, Serena and Whitney—and a baby who was sleeping through the whole thing. "They seem…nice," Whitney ventured.

"Lucy doesn't really like us," Frances explained over the lip of her beer. She was the only one drinking. "Which happens in this family. Every time Dad married a new wife, the new one would bad-mouth the others. That's why Toni isn't comfortable around us, either. Her mom told her we were all out to get her."

"And," Serena added, giving Frances a sharp look, "if I understand correctly, you *were* out to get her when you were a kid."

Frances laughed. "Maybe," she said with a twinkle in her eye. "There might have been some incidents. But that was more between Lucy and Toni. I was too old to play with *babies* by that point. Besides, do you know how much crap Phillip used to give me? I swear, he'd put me on the meanest horse he could find just to watch me get bucked off and cry. But I showed him," she told Whitney. "I learned how to stay on and I don't cry."

Serena rolled her eyes and looked at Whitney. "It's a strange family."

Whitney nodded and smiled as if it were all good fun, but she remembered Matthew telling her how his older brothers used to blame him for, well, *everything*.

"Okay, yeah," Frances protested. "So we're all a little nuts. I mean, I'm never going to get married, not after having *that* many evil stepmothers. Never going to happen. But that's the legacy we were born into as Beaumonts—all except Matthew. He's the only one who was ever nice to all of us. That's why Lucy and Toni were here today—he asked them to come. Said it was important to the family, so they came. The only person who doesn't listen to him is Eliza, Chadwick and Phillip's mom. Everyone else does what he says. And seriously? That man not only wouldn't let me take you guys to the hottest club, but he wouldn't even let me hire a stripper." She scoffed while rolling her eyes, a practiced gesture of frustration. "He can be such a control freak. He probably even picked out your shoes or something."

There was a pause, and then both Frances and Serena turned to look at Whitney.

Heat flooded Whitney's cheeks. Matthew had, in fact, picked out her shoes. And her hairstyle. And her lipstick. Right before he'd mussed them all up. She wasn't about to argue the control-freak part. But then, he'd also let her tie him up. He'd kept up the illusion even though her knot hadn't held. Just so she could be in control.

"So," Frances said in a too-bright tone. "You *have* met Matthew."

"Yes." The one word seemed safer. She wasn't used to kissing and telling. Heck, she was still getting used to the kissing thing. She was absolutely not going to tell anyone about it.

"And?" Frances looked as if she were a lioness about to pounce on a wounded wildebeest.

Whitney hated being the wildebeest. "We're just working to make sure that the wedding goes smoothly. No distractions." She thought it best not to mention the shoes. Or the ties.

Serena nodded in appreciation, but Frances made a face of exasperation. "Seriously? He's had a huge crush on you for, like, forever! I bet he can barely keep his hands off you. And frankly, that man could stand to get distracted."

"Frannie!" Jo and Serena said at the same time. The baby startled and began to mew in tiny-baby cries.

"Sorry," Serena said, draping a blanket over her shoulder so she could nurse, Whitney guessed.

"Well, it's true! He's been driving us all nuts with this wedding, insisting it has to be perfect. Honestly," Frances said, turning her attention back to Whitney, "I'm not sure he ever just does something for fun. It'd be good for him, you know?"

Whitney was so warm she was on the verge of sweating. She thought of the way he'd ignored his phone while they cuddled on the couch, watching a Christmas movie. Was that fun?

"He had a crush on Whitney Wildz," she explained, hoping her face wasn't achieving a near-fatal level of blush. "That's not who I am."

They'd cleared that up before the clothes had started to come off. He knew that she was Whitney Maddox. He liked her for being her, not because she'd once played someone famous. End of discussion.

Except…Matthew was, in fact, having trouble keeping his hands off her. Off *her*, right? Not Whitney Wildz?

She didn't want the doubt that crept in with Frances's knowing smile. But there it was anyway. She couldn't be 100 percent sure that Matthew wasn't sleeping with Whitney Wildz, could she? Just because he'd called her Ms. Maddox a few times—was that really all the proof she needed?

"Sure," Frances said with a dismissive wave of her hand. "Of course."

"You're being obnoxious," Serena said. Then she added to Whitney, "Frances is good at that."

"I'm just being honest. Matthew's way too focused on making sure we all do what he thinks we should. This is a rare opportunity for him to do something for himself. Lord knows the man needs more fun in his life. You two should go out." She paused, a smile that looked way too familiar on her face. "If you haven't already."

This was it. After all these years, all those headlines and horrible pictures and vicious, untrue rumors, Whitney was finally going to die of actual embarrassment. She'd have thought she couldn't feel it this much anymore—that she was immune to it—but no. All it took was one affair with a Beaumont and an "honest" conversation with his little sister and *boom*. It was all over.

Jo sighed. "Are you done?"

"Maybe," Frances replied, looking quite pleased with herself.

"Because you know what Matthew's going to do to you when he finds out you're treating my best friend like this, don't you?"

At that, a look of concern managed to blot out Frances's satisfied smile. "Well...hey, I've been on my best behavior ever since you guys decided to get married. No headlines, no trouble. I leave that to Byron."

And Byron had gotten into trouble only because Matthew had asked him to. For her. There was a moment of silence, during which Whitney considered getting her coat and going. Except she couldn't leave without Jo. Damn it.

Then the silence was broken. "But what about—?" Serena said, joining the fray.

"Or the one time when you—" added Jo.

"Hey!" Frances yelped, her cheeks turning almost as red as her hair. "That's not fair!"

"We're just being honest," Serena said with a grin that bordered on mean.

Jo nodded in agreement, giving Whitney an encouraging grin. "What did Phillip tell me about that one guy? What did he call you? His Little Red—"

Frances's phone chimed. "Sorry, can't listen to you make fun of me. Must answer this very important text!" She read her message. "Byron says he can't believe that's really Whitney Wildz." She began to type a reply.

"What are you going to tell him?" Whitney asked.

"What do you think?" Frances winked at her. "That your name is Whitney Maddox."

"Is that…Whitney Wildz?" Byron held his phone up to his good eye. "Seriously?"

"What?" Matthew grabbed the phone away from his brother. "Jesus." It was, in fact, Whitney, standing next to Frances, smiling for the camera. She looked good. A little worried but that was probably because Frances had a death grip on her shoulders.

He was going to kill both of them. Why would Whitney let anyone take her picture? And hadn't he warned Frances not to do anything stupid? And didn't taking a picture of Whitney and plastering it all over the internet count as stupid?

The phone chimed as another message popped up.

Tell Matthew that she made me promise to only send it to you. No social media.

Matthew exhaled in relief. That was a smart compromise. He could only hope Frances would hold up her end of that promise. He handed the phone back over, hoping he appeared nonchalant. "That was a character she played," he said in his most diplomatic tone. "Her name is Whitney Maddox." He shot a look at Phillip, who was enjoying a cigar on Matthew's private deck.

Phillip gave him his best innocent face, then mimed locking his lips and throwing away the key.

The guys had managed to arrive at Matthew's place without notice. It was just the five of them. Byron didn't get along with their other half brothers David and Johnny at all and Mark was off at college. Matthew had decided to keep the guest list to the wedding party. Just the four Beaumont men who could tolerate each other. Most of the time.

Plus the sober coach, Dale. When Phillip was out on the farm, he was fine, but he'd been sober for only seven months now and with the pressure of the wedding, no one wanted a relapse. Hands down, that would be the worst thing to happen to the wedding. There would be no recovering from that blow to the Beaumont image and there would be no burying that lead. It would be game over.

Matthew and Phillip had made sure that Dale would be available for any event that took place away from the farm. Currently, Dale was sitting next to Phillip, talking horses. This was what the Beaumont men had come to—soda and cigars on a Saturday night. So this was what getting old was like.

"Who?" Chadwick asked, taking the phone.

"Whitney Wildz." Byron was studying the picture. "She was this squeaky-clean girl who starred in a rock-and-roll update of *The Partridge Family* called *Growing Up Wildz*. Man," he went on, "she looks *amazing*. Do you know if she's—?"

"She's not available," Matthew said before he could stop himself. But Byron was a Beaumont. There was no way Matthew wanted his little brother to get it into his head that Whitney was fair game.

All three of his brothers gave him a surprised look. Well, Chadwick and Byron gave him a look. Phillip was trying too hard not to laugh, the rat bastard. "I mean, if anyone tried to hit on her, it'd be a media firestorm. Hands off."

"Wait," Chadwick said, studying the picture again. "Isn't this the woman who's always stoned or flashing the camera?"

"She's not like that," Matthew snapped.

"What Matthew means to say," Phillip added, "is that in real life, Whitney raises prize-winning horses and lives a fairly quiet life. She's definitely *not* a fame monster."

"*This* is the woman who's the maid of honor?" Chadwick's voice was getting louder as he glared at the phone. "How is this Whitney Wild person not going to make this wedding into a spectacle? You know this is the soft opening for Percheron Drafts, Matthew. We can't afford to have anything compromise the reception."

"Hey—easy, now, Chad." Chadwick flinched at Phillip's nickname for him. Which Phillip used only when he was trying to piss off the oldest Beaumont. Yeah, this little bachelor party was going downhill, fast. "It's going to be fine. She's a friend of Jo's and she's not going to make a spectacle of anything. She's perfectly fine. Matthew was worried, too, but he's seen that she's just a regular woman. Right?" He turned to Matthew. "Back me up here."

"Phillip's correct. Whitney will be able to fulfill her role in the wedding with class and style." *And*, he added mentally, *with a little luck, some grace*. He hoped he'd put her in the right shoes. "She won't be a distraction. She'll help demonstrate that the Beaumonts are back on top."

Funny how a few days ago he'd been right where Chadwick was—convinced that a former star would take advantage of the limelight that went with a Beaumont Christmas wedding and burn them all. Now all Matthew was worried about was Whitney getting down the aisle without tripping.

He glanced up to see Byron staring at him. "What?"

It was Chadwick who spoke first. "We can't afford any *more* distractions," he said, half punching Byron on the arm. "I'm serious."

"Fine, fine. I prefer to eat my own cooking anyway." Byron walked off to lean against the railing on the balcony. Then he looked back at Matthew.

Matthew knew what that meant. Byron wanted to talk. So he joined his little brother. Then he waited. It was only when Phillip distracted Chadwick by asking about his baby daughter that Matthew said, "Yes?"

"Did you ask Harper?" Byron kept his voice low. Yeah, there was no need to let Chadwick in on this conversation. If Chadwick knew that they'd asked his nemesis to the wedding... Well, Matthew hated bailing people out.

"I did. He refused. The Harpers will not be joining us at the reception."

"Not even...?" Byron swallowed, staring out at the mountains cloaked in darkness. "Not even his family? His daughter?"

Suddenly, Matthew understood. "No. Is she the reason you've got a black eye?"

Byron didn't answer. Instead, he said, "Is Whitney Wildz *your* reason?"

"Her name," Matthew said with more force than he probably needed, "is Whitney Maddox. Don't you forget it."

Byron gave him the look—the same look all the brothers shared. The Beaumont smile. "Exactly how 'not available' is she, anyway?"

Deep down, Matthew had to admire how well his little brother was handling himself. In less than a minute, he'd completely redirected the conversation away from Harper's daughter and back to Matthew and Whitney. "Completely not available."

"Well," Phillip announced behind them, "this has been

lovely and dull, but I've got a bride-to-be waiting for me who's a lot more entertaining than you lot."

"And I've got to get home to Serena and Catherine," Chadwick added.

"I swear," Byron said, "I leave for one lousy year and I don't even know you guys anymore. Chadwick, not working? Phillip, sober and monogamous? And you?" He shot Matthew a sidelong glance. "Hooking up with Whitney Wild—"

"Maddox," Matthew corrected.

Byron gave him another Beaumont smile and Matthew realized what he'd just done—tacitly agreed that he was, in fact, hooking up with Whitney. "Right. You hooking up with anyone. Next thing you know, Frances will announce she's joining a nunnery or something."

"We can only hope," Chadwick grumbled before he turned to Phillip and Dale. "You okay to get home?"

Dale spoke. "You're going straight home to the farm?"

"Yeah," Phillip replied, slapping the man on the shoulder. "Jo's waiting on me. Thanks for—"

Matthew cut him off. "I'll see that he gets home."

"What—" Phillip demanded. He sounded pissed.

Matthew didn't look at him. He focused on Dale and Chadwick. "There's been a lot of pressure with this wedding. We can't be too careful."

"—the hell," Phillip finished, giving him a mean look.

Matthew refused to flinch even as he wondered what he was doing. At no point during the wedding planning had Phillip been teetering on the brink of dependency. Why was Matthew implying that he suddenly needed a babysitter?

Because. He wanted to see Whitney.

"Good plan," Chadwick said. "Dale, is that okay with you?"

"Yeah. See you tomorrow at the rehearsal dinner." Dale took off.

When it was just the four brothers, there was a moment of

awkward silence. Then the awkwardness veered into painful. What was Matthew doing? He could see the question on each man's face. Byron's black eye. Casting doubts on Phillip's sobriety. That wasn't who Matthew was. He was the one who did the opposite—who tried to make the family sound better, look better than it really was. He put the family name first. Not his selfish desire to see a woman who was nothing but a PR headache waiting to happen.

Phillip glared at him. Yeah, Matthew had earned that. "Can we go? Or do you need to take a potshot at Chadwick, too?"

Chadwick paused. He'd already headed for the door. "Problem?"

"No. Nothing I can't handle," Matthew hurried to say before Byron and Phillip could tattle on him.

He could handle this. His attraction to Whitney? A minor inconvenience. A totally amazing, mind-blowing inconvenience, but a minor one. He could keep it together. He had to. That was what he did.

Chadwick nodded. That he was taking Matthew at his word was something that should have made Matthew happy. He'd earned that measure of trust the hard way. It was a victory.

But that didn't change the fact that he was, at this exact moment, undermining that trust, as well.

Yeah, he could handle this.

He hoped like hell.

Fourteen

The drive out to the farm was fast and tense.

"After this wedding," Phillip finally said as he fumed in the passenger seat, "you and I are going to have words."

"Fine." Matthew had earned it, he knew.

"I don't get you," Phillip went on, clearly deciding to get those words out of the way now. Matthew thought that it'd be better if they could just fight and get it over with. "If you wanted to come out to the farm and see her, you could have just come. Why'd you have to make it sound like I had my finger on the trigger of a bottle? Because I don't."

"Because."

"What the hell kind of answer is that?"

Matthew could feel Phillip staring at him. He ignored him. Yeah, he'd bent the truth. That was what he did. Besides, he'd covered up for Phillip so many times they'd both lost count.

"You don't have to hide her. Not from us. And certainly not from me. I already know what's going on."

The statement rankled him. The fact that it was the truth? That only made it worse. "I'm not hiding."

"Like hell you're not. What else would you call that little show you put on back there? Why else does Byron have a black eye? You can dress it up as you're protecting her because that's what you do but damn, man. There's nothing wrong with you liking the woman and wanting to spend time with her. You think I'd hold that against you?"

"You would have. In the past."

"Oh, for crying out loud." Phillip actually threw his hands up. "There's your problem right there. You're so damn concerned with what happened last year, five years ago—thirty-five years ago—that you're missing out on the *now*. Things change. People change. I'd have thought that hanging out with Whitney would have shown you that."

Matthew didn't have a comeback to that. He didn't have one to any of it.

Phillip moved in for the kill. Matthew wasn't entirely used to the new, improved, changed Phillip being this right and certainly not right about Matthew. "Even Chadwick would understand if you've got to do something for *you*. You don't have to manage the family's image every single minute of your life. Figure out who you are if you're not a Beaumont."

Matthew let out a bark of laughter. "That's rich, coming from you."

If he wasn't a Beaumont? Not happening. He'd fought too hard to earn his place at the Beaumont table. He wasn't going to toss all that hard work to "figure out" who he was. He already knew.

He was Matthew Beaumont. End of discussion.

"Whatever, man. But the next time you want to cover your tracks, don't use me as a human shield. I don't play these games anymore."

"Fine."

"Good."

The rest of the drive was silent.

Matthew was mad. He was mad at Phillip—but he wasn't sure why. Because the man had spoken what felt uncomfortably like the truth? And Byron—he'd gotten that damn black eye. Because Matthew had asked him to do something dramatic.

And he was—he was mad at Whitney. That was what this little verbal skirmish was about, wasn't it? Whitney Maddox.

Why did she have to be so—so—so *not* Whitney Wildz? Why couldn't she be the kind of self-absorbed celebrity he knew how to manage—that he knew how to keep himself distant from? Why did she have to be someone soft and gentle and—yeah, he was gonna say it—innocent? She shouldn't be so innocent. She should be jaded and hard and bitter. That way he wouldn't be able to love her.

They pulled up at the farmhouse. Matthew didn't want to deal with Phillip anymore. Didn't want to deal with any of it. He was not hiding her, damn it.

He strode into the house as if he owned the thing, which he didn't. Not really. But it was Beaumont Farms and he was a Beaumont, so to hell with it.

He found Jo and Whitney on the sofas, watching what looked like *Rudolph the Red-Nosed Reindeer*, the one he'd watched back when he was a kid. Whitney was already in her pajamas. Jo's ridiculous donkey, Betty, was curled up next to Whitney. She was petting Betty's ears as if it were a normal everyday thing.

Why didn't he feel normal anymore? Why had he let her get close enough to change him?

"Hi," she said in surprise when she looked up. "Is everything—?"

"I need to talk to you." He didn't wait for a response. Hell, he couldn't even wait for her to get up. He scooted Betty out of the way and pulled Whitney to her feet.

"Are you—*whoa!*"

Matthew swept her legs up and, without bothering to look back at where Phillip was no doubt staring daggers at him— hell, to where the donkey was probably staring daggers at him—he carried Whitney up the stairs.

She threw her arms around his neck as he took the steps two at a time. "Are you okay?"

"Fine. Just fine." Even as he said it, he knew it wasn't true. He wasn't fine and she was the reason.

But she was the only way he knew how to make things fine again.

"Bachelor party went okay?" she asked as he kicked open the door to her room.

"Yeah. Fine." He threw her down on the bed and wrenched off his tie.

Her eyes went wide. "Matthew?"

"I—I missed you, okay? I missed you." Why did saying it feel like such a failure? He didn't miss people. He didn't miss women. He didn't let himself care enough to miss them.

But in two damn days, he'd missed her. And it made him feel weak. He wrapped the tie around his knuckles and pulled, letting the bite of silk against his skin pull him back. Pull him away from her.

She clambered up to her knees, which brought her face almost level with his. "I missed you, too."

"You did?"

She nodded. Then she touched his face. "I…I missed waking up with you."

At her touch—soft and gentle and innocent, damn it all—something in him snapped. "I don't want to talk."

She was the reason he was the mess he was. He had to—he didn't know. He had to put her in her place. He *had* to keep himself distanced from her, for his own sanity. And he couldn't do that while she was touching him so sweetly, while she was telling him she missed him.

One eyebrow notched up. Too late, he remembered announcing that the whole reason he was sweeping her off her feet was to talk to her.

But she didn't say anything. Instead, she pushed herself up onto her feet and stripped her pajama top off. Then, still standing on the bed—not tipping over, not accidentally kicking him—she shimmied out of her bottoms, which was fine because it was damnably hard to think the lustful thoughts he was thinking about someone who was wearing pink pants covered with dogs in bow ties. Then she sank back down to her knees in front of him.

No talking. No touching. He would keep a part of himself from her, just as he did with everyone else. No one would know what she meant to him. Not even him.

Then he had her on her back, but that was still too much. He couldn't look into her eyes, pale and wide and waiting for him. He couldn't see what he meant to her. He couldn't risk letting her see what she meant to him. So he rolled her onto her belly and, after getting the condom, buried himself in her.

She didn't say a word, not even when her back arched and her body tightened down on his and she grabbed the headboard as the climax rolled her body. She was silent as he grabbed her hips and drove in deep and hard until he had nothing left to give her.

They fell onto the bed together, panting and slick with sweat. He'd done what he needed to—what a Beaumont would. This was his birthright, wasn't it? White-hot affairs that didn't involve feelings. His father had specialized in them. He'd never cared about anyone.

Matthew needed to get up. He needed to walk away from Whitney. He needed to stay a Beaumont.

Then she rolled, looped her arms over his neck and held him. No words. Just her touch. Just her not letting him go.

How weak was he? He couldn't even pull himself away from her. He let her hold him. Damn it all, he held her back.

It was some time before she spoke. "After the wedding... after Christmas morning..."

He winced. "Yes?" But it was surprisingly hard to sound as if he didn't care when his face was buried in the crook of her neck.

"I mean," she hurried on, her arms tightening around his neck, "that'll be... We'll be..."

It. That'll be it. *We'll be* done. That was what she was trying to say. Then—and only then—did he manage to push himself up. But he couldn't push himself away from her. "My life is here in Denver, and you..." He swallowed, wishing he were stronger. That he could be stronger for her. "You need the sun."

She smiled—he could see her trying—but at the same time, her eyes began to shine and the corners of her mouth pulled down. She was trying not to cry. "Right."

He couldn't watch her, not like this. So he buried his face back against her neck.

"Right," he agreed. *Fine*, he thought, knowing it wasn't. At least that would be clean. At least there wouldn't be a scene that he'd have to contain. He should have been relieved.

"Anytime you want to ride the Trakehners," she managed to get out, "you just let me know."

Then—just because she made him so weak—he kissed her. Because no matter how hard he tried, he couldn't hold himself back. Not around her.

Fifteen

They spent the next morning looking over the carriage that would pull Phillip and Jo from the chapel to the reception. The whole thing was bedecked with ribbons and bows of red-and-green velvet, which stood out against the deep gray paint of the carriage. Whitney wasn't sure she'd ever really grasped what the word *bedecked* meant, but after seeing the Beaumont carriage, she understood completely. "It's a beautiful rig."

"You like it?" Matthew said. He'd been quiet all morning, but he'd held her hand as they walked around the farm together. In fact, he had hardly stopped touching her since they'd woken up. His foot had been rubbing against her calf during their breakfast; his hands had been around her waist or on her shoulders whenever possible.

Whitney had been worried after last night. Okay, more than worried. She'd originally thought that he was mad at her because of the picture with Frances, but there'd been something else going on.

After the intense sex—and the part where he'd agreed that this relationship was short-term—she had decided that it wasn't her place to figure out what that "something else" was. If he wanted to tell her, he would. She would make no other claims to him.

She would try not to, anyway.

"I do." She looked at the carriage, well and truly bedecked. "It's going to look amazing. And with Jo's dress? *Wow.*"

He trailed his hand down her arm. She leaned into his touch. "Do you have a carriage like this?"

She grinned at him. He really didn't know a whole lot about horses, but he was trying. For her. "Trakehners aren't team horses, so no."

He brushed his gloved fingertips over her cheek. She could feel the heat of his touch despite the fabric. "Want to go for a ride?"

She pulled up short. "What?"

"I'll have Richard hook up the team. Someone can drive us around."

"But…it's for the wedding."

"I know. You're here *now.*" Then he was off, hunting up a hired hand to take them on a carriage ride around Beaumont Farms.

Now. Now was all they had. Matthew gallantly handed her up into the carriage and tucked the red-and-green-plaid blankets around her, then wrapped his arm around her shoulder and pulled her into him. Then they were off, riding over the snow-covered hills of the farm. It was…magical.

She tried not to overthink what was happening between them—or, more to the point, what wasn't going to happen in a few days. What was the point of dwelling on how she was going to go back to her solitary existence, with only her animals and crazy Don to break up the monotony?

This was what she wanted—a brief, hot Christmas-vacation romance with a gorgeous, talented man. A man who would make her feel as if Whitney Maddox was a woman who didn't have to hide anymore, who could take lovers and have relationships. This was getting her out of the safety of her rut.

This time with Matthew was a gift, plain and simple. She couldn't have dreamed up a better man, a better time. He was, for lack of a better word, *perfect*.

That had to be why she clung to him extra hard as they rode over the ice-kissed hills, the trees shimmering under the winter sun. This was, hands down, the most romantic thing she'd ever done—even though she knew the score. She had him now. She didn't want to miss any of that.

So when it was time to go to the rehearsal, she went early with Matthew. They were supposed to eat lunch, but they wound up at his palatial apartment, tangled up in the sheets of his massive bed, and missed lunch entirely. Which was fine. She could eat when she was alone. And the dinner after the rehearsal would be five-star, Matthew promised.

They made it to the chapel for the rehearsal almost an hour ahead of everyone else—of course they did. The place was stunning. The pews were decorated with red-and-gray bows that matched the ones on the carriage perfectly atop pine garlands, making the whole place smell like a Christmas tree. The light ceilings had dark buttresses and the walls were lined with stained-glass windows.

"We're going to have spotlights outside the windows so the lights shine at dark," Matthew explained. "The rest of the ceremony will be candlelit."

"Wow," Whitney breathed as she studied the chapel. "How many people will be here for the wedding?"

"Two hundred," he said. "But it's still an intimate space. I've been working with the videographers to make sure they don't overtake the space. We don't want anything to distract from the happy couple."

She took a deep breath as she held an imaginary bouquet in front of her. "I should practice, then," she said as she took measured steps down the aisle. "Should have brought my shoes."

Matthew skirted around her and hurried to the altar. Then he waited for her. Her cheeks flushed warm as an image of her doing this not in a dove-gray gown but a long white one forced its way across her mind.

Now, she thought, trying not to get ahead of herself. *Stay in the now.*

That got harder to do when she made it up to the altar, where Matthew was waiting. He took her hands in his and, looking down into her eyes, he smiled. Just a simple curve of the lips. It wasn't rakish; it wasn't predatory—heavens, it wasn't even overtly sexual.

"Ms. Maddox," he said in a voice that was as close to reverent as she'd ever heard him use.

"Mr. Beaumont," she replied because it seemed like the thing to do. Because she couldn't come up with anything else, not when his gaze was deepening in its intensity.

It was almost as if, standing here with Matthew, in this holy place...

No. She would not hope, no matter how intense his gaze was, no matter how much his smile, his touch affected her. She would not hope, because it was pointless. She had three more days before she left for California. Tonight, Christmas Eve and maybe Christmas morning. That was it. No point in thinking about something a little more permanent with him.

He leaned forward. "Whitney..."

Say something, she thought. *Something to give me hope.*

"Hello? Matthew?"

To his credit, he didn't drop Whitney's hands. He did lean back and tuck her fingers into the crook of his arm. "Here," he called down the aisle as the wedding planner came through the doors. Then, to Whitney, he said, "Shall we practice a few times before everyone gets here?"

"Yes, let's." Which were not words of hope.

That was fine. She didn't want any.

Really.

* * *

Against his will, Matthew sent Whitney home with Jo and took Phillip back to his place. Even though they were going to shoot photos before the ceremony, Jo had decided that she wanted to at least get ready without Phillip in the house.

Phillip wasn't exactly talking to Matthew, which was fine. Matthew had things to do anyway. The press was lining up, and Matthew had to make sure he was available for them before they wandered off and started sniffing around.

This was his job, his place in this world. He had to present the very best side of the Beaumonts, contain any scandals before they did real damage and...

His mind drifted back to the carriage ride across the farm with Whitney—to the way she'd looked standing hand in hand with him at the altar.

For such a short time, it hadn't mattered. Not the wedding, not the public image—not even the soft launch of Percheron Drafts. His showroom-ready apartment, his fancy cars—none of that mattered.

What had mattered was holding a beautiful woman tight and knowing that she was there for him. Not for the family name, the fortune, the things.

Just him.

And now that time was over and he was back to managing the message. The good news was that Byron's little brawl had done exactly what Matthew had intended it to—no one was asking about Whitney Wildz.

He checked the social media sites again. Whitney had insisted on keeping her hat on during the rehearsal and the following dinner and had only talked with the embedded press representatives when absolutely required. He knew he should be thankful that she was keeping her profile as low as possible, but he hated that she felt as if she had to hide.

All was as calm as could be expected. As far as he could tell, no one in attendance had connected the quiet maid of honor with Whitney Wildz. Plus, the sudden influx of famous people eating in restaurants and partying at clubs was good press, reinforcing how valuable the Beaumont name was without Matthew being directly responsible for their actions.

It wouldn't last, he knew. He sent out the final instructions to the photographer and videographer, which was semipointless. Whitney was in the wedding party, after all. And he hadn't let her change her hair. They'd have to take pictures of her. But reminding the people on his payroll what he expected made him feel better anyway.

They just had to get through the wedding. Whitney had to make it up the aisle and back down without incident.

Just as she'd done today. She'd been downright cute, miming the action in a sweater and jeans and that hat, of course. But tomorrow?

Tomorrow she'd be in a gown, polished and proper and befitting a Beaumont wedding. Tomorrow she'd look perfect.

He could take a few days after the wedding, couldn't he? Even just two days off. This thing had swallowed his life for the past few months. He'd earned some time. Once he got Phillip and Jo safely off on their honeymoon and his siblings and stepmothers back to their respective corners, once he had Christmas dinner with his mom, he could...

He could go see Whitney. See her in the sun. Ride her horses and meet her weird-looking dogs and her pop-singer cats.

This didn't change things, he told himself as he began to rearrange his schedule. This was not the beginning of something else, something *more*. Far from it. They'd agreed that after the wedding, they were...done.

Except the word felt wrong. Matthew had never had a problem walking away from his lady friends before. When it was over, it was over. There were no regrets, no looking back and absolutely no taking time off to spend a long weekend together.

It was close to midnight when he found himself sending her a text. What are you doing? But even as he hit Send, he knew he was being foolish. She was probably in bed. He was probably waking her up. But he couldn't help himself. It'd been a long day, longer without her. He just wanted… Well, he just wanted her.

A minute later, his phone pinged and there was a blurry photo of Whitney with a tiny donkey in her lap. He could just see the silly dogs in bow ties on her pajama pants. Jo had leaned over to grin into the frame, but there was no missing Whitney's big smile. Watching Love Actually and eating popcorn, came the reply.

Good. Great. She was keeping a low profile and having fun at the same time.

Then his phone pinged again.

Miss you.

He could take a couple of days. Maybe a week. Chadwick would understand. As long as they made it through the wedding with no big scandals—as long as all the Beaumonts stayed out of the news while he was gone—he could spend the time with Whitney.

Miss you, too, he wrote back. Because he did.

He was pretty sure he'd never missed anyone else in his life.

The day of the wedding flew by in a blur. Manicures, pedicures, hairstylists, makeup artists—they all attacked Whitney and the rest of the wedding party with the efficiency of a long-planned military campaign. Whitney couldn't tell if that was because Matthew had everything on a second-by-second schedule or if this was just what happened when you had the best of the best working for you.

She finally met Byron Beaumont, as he was next in the makeup artist's chair after they finished painting Whitney's lips scarlet-red. She winced as she looked at the bruise around his face that was settling into purples and blues like a sunset with an attitude.

"Ms. Maddox," he said with an almost formal bow. But he didn't touch her and he certainly didn't hug her, not as Frances had. Heck, he didn't even call her Whitney Wildz. "It's an honor."

"I'm sorry about your eye," she heard herself say, as if she were personally responsible for the bruising. Byron looked a great deal like Matthew. Maybe a few inches shorter, and his eyes were lighter, almost gray. Byron's hair was almost the same deep auburn color as Matthew's, but his hair was longer with a wave to it.

Byron grinned at her then—almost the exact same grin that Matthew had and that Phillip had. "Anything in the service of a lady," he replied as he settled into the chair, as if he had his makeup done all the time.

By four that afternoon, the ladies were nibbling on fruit slices with the greatest of care to sustain them through the rest of the evening. "We don't want anyone to pass out," the wedding planner said as she stuck straws into water bottles and passed them around.

Then they were at the chapel, posing for an endless series of photos. She stood next to Jo, then next to Frances, then between Frances and Serena. They took shots with Jo's parents, her grandmother, her aunt and uncle. Since Toni Beaumont was singing a song during the wedding, they had to have every permutation of who stood where with her, too.

Then the doors to the chapel opened, and Whitney heard Matthew say, "We're here." The men strode down the aisle as if they owned the joint. At first she couldn't see them clearly. The chapel wasn't well lit and the sunlight streaming in behind them was almost blinding. But then, suddenly, Matthew was leading the Beaumont men down the aisle.

She gasped at them. At him. His tuxedo was exquisitely cut. He could have been walking a red carpet, for all the confidence and sensuality he exuded.

"We're keeping to the schedule, right, people?" he demanded. Then their gazes met and the rest of the world—the stylists and wedding planner chatting, the photographer bossing people around—all of it fell away.

"Perfect," he said.

"You, too," she murmured. Beside her, Frances snickered. Oh, right—they weren't alone. Half the Beaumont family was watching them. She dropped her gaze to her bouquet, which was suddenly very interesting.

Matthew turned his attention to the larger crowd. "Phillip's ready for the reveal."

"Everyone out," the photographer announced. "I want to get the bride and groom seeing each other for the first time. Joey," he said to Jo. He'd been calling her that for half an hour now. Whitney was pretty sure it wouldn't be much longer before Jo cracked and beat the man senseless with his own camera. "You go back around and walk down the aisle."

Jo glanced at Whitney and rolled her eyes, which made them both giggle. Whitney gathered up Jo's train, and they hurried down the aisle as fast as they could in these dresses. It was only when they had themselves tucked away that Frances gave the all clear.

Whitney and Frances peeked as Jo made her way up the aisle to where Phillip was waiting for his bride. "I don't know if I've ever seen him that happy," Frances whispered as Phillip blinked tears of joy out of his eyes. "I hope it lasts."

"I think it will," Whitney decided.

"I just…" Frances sighed. "I just wish we could all stop

living in our father's shadow, you know? I wish I could believe in love. Even if it's just for them."

"Your time will come," Whitney whispered as she looked at Frances. "If you want it to."

"I don't. I'm never getting married," Frances announced. Then, standing up straighter, she added, "But if you want to marry Matthew, can I be your bridesmaid?"

Whitney opened her mouth and then closed it because as much as she wanted to tell Frances her head was in the clouds and that after tonight Whitney and Matthew were going their separate ways, she couldn't dismiss the image of him standing with her at the very same altar where Jo and Phillip now stood. For that brief moment—when she'd wanted him to say something that would give her hope that they weren't done after this. When she'd thought he was going to do just that. And then they'd been interrupted.

Finally, she got her mouth to work. "I'm not going to marry Matthew."

"Pity," Frances sniffed. "I saw how he looked at you. Trust me, Matthew doesn't look at other people like that."

So everyone had seen that look. Whitney sighed. But before she could respond, a deep voice behind them said, "Like what?"

The women spun around at Matthew's voice. Whitney teetered in her shoes, but Matthew caught her before she could tip forward. Then his arms were around her waist, and he was almost holding her. But not quite. They managed to keep a glimmer of space between them.

"Hi," Whitney breathed. She wanted to tell him how much she'd missed him. She wanted to ask if they could spend this last night together, after the reception, so that their Christmas morning could start off right. She wanted to tell him that he was the most handsome man she'd ever seen.

She didn't get the chance.

"Like that," Frances said with obvious glee.

"Frannie." Matthew's voice was as clear a warning as Whitney had heard since that very first night, when he'd realized who she'd once been. The space between him and Whitney widened ever so slightly. "Go make sure Byron stays out of trouble, please."

Frances rolled her eyes. "Fine. I'm going, I'm going. But he's not the one I'm worried about right now." Then, with a rustle of silk, she was gone.

And they were alone in the vestibule. "You look amazing," she managed to get out.

"So do you," he said as his arms tightened around her. "I'd kiss you, but..."

"Lipstick," he agreed. "We're going to have to go out for more photos soon."

A quick moment. That was all they had. But she wanted more. She at least wanted tonight. One more night in his arms. Then, somehow, she'd find a way to let him go. "Matthew..." she said.

At the same time, he said, "Whitney..."

They paused, then laughed. But before she could ask for what she wanted, the photographer called out, "The best man and maid of honor? Where are you, people?"

"Tonight," Matthew said as he looped his arm through hers. "We'll talk at the reception, all right?"

All she could do was nod as they walked down the aisle together, toward the happy couple and the bossy photographer.

Whitney didn't trip.

Sixteen

Everything went according to plan. After they finished the photos in the chapel—including a series of shots with Betty in her flower-girl-slash-ring-bearer harness—the whole party went to a nearby park and took shots with snow-covered trees and ground as the backdrop. They also did the shots of Jo and Phillip getting into and out of the carriage.

Then, just because everything was going so smoothly, Matthew asked the photographer to take pictures of each of the couples with the carriage, just so he and Whitney could have a photo of the two of them with the Percheron team. So they'd have something to remember this week by.

Serena and Chadwick didn't mind, but Frances and Byron clearly thought he was nuts and Matthew didn't miss the look Phillip gave him.

He wasn't hiding how he felt about Whitney, okay? He *wasn't*. That wasn't why he had the photographer take extra shots of all the couples by themselves. He reasoned that Chadwick and Serena had had a small ceremony—absolutely no pomp and circumstance had been allowed. True, Serena had been about seven months pregnant and, yes, Chadwick had already had a big wedding for his first marriage. Serena's parents had walked her down the aisle while Phillip,

Matthew and Frances stood as witnesses. Cell phone photos didn't count. So Matthew was really doing this for Chadwick and Serena, so they'd have beautiful photos of them at their very best. And if Matthew and Whitney got some memories out of it, so much the better.

And because he was not hiding how he felt about her, he had his arms on her while the photographer snapped away. An arm around her waist when they leaned underneath the evergreen tree, its branches heavy with glistening snow. Handing her up into the carriage. Tucking her against his waist.

For their part, his family was...okay with it. Byron had slapped him on the back and said, "Some women are worth the bruises, huh?" Matthew had ignored his baby brother.

Chadwick's big comment was, "The situation is under control, correct?"

To which Matthew had replied, "Correct." Because it was.

For the moment, anyway.

"You doing okay?" Matthew whispered to Phillip as they stood at the front of the chapel. He could see that Phillip had started to fidget.

"Why is everything going so slow?" Phillip whispered back as Frances did the "step, pause, step, pause" walk down the aisle to Pachelbel's *Canon in D.* "I want Jo."

"Suck it up and smile. Remember, the cameras are rolling."

Matthew looked out over the full house in the chapel. Phillip's mother had a place of honor in the front, although she had chosen not to sit with Jo's family. Which didn't surprise Matthew a bit. Eliza Beaumont was not a huge fan of anything that had to do with the Beaumont family, a list that started with Matthew and went on for miles.

But Phillip had wanted his mother at his wedding and Matthew had the means to make it happen, so the woman was sitting in the front row, looking as relaxed as a prisoner before a firing squad and pointedly ignoring everyone.

Serena was headed down the aisle now, although she was moving at a slightly faster clip than Frances had been. "Beautiful," Chadwick whispered from the other side of Matthew. "I have to say, I'm impressed you pulled this off."

"Don't jinx it, man," Matthew hissed through his smile.

Then Serena was standing next to Frances and everyone waited.

Matthew could see Whitney, standing just inside the doors. *Come on, babe,* he thought. *One foot in front of the other. You can do it. It'll be fine.*

Then the music swelled and she took the first step. Paused. Second step. Paused. Each foot hit the ground squarely. She didn't wobble and she didn't trip on her hem. She *glided* down the aisle as if she'd been born with a bouquet in her hand and a smile on her face. The whole time, she kept her gaze fastened on him. As though she was walking not just to him but *for* him.

God, she was *so* beautiful. Simply perfect. But then, the woman in her doggy pajamas had been perfect, too. Even when she was klutzy and nervous and totally, completely Whitney, she was absolutely perfect.

How was he going to let her go?

She reached the altar and took her place. He could see how pleased she was with herself, and frankly, he was pretty damn happy, too.

Then there was a moment that should have been silent as the music changed to the wedding march and Jo made her big entrance.

Except it wasn't silent. A murmur ran through the crowd—the highest of Denver's high society, musicians and actors and people who were famous merely for being famous.

Then he heard it. "...Whitney Wildz?" Which was followed by "...that hair!" More murmurs followed. Then a click. The click of a cell phone snapping a picture.

He looked at Whitney. She was still smiling, but it wasn't

the same natural, luminous thing it'd been earlier. Her face was frozen in something that was a mockery of joy.

It'll be okay, he wanted to tell her. He wanted to believe it.

Then the music swelled up, drowning out the whispers and the clicks. Everyone stood and turned to the entrance. Betty tottered down the aisle as the daughter of one of the brewery's employees tossed rose petals onto the ground. Betty should have held everyone's attention.

But she didn't. Not even a mini donkey wearing a basket and a crown of flowers over her floppy ears could distract from Whitney Wildz. People were holding their devices high to get the best shot of her.

Jo came down the aisle on the arms of her parents. Matthew took advantage of this to get the wedding rings untied from the small pillow on Betty's back, and then the farm manager, Richard—looking hilariously uncomfortable in a suit—led the small animal off before she started munching on the floral arrangements.

When he stood back up, Matthew caught Whitney's eye as Jo took her place at the altar. He gave her an encouraging nod, hoping that she'd get the message. *Ignore them. Don't let them win.*

When the music stopped this time, the murmuring was even louder. The preacher took his place before the happy couple. Jo handed Whitney her bouquet.

The murmuring was getting louder. People weren't even trying to whisper now. Matthew wanted to shout at the crowd, *This is a wedding, for God's sake! Have some decency!* But he'd long since learned that you didn't feed the fire like that. Ignoring the excited whispers was the only way to make it through this.

"Matthew," Chadwick said in the quietest of whispers, and Matthew knew what his older brother was thinking. This was having the situation under control? *This* was handling it?

The preacher began to talk about vows and love, but he had to stop and pitch his voice up in volume to be heard.

Matthew kept his attention on the happy couple—and on Whitney. She was blinking too fast, but her smile was locked. Her face looked as if it were going to crack in half. She didn't look at him, but she didn't need to. He could read her well enough.

This was just like the restaurant all over again. She'd done nothing—not even tripped, much less fallen, and yet she was setting off a media firestorm. He had the sinking feeling that if he got out his phone and checked social media, Whitney would already be trending.

Then, out of the corner of his eye, he saw it. Movement, in the aisle. As best he could without turning and staring, he looked.

Oh, hell. People were getting up and exiting the pews—coming into the aisles. Phones and cameras were raised. They were jostling—yes, jostling—for a better shot. Of Whitney. Of someone they thought was Whitney Wildz.

"If I may," the preacher said in a tone better suited for a fire-and-brimstone Sunday sermon than a Christmas Eve wedding. "If I may have *silence*, please."

That was when Whitney turned her stricken face to his. He saw the tears gathering, saw how fast she was breathing. "I'm sorry," she said, although he couldn't hear her over the crowd. He read her lips, though. That was enough.

"No," he said, but she didn't hear him. She was already turning to hand Jo's bouquet to Serena and then she was running down the aisle, arms stiffly at her side.

Gone.

Oh, hell.

"Ms. Maddox?"

Whitney realized that she was outside.

The horse-drawn carriage was parked in front of the chapel, waiting for the happy couple. The happy couple whose wedding she'd just ruined. She vaguely recognized the driver as one of the farmhands, but he wasn't wearing jeans and flannel. "Is everything okay?"

"Um…" No. Nothing was okay. And worse? She didn't know when it would start being okay again. The chapel was on a college campus. She had to walk…that way to get to a main road?

Snow began to fall on her bare shoulders. She hadn't even managed to snag her cape, but who cared. She wasn't going back in there. She was going…

Home. That was where she was headed. Back to her solitary ranch where she could live out her solitary life. That was where she belonged. Where she wouldn't embarrass herself, which was bad enough. She was used to that.

She'd ruined Jo's wedding. Her best friend—hell, her only friend—and Whitney had ruined the wedding. She hadn't fallen, hadn't even dropped her bouquet.

She'd just been herself.

Why had she ever thought she could do that?

She wrapped her arms around her waist to try and keep warm as she walked away from the carriage and the driver. She didn't really have a plan at this point, but she knew she couldn't take off in the wedding carriage. The very carriage she'd ridden in yesterday, snuggled in Matthew's arms. She'd already messed up the wedding. She drew the line at stealing the carriage.

"Ms. Maddox?" the driver called behind her, but she ignored him. She needed to get back to the farm so she could get her things and go—and there was no way the horse and carriage could get her there.

She'd walk to the main road and catch a taxi. Taxis could get her to the farm and from there, she could leave. There. That was a plan.

The snow was coming down thick and fast, each flake

biting into her bare shoulders with what felt like teeth. It felt as if it were trying to punish her, which was fine. She deserved it.

She'd tried. She'd tried *so* hard. She'd offered to step aside. She'd tried to convince Matthew to let her change her hair. And she damn well had on panties today. Industrial-strength Spanx in opaque black, just to be extra sure.

But it wasn't enough. It would never be enough. She would *always* be Whitney Wildz. And every time she got it into her foolish little head that she wasn't—that she could be whoever she wanted to be—well, this was what would happen. If she didn't hurt herself, she'd hurt the people she cared for. People like Jo.

People like Matthew.

God, she couldn't even think of him without pain. She'd *told* him she was going to ruin the wedding, but the man had decided that through the sheer force of his will alone, she wouldn't. He'd been bound and determined—literally—to have the perfect Beaumont wedding. He was a man who was used to getting what he wanted. He'd given her a chance to show him—to show everyone—that she was Whitney Maddox. For a beautiful moment—a too-short moment—she'd thought they had succeeded.

But that'd been just an illusion and they were both the poorer for indulging in it. He had to hate her now. She was living proof that he couldn't control everything. He'd never be able to look at her and see anything but imperfection.

She slipped but managed not to fall. The sidewalks were getting slicker by the second and these shoes weren't suited for anything other than plush carpeting. She could hear the sounds of traffic getting closer, and she trudged on. Good. The farther she could get from the wedding, the better.

Her stomach turned again. She hoped Jo and Phillip were still *able* to get married. What if the whole thing had devolved into a brawl or something? What if the preacher decided Whitney's running was a sign from God that Jo and Phillip shouldn't be married? It was on her head. All of it.

She'd just come upon the main street when she heard "Whitney?" from behind her.

Matthew. No, God, please—not him. She couldn't look at him and see his failure and know it was hers.

She waved her hands, hoping there was a taxi somewhere. Anywhere. And if there wasn't, she'd keep walking until she found one.

"Whitney, wait! Babe," she heard him shout. Damn it, he was getting closer.

She tried to hurry, but her foot slipped. Stupid heels on the stupid snow. The whole universe was out to get her. She thought she would keep her balance but she hit another slick spot and started to fall. Of course. Maybe someone would get a picture of it. It'd make a great headline.

Instead of falling, though, she was in his arms. The warmth of his body pushed back against the biting cold as he held her tight. It was everything she wanted and nothing she deserved. "Let me go," she said, shoving against him.

"Babe," he said, pointedly not releasing her from his grip. If anything, he held on tighter. "You're going to freeze. You don't even have your cape."

"What does it matter, Matthew? I ruined the wedding. You saw how it was. You and I both knew it was going to happen and…and we let it." The tears she'd been trying not to cry since the first whisper had hit her ears threatened to move up again. "Why did I let it happen?"

He came around to her front and forced her to look at him. He was not gentle about it. "Because you're Whitney Maddox, damn it. And I don't care about Whitney Wildz. You're enough for me."

"But I'm not and we both know it. I'm not even enough for me. I can never be the perfect woman you need. I can never be perfect." The tears stung at her eyes almost as much as the snow stung against her skin. And that, more than anything else, hurt the most.

"You *are*," he said with more force. "And you didn't ruin the wedding. Those people—they did. This is on them. Not you."

She shook her head, but before she could deny it—because Matthew had never been more wrong in his life—shouts of "Whitney? Whitney!" began to filter through the snow.

A taxi pulled up next to them and the cabbie shouted, "You need a cab, lady?"

Matthew got a fierce look on his face. "Let me handle them," he said as he stripped off his tuxedo jacket and wrapped it around her shoulders. "Follow my lead. I can fix this."

She wanted to believe it. She wanted him to protect her, to save her from herself.

But she couldn't. She couldn't let him throw away everything he'd worked for because of her. She wasn't worth it.

"Don't you see? I can't be another mess you have to clean up. I just can't." She ducked under his arm and managed to get the taxi door open on the second try. "It has to be this way," she told him.

Before the press could swarm, she got in the taxi and slammed the door. Matthew stood there, looking as if she'd stabbed him somewhere important. It hurt to look, so she focused on the cabbie.

"Where to, lady?" he asked.

"Can you take me to the Beaumont Farms? Outside the city?"

The cabbie stared at her dress, then at Matthew and the press, complete with flashing cameras and shouting. "You can pay?"

"Yes."

The fare would be huge, but what did it matter?

This evening had already cost her everything else.

Seventeen

Matthew was going to punch something. Someone. Several someones.

Hard.

Whitney's taxi sped off, its wheels spinning for traction on the newly slick streets. Then the press—the press *he* had invited to the wedding—was upon him like hungry dogs fighting over the last table scrap.

"Matthew, tell us about Whitney!"

"Matthew! Did you see Whitney Wildz drinking before the wedding? Can you confirm that Whitney Wildz was drunk?"

"Was she on drugs?"

"Is there something going on, Matthew? Are you involved with Whitney Wildz?"

"Did Whitney have a baby bump, Matthew? Who's the father?"

"Is Byron the father? Is that why he has a black eye? Did you two fight over her?"

The snow picked up speed, driving into his face. It felt good, the pain. It distracted him from the gut-wrenching agony of Whitney's face right before she ran down the aisle. Right before she got into the taxi.

"Ladies and gentlemen," he said in his meanest sneer. There were no such people before him. Just dogs with cameras.

No one blinked. The sarcasm was lost on them entirely. They just crowded closer, microphones in his face, cameras rolling. For a moment, he felt as if he were back in college and, at any second, someone was going to ask him what he thought about those photos of his father with his pants around his ankles.

Panic clawed at him. No one had ever asked if he wanted to manage the Beaumont public image. It was just something he'd fallen into and, because he was good at it, he'd stuck with it. Because it earned him a place in the family. Because defending his father, his brothers, his stepmothers—that was what made him a Beaumont.

Figure out who you are if you're not a Beaumont.

Phillip's comment came back to Matthew, insidious little words that Matthew had thought were Phillip's attempt at chipping away at Matthew's hard-won privilege.

But if being a Beaumont meant he had to throw Whitney to the dogs...could he do that? Did he want to?

No. That was not what he wanted. It'd never been, he realized. Hadn't he asked Byron to generate some press? Hadn't that been putting Whitney first?

Who am I? Her voice whispered in his ear. *Who am I to you?*

She'd said those words to him in the front seat of his car, right before he'd tied her to the bed.

She was Whitney Maddox. And she was Whitney Wildz. She was both at the same time.

Just as he was Matthew Beaumont and Matthew Billings. He'd never stopped being Matthew Billings. That lost little boy had always been standing right behind Matthew, threatening to make him a nobody again.

Because if he wasn't a Beaumont, who was he? He'd always thought the answer was a nobody. But now?

Who was *he* to *her*?

Who was he?

He was Matthew Beaumont. And being a Beaumont was saying to hell with what people thought of you—to hell with even what your family thought of you. It was not giving a rat's ass what the media said.

Being a Beaumont was about doing what you wanted, whenever you wanted to do it. Wasn't that what was behind all of those scandals he'd swept under the rug for all these years? No one else in his family ever stopped to think. They just *did*. Whatever—whoever—they wanted.

He looked at the cameras still rolling, the reporters all jostling for position to hear what juicy gossip he was going to come up with. The headlines tomorrow would be vicious—but for the first time in his life, he didn't care.

"Ladies and gentlemen," he began again, "I have no comment."

Dead silence. Matthew smirked. He'd truly managed to stun the lot of them into silence.

Then he turned and hailed a cab. Mercifully, one pulled right up to the curb.

"Where to, buddy?" the cabbie asked as Matthew shut the door on the gaping faces of the press.

Who was he? What did he want?

Whitney.

He had to get her. "The Beaumont Farms, south of the city."

The cab driver whistled. "That's gonna cost you."

"Doesn't matter." Then, with a smile, he added, "I'm a Beaumont."

Eighteen

"Ms. Maddox?" The guard stepped out of the gate when Whitney climbed out of the taxi. "Is everything all right?"

She really wished people would stop asking that question. Wasn't the answer obvious? "I...I need to pay him and I don't have any money. On me. I have some cash in the house..." She shivered. The cabbie had turned the heat on full blast for her, but it hadn't helped. Matthew's jacket wasn't enough to fend off the elements. The snow was coming down thick and fast and the cabbie was none too happy about the prospect of making it home in this weather.

The guard stared at her with obvious concern. Then he ushered her into the guard house. "I'll pay the driver and then get a truck and take you to the house. Don't move."

He said it as if he was afraid she might go somewhere, but she didn't want to. There was heat in this little building.

Plus, she was almost back to the farmhouse. This nice guard would take her the rest of the way. She'd get out of this dress and back into her own clothes. She didn't have much. She could be packed within twenty minutes. And then...

If she left immediately, she could be home by tomorrow afternoon. Back to the warmth and the sun and her animals and crazy Donald, none of whom would ever care that she'd ruined the Beaumont Christmas wedding. Yes. Back to the safety of solitude.

The guard came back with a truck and helped her into the passenger seat. He didn't tell her how much it had cost to get the cabbie to drive away. She'd pay it back, of course. She'd use the money from the royalty checks for *Whitney Wildz Sings Christmas, Yo*. Fitting.

"I'm going home," she told him when he pulled up in front of the house and got out to unlock the front door for her. "Tonight."

"Ms. Maddox, the snow is going to continue for some time," he said, the worry in his voice obvious. "I don't think—"

"I can drive on snow," she lied. She couldn't stay here. That much she knew.

"But—"

Whitney didn't listen. She said, "Thank you very much," and shut the door in the man's face. Which was a diva thing to do, but it couldn't be helped.

She didn't get lost on her way back to what had been her room and Matthew's room. Their room. Well, it wasn't that anymore.

She changed and started throwing things into her bags. She'd have time when she got home to shake out the wrinkles. She didn't have that time now.

The dress…it lay in a heap on the floor, as if she'd wounded it in the line of duty. She'd felt beautiful in the dress. Matthew had thought so. She'd felt…

She'd felt like the woman she was supposed to be when she'd worn it. Glamorous and confident and sexy and worthy. And not scandalous. Not even a little.

She picked it up, shook it out and laid it on the bed. Then she did the same with his tuxedo jacket. In her mind's eye, she saw the two of them this afternoon, having their pictures taken in a park, in a carriage bedecked in Christmas bows.

They hadn't even gotten to walk down the aisle together. She'd ruined that, too.

Her bags were heavy and, because she hadn't packed carefully, extra bulky. Getting them both out of the door and down the hall was bad enough. She was navigating the stairs one at a time when she heard the front door slam open.

"Whitney?"

Matthew. *Oh, no.* That was all that registered before she lost her grip on one of her bags. It tangled with her feet and suddenly she was falling down the last few stairs.

And right into his arms. He caught her just as he had before—just as he was always doing.

Then, before she could tell him she was sorry or that she was leaving and she'd pay back the cab fare, he was kissing her. His hair was wet and his shirt was wet and he was lifting her up to him, sliding his hands around her waist and holding her.

And he was kissing her. She was so stunned by this that she couldn't do anything but stare at him.

He pulled away, but he didn't let her go. Hell, he didn't even set her on her feet. He just held her as though his life depended on it.

She needed to get out of his arms so she could go back to being invisible Whitney Maddox. But she couldn't. Was it wrong to want just a few more minutes of being someone special? Was it wrong to want that hope, even if she was going to get knocked down for daring to hope almost immediately?

Matthew spoke. "*Always* kiss me back," he said, as if this were just another wild Tuesday night and not the ruination of everything. Then her bags—which had come crashing down after her—seemed to register with him. "Where are you going?"

"Home," she told him. She would not cry. Crying solved

nothing. And really, this was everything she'd expected. "I don't belong here. I never did."

"That's not true."

Oh, so they were just going to deny reality? Fine. She could do that. "Why are *you* here? Why aren't you at the wedding?" Then, because she couldn't help herself— because she might never get another chance to have him in her arms—she placed her palm on his cheek.

He leaned into her touch. "I had this revelation," he said as he touched his forehead to hers. "It turns out that I'm not a very good Beaumont."

"What?" she gasped. She'd heard him say how hard it was to earn his place at the table—at the altar. Why would he say that about himself? "But you're an amazing man— you take care of people and you took your sister and brother to my concert and the whole wedding was *amazing*, right until I ruined it!"

His grin was sad and happy and tired, all at the same time. Her feet touched the ground, but he didn't let her go.

"A Beaumont," he said with quiet conviction, "wouldn't care what anyone else thought. They wouldn't care how it played in the media. A Beaumont would do whatever he wanted, whenever he wanted, consequences be damned. That's what makes a Beaumont. And I've never done that. Not once." He paused, lifting her up even closer. "Not until I met you."

Hope. It was small and felt foreign in her mind—so foreign that she almost didn't recognize it for what it was. "Me?"

"You. For the first time in my life, I did something because I wanted to, regardless of how it'd play in the press." He touched her hair, where the bejeweled clip still held her stubborn white streak in place. "I fell in love with you."

Her heart stopped. Everything stopped. Had he just said… that he'd fallen in love with her? "I—" But she didn't have anything else.

Then, to her horror, she heard herself ask, "Who am I to you?"

He gave her a little grin, as if he'd known she was going to ask the question but had hoped she wouldn't. "You're a kind, thoughtful, intelligent woman who can get clumsy when you're nervous. You'd do anything for your friends, even if it puts you in the line of fire."

"But—"

He lifted her face so she had to look at him. "And," he went on, "you're beautiful and sexy and I can't hold myself back when I'm around you. I can't let you go just because of how it'll look in a headline."

"But the press—tomorrow—" She shuddered. The headlines would be cruel. Possibly the worst in her life, and that was saying something. The Beaumont public image would be in tatters, thanks to her. "Your family... I ruined *everything*," she whispered. Why couldn't he see that?

His grin this time was much less sweet, much more the look of a man who could bend the press to his will. "You merely generated some PR, that's all. And there's no such thing as bad PR."

"That's not— What?"

"Don't let the guessing games that complete strangers play hold you back, Whitney. Don't let a manufactured scandal keep us apart."

"But—but—but your life is here. And I need the sun. You said so yourself."

"The Beaumonts are here," he corrected her. "And we've already established that I'm not a very good Beaumont."

The thing that was hope began to grow inside of her until it was pulsing through her veins, spreading farther with each heartbeat. "What are you saying?"

"Who am I?" His voice was low and serious. It sent a chill up her spine that had nothing to do with his wet shirt. "If I'm not a Beaumont, who am I to you?"

"You're Matthew." He swallowed, his Adam's apple bobbing nervously. "It never mattered to me what your name is—Billings, Beaumont—I don't care. I came here thinking it'd be nice to meet a man who could look at me without thinking about Whitney Wildz or all the headlines. A man who could make me feel sexy and wanted, who could give me the confidence to maybe start dating. Who could show me it was even possible."

He cupped her face in his hands, his thumbs stroking her cheeks. "And?"

"And...that man was you. Eventually," she added with an embarrassed smile, remembering the first time she'd fallen into his arms. "But now the wedding's over. And I—" Her voice caught. "I can't be another mess you have to manage, Matthew. And I can't ever be perfect. You know I can't."

"I know." For the briefest of seconds, it felt like a book being slammed shut. "But," he added, "I don't want perfection. Because I'll never get it. I can try and try to be the perfect Beaumont until I lie down and die and I'll never make it. That's what you've shown me."

A little choked sob escaped her lips. No matter what she did, she'd never be perfect, either. Not even to him. "Great. Glad to help."

"Be *not* perfect with me, Whitney. Let me be a part of your life. Let me catch you when you fall—and hold me up when I stumble."

"But...the press—the headlines—"

"They don't matter. All that matters is what you and I know. And this is what I know. I have never *let* myself fall in love before, because I've been afraid that loving someone else will take something away from me. Make me less of a man, less of a Beaumont. And you make me more than that. More than my name. You make me whole."

The impact of his words hit her hard. Suddenly, those tears that she hadn't allowed herself to cry because the disappointment and shame were always to be expected—suddenly, those tears were spilling down her cheeks. "I didn't expect to find you. I didn't expect to fall in love with you. I don't—I don't know how to do this. I don't want to mess this up. More than I already have."

"You won't," he said, brushing his lips over hers. "And if you try, I'll tie you to the bed." She giggled, and he laughed with her. "We will make this work because I'm not going to let you go. You will always be my Whitney. Although," he added with a wicked grin, "I was thinking—you might want to try out a new last name. Maybe something that starts with a *B*."

"What are you saying?"

"Marry me. Let me be there for you, *with* you."

"Yes. Oh, God—*Matthew*." She threw her arms around his neck. The tears were coming faster now, but she couldn't hold them back. It was messy and not perfect but then, so was life. "You see me as I really am. That's all I ever wanted."

"I *love* you as you really are." He swept her feet out from underneath her and began to climb the stairs back to his room. Their room. "Love me back?"

"Always," she told him. "Always."

* * * * *

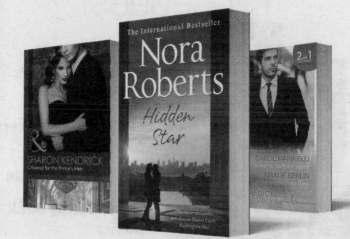